DARK FORCES

STEPHEN LEATHER

ISIS
LARGE
PRINT

First published in Great Britain 2016
by
Hodder & Stoughton

First Isis Edition
published 2020
by arrangement with
Hodder & Stoughton
An Hachette UK company

ISBN 978–1–78541–891–4

Published by
Ulverscroft Limited
Anstey, Leicestershire

Set by Words & Graphics Ltd.
Anstey, Leicestershire
Printed and bound in Great Britain by
T. J. International Ltd., Padstow, Cornwall

This book is printed on acid-free paper

DARK FORCES

A violent South London gang will be destroyed if Dan "Spider" Shepherd can gather enough evidence against them while posing as a ruthless hitman. What he doesn't know is that his work as an undercover agent for MI5 is about to intersect with the biggest terrorist operation ever carried out on British soil. Only weeks before, Shepherd witnessed a highly skilled IS sniper escape from a targeted missile strike in Syria. But never in his wildest dreams did he expect to next come across the shooter in a grimy East London flat. Spider's going to have to proceed with extreme caution if he is to prevent the death of hundreds of people — but at the same time, when the crucial moment comes, he will have to act decisively. The clock is ticking . . .

For Sam

The man's name was Mohammed al-Hussain, a common enough name in Syria. But the Mohammed al-Hussain lying prone on the roof of the two-storey building was no ordinary man. He was a sniper, one of the best in the world. He had 256 kills to his credit, each one meticulously recorded in the small cloth-bound notebook he kept in his back pocket. Each entry detailed the nature of the target, the location and the distance. Almost all of his kills were Syrian government soldiers.

He was twenty-two years old, his skin the colour of weak coffee with plenty of milk. He had soft brown eyes that belonged more to a lovesick spaniel than the tried and tested assassin he was. His beard was long and bushy but his nails were neatly clipped and glistened as if they had been varnished. Around his head was a knotted black scarf with the white insignia of Islamic State, the caliphate that claimed authority over all Muslims around the world. His weapon was lying on a sandbag.

When he had first started sniping, he had used a Russian-made Dragunov SVD rifle, accurate up to six hundred metres. It was a lightweight and reliable weapon, capable of semi-automatic fire and equipped with a ten-round magazine. Most of his kills back then had been at around two hundred metres. His commander had spotted his skill with the weapon and had recommended him for specialist training. He was pulled off the front line and spent four weeks in the desert at a remote training camp.

There, he was introduced to the British L115A3 sniper rifle. It was the weapon of choice for snipers in the British SAS and the American Delta Force, and it hadn't taken al-Hussain long to appreciate its advantages. It had been designed by Olympic target shooters and fired an 8.59mm round, the extra weight resulting in less deflection over long ranges. In fact, in the right hands the L115A3 could hit a human-sized target at 1,400 metres, and even at that distance the round would do more damage than a magnum bullet at close range.

The L115A3 was fitted with a suppressor to cut down the flash and noise it made. No one killed by a bullet from his L115A3 ever heard it coming. It was the perfect rifle for carrying around — it weighed less than seven kilograms and had a folding stock so it could easily be slid into a backpack.

It had an adjustable cheek-piece so that the marksman's eye could be comfortably aligned with the Schmidt & Bender 25 x magnification scope. Al-Hussain put his eye to it now and made a slight adjustment to the focus. His target was a house just over a thousand metres away. It was home to the mother of a colonel in the Syrian Army, and today was her birthday. The colonel was a good son and, at just after eight o'clock, had arrived at the house to have breakfast with his mother. Fifteen minutes later, al-Hussain had taken up position on the roof. The colonel was a prime target and had been for the best part of a year.

The L115A3 cost thirty-five thousand dollars in the United States but more than double that in the Middle East. The Islamic State was careful who it gave the weapons to, but al-Hussain was an obvious choice. His notepad confirmed the benefits of using the British rifle. His kills went from an average of close to two hundred metres with the Dragunov to more than eight hundred. His kill rate increased too. With the Dragunov he averaged three kills a day on active service. With the L115A3, more often than not he recorded at least five. The magazine held only five shells but that was enough. Firing more than two shots in succession was likely to lead to his location being pinpointed. One was best. One shot, one kill. Then wait at least a few minutes before firing again. But al-Hussain wasn't planning on shooting more than once. There were two SUVs outside the mother's house and the soldiers had formed a perimeter around the building but the only target the sniper was interested in was the colonel.

"Are we good to go?" asked the man to the sniper's right. He was Asian, bearded, with a crooked hooked nose, and spoke with an English accent. He was one of thousands of foreign jihadists who had crossed the border into Syria to fight alongside Islamic State. The other man, the one to the sniper's left, was an Iraqi, darker-skinned and wearing glasses.

Al-Hussain spoke good English. His parents had sent him to one of the best schools in Damascus, the International School of Choueifat. The school had an indoor heated pool, a gymnasium, a grass football pitch, a 400-metre athletics track, basketball and tennis courts. Al-Hussain had been an able pupil and had made full use of the school's sporting facilities.

Everything had changed when he had turned seventeen. Teenagers who had painted revolutionary slogans on a school wall had been arrested and tortured in the southern city of Deraa and thousands of people took to the streets to protest. The Syrian Army reacted by shooting the unarmed protesters, and by the summer of 2011 the protests had spread across the country. Al-Hussain had seen, first hand, the brutality of the government response. He saw his fellow students take up arms to defend themselves and at first he resisted, believing that peaceful protests would succeed eventually. He was wrong. The protests escalated and the country descended into civil war. What had been touted as an Arab Spring became a violent struggle as rebel brigades laid siege to government-controlled cities and towns, determined to end the reign of President Assad.

By the summer of 2013 more than a hundred thousand people had been killed and fighting had reached the capital, Damascus. In August of that year the Syrian government had killed hundreds of people on the outskirts of Damascus when they launched rockets filled with the nerve gas Sarin.

Al-Hussain's parents decided they had had enough. They closed their house in Mezze and fled to Lebanon with their two daughters, begging Mohammed to go with them. He refused, telling them he had to stay and fight for his country. As his family fled, al-Hussain began killing with a vengeance. He knew that the struggle was no longer just about removing President Assad. It was a full-blown war in which there could be only one victor.

Syria had been run by the president's Shia Alawite sect, but the country's Sunni majority had been the underdogs for a long time and wanted nothing less than complete control. Russia and Iran wanted President Assad to continue running the country, as did Lebanon. Together they poured billions of dollars into supporting the regime, while the US, the UK and France, along with Turkey, Saudi Arabia, Qatar and the rest of the Arab states, supported the Sunni-dominated opposition.

After the nerve gas attack, al-Hussain's unit switched their allegiance to Islamic State, which had been formed from the rump of al-Qaeda's operations in Iraq. Led by Abu Bakr al-Baghdadi, Islamic State had attracted thousands of foreign jihadists, lured by its promise to create an Islamic emirate from large chunks of Syria and Iraq. Islamic State grew quickly, funded in part by captured oilfields, taking first the provincial Syrian city of Raqqa and the Sunni city of Fallujah, in the western Iraqi province of Anbar.

As Islamic State grew, Mohammed al-Hussain was given ever more strategic targets. He was known as the sniper who never missed, and his notebook was filled with the names of high-ranking Syrian officers and politicians.

"He's coming out," said the Brit, but al-Hussain had already seen the front door open. The soldiers outside started moving, scanning the area for potential threats. Al-Hussain put his eye to the scope and began to control his breathing. Slow and even. There was ten feet between the door and the colonel's SUV. A couple of seconds. More than enough time for an expert sniper like al-Hussain.

A figure appeared at the doorway and al-Hussain held his breath. His finger tightened on the trigger. It was important to squeeze, not pull. He saw a headscarf. The mother. He started breathing again, but slowly and tidally. She had her head against the colonel's chest. He was hugging her. The door opened wider. She stepped back. He saw the green of the colonel's uniform. He held his breath. Tightened his finger.

The phone in the breast pocket of his jacket buzzed. Al-Hussain leapt to his feet, clasped the rifle to his chest and headed across the roof. The two spotters looked up at him, their mouths open. "Run!" he shouted, but they stayed where they were. He didn't shout again. He concentrated on running at full speed to the stairwell. He reached the top and hurtled down the stone stairs. Just as he reached the ground floor a 45-kilogram Hellfire missile hit the roof at just under a thousand miles an hour.

Dan "Spider" Shepherd stared at the screen. All he could see was whirling brown dust where once there had been a two-storey building. "Did we get them all?" he asked.

Two airmen were sitting in front of him in high-backed beige leather chairs. They had control panels and joysticks in front of them and between them was a panel with two white telephones.

"Maybe," said the man in the left-hand seat. He was Steve Morris, the flying officer in command, in his early forties with greying hair. Sitting next to him was Pilot Officer Denis Donoghue, in his thirties with ginger hair, cut short. "What do you think, Denis?"

"The sniper was moving just before it hit. If he was quick enough he might have made it out. We got your two guys, guaranteed. Don't think they knew what hit them."

"What about IR?" asked Shepherd.

Donoghue reached out and clicked a switch. The image on the main screen changed to a greenish hue. They could just about make out the ruins of the building. "Not much help, I'm afraid," said Donoghue. "There isn't a lot left when you get a direct hit from a Hellfire."

"Can we scan the surrounding area?"

Morris turned his joystick to the right. "No problem," he said. The drone banked to the right and so did the picture on the main screen in the middle of the display. The two screens to the left of it showed satellite images and maps, and above them was a tracker screen that indicated the location of the Predator. Below that was the head-up display that showed a radar ground image. But they were all staring at the main screen. Donoghue pulled the camera back, giving them a wider view of the area, still using the infrared camera.

The drone was an MQ-9, better known as the Predator B. Hunter-killer, built by General Atomics Aeronautical Systems at a cost of close to 17 million dollars. It had a 950-shaft-horsepower turboprop engine, a twenty-metre wingspan, a maximum speed of 300 m.p.h. and a range of a little more than a thousand miles. It could fly loaded for fourteen hours up to a height of fifteen thousand metres, carrying four Hellfire air-to-surface missiles and two Paveway laser-guided bombs.

One of the Hellfires had taken out the building, specifically an AGM-114P Hellfire II, specially designed to be fired from a high-altitude drone. The Hellfire air-to-surface missile was developed for tank-hunting and the nickname came from its initial designation of Helicopter Launched, Fire and Forget Missile. But the armed forces of the West soon realised that, when fired from a high-flying drone, the Hellfire could be a potent assassination tool for taking out high-value targets. It was the Israelis who had first used it against an individual when their air force killed Hamas leader Ahmed Yassin in 2004. But the Americans and British had taken the technique to a whole new level, using it to great effect in Pakistan, Somalia, Iraq and Syria. Among the terrorists killed by

Hellfire missiles launched from drones were Al-Shabaab leader Ahmed Abdi Godane, and British-born Islamic State terrorist Mohammed Emwazi, also known as Jihadi John.

The Hellfire missile was efficient and, at less than a hundred thousand dollars a shot, cost-effective. It was just over five feet long, had a range of eight thousand metres and carried a nine-kilogram shaped charge that was more than capable of taking out a tank. It was, however, less effective against a stone building. While there was no doubt that the men on the roof would have died instantly, the sniper might well have survived, if he had made it outside.

Shepherd twisted in his seat. Alex Shaw, the mission coordinator, was sitting at his desk in front of six flat-screen monitors. He was in his early thirties with a receding hairline and wire-framed spectacles. "What do you think, Alex? Did we get him?"

"I'd love to say yes, Spider, but there's no doubt he was moving." He shrugged. "He could have got downstairs and out before the missile hit but he'd have to have been moving fast."

Shepherd wrinkled his nose. The primary target had been a British jihadist, Ruhul Khan and it had been Khan they had spent four hours following until he had reached the roof. It was only when the sniper had unpacked his rifle that Shepherd realised what the men were up to. While the death of the British jihadist meant the operation had been a success, it was frustrating not to know if they'd succeeded in taking out the sniper.

Shaw stood up and stretched, then walked over to stand by Shepherd. Donoghue had switched the camera back to regular HD. There were several pick-up trucks racing away from the ruins of the building, and a dozen or so men running towards it. None of the men on the ground looked like the sniper. It was possible he'd made it to a truck, but unlikely. And if he had made it, there was no way of identifying him from the air.

"We'll hang around and wait for the smoke to clear," said Shaw. "They might pull out the bodies. Muslims like to bury their dead within twenty-four hours." He took out a packet of cigarettes. "Time for a quick smoke."

"Just give me a minute or two, will you, Alex?" asked Shepherd. "Let's see if we can work out what the sniper was aiming at."

"No problem," said Shaw, dropping back into his seat.

"Start at about three hundred metres and work out," said Shepherd.

"Are you on it, Steve?" asked Shaw.

"Heading two-five-zero," said Morris, slowly moving his joystick. "What are we looking for?"

"Anything a sniper might be interested in," said Shepherd. "Military installation. Army patrol. Government building."

"It's mainly residential," said Donoghue, peering at the main screen.

Shepherd stared at the screen. Donoghue was right. The area was almost all middle-class homes, many with

10

well-tended gardens. Finding out who the occupants were would be next to impossible, and there were dozens of houses within the sniper's range. There was movement at the top of the screen. Five vehicles, travelling fast. "What's that?" he asked.

Donoghue changed the camera and zoomed in on the convoy. Two army jeeps in front of a black SUV with tinted windows, followed by an army truck with a heavy machine-gun mounted on the top followed by a troop-carrier. "That's someone important, right enough," said Donoghue.

Shepherd nodded. "How far from where the sniper was?"

"A mile or so." Donoghue wrinkled his nose. "That's a bit far, isn't it?"

"Not for a good one," said Shepherd. "And he looked as if he knew what he was doing." He pointed at the screen. "They're probably running because of the explosion. Whoever that guy is, he'll probably never know how close he came to taking a bullet."

"Or that HM Government saved his bacon," said Shaw. He grinned. "Well, not bacon, obviously."

"Can we get back to the house, see if the smoke's cleared?" said Shepherd. He stood and went over to Shaw's station. "Can you get me close-ups of the sniper and his gun?"

"No problem. It'll take a few minutes. I'm not sure how good the images will be."

"We've got technical guys who can clean them up," said Shepherd.

"Denis, could you handle that for our guest?" said Shaw, then to Shepherd: "Thumb drive okay?"

"Perfect."

"Put a selection of images on a thumb drive, Denis, while I pop out for a smoke." Shaw pushed himself up out of his chair.

"I'm on it," said Donoghue.

Shaw opened a door and Shepherd followed him out. The unit was based in a container, the same size and shape as the ones used to carry goods on ships. There were two in a large hangar. Both were a dull yellow, with rubber wheels at either end so that they could be moved around, and large air-conditioning units attached to keep the occupants cool. The hangar was at RAF Waddington, four miles south of the city of Lincoln.

Shaw headed for the hangar entrance as he lit a cigarette. On the wall by the door was the badge of 13th Squadron — a lynx's head in front of a dagger — and a motto: ADJUVAMUS TUENDO, "We Assist by Watching". It was something of a misnomer as the squadron did much more than watch. Shaw blew smoke at the mid-morning sky. "It was like he had a sixth sense, wasn't it? The way that sniper moved."

"Could he have heard the drone?"

Shaw flashed him an admonishing look. The men of 13th Squadron didn't refer to the Predators as drones. They were RPAs, remotely piloted aircraft. Shepherd supposed it was because without the word "pilot" in there somewhere, they might be considered surplus to

12

requirements. Shepherd grinned and corrected himself. "RPA. Could he have heard the RPA?"

"Not at the height we were at," said Shaw.

"Must have spotters then, I guess."

"The two men with him were eyes on the target. They weren't checking the sky."

"I meant other spotters. Somewhere else. In communication with him via radio or phone."

"I didn't see any of them using phones or radios," said Shaw.

"True," said Shepherd. "But he could have a phone set to vibrate. The phone vibrates, he grabs his gun and runs."

"Without warning his pals?"

"He could have shouted as he ran. They froze. Bang."

"Our target was one of the guys with him. The Brit. Why are you so concerned about the one that got away?"

"Usually snipers have just one spotter," said Shepherd. "Their job is to protect the sniper and help him by calling the wind and noting the shots. That guy had two. Plus it looks like there were more protecting him from a distance. That suggests to me he's a valuable Islamic State resource. One of their best snipers. If he got away, I'd like at least to have some intel on him."

"The Brit who was with him. How long have you been on his tail?"

"Khan's been on our watch list since he entered Syria a year ago. He's been posting some very nasty stuff on Facebook and Twitter."

"It was impressive the way you spotted him coming out of the mosque. I couldn't tell him apart from the other men there."

"I'm good at recognising people, close up and from a distance."

"No question of that. I thought we were wasting our time when he got in that truck but then they picked up the sniper and went up on the roof. Kudos. But how did you spot him?"

"Face partly. I'd seen his file in London and I never forget a face. But I can recognise body shapes too, the way people move, the way they hold themselves. That was more how I spotted Khan."

"And what is he? British-born Asian who got radicalised?"

"In a nutshell," said Shepherd. "A year ago he was a computer-science student in Bradford. Dad's a doctor, a GP. Mum's a social worker. Go figure."

"I don't understand it, do you? What the hell makes kids throw away their lives here and go to fight in the bloody desert?"

Shepherd shrugged. "It's a form of brainwashing, if you ask me. Islamic State is a cult. And like any cult they can get their believers to do pretty much anything they want."

Shaw blew smoke at the ground and watched it disperse in the wind. "What sort of religion is it that says booze and bacon are bad things?" he said. "How can anyone in their right mind believe for one moment that a God, any God, has a thing about alcohol and pork? And that women should be kept covered and

14

shackled? And that old men should have sex with underage girls? It's fucking mad, isn't it?"

"I guess so. But it's not peculiar to Islam. Jews can't eat pork. Or seafood. And orthodox Jews won't work on the Sabbath."

"Hey, I'm not singling out the Muslims," said Shaw. "It's all religions. We've got a Sikh guy in the regiment. Sukhwinder, his name is, so you can imagine the ribbing he takes. Lovely guy. Bloody good airman. But he wears a turban, doesn't cut his hair and always has to have his ceremonial dagger on him. I've asked him, does he really believe God wants him not to cut his hair and to wear a silly hat?" Shaw grinned. "Didn't use those exact words, obviously. He said, yeah, he believed it." He took another pull on his cigarette. "So here's the thing. Great guy. Great airman. A true professional. But if he really, truly, honestly believes that God wants him to grow his hair long, he's got mental-health issues. Seriously. He's as fucking mad as those nutters in the desert. If he truly believes God is telling him not to cut his hair, how do I know that one day his God won't tell him to pick up a rifle and blast away at non-believers? I don't, right? How the hell can you trust someone who allows a fictional entity to dictate their actions?"

"The world would be a much better place without religion — is that what you're saying?"

"I'm saying people should be allowed to believe in anything they want. Hell, there are still people who believe the earth is flat, despite all the evidence to the contrary. But the moment that belief starts to impact on others . . ." He shrugged. "I don't know. I just want the world to be a nicer, friendlier place and it's not, and it feels to me it's religion that's doing the damage. That and sex."

Shepherd smiled. "Sex?"

"Haven't you noticed? The more relaxed a country is about sex, the less violent they are. The South Americans, they hardly ever go to war."

"Argentina? The Falldands?"

"That was more of a misunderstanding than a war. But you know what I mean. If you're a young guy in Libya or Iraq or Pakistan, your chances of getting laid outside marriage are slim to none. They cover their women from head to toe, for a start. So all that male testosterone is swilling around with nowhere to go. Of course they're going to get ultra-violent."

"So we should be sending hookers to Iraq and Libya, not troops?"

"I'm just saying, if these Islamic State guys got laid more often they wouldn't be going around chopping off so many heads. If Khan had been getting regular sex with a fit bird in Bradford, I doubt he'd be in such a rush to go fighting in the desert."

"It's an interesting theory," said Shepherd. "But if I were you I'd keep it to myself."

"Yeah, they took away our suggestions box years ago," said Shaw. He flicked away the remains of his cigarette. "I'll get you your thumb drive and you can be on your way."

They went back inside the container. Donoghue had the thumb drive ready and handed it to Shepherd, who thanked him and studied the main screen. The dust and smoke had pretty much dispersed. The roof and upper floor had been reduced to rubble but the ground floor was still standing. "No sign of any bodies?" asked Shepherd.

"Anything on the roof would have been vaporised, pretty much," said Morris. "If there was anyone on the ground floor, we won't know until they start clearing up, and at the moment that's not happening. They're keeping their distance. Probably afraid we'll let fly a second missile. We can hang around for a few hours but I won't be holding my breath."

"Probably not worth it," Shepherd said. "Like you say, he's either vaporised or well out of the area." He looked at his watch and flashed Shaw a tight smile. "I've got to be somewhere, anyway."

"A hot date?" asked Shaw.

"I wish," said Shepherd. He couldn't tell Shaw he was heading off to kill someone and this time it was going to be up close and personal.

Mohammed al-Hussain was driven to see his commander in the back of a nondescript saloon car, a twelve-year-old Toyota with darkened windows. The commander was based in a compound on the outskirts of Palmyra, pretty much in the middle of Syria. Palmyra had been gutted by the fierce fighting between the Syrian government and Islamic State fighters. The city's historic Roman theatre had been left virtually untouched and was now used as a place of execution, the victims usually forced to wear orange jump-suits before they were decapitated, often by children.

The commander was Azmar al-Lihaib, an Iraqi who had been one of the first to join Islamic State. His unit worked independently, often choosing its own targets, though special requests were regularly handed down from the IS High Command.

Al-Hussain was dog-tired. He hadn't slept for more than thirty-six hours. The *khat* leaves he was chewing went some way to keeping him awake but his eyelids kept closing as he rested his head against the window. He must have dozed for a while because the car lurched to a halt unexpectedly causing him to jerk upright, putting his hands up defensively. They had arrived at al-Lihaib's compound. The men in the unit never wore uniforms and the Toyota's occupants were checked by two men in flowing gowns, holding Kalashnikovs, with ammunition belts strung across their chests.

They drove through the gates and parked next to a disused fountain. Al-Hussain climbed out and pulled the backpack after him. He never went anywhere without his rifle and even slept with it by his side. He spat out what was left of the *khat*, and green phlegm splattered across the dusty ground.

Two more guards stood at either side of an arched doorway and moved aside to allow him through. He walked down a gloomy corridor, his sandals scuffing along the stone floor. There was a pair of double wooden doors at the far end with another two guards. One knocked and opened them as al-Hussain approached. He hesitated for a second before he went through.

18

It was a large room with thick rugs on the floor and heavy purple curtains covering the window. Commander al-Lihaib was sitting cross-legged beside an octagonal wooden table inlaid with mother-of-pearl on which stood a long-spouted brass teapot and two small brass cups. Even when he was sitting down it was obvious that al-Lihaib was a big man and tall, while his Kalashnikov, on a cushion beside him, looked like a toy against his shovel-sized hands. He was in his forties with hooded eyes and cheeks flecked with black scars that looked more like a skin condition than old wounds. Like many Islamic fighters his beard was long and straggly, and the backs of his hands were matted with hair. His fingernails were yellowed and gnarled and his teeth were chipped and greying. He waved al-Hussain to the other side of the table, then poured tea into the cups as the younger man sat and crossed his legs.

Al-Lihaib waited until they had both sipped their hot mint tea before he spoke. "You had a lucky escape," he said.

"Allah was looking over me," said al-Hussain.

"As were your team, thankfully," said al-Lihaib. "It is rare actually to see a drone but one of the men caught the sun glinting off it, then the missile being launched."

"I barely made it off the roof," said al-Hussain. "I'm sorry about the men who were with me. I shouted a warning but they froze."

"They had been briefed?"

"They had been told to follow my orders immediately. As I said, they froze."

"You had only seconds in which to act," said al-Lihaib.

"The question is, how did they know where I would be?" said al-Hussain. "I was told of the location only an hour before I got there."

"And we learned of the colonel's visit only that morning, by which time the drone was almost certainly in the air." Al-Lihaib sipped his tea.

"Could the drone have been protecting the colonel?" asked al-Hussain.

"Out of the question," said the commander. "The Americans and the British do not use their drones to protect foreigners, only to attack their enemies."

"Then how did they know I would be on the roof?"

"They didn't," said al-Lihaib. "They couldn't have."

"Then why?"

Al-Lihaib took another sip of his tea. "It could only have been the British jihadist they were after," he said. "The British have been using the drones to track and kill their own people. They must have been following him, watched him join you and go to the roof. Once they had a clear shot, they launched their missile." He smiled grimly. "You were in the wrong place at the wrong time. It was the Brit they wanted to kill. You would have been collateral damage."

Al-Hussain drank some tea.

"Your parents are in Lebanon?" asked al-Lihaib.

Al-Hussain nodded. "They fled in 2013."

"They are safe?"

Al-Hussain shrugged. "I haven't spoken to them since they left. I told them they should stay. We are Syrians, this is our country. We should fight for it."

"Sometimes we have to take the fight to the enemy," said al-Lihaib. "Like the martyrs did on Nine Eleven. The whole world took notice. And in Paris. We hurt the French, we made them bleed. They learned a lesson — you hurt us and we hurt you. An eye for an eye."

Al-Hussain nodded but didn't say anything. Al-Lihaib reached inside his robe and took out a passport. He placed it on the table in front of al-Hussain.

"What's that?"

The commander waved for him to pick it up. It was a British passport. The man in the photograph was strikingly similar to al-Hussain but, according to the printed details, he was called Hammad Rajput. He was two years older than al-Hussain and had been born in Birmingham. The beard in the picture was shorter and well-trimmed, but the likeness was so close they might have been brothers.

"I don't understand," he said.

"We're sending you to England, brother. We have a special job for you." He gestured at the passport. "A brother in England is allowing you to use his identity to get into the country. You look very like him so you will not be stopped, and your English is good enough to pass muster. We will get you into Europe and then to London."

Al-Hussain chose his words carefully. Islamic State did not take kindly to those who did not follow orders without question. "I always feel that I can do my best work here," he said. "I have support, I know the territory. No one has more kills than me."

"You are one of our best snipers," agreed al-Lihaib.

Al-Hussain wanted to correct him. He was the best sniper in the country, by far. No one else came close. But pride was not a quality that IS encouraged so he bit his tongue.

"That is why we need you in England. We have a job that only you can do."

"But I can come back? Afterwards?"

Al-Lihaib smiled slyly. "Do you fear becoming a *shahid*, brother? Do you fear dying for Allah?"

"I would die in an instant for Allah and for my country," said al-Hussain. "Without hesitation and with a smile on my face."

"No one is asking you to die, brother," said al-Lihaib. "We have gone to a lot of time and trouble to train you. No one is prepared to throw that away."

"But I can do so much more here," said al-Hussain. "I can be efficient. And the targets I take out here are our enemy."

"The British are also our enemy, brother. They are killing our people from the air. They invaded Afghanistan and killed our brothers and sisters. They did the same in Iraq. The British are our enemies, and what better way to hurt our enemy than to attack him on his own territory?"

Al-Hussain considered his words carefully. Al-Lihaib was smiling but he knew he had to tread carefully. He felt that he had already said too much but he had to give it one more try. "It's a long way to go. Is the target so very important?"

Al-Lihaib's eyes hardened. "The importance of the target is not for you to decide, Mohammed al-Hussain. You are a soldier and you will obey orders. You will obey this order, will you not?"

Al-Hussain returned the man's stare for several seconds, then lowered his eyes. "I will," he said. "*Inshallah*." God willing.

"This is fucking bullshit," said the man. He was standing in a hastily dug grave, just over three feet deep. His name was Laurence McGovern but most people called him Larry. "You're going to shoot me here?"

"It's got to be done, Larry. Stop complaining," said Shepherd. He was holding a revolver, a Smith & Wesson 627 loaded with eight .357 rounds.

McGovern looked down. "It's fucking muddy as hell. And this is a two-thousand-quid Hugo Boss suit."

Shepherd pointed the gun at McGovern's chest. "Would you stop complaining?" he said. "This is for your own good."

"Shooting me in the middle of the New Forest is for my own good? You are one mad bastard."

Shepherd grinned. "It has to look good or it's not going to work."

"But the suit . . ." McGovern raised his arms. "You could at least let me change into something cheaper."

"That's the suit you left home in," said Shepherd. "That's the suit you're going to die in. Now, stop moaning." He looked over his shoulder at the two men standing behind him. "Are we good to go?" he asked.

"Ready when you are," said the older of the two men. Philip Duff was one of MI5's most able technicians and was holding the trigger that would set off the small explosive charges on the vest under McGovern's shirt. His assistant was a younger man and his main role seemed to be to carry Duff's bags.

Shepherd looked back at McGovern. "Don't fuck this up, Larry," he said. "If you do, we'll only have to ruin another suit."

"Just pull the trigger and get it over with," said McGovern.

"Don't over-egg it, that's what I'm saying," said Shepherd. "Bang. You react. Bang. Bang. You go down. Keep your eyes closed and don't breathe." He took out his mobile phone with his left hand.

"I'm not stupid," said McGovern.

Shepherd opened the phone's camera and pressed the button to start video recording. "Just so you know, Tommy and Marty want to say goodbye."

"Mate, you don't have to do this," said McGovern. "Whatever they're paying you, I'll match it. I'll double it." He held up his hands. "Just name your price."

"I've been paid," said Shepherd. He pulled the trigger. Fake blood burst from McGovern's chest. He looked down, his mouth open. Shepherd pulled the trigger twice in quick succession and two more blood spouts erupted at the top of McGovern's shirt. McGovern slumped to his knees, then fell forward into the grave. Shepherd walked slowly to the grave and shot a few seconds of McGovern lying face down, then he switched off the phone. "All done, Larry," he said. "Up you get."

McGovern pushed himself to his knees. His face was splattered with mud and he spat noisily. Shepherd looked at Duff. "How did it look?" He held out the gun.

"Perfect," said the technician. He took the weapon and handed it to his assistant, who placed it in a metal case.

"The blood was good?"

Duff nodded.

McGovern peered down at his mud-soaked jacket. "For fuck's sake," he said. He undid it and stared at the blood dripping through the holes in his shirt, then did it up again. "This suit is fucking ruined."

"I thought you'd fall on your back," said Shepherd.

"I thought forward would be more real," said McGovern. He held out his hand. Shepherd grabbed it and pulled him out of the grave.

"Think it'll convince them?" asked McGovern.

Shepherd held out the phone and replayed the video. "Looks good to me."

McGovern was staring at his mud-soaked knees. "Who's going to pay for the suit?" he asked.

"Just get it dry-cleaned," said Shepherd. "It'll be fine."

"It's fucked," said McGovern.

"Larry, if anyone else had taken this contract you'd be fucked, never mind your suit." He pointed at the gold bracelet on McGovern's right wrist. "I'll need that. They'll want proof."

McGovern put his hand over the bracelet. "My wife gave me this."

"She divorced you five years ago."

"Yeah, but it's worth a couple of grand."

"They'll know it's yours and that you wouldn't have given it up without a fight." Shepherd held out his hand and clicked his fingers. "Come on, don't fuck about."

McGovern grimaced but unhooked the bracelet and handed it over.

"The guys will want their equipment back," said Shepherd.

McGovern took off his jacket. Duff's assistant unbuttoned McGovern's shirt and helped him take it off, then removed the wiring, battery pack and transmitter that had been taped to his body. He put the shirt in one plastic bag and the equipment in another. Duff handed McGovern a sweatshirt.

McGovern looked at it contemptuously. "Are you serious? What did you do — raid your wardrobe?"

"Play nice, Larry," said Shepherd. "Everyone here is trying to help you."

"Because you want to put the O'Neills behind bars," said McGovern.

"And keep you alive," said Shepherd. "Let's not forget that."

McGovern pulled on the sweatshirt. "Now what?"

"Now we take you to a safe house," said Shepherd.

"Which is where?"

"One of the reasons it's safe is because you won't know where it is," said Shepherd. "No phone, no Wi-Fi, no nothing."

"I wasn't planning on tweeting that I was still alive," said McGovern.

"We need you out of sight, out of mind," said Shepherd.

"For how long?"

"As long as it takes," said Shepherd. He gestured at a waiting SUV. "Time to go."

"Days, right?"

"I don't know, Larry. I can't be making promises at this stage. The O'Neills wanted you dead and were prepared to pay good money for that. Luckily we got wind of it and I took the contract. We tipped you off, which is why we're all here now. But how it moves forward . . ." He wrinkled his nose. "I really don't know. I hope that after this the O'Neills will trust me and invite me in. If so, all well and good. But it might just be one of a series of tests, in which case it could drag on."

"That's not on," said McGovern. "I can't stay hidden for months. I've got a life."

Shepherd's eyes hardened. "Larry, you've got a life because I gave you one. If anyone else had taken the contract, you'd be lying in that hole for real."

"And don't think I'm not grateful for that. But the world's going to think I'm dead. It's going to fuck up my finances for one thing. My lawyer's going to hear I'm dead, which means my will gets opened. My business is going to fall apart."

"Larry, you're a gangster, not a businessman."

McGovern pointed a finger at Shepherd's face. "I have legitimate businesses," he said. "I have two dry-cleaning firms, a pub, a car wash, a florist."

"Cash businesses to launder money," said Shepherd.

"They're still legit, and if I'm dead they'll fall apart."

"I don't think the O'Neills are going to broadcast the fact that they've had you killed," said Shepherd. "So far as the world's concerned, you're missing."

McGovern scowled, still not convinced. Shepherd put his arm around his shoulder. "Larry, trust me, I don't want this to drag on one minute longer than necessary." He walked him to the SUV. There were two men in the front, MI5 heavies. Shepherd knew they were both armed. The rear passenger windows were impenetrably dark. He opened the offside back door for McGovern to get in. "You'll be fine, Larry. Cable TV, decent food, and your booze bill is on us."

"Hookers?"

Shepherd laughed. "You're dead, Larry. You won't be needing hookers."

McGovern climbed in and Shepherd slammed the door. The SUV drove off through the forest. Shepherd pulled out his phone and replayed the video. It looked convincing. He just hoped it would convince the O'Neill brothers.

It was a five-hour drive north along Route 6 from Palmyra to Tel Abyad. There had been three white SUVs. Mohammed al-Hussain had sat in the middle vehicle, armed IS fighters front and back. They had switched vehicles in Tel Abyad after stopping at a café down a quiet alley where al-Hussain had been given time to use a foul-smelling bathroom with an open toilet that was nothing more than a hole in the ground. After he had washed as best he could, an old man appeared with a pair of scissors and an open razor and spent twenty minutes carefully trimming al-Hussain's beard until it matched the photograph in the British passport. Afterwards al-Hussain and the other men had prayed on threadbare carpets, then eaten a quick meal of chicken, hummus and flatbread, with iced water, sitting at a table, while above them an old wall-mounted TV showed an Al-Jazeera news programme with the sound muted.

After the meal they had given al-Hussain fresh clothes to change into. They were clearly used but had been cleaned. There was a denim shirt, faded jeans, socks, underwear and almost-new Nike trainers. His old clothes were taken from him and put into a black plastic rubbish bag. He kept the British passport that Commander al-Lihaib had given him, his prayer beads and his wristwatch, a TAG-Heuer that had been an eighteenth-birthday present from his parents.

"I need to see the watch," said the fighter who headed the security team. He was in his late fifties, his skin the colour of teak, his right hand covered with scar tissue. His name was Ahmadi but everyone called him Al Am, the Uncle. His orders were obeyed without question.

Al-Hussain took it off and handed it to him. Al Am looked at it and turned it over. As he did so, al-Hussain remembered the engraved inscription on the back: "To a wonderful son, from his proud parents. May Allah protect him." Al Am looked at him and shook his head.

"I understand," said al-Hussain.

"And the bag. We must take it from you now." He held his hand out for al-Hussain's backpack. He took it off and held it for a while, like a newborn baby, cradled against his chest, his head resting on the top. He didn't want to let go of his weapon, but knew he had no choice. If he was discovered with a sniper's rifle, his cover would be destroyed and he'd be shot or worse. The notebook had to go. In fact everything, every single thing, that connected him to his former life had to be handed over to the IS fighter. To keep anything that gave away his true identity risked exposing him and ending the mission. And the mission was all that mattered.

"You will take good care of my bag," said al-Hussain, as he took it off. "You will take it back to Commander al-Lihaib. You are to give it to him and no one else."

"I will do that," said Al Am. "*Inshallah*." If Allah wills.

Al-Hussain held out the bag. His fingers stayed touching the nylon material for several seconds and he sighed audibly as it was taken from him. "Now tell me your name," said Al Am.

"My name?"

"Who are you?"

Al-Hussain frowned. "I am Mohammed al-Hussain."

Al Am shook his head. "You are not. From now on you are Hammad Rajput. From England. Until this mission is over you must put all thoughts of Mohammed al-Hussain out of your head."

Al-Hussain grimaced at his mistake, but said nothing.

Al Am placed the wristwatch inside the bag, then slung it over his shoulder. "It is time to go."

"Thank you for getting me this far."

"It has been an honour and a privilege," said Al Am, bowing his head.

Mohammed al-Hussain was put into the back of a rusting black pick-up truck. The two IS fighters who had driven him from Palmyra sat in the front and he was joined by another man, in his late twenties with skin burned almost black by the sun, who cradled an AK-47 with a folding metal stock in his lap. He turned to al-Hussain and smiled, revealing several missing teeth.

"*Assalamu alaykum*," said the man. "*Kayfa anta?*" How are you?

"*Bi-khair alhamdulillah.*" Fine, praise be to Allah.

"There's water under the seat if you're thirsty."

Al-Hussain nodded. "I'm grateful, thank you."

Shepherd had the black cab drop him outside Selfridges. He went inside and spent fifteen minutes wandering around, reassuring himself that he wasn't being followed. He headed outside and grabbed the third cab that drove by with its light on and said, "Paddington station," in a loud voice as he climbed in. As soon as the vehicle pulled away from the kerb he asked the driver to drop him at the Mayfair Hotel.

Howard Wedekind was sitting at a corner table with a vodka and tonic in front of him. He looked like a typical accountant, balding and wearing a rumpled suit with a scuffed briefcase at the side of his chair. He had the yellowing fingers of a smoker and, from the way he was tapping them on the table, Shepherd figured it had been a while since he'd had a cigarette.

"You're late," said Wedekind.

"I said four-ish," said Shepherd, sitting down.

Wedekind glanced at his watch, a cheap black plastic Casio. "It's half past." There was something off about his left eye. It was slightly closed and the pupil seemed a bit further to the side than it should have been.

"Which is four-ish," said Shepherd. "In a few more minutes it'll be five-ish and I'll be officially late." He smiled at a waitress in a short skirt. "Bombay gin, Schweppes tonic, lime and ice," he said. She smiled and tottered away on impossibly high heels. Shepherd turned to watch her, playing the ladies' man for Wedekind's benefit. "I'd give her one," he said.

"How did it go?" asked Wedekind.

"Same as it always goes. He begged me not to shoot him, he offered me money, then I shot him." He shrugged. "Same old, same old."

"As easy as that?"

"I didn't say it was easy," said Shepherd, "but there's a predictability about it. First they don't believe it's happening, then they try to negotiate or threaten their way out of it, and finally they accept it. Or they try to rush you. But Larry wasn't a rusher. You've got my money?"

"Obviously I'd like proof of death," said Wedekind, his voice a low whisper.

Shepherd reached into his jacket pocket and pulled out the gold bracelet he'd taken from McGovern. He gave it to Wedekind, who smiled as he weighed it in the palm of his hand. "He loved this, Larry did. Never took it off."

"Yeah. Well, not any more." He fished a small memory card out of his wallet. "If the lads want to see McGovern's final seconds, show them this."

Wedekind stared at it in amazement. "You're joking."

"Serious as cancer."

"You filmed it?"

"Howard, there's a reason they call it a handgun. One hand is all you need."

"This is a fucking first," said Wedekind, taking the card.

The waitress returned with Shepherd's gin and tonic. She bent down low, giving him a fairly decent view of her impressive cleavage and flashed him a smile, then straightened up and tottered away.

"I can't believe you filmed it," said Wedekind, putting the card into his wallet. "The boys are going to love that. And no one will ever find the body?"

"Buried deep in the New Forest," said Shepherd. "I've put a dozen in the woods and no one's ever the wiser. You've got to bury them deep enough so dogs don't get the scent, but other than that it's easy-peasy." He raised his glass in salute and took a long drink.

"You're a pro all right," said Wedekind. "A breath of fresh air in this business."

"That's why they call me the Hammer," said Shepherd. "I nail it every time."

Wedekind bent down, opened his briefcase and took out a brown envelope. He handed it to Shepherd. "Your fee."

Shepherd took it and put it into his inside pocket.

"You don't want to check it?" asked Wedekind.

"I know you can afford it, and I also know you know what would happen if you tried to short-change me," said Shepherd. He grinned as Wedekind's eyes tightened. "I'm just messing with you," he said. "This is a long-term thing, Howard. I'd rather work for your firm than a succession of strangers. Strangers can be a liability. I know you, you know me, there's a bond. Trust."

"I hear you," said Wedekind.

"I mean it. This job I just did, it was by way of a test. It wasn't about the money. It was about me proving to you that I do what I say I'll do." He patted the pocket containing the money. "And proving to myself that you'll pay for my services. The big question is, where do we go from here?"

"I'll be in touch, you can count on it," Wedekind said.

"Good to know."

The pick-up truck left the road before they reached the Turkish border, about an hour after darkness had fallen, as quickly as if a black sheet had been thrown over the desert. They drove for five miles, then saw another pick-up, this one a mud-spattered red. Four men in long robes stood around it, holding Kalashnikovs.

The truck slowed to a halt about fifty feet from the other vehicle. The driver twisted in his seat. "Stay here," he said. He climbed out, as did the fighter in the passenger seat. The man sitting next to Mohammed al-Hussain slipped his finger onto the trigger.

"Is there a problem?" al-Hussain asked him.

The man smiled, showing the gaps between his teeth. "No," he said. "*Inshallah*." God willing.

The two fighters walked to the other four and the driver said something. One of the men replied, and shortly afterwards they all embraced. The man beside al-Hussain slid his finger off the trigger and visibly relaxed.

Their driver indicated that they should get out of the car and beckoned them over. They did as they were told and he came to talk to them. The sky overhead was a carpet of stars, and a chilling breeze blew from the north. The terrain ahead was bleak desert, sand and rocks. The only indication that Syria would become Turkey was a concrete wall topped by razor wire. The Turkish border town of Akçakale lay a few miles away on the other side. Behind them, half an hour's drive, was Tel Abyad. "Everything is good," said the driver. "They will take you over the wall into Turkey and another vehicle will pick you up there."

"Thank you for bringing me this far," said al-Hussain. "*Assalamu alaykum*." Peace be upon you.

The man hugged him. "*Assalamu alaykum wa rahmatu Allahi wa barakaatuhu*," he said. Peace be upon you and Allah's mercy and blessings. He hugged him again, this time kissing him softly on both cheeks. "It's time for you to go." He directed him to the second pick-up truck. Al-Hussain walked slowly towards the four men. For a wild moment he wondered if it was some sort of trap and they were about to kill him in the desert, but they greeted him warmly.

Two of them pulled a tarpaulin loose in the back of the truck to reveal two aluminium folding ladders. They seized one each and carried them to the wall. Al-Hussain followed them, shivering in the cold night air.

One of the men placed his ladder against the wall and hurried up it. He used clippers to cut away a section of the razor wire, then waved for al-Hussain to join him. Al-Hussain went up the ladder carefully and sat on the top of the wall. He helped lift the second ladder up and the fighter at the top placed it on the other side. He went down first, then waved for al-Hussain to follow him.

He stepped carefully over the top of the wall making sure not to catch his shirt on the razor wire, then hurried down to join the other man, who was already jogging over to the final barrier, a wire fence again topped by razor wire. It was only eight feet high but they didn't intend to climb over it: the fighter already had his wire clippers in his hand and bent down to cut a hole.

Al-Hussain stood with his hands on his hips and surveyed the scene ahead. He stiffened as he spotted a dark SUV. He shifted his head from side to side, trying to get a clearer view, and realised two figures were standing at the rear of the vehicle. He bent down. "Are they waiting for me?" he whispered.

"Of course," said the man. He snipped another strand of wire. In less than three minutes he had cut enough to force a hole in the fence big enough for both men to slip through. He held the wire back for al-Hussain. "Be careful," he said, holding al-Hussain's arm. "There is a ditch."

They went down slowly into the sandy ditch and crawled up the far side, then hurried to the SUV. The fighter with al-Hussain exchanged a few words with the men, then hugged them both. "This is the cargo," he said, waving his hand at al-Hussain. "It is to be protected at all costs."

The SUV had four doors and a man opened one of the rear doors for al-Hussain. "There's food in the back, and water," said the man, "with a blanket and a pillow, if you wish to sleep. We'll be driving for some time."

Al-Hussain thanked him and climbed in. The door slammed behind him. As he watched through the window the three men outside embraced again, then the IS fighter headed back to the border. Two minutes later the SUV was bouncing along the rough ground. The driver and the second man had both donned night-vision goggles and kept the headlights off. There was a cloth package on the seat next to him, which al-Hussain unwrapped. Inside he found a small loaf of hard bread, some olives and soft goat's cheese. Another, smaller, package contained a bundle of *khat*.

Al-Hussain put aside the food and started to chew the leaves.

Omar Hassan lived in Salford, just five miles south of the park where he was to meet his contact. It would have taken just twelve minutes by taxi but he travelled by bus, tram and then on foot. The journey took him almost an hour but gave him plenty of opportunity to check that he wasn't being followed.

The instructions detailing where he was to go and whom he was to meet had been placed in a mail folder in a Yahoo account. It was the way he had communicated with his Islamic State handlers for more than five years, ever since he had returned from a training camp on the Pakistan border. Hassan had flown to Islamabad in 2010 with four of his friends from Greater Manchester, ostensibly to attend a wedding, then to spend time getting to know the culture of the country their parents had come from. All five were British-born, the sons of parents who had emigrated to the UK during the fifties and sixties.

They had been teenagers when they had made the long trip to Pakistan, and Hassan's parents had expressed their reservations. Hassan was the youngest of five, four boys and a girl, and was the only one who had ever expressed any interest in connecting with his Pakistani heritage. The local imam had come to see his parents to ask their permission for him to go. What they didn't know was that the imam was a recruiter for al-Qaeda, selecting men suitable for jihadist training. He was a kindly man, well known in the area for his charitable works, and he had sat in the Hassan house for more than an hour drinking hot mint tea as he explained how beneficial the trip would be for Omar's Islamic studies, that a Saudi Arabian charity would bear the costs and pay him a handsome stipend.

Eventually Hassan's parents agreed, and he flew to Pakistan a month later. He attended the wedding and returned with lots of photographs of the ceremony and the celebrations afterwards. There were also photographs of him visiting sights of cultural interest, and attending various mosques. But there were no photographs of the place where he and his companions had spent most of the trip: an al-Qaeda training camp across the border in the rugged mountains of Afghanistan. There, Hassan had been trained to fire a range of weapons, from handguns to shoulder-mounted ground-to-air missiles, and instructed on how to deal with explosives, from making small IEDs to constructing landmines large enough to destroy a tank. His instructors had groomed him in tradecraft as well, explaining how to arrange a clandestine meeting, how to detect a tail, and how to remain undercover and invisible for years.

Hassan had been an eager pupil and had returned to Salford fired up and ready to fight for the cause, to kill the infidel and avenge Muslims who had been persecuted and murdered around the world. His instructions had been to return to his regular life until he was called upon to serve the cause. Each day he was to check a Yahoo account that had been specially set up for him. He was not to send emails from the account, or to receive any on it, but messages could be left in the drafts folder. It was a foolproof system that neither the Americans nor the British could spy on, no matter how hard they tried. Messages that were not sent could not be intercepted. But days turned to weeks, weeks turned to months and eventually became years. Each day he would check the drafts folder, and each day he would be disappointed.

When the Americans killed al-Qaeda leader Bin Laden, Hassan was sure he would be called to arms, but the call never came. What he didn't know was that after Bin Laden's death there had been a leadership struggle for control of the jihadist battle in the Middle East, with the relatively young jihadists of Islamic State eventually becoming dominant. The men who had trained Hassan had switched sides early on and expanded their training programme. Dozens of young jihadists were trained and sent back to their own countries, and still Hassan waited. Several times he would leave a message in the draft folder: I AM READY. PLEASE USE ME. Each time, the reply was always the same: BE PATIENT, BROTHER.

Eventually, some five years and six months after his return from Pakistan, Hassan received a message telling him to report for a meeting in Heaton Park the following day. After he'd read it, Hassan could barely concentrate on his work, servicing engines at the family's garage. He couldn't eat because his stomach was churning, and that night he tossed and turned, unable to sleep.

He walked past the entrance, then doubled back, checking carefully to see if he had wrong-footed any

40

followers, but he was sure he wasn't being tailed. He went into the park.

Heaton Park covered more than six hundred acres and was the biggest council park in Europe, with an eighteen-hole golf course, a boating lake, tennis courts, woodlands, ornamental gardens and a petting zoo. The instructions said that Hassan was to wait on a bench overlooking the lake. He did a complete circuit of the lake, then sat down on the bench. Two minutes later he was joined by an Asian man in his fifties, bearded and wearing a skull cap. In his right hand he carried a small copy of the Koran. He had the look of an imam. He undid the top two buttons of his coat and sat down on the far side of the bench. They were silent for a minute or so. Then: "Did you see the match last night?" said the man, quietly, as he looked out across the lake.

"Which one?"

"City."

"Five — two," said Hassan.

Manchester City hadn't played since the previous weekend and the game had been a draw. The brief conversation had been prearranged and confirmed that both men were who they claimed to be. The man looked at Hassan and smiled. "The time has come for you to serve, brother."

"I'm ready," said Hassan.

The man glanced around, then took a folded piece of paper from his pocket. On it were five pictures of a vehicle. The front, the back, the two sides and an overhead view. Hassan raised his eyebrows when he realised what it was. "Are you serious?"

"The markings and colours must be identical," said the man. "We'll need four."

"How soon?"

"Three weeks. Maximum. You'll be supplied with registration numbers the day before the vehicles are required."

"And — what? I steal them?"

"Not necessarily," said the man. "They are often sold second hand after they have outlived their usefulness. But they must be roadworthy and they must look like the photographs. See what's available around the country. Use false names when you buy. If you have to steal, make sure you steal from different counties."

"What about the insides?"

"They should look the part but they don't have to function. They must be driveable, obviously."

"They won't be cheap, brother, not if we buy them."

The man smiled and took out a thick envelope. "We'll require receipts," he said.

Hassan slipped the envelope inside his jacket.

"If you need more money, ask. But, as I said, we'll require receipts. How many men will you be using?"

"The engines and mechanical work I can take care of myself," he said. "I'll only be buying runners so it should just be a matter of tuning them up. I'm assuming we don't need insurance or MOTs."

The man nodded. "They'll be used only once, and they're to stay off the road until they're needed."

"Then I can probably get away with one guy to do the paintwork and the signs," he said.

"The lights?"

"I'm good with electrics."

The man smiled his approval. "That is why you were chosen, brother. You have the skills."

"But if we have to steal them, I'll need help."

"You have the people?"

"I do."

"And they can be trusted?"

"Absolutely. With my life."

"Use them if you must, but say nothing until the time is at hand," he said.

"Where do I keep them? There isn't room in my garage — or not enough to keep them hidden."

"You will be contacted by someone with premises. Through the mail folder." He stood up. "This is a great thing we're doing, brother," he said.

"I realise that," said Hassan.

"Be careful."

"I will."

The two men embraced, then walked off in different directions.

The black cab dropped Shepherd at the main entrance to the British Museum but he walked around the side towards an office area clearly marked EMPLOYEES ONLY. There was a black door with an intercom on the wall next to it. He pressed the button and looked up at the CCTV camera covering the area. The lock buzzed and Shepherd pushed the door open. He stepped into a carpeted corridor with more doors leading off both sides. He knocked on the third to the left.

"Enter!" It was the tone of a headmaster summoning a schoolboy and Shepherd had half a mind to turn and walk away. Instead he twisted the handle and pushed open the door. Jeremy Willoughby-Brown was sitting behind a large desk in a high-backed executive chair, his feet on a window-sill. "Daniel, welcome, grab yourself a pew." He waved at two straight-backed chairs facing him, and Shepherd took the one on the left. Willoughby-Brown was halfway through one of his favourite small cigars and he had opened a window behind him to allow the smoke to escape, though Shepherd knew that that didn't make what he was doing any less illegal. "No refreshments, I'm afraid," he said. "This is all I could get at short notice."

"I'm good," said Shepherd, though actually he could have done with a coffee.

"There's no reason we couldn't have done this in Thames House," said Willoughby-Brown.

"I'm undercover. I can't risk being spotted walking into MI5's HQ."

"You're being over-cautious," said Willoughby-Brown, flicking ash into the pot of what seemed to be a plastic plant. "What are the odds that anyone connected to a South London crime family would be passing Thames House at the exact moment you decided to pay us a visit?"

"It doesn't matter what the odds are. I'm not prepared to take the risk. And it's my call."

Willoughby-Brown raised his hands in surrender. "Daniel, whatever it takes to keep you happy is fine by me. So, how are we fixed with the O'Neills?"

"All good. So far as they know, I'm a stone-cold killer who's happy to be on their payroll. Give it a few days and I'll mention the money thing, see if I can get them to bring me into their laundering. At that point I'm going to need some cash."

"How much?"

"It'll have to be a lot or they won't take me seriously."

"How much is a lot?"

"Half a mill would get their attention."

Willoughby-Brown grimaced. "That's a big wedge, Daniel."

"You don't need money-laundering for a few grand. If you want me to blow the whole organisation apart, we need to be able to follow the money."

"You can understand my reluctance to give London's biggest gangster firm half a million pounds of Her Majesty's money. What if they rip you off?"

"They're convinced I'm a professional assassin. I'm the last person they're going to be thinking about ripping off. Any less than that and they're not going to introduce me to their money men. But with half a mill I can demand a sit-down. Then we can put names to faces so that when we take them down we can get their assets, too."

"And it has to be cash?"

Shepherd sighed in exasperation. "I can hardly give them a cheque, can I? The whole point is that I want to get cash into the system."

"Yes, I know that," said Willoughby-Brown, archly. "But I'm sure you understand my reservations."

"You don't make an omelette without breaking eggs," said Shepherd.

"This isn't about a dozen eggs, though, is it? This is the whole hen-house."

"If Five is serious in wanting to destroy the O'Neills as a criminal force, they have to put in the effort. So far we have enough on tape to put half a dozen of them behind bars but not Tommy and Marty, not yet. And even if we do move against them with what we have, we don't know where most of the money is. There's the house in Bromley but that's in Tommy's wife's name. The cars are leased, the businesses in shell companies. They never use credit or debit cards."

"We can get Tommy and Marty on conspiracy to murder," said Willoughby-Brown.

"Not without me standing in the witness box, and that's not going to happen," said Shepherd. "You know how it works. I gather evidence but I'm never in court."

"We could put you behind a screen. Work up a disguise for you. It's been done before."

"Not with me it hasn't."

"Okay, I take your point. We need to bait the trap and a few crumbs of cheese won't do it. I'll get the money sorted. Pounds, I suppose?"

"Some pounds, some euros. The Hammer works Europe-wide."

"Seriously? You call yourself the Hammer?"

"It makes what I do more memorable."

"I suppose you know best," said Willoughby-Brown. "The money might take a day or two — we'll need the numbers registered."

"No consecutive ones," said Shepherd.

Willoughby-Brown flashed him a tight smile. "I'm not exactly a virgin at this, Daniel. Please give me some credit. What about when you give them the money? Can you be wired up?"

"Not if Tommy and Marty are anywhere nearby," Shepherd said. "They use the latest counter-eavesdropping technology. And Tommy's hardly ever here, these days. He's almost always in Dubai. There's no way he'll be going anywhere near the money."

"What about the wife? Can we get to her?"

Shepherd shook his head. "They're solid. They lead separate lives pretty much but she's still Mrs O'Neill."

"What about getting Marty to talk on tape? We can be creative. I'd like some record of the money being handed over. I don't suppose there's any way we could get them to go with you when you do it?"

"They'll probably insist on using a third party. But let me play it by ear."

"How long have we been after the O'Neills? It's going on six months, right?"

Shepherd nodded. "Since I first got introduced to Marty."

"Softy softly, catchee monkey."

"Has to be that way, obviously. Can't be seen to be too keen. It has to look like their idea."

"And what about Marty? How do you feel about him?"

Shepherd's eyes narrowed. "What do you mean?"

"It must be strange, cosying up to him when he's the enemy."

"He's not really an enemy," said Shepherd. "He's a target. 'Enemy' suggests there's bad feeling between us. There's nothing like that. He's a criminal. I work for an organisation that tries to put criminals out of business."

"But to do that, you have to befriend him, don't you?"

Shepherd shrugged but didn't answer.

"And then you have to betray him. All of them, in fact. How does that make you feel?"

Shepherd held the man's eyes for several seconds before he spoke. "What was your degree in?"

"PPE. Philosophy, politics and economics. Why?"

"Not psychology, then?"

"Very droll, Daniel. No, not psychology."

"So maybe we should leave any psychological evaluation in the hands of the experts."

"I was just asking, out of interest."

"To be blunt, how I feel about what I do is absolutely no concern of yours. All you need to worry about is how well I do my job and how I deal with the tasks I'm given. The O'Neill investigation is going as planned and that's all you have to know."

"You sound defensive," said Willoughby-Brown, leaning back in his seat and steepling his fingers under his chin.

"It's a natural reaction when somebody suggests I'm not capable of carrying out my job effectively," said Shepherd. "I hang out with Marty and his mates, I drink with them and chat with them, but I never lose sight of the fact that they're my targets, and at the end of the day, if I do my job properly, they'll be behind bars. But that's down to the choices they've made. No one forced them to become criminals."

"And how do you think they'll feel when they eventually find out who you are?"

"They won't," said Shepherd. "Not if you do your job properly."

"They'll suspect, surely."

"Again, it's a question of making sure that doesn't happen." He frowned. "I hope you're not serious, Jeremy. They must never even suspect my role in this."

"It wouldn't be the end of the world — they'll be behind bars for a long time."

"You think that'll stop them running things? They'll still have money and they'll have the contacts. They can put out a hit on me from a cell in Belmarsh as easily as they can from the Mayfair bar."

"Do you have an exit strategy?"

"I might have to die, like McGovern. We'll see."

"Whatever you're comfortable with, Daniel."

"I'll keep you posted. Meanwhile, there's something I wanted to run by you," said Shepherd. He took the RAF thumb drive from his pocket and held it out. "I've got pictures of three guys on the roof, just before the missile hit. You'll be able to confirm that our two targets are there, but the sniper might have got away."

Willoughby-Brown took it. "Can't win 'em all."

"Be handy if you could ID the sniper. Get the technical boys on it."

"Syria's full of snipers," said Willoughby-Brown. "It's not really our problem. We're more interested in the

British jihadists and, so far as I'm aware, there are no Brit snipers out there."

Shepherd gestured at the thumb drive. "That guy's special," he said. "He was looking at a shot of a mile or so. And there were two men on the roof with him. Two spotters is unusual. And I think he had even more jihadists watching out for him. That was how he managed to avoid the explosion. It looks to me like IS were going out of their way to protect him, which would make him a high-value target."

"But not for us."

"The Americans, then. I'm serious, Jeremy. There's no way of knowing how many guys that sniper has killed. At least get your people to do facial recognition on the pictures, see if he's known."

"Okay," said Willoughby-Brown, but Shepherd had heard the lack of conviction in his voice.

"What now?" he asked. "I'm getting a bit tired of sitting in that container watching video feeds."

Willoughby-Brown grinned. "I can remedy that," he said. "I need you out in Turkey."

"Since when has Five operated in Turkey?"

"We're liaising with Six."

"They don't have their own people?"

Willoughby-Brown grimaced. "Why are you giving me a hard time, Daniel? I thought you might jump at a bit of overseas travel. Get you out of your rut."

"What rut?"

"I just meant a change is as good as a rest. Revitalise the old batteries while serving Queen and country. But the threat is a UK one. We have a source in a refugee camp, a chap by the name of Yusuf Yilmaz. He's made contact and is offering us names and photographs of Islamic State fighters who have passed through the camp pretending to be Syrian refugees. He helped them get the paperwork. He says they're on their way to Europe. The UK in particular."

"So fly him over and debrief him in Thames House."

"I wish it was that easy," said Willoughby-Brown. "He has a number of demands, including fast-track to British citizenship and rather a lot of money."

"If the intel's good, what's the problem?"

"Because we don't have the intel. All we've got is an initial contact, via an agent of ours who works for an NGO out there. We need someone to go and talk to him, to see if he's offering us gold or shit."

"You can send anyone. A bloody intern could handle it. Check out the intel. If it's good, put him and his family on a plane."

"Our local guy has met with Yusuf but I need someone more experienced to sit down with him."

"So he's a people-trafficker, this Yusuf?"

"It sounds like it. As I said, at the moment we have little in the way of hard information. But if he has what he says he has, we could have a major Islamic State cell, or cells, already in place in the UK."

Shepherd sighed. "Okay. When do I leave?"

"I'm having your John Whitehill legend refreshed for you as we speak. The documents should be ready within the hour. The Hampstead flat still works as Whitehill's address and we've been placing various

51

bylined stories in magazines and on websites so it's the perfect cover. Have you heard of Suruç?"

Shepherd nodded. "The Turks have one of their largest refugee camps there. Forty thousand Syrians, last I heard."

"It's a massive set-up," said Willoughby-Brown, "basically a huge tent city with two hospitals, seven clinics, and enough schools for ten thousand kids. It's just over the border from Syria, close to where Kurdish forces have been battling it out with Islamic State."

"How many refugees are there in Turkey now?"

"Around three million," said Willoughby-Brown. "Even if just one in a thousand of those are Islamic State bad guys then we're looking at three thousand potential Islamic militants in Europe. Suruç itself is relatively safe though there was a bombing there in July 2015 that killed thirty-two people."

"At the camp?"

Willoughby-Brown shook his head. "Outside a cultural centre."

"Nice," said Shepherd.

Willoughby-Brown slid a photograph across the desk. "This is our agent, Craig Parker. He's been on Six's payroll for the past ten years but he's gainfully employed by Refugee Rescue, an NGO that's funded mainly out of the US and the EU. Parker was in the former Yugoslavia when Six first spotted him but latterly he's been all over the Middle East, Afghanistan, Iraq, Libya, then Syria and Turkey as of last year. He's reliable, a bit of a lefty, but he helps us if he thinks it's the right thing to do."

52

"Be nice if we could all be as choosy as that."

Willoughby-Brown chuckled drily. "It's just a question of phrasing our requests in the right way," he said. "But in this case he was on the phone to us as soon as Yusuf made the approach."

"So Yusuf knows Parker's with Six?"

"Oh, God, no. Yusuf was just mouthing off and Parker said he might know someone who could help. He put him in touch with one of our people from the embassy in Ankara. That guy did the preliminary interview but Yusuf is insisting on talking to someone from London. That plays into our hands because it means you can take a look at whatever he's got."

"What do we know about him?"

"Not much. He's just a run-of-the-mill people-trafficker, so far as we know. No links to terrorism."

"Do the Americans know about him?"

"We haven't checked with them yet."

"Yet?"

"We don't go running to the Americans every time we get a piece of intel. This is exclusive to us and we'd like to keep it that way."

"Sure, but the Americans have way more intel on what's going on in Turkey and Syria than we do. It would be handy to know if Yusuf is naughty or nice."

"Well, yes, but it's the quality of the intel that matters at the end of the day, not the source."

"I'm more concerned about my safety, frankly," said Shepherd.

"Turkey isn't a war zone."

"It's right next to one," said Shepherd. "How do we know Yusuf isn't part of some greater plan to put an MI5 officer in an orange jumpsuit and behead him on YouTube?"

"Shuttleworth said he seemed kosher." He grinned. "Well, not kosher obviously. But there were no red flags."

"Shuttleworth?"

"Our man in the embassy. Derek Shuttleworth. He interviewed him, covered the basics, and now it's time for us to take over." He took a drag on his cigar and flicked more ash. "We can give you protection out there, I'm sure."

"Bodyguards?"

"Army, if you prefer. Just let me know what you need."

"First sign of anything and I'm out," said Shepherd.

"Absolutely. Wouldn't have it any other way," said Willoughby-Brown. "Your safety is paramount, as always."

Shepherd didn't reply. He doubted that his personal safety was of the slightest interest to Willoughby-Brown.

"So we're good?" asked Willoughby-Brown.

"When?"

"Soon as."

"There's a boxing do tonight. Black tie. Marty will be there."

"What about Tommy?"

"No one's mentioned it, but they never do. He flies in and out, like the Scarlet Pimpernel. But he's a big boxing fan so my guess is that he'll be there."

54

"So, fly tomorrow. I'll get you on the BA flight, direct. It's less than four hours. Leave in the morning and you'll be in Suruç before dark."

"Get me a stopover. Schiphol, Frankfurt or Paris."

"Because?"

"Because if I'm being tailed it'll be that much harder to follow me."

"If that's what you want."

"Yes, it's what I want, Jeremy," said Shepherd.

He shrugged. "So mote it be."

Shepherd frowned. It was a strange expression for the man to use. "So mote it be" was a phrase Freemasons used at the end of prayers instead of "amen". Was Willoughby-Brown a Freemason? A lot of police officers were but he hadn't come across it in the security services.

"I'll get the flights fixed. And what about tonight? Do you need any equipment?"

Shepherd shook his head. "It's social."

Omar Hassan arrived at the family garage just after lunch. As always, it was busy, with his three brothers hard at work. "Where've you been?" asked Zack, the eldest, who was in charge when their father wasn't there.

"I told Dad I'd be late. He was cool with it," said Omar.

"I didn't ask whether you'd told him, I asked where you'd been."

Zack was almost ten years older than Omar and a good two inches taller. As the eldest he was supposed to be accorded respect, but Omar despised him. He was weak and flabby, too fond of Coke and fast food. He was a bad Muslim, too, often missing prayer time while working in the garage. Worse, much worse, he was dating an English girl. A *kafir*. For that alone he deserved to be treated with contempt. But Omar's trainers had taught him well. He smiled and put up his hands to apologise. "I'm sorry, bruv. I was at the dentist's. One of my back teeth was playing up."

"Okay now?"

Omar pulled a face. "He gave me an injection, said it should quieten the nerve down. But if it doesn't get better I might need the root working on."

"Unlucky, bruv," said Zack, ruffling his brother's hair. He gestured at a white Transit van. "New brake linings. And the steering's loose."

"I'm on it," said Omar. He hurried to the locker room.

Another of his brothers, Toby, was bent over the engine of another Transit. "You okay, bruv?" he asked, as Omar went by.

"Yeah, all good," said Omar. Toby was a couple of years older than Omar, and had thought he might one day become a jihadist. But the imam who had groomed Omar was less convinced by the older brother. He had spoken to Toby at length over a six-month period not long before Omar had gone to Pakistan and pronounced him too weak and too corrupted by the West. Omar knew that the imam had a point. Toby prayed every day, but never more than once or twice. He liked pop music and had posters of Beyoncé and

56

Rihanna on his bedroom wall. He abused himself every night. Omar knew that to be the case because his bedroom was next to Toby's and he could hear him through the wall.

"When you're done with the Transit, I could do with a hand here. We've got a rush on."

"We've always got a rush on," said Omar. "Dad takes on too much work. He's killing us."

"Make hay while the sun shines, bruv," said Toby, wiping his forehead with his sleeve. "We'd be moaning if we didn't have any work. At least this way we're earning."

Omar's father had set up the garage a few years after arriving in the UK, funded with money he'd borrowed from family and friends. The early years had been a struggle but he was a good, honest mechanic and had a lot of return business, mainly from within the local Pakistani community. But it was the boom in online shopping that had taken the business to a whole new level. With more and more people ordering online, courier firms sprang up around the country, with fleets of vehicles that needed repairing and servicing. Omar's father had landed half a dozen lucrative contracts and the garage had been working at full capacity for the past two years. Now he was searching for larger premises.

All four of the Hassan brothers worked as mechanics and their sister Jasmine ran the office, a small windowless cubby-hole in the far corner of the garage. Omar's father had also hired a bodywork specialist, a Pakistani who had been in the country for just two years and was claiming asylum as an Afghan refugee.

His name was Faisal and he was in his thirties. He had left his wife and two children in Pakistan and planned to bring them over once he had been granted leave to remain, which his lawyer thought would take three more years at most.

Faisal did most of his work at the far end of the garage in an area closed off with plastic sheeting. He was preparing to respray a door he'd recently repaired. When he saw Omar, he took off his mask and waved at him. Omar waved back. Faisal was a good Muslim, a true Muslim, and, like Omar, a committed jihadist. He trusted Faisal completely. He had told him about his al-Qaeda training and that one day he hoped to bring the jihadist fight to England. Faisal had nodded enthusiastically and promised to help.

Just as Omar pulled open the door to the locker room, his third brother, Aidan, came out, zipping up his overalls. "Hi, bruv," said Aidan. "Where've you been?" He was seventeen and getting ready to go to university, though he had applied to study in Manchester so that he could continue to work part-time in the garage. He had a black eye and a scrape across his nose from where a badly secured van bonnet had crashed down on him two days earlier.

"Dentist," said Omar.

"You okay?"

"He gave me an injection."

"Sorry, bruv."

"Aidan, get over here!" shouted Toby. "How long does a dump take?"

Aidan grinned at Omar. "He's a charmer, isn't he?" He jogged over to Toby.

Omar went into the locker room, which contained a dozen rusting metal lockers that his father had picked up cheaply at a government auction years earlier. There was a bench against one wall and a door leading to the bathroom. It was a men-only affair and rarely cleaned. Jasmine had her own facilities next to her office and guarded them jealously — she had the only key. Omar pulled his key-ring from the pocket of his jeans and opened his locker. He took out the envelope of cash and rifled through it: there were at least a hundred fifty-pound notes. He put it on the shelf, covered it with a copy of *Motorcycle News*, then changed into his overalls, which were blue, with the name of the garage on the back. His heart was pounding. He was finally doing it. He was finally on a mission. His life was about to change for ever.

Shepherd squared his shoulders, took a deep breath, and walked towards the hotel entrance. A dozen men in black tie, laughing and smoking cigarettes, were standing outside. Shepherd was wearing black tie, too, an Armani suit that had cost the best part of three thousand pounds. Willoughby-Brown had balked at that but Shepherd had explained there was no way he could turn up in a rented tux. The Rolex Daytona on his wrist was real and his shoes had cost close to five hundred pounds. Men like Tommy and Marty O'Neill could spot a fake from a hundred yards and that went for people as much as clothes and watches.

To the left of reception a sprawling bar area was packed with another couple of hundred men in dinner jackets. There were lots of shaved heads and gold chains. They turned to check Shepherd as he walked by, nothing aggressive, just alpha males wanting to know who the competition was.

Shepherd scanned the room and spotted Paul Evans almost immediately. Evans had been his introduction to the O'Neill family. He was an enforcer, one of the guys who were sent around to collect bad debts. Some debt-collectors used guns, others blunt instruments, but Evans was a big hard man whose intimidating presence and dead-fish stare were often enough to persuade people to pay up. When he wasn't working, Evans was affable and good company, and had a plethora of funny stories about his childhood, usually ending with his Welsh miner father taking off his belt and giving him a good thrashing. Like a lot of villains, Evans could turn on the hard stare at will, switching from laughing *bon viveur* to menacing thug in a fraction of a second. Most of the men in the room had that quality, and while there was lots of laughter and good-natured back-slapping, there was an underlying tension, a sense that violence could kick off at any moment, leaving blood on the highly polished parquet floor.

Evans spotted Shepherd and waved him over. A chunky gold bracelet glinted on his right wrist with two large sovereign rings on his fingers — they functioned as an efficient knuckleduster when needed. Evans had close-cropped bullet-grey hair and a nose that had

60

clearly been hit a few times. The slightly swollen left ear testified to his years as an amateur boxer, before he'd discovered that he could be paid handsomely for hitting people out of the ring.

"Terry, good to see you, mate." Evans hugged Shepherd. "It's going to be a fun night. What do you want?"

"Gin and tonic," said Shepherd.

"Double?"

"At least."

Evans headed for the bar. Shepherd knew the two men he was drinking with. The bigger of them was Jon Cooper, a second-hand-car dealer with a chunky diamond in his left ear. The other was a drug-trafficker, who split his time between a large detached house in Croydon and a villa with a pool outside Marbella. His name was Ricky Carter and Shepherd knew that the police had been after him for years, but as he never did any business when he was in the UK, he had never been caught. Cooper and Carter often hung out with Evans, and Shepherd always found them good company. He was pretty sure that would change if they ever found out he was an undercover MI5 officer.

"You ever box, Terry?" asked Cooper.

"Never in a ring," said Shepherd. "But I've had the odd moment."

Cooper laughed. "Yeah, I bet you have."

"I boxed a bit when I was a kid," said Carter, "but I didn't want to mess with my good looks." He laughed and clapped Shepherd on the back. "Now if anyone needs punching I get someone else to do it."

"Always the best way," said Cooper. "You know, if you hit someone in the face, you're more likely to break a bone in your hand than to hurt them. That's why boxers wear gloves. I always thought it was so they wouldn't hurt the guy too much but, nah, it's to stop them breaking their hands."

"That's why God invented knuckledusters, innit?" said Carter, and all three men laughed.

Evans returned with Shepherd's drink. Shepherd took a sip and winced. "Double? More like a treble."

"They water the gin down here anyway," said Evans. "The more the fucking merrier."

"Just telling Terry, boxers wear gloves to protect their own hands, not the other guy's face," said Cooper.

Evans nodded. "True enough," he said. "Worst injury I had was in Brighton. Can't remember how it started but I was up against two big chaps and I hit one of them right on the chin. He went down but I broke half a dozen bones in my hand. Took months to fix."

"What about the guy you hit?" asked Shepherd.

"Yeah, well, he went out like a light, obviously. But he'd have been up and about with nothing more than a sore chin. I was in pain for fucking days and couldn't hit anyone for months." He held up his right hand and flashed the bulky rings. "Now these do the trick nicely. I don't even have to hit hard, just make sure I twist as the fist goes in and the flesh gets ripped up nicely."

Cooper shook his head, chuckling. "You're an evil bastard, Paul."

"Just taking care of Number One, mate," said Evans. "Same as it ever was."

Shepherd sipped his drink again. His eyes narrowed as he recognised someone over Carter's shoulder. He hadn't seen the man for more than ten years but his memory kicked in as accurately as if the police file was in front of him. Jeff Owen. Armed robber. He was in his late thirties now and had put on weight and lost some hair, but it was definitely him. Shepherd had been undercover, penetrating the gang Owen was in, when they had been busted. The guy who ran it, Ted Verity, was a nasty piece of work and had gone down for twenty-five years. Owen had been given fifteen, which meant that with good behaviour he would have been out in eight.

Shepherd's mind raced. He had been working for a police unit back then and using the alias Bob Macdonald, a former squaddie who had turned to crime. He hadn't given evidence against Owen and Verity and there was nothing in the police or CPS files that suggested Bob Macdonald was an undercover cop. But the final robbery hadn't gone as planned, and at the last minute Shepherd had had to step in to make sure that civilians didn't get hurt. He'd flattened Verity and threatened to shoot Owen. The script that Shepherd had stuck to was that he wasn't happy with Verity's plan to hurt the civilians and wanted out. So far as he knew the gang had believed it and no one had suspected he was a cop, but that didn't mean they were likely to forgive and forget.

Shepherd considered his options. Jeff Owen might not recognise him — not everybody had his memory for faces. But ten years wasn't a long time in the grand scheme of things and Shepherd hadn't changed much over the past decade. Owen might have calmed down while he was in prison but Shepherd doubted it. Owen had personally vouched for Bob Macdonald and had brought him into the gang. They had become quite close over the months it had taken Shepherd to earn the man's trust.

If Owen spotted Shepherd and confronted him, the O'Neill operation would go down in flames. There was no way he could explain how Owen knew Terry Taylor as Bob Macdonald, not in any way that would convince the O'Neills that something wasn't wrong. It was just about possible that Macdonald had changed his name but if Taylor was a stone-cold hitman why would he be so coy about his armed-robbery past? And if Owen told them about the bust, how could he explain his decision to poleaxe the leader of the gang? Shepherd might, just might, be able to talk his way out of a beating, or worse, but the O'Neills would never trust him again.

"So, you been busy?" asked Evans.

Shepherd grinned. "Ducking and diving."

"A little bird tells me you were out in the New Forest."

Shepherd kept smiling but his mind was racing. How much did Evans know? "You been following me, mate?"

Evans grinned and put his mouth close to Shepherd's ear. "I was chatting to Marty earlier. He said you'd done him a favour. Taken care of some business."

"Fuck me, Paul, I was hoping there'd be some client confidentiality in operation."

Evans laughed. "Your secret's safe with me, mate. And I love that crack — they call you the Hammer because you nail it every time. That's a fucking classic."

"What else did he tell you?"

"No details, mate, don't worry." He gestured at the door. "Now, come on. They're going in."

Evans guided Shepherd into the main dining room. There were a couple of dozen tables, each seating twelve, around a boxing ring, plus a long table for the main guests facing the action.

Shepherd glanced over his shoulder. Owen was lost in the crowd. "Give me a minute, just want to see where a pal of mine's sitting."

"See you at the table," said Evans.

Shepherd hurried to a whiteboard with two sheets of paper stuck to it. He ran his finger down the first page, then found Jeff Owen halfway down the second. He was on table eighteen. There was a map of the seating plan. Evans had table three, which put them on the opposite side of the boxing ring. As long as Owen stayed seated, he wouldn't see Shepherd. But if he decided to take a trip to the toilet, there was a fair chance he'd walk by Shepherd's table. He cursed under his breath. He had to do something, and quickly.

He took another look around, then headed for the hotel reception area, which was still packed with dinner-jacketed men holding invitations. Shepherd went outside. There were fewer smokers than before, now split into two groups. Cigars seemed to outnumber cigarettes. Shepherd took out his phone, jogged across the road and tapped in Jimmy Sharpe's number. He kept none on his phone, called everyone from memory and made a habit of deleting his call history. "Hi, Razor, where are you?"

"What are you? My mother?" growled Sharpe.

"I'm in deep shit and you're the only person who can get me out of it. Where are you?"

"A curry house in the East End with a mate from the Fraud Squad," said Sharpe, his tone suddenly serious. "What do you need?"

"I'm at a boxing do in the West End with a few hundred faces, most of them from south of the river. One might recognise me and if I don't do something my case is going to fall apart."

"Who's the face?"

"Blagger by the name of Jeff Owen. He was number two in a crew run by Ted Verity. I put them away more than ten years ago and it looks like Owen's out."

"What do you want me to do?" asked Sharpe.

"I need him taken away for a few hours."

"I'll happily come around and flash my warrant card, but if he tells me to fuck off what can I do?"

"It has to be more official than that or he'll wonder what's going on. Here's my thought. He was given fifteen years, which means he's out on licence. I'm sure under the terms of his parole he's not allowed to mix with criminals and they're wall to wall here. There's three on his table alone. I'm thinking get his probation officer involved and have him hauled into a local station for questioning."

"That might mean him getting sent back to prison."

"He's a nasty piece of work, Razor. He deserved more than an eight stretch."

"This'll have to be official — you know that? I can't start commandeering police stations and probation officers."

"Can you run it by Sam Hargrove? You're still working for him, right?"

"Sure."

"He knows this Owen character and he'll remember the case."

"I remember it," said Sharpe. "Drug-dealer running his operation from behind bars."

"That's the one. Fill Hargrove in and get him on the case. It needs to be quick, Razor. We're just sitting down to eat."

"I'm on it," said Sharpe.

Shepherd ended the call and walked back to the hotel. The last of the smokers were finishing up and most of the tables were filled. There were now a dozen men sitting at the top table, a mix of former champion boxers, Catholic priests and two actors who'd had minor roles in Cockney gangster movies. Shepherd kept his head turned away from the table where Owen was sitting as he headed to his seat. He was between Evans and Cooper, Carter opposite. Including himself, there were a dozen men at the table and Shepherd knew all of the others by name and reputation. He shook hands with the four he hadn't met and introduced himself. No one asked what he did or where he was from: it was taken for granted that he was one of them. If he was anything but, he wouldn't have been there.

There were six bottles of wine opened on the table, three red and three white, and Shepherd could see that they were all good vintages. But the wine stayed untouched. Evans waved over a middle-aged waiter with a neatly-trimmed beard and ordered a round of drinks. Everyone wanted beer or spirits. He automatically ordered Shepherd a gin and tonic. Shepherd took a quick look around. It was pretty much an all-male affair, though off to his left there was a women-only table, which looked as if wives had been parked there by their husbands. The women were in their thirties with over-styled hair, too much make-up and jewellery, and their painted nails glistened like talons.

The doors from the kitchen burst open and Evans flinched, then grinned shame-facedly as waiters poured into the room, laden with trays. There were several hundred people to be fed and the serving staff worked with military precision as they placed the starter on the tables. It was pate with toast and a limp salad. Shepherd didn't feel like eating and pushed the food around the plate until everyone had finished. Evans was constantly summoning waiters and ordering more drinks. The wine stayed untouched, as it seemed to be on most of the tables. Even the wives had ignored it and ordered themselves Cristal champagne. Shepherd kept an eye on the far side of the room but the tables were hidden from view by the boxing ring.

Plates were cleared, and after ten minutes, the army of white-shirted, black-trousered waiters returned with

68

stainless-steel trays and the main course: roast beef, which proved to be surprisingly good, with a selection of vegetables. Evans ordered another round of drinks. Gin and tonic was a good drink when he was undercover because no one could tell how much alcohol was in the glass. Whenever Shepherd was sure he wasn't being watched he'd slosh some water into it.

Evans was holding court at the table, and as he was paying, his guests were happy enough to eat and listen. He told stories about his boxing days, and the great fighters he'd met over the years. He was a huge fan and spent tens of thousands flying around the world to get ringside seats at all the major bouts. Shepherd kept looking over each time anyone walked by on the far side of the ring, but while plenty of people were heading back and forth to the toilets, Owen's bladder seemed to be made of sterner stuff.

As the plates were being cleared away, a black-suited man in his fifties walked purposefully across the room. He had the look of a manager, and a minute or two later he went back to the door, this time accompanied by Owen. Shepherd raised his napkin and dabbed his lips but Owen didn't look in his direction.

When the manager opened the door Shepherd saw two uniformed policemen. One spoke to Owen, who threw up his arms angrily but after a few seconds he appeared to calm down and the door was closed. Dessert was served. Some sort of mousse with thawed frozen berries. Shepherd picked at it as he listened to Evans tell the story of how he had met Muhammad Ali in Las Vegas.

Shepherd's phone vibrated and he fished it out of his pocket. It was a text message from Razor. *Sorted*. And a smiley face. Shepherd grinned and put it away.

"Good news?" asked Evans.

Shepherd hadn't realised the man had been watching him. "Another job," he said.

"Back to the New Forest?"

Shepherd pointed a warning finger at the man's face, but he was still smiling. "Mum's the word, mate."

Evans held up his pint glass. "Your secret's safe with me."

The two men clinked their glasses together. "I hope so," said Shepherd.

Evans narrowed his eyes. "You saying I'd grass you up?"

"Of course not," said Shepherd. "What the fuck, Paul?"

Evans burst out laughing. "I'm busting your balls, Terry, you soft bastard. Now, are you coming to the big match? I've got a dozen ringside seats and your name's on one of them. We're all going for a steak first and we'll hit the Mayfair afterwards."

The boxing match was due to be one of the biggest of the year, a rematch between the Russian heavyweight champion Konstantin Kuznetsov and British champion Barry "Face-Down" Hughes, who got his nickname after three consecutive opponents fell in that way early in his career. The match was taking place at an East End football stadium where more than twenty-five thousand boxing fans were expected. The cable TV pay-per-view rights were said to be worth tens of millions. Shepherd had heard that ringside seats were selling for five thousand pounds each. He raised his glass to Evans. "Try to keep me away," he said.

Evans raised his own. "You the man."

Shepherd grinned, pretending to be a bit drunker than he actually was. "No, you the man."

"Fuck off!" shouted Evans. "You the man."

"Okay. I'm the man," said Shepherd. They clinked glasses and drank. Evans waved a waiter over and ordered another round.

A big man in a too-tight tuxedo stepped into the ring. He was holding a microphone and started to introduce the men sitting at the top table. Shepherd jumped as a hand fell on his shoulder. "Terry, good man." He looked up to see Marty O'Neill grinning down at him. He squeezed, hard enough to hurt. Marty was a big man, a couple of inches taller than Shepherd. He had rock-hard forearms — Shepherd could imagine generations of O'Neill men laying tarmac or working down the mines — and while he was a good twenty kilos heavier than Shepherd there wasn't an ounce of fat on him. Marty's hair was an unnatural shade of chestnut, except round his temples, which remained grey. He had a strong jaw, and teeth that Shepherd assumed had been professionally whitened. Marty favoured Armani suits and recognised Shepherd's tuxedo for what it was. "Nice," he said, running his hand down the sleeve. "Cashmere?"

"Yeah, he does a good suit does Giorgio," said Shepherd.

"Not a hundred per cent, though?" said Marty. "Cashmere wool mix, right?"

"Twenty per cent, I think."

"I met him, once, Armani."

"You serious?"

"In a club in Piccadilly. Sent him over a bottle of Cristal. Nice guy. Real gentleman."

"Did you ask him for a discount?"

Marty chuckled. "Fuck me, I didn't think of that. Look, Tommy and I are going for a quick smoke. Keep us company, yeah?"

"Sure," said Shepherd. He stood up and Marty waved at his brother. Tommy got up and the two men walked outside. Tommy was older than Marty by a couple of years but he was shorter and slighter. Unlike Marty, Tommy had allowed his hair to grey while his teeth showed the effects of smoking and red wine. The only jewellery he wore was a simple gold wedding band and he tended to buy his clothes from chain stores. He always seemed slightly the worse for wear: his hair was unruly and there was generally a greyness to his skin as if he was short of a few essential vitamins.

Character-wise, Tommy and Marty were chalk and cheese. Marty was loud and ebullient, always cracking jokes and teasing people. Tommy was much quieter, and there was always a short pause before he spoke, as if he was running his comments through some internal checking mechanism. Marty had a quick temper but Tommy was always ice cold, almost lizard-like. Shepherd had met the older brother only a few times but he had never seen him anything other than totally calm. But of the two men, it was Tommy who made him the more nervous. Marty could fly off the handle when something upset him, but he was just as quick to calm down. Tommy was much harder to gauge, and Shepherd always felt he was walking on eggshells when he was in his presence.

Shepherd followed them, wondering if the invitation was connected to the cops taking Owen away. A dozen or so men were already smoking, split into three groups, but Marty and Tommy walked into the car park so they wouldn't be overheard. Tommy reached inside his jacket and pulled out a leather cigar case. He opened it and offered it to Marty. Marty took a cigar and Tommy held the case out to Shepherd. Shepherd wasn't a smoker but he took one. Marty had produced a gold cigar cutter and a Dunhill lighter but Tommy had already bitten the end off his and spat it onto the ground.

"Classy," said Marty, carefully cutting his.

"Poncy," said Tommy, gesturing at the cigar-cutter.

Marty held it up. "This, gentlemen, is an instrument of torture. Put a guy's pecker in the hole and he'll sing like a fucking canary."

He held it out to Shepherd, who grinned. "Mate, I've got to be honest, my dick's way too big to fit in there." He gave it back and bit the end off his cigar, then followed Tommy's example and spat it on the ground.

Tommy roared with laughter, pulled out a box of matches and handed it to Shepherd. He lit a match but held it out so that Tommy could light his cigar from it. He could see from the man's smile that he appreciated the gesture of respect. Marty used his lighter to get his cigar going and both men puffed contentedly as Shepherd lit another match and attended to his own.

"Thanks for taking care of that thing for us," said Tommy, his voice a low growl.

"Happy to help," said Shepherd.

"The bracelet and the video were nice touches."

"I figure that when there's no body, proof of death is always appreciated."

Marty blew a thick cloud of smoke at the night sky. "He was a bastard — he had it coming."

"No question," said Tommy. He flicked ash onto the ground. "Howard said you were keen to do more work for us."

"Sure," said Shepherd.

"We don't do that sort of thing often. Once in a blue moon."

Shepherd shrugged. "That's OK. But I meant it in a wider context. You could get me more involved in the business."

"Why would you want that, though?" asked Tommy, quietly. "You're good at what you do. You're a freelance so you can work as and when you want. Why tie yourself down to one crew?"

"It's the fact that I'm a freelance that worries me," said Shepherd. "A lot of the time I'm dealing with people I don't know. Okay, jobs come in by word of mouth and a new client always has to be vouched for, but one day maybe I'll get approached by a wrong 'un, someone trying to stitch me up."

"An undercover cop?"

74

"It happens. So far I've been lucky, I'm below the radar, but then some smart arse began calling me the Hammer, and once you've got a nickname the cops start taking an interest." He took a short pull on his cigar and blew smoke. "Look, here's the thing. You run a slick operation. No one fucks with you. The cops don't bother because they know you're untouchable, right?"

Marty grinned. "Pretty much, yeah."

"I'm guessing that part of the reason is you have a few top cops in your pocket. The odd judge, maybe."

Marty's grin widened. "We couldn't possibly comment," he said.

"And it's none of my business, obviously," said Shepherd. "But my point is, I'd rather be inside the tent than outside. I'd prefer to be part of a team, that's all. And you're the best team around."

"No need to go blowing smoke up our arses, Terry," laughed Tommy, but there was an edge to the laughter that made it a casual threat.

"You know what I mean, though," said Shepherd. "My money's good, no question of that. But it's erratic. And the more jobs I do, the more I'm putting myself at risk. If I'm part of a crew, especially a successful one like yours . . ."

"I hear you, Terry," said Tommy. He looked at his brother. "What do you think, Marty?"

"Give him a go. What have we got to lose?"

Tommy turned back to Shepherd. He paused for a few seconds, staring at him with unblinking eyes.

"We've got a bit of a problem on the Rock. Do you fancy flying over and sorting it out for us?"

"Sure. What's the story?"

Another short pause, then just a hint of a nod. "I'll have Howard run it by you. Let him know if you need any more people. He'll sort it." He drew on his cigar as he studied Shepherd's face. "You been to Gibraltar before?"

Shepherd shook his head. "Spain. But never Gibraltar." That was a lie, but a necessary one. Shepherd had visited Gibraltar several times, but always in transit with the SAS on a Hercules, usually en route to Belize.

Tommy nodded. "If you feel like a curry while you're there, pop into Raj's Curry House. That's what it's called, no shit. Ragged Staff Wharf. Best curries I've ever had. Place looks a bit run-down but you can't beat the food."

Marty nodded in agreement.

"Mind you, if you want to try some decent food, come out to Dubai."

"I might take you up on that," said Shepherd.

"Gordon Ramsay's new place is shit hot," said Tommy.

"So you're there for the food, not the lack of an extradition treaty?" said Marty.

Tommy punched his brother softly on the arm and laughed. "Bit of both, truth be told."

A roar went up inside and Tommy gestured at the hotel entrance. "Let's get back inside," he said. "Wouldn't want to miss the fights."

Omar Hassan was sitting with his family in the large dining room. His mother insisted that the family ate together as often as possible and that was no hardship because she was an amazing cook. His father was at the head of the table, his wife facing him and closest to the door. Omar was between his father and Aidan, with Toby and Zack opposite. Jasmine carried in the last of the food, then took her seat between Aidan and their mother.

Omar's mother had been working in the kitchen for most of the afternoon, joined by Jasmine when she got back from the garage. While the men had showered and changed their clothes, the women had put the finishing touches to the meal. There were succulent lamb kebabs, goat curry with okra and aubergine, aloo gosht and chicken Korma. Plates of freshly made naan bread were scattered along the table, with a bowl of steaming rice and a larger one of salad.

Omar was famished but he waited for his father to help himself before heaping food onto his plate. There was water and fruit juice to drink and Omar washed his food down with both. The talk was usually about football or work, but *The Voice* was on later that night and they were all backing their favourites. Toby, of course, was championing the blonde with big breasts even though two of the contestants were Asian. Omar didn't join in the discussion as he bolted his food. All he could think about was his mission. The piece of paper with the photographs of the vehicles he was to purchase was in his back pocket and he had constantly to fight the urge to take it out and look at it.

"That injection must have worked," said his father.

"Excuse me?" Omar had only half heard him.

His father pointed at his mouth. "The way you're wolfing your food, your tooth must be a lot better."

Omar remembered his lie and put his hand up to his lips. "Still a bit sore. I'm just hungry. I missed breakfast."

"You need to eat more vegetables," said his mother. "They're good for teeth."

"It's true," said Jasmine. "Rabbits have great teeth and that's all they eat."

"What time's *The Voice* on?" asked Omar, desperate to change the subject. His ruse worked and within minutes they were all arguing about singers again.

Omar went to his room at just after nine. His mother asked him if his tooth was still bothering him. He hated lying to her but he forced a brave smile and said that it was, a bit. He went upstairs and booted up his laptop. He was up until midnight, searching the internet for the vehicles he needed. He found two almost immediately, one in Newcastle and another in Birmingham. One was offered for sale at just over four thousand pounds, the other for three thousand. From the photographs the vendors had put on line all they needed was new lights and some signage. One in Scotland looked similar but wasn't identical to the pictures he'd been given and another in Durham had no picture or price. He sent off emails asking when he could see the vehicles, left a message in the draft mail folder, then showered and went to bed. He was asleep as soon as his head touched the pillow.

It was close to two o'clock in the morning when Shepherd phoned Sharpe. The boxing had finished at eleven, then everyone had sat around until midnight. Tommy O'Neill had waved Shepherd and Evans to his table and they had drunk with him for an hour before he and Marty announced they were heading off for more drinks at the Mayfair. Evans and Shepherd had piled into a black cab with the O'Neills and were the first to arrive at the bar. The maitre d' had recognised Marty and ushered them through into the VIP area. Marty ordered a bottle of Cristal, had second thoughts and ordered two. "Might as well celebrate," he said. He punched Shepherd's shoulder. "Job well done, mate. Job well fucking done."

"I said Terry was all right," said Evans.

Within fifteen minutes another dozen or so men in black tie arrived and the VIP area was heaving. Shepherd didn't hear anyone mention Owen or what had happened to him, which he took as a good sign. He wasn't happy about having to drink champagne and he was pretty sure that Willoughby-Brown would be even less happy when he got the expenses claim for four bottles of Cristal, but he had to play the role of Terry Taylor to the full. Shepherd wasn't the first to leave the bar and he wasn't the last. He hugged the O'Neills and Evans, pretending to be drunker than he was, then caught a black cab to the Battersea flat he was using as part of his legend. It was in a modern block with floor-to-ceiling windows that provided a view of the Thames and north London beyond. It was expensive but the security alone made it worth the price. The reception desk was manned twenty-four/seven and there was extensive CCTV, with an underground car park that required a keycard to access it. Shepherd was dealing with men who wouldn't think twice about killing him if they discovered who he was, and he slept easier knowing that his apartment was secure.

One of MI5's top dressers had kitted out the flat with items that fitted the Terry Taylor legend, including holiday snaps, well-thumbed books and a surprisingly decent CD and DVD collection, even though Shepherd had no plans to bring anyone home with him. There was always a chance that the O'Neills or one of their people would check up on him so he had to be prepared. That was what made undercover work so stressful: he could never, ever, let his guard down.

He waited until he had switched the kettle on before calling Sharpe. "Thanks for that," he said. "Any problems?"

"Smooth as silk," said Sharpe. "As it happens, Owen had missed his last two scheduled appointments with his probation officer so he was already red-flagged. One of the cops took the seating plan with him and Owen doesn't have a leg to stand on. Like you said, his table alone was enough to send him back behind bars. And there were half a dozen other convicted armed robbers at that dinner so he's got a lot of explaining to do."

"A good lawyer might be able to keep him out," said Shepherd, "but you dragged my nuts out of the fire, so I owe you one."

"Another one," corrected Sharpe. "Are you around for a drink tomorrow?"

"I can't. I'm off to Turkey."

"Rather you than me."

"Ours not to reason why."

Sharpe laughed. "You still working for that shithead Willoughby-Buggery?"

"Willoughby-Brown. Yeah."

"Then watch your back — that bastard will throw you to the wolves as soon as look at you."

"Razor, mate, you never trusted Charlie either." Charlotte Button was Willoughby-Brown's predecessor, thrown out of MI5 after using professional contacts to resolve personal issues, which was a polite way of saying she had used government money to pay for the assassination of the men who had killed her husband.

"I'd trust the fragrant Ms Button over Willoughby-Buggery any day of the week," said Sharpe.

"I'll tell her that next time I see her."

"You two still close?"

"Unfortunately not," said Shepherd. "We haven't been in touch since she left."

"Probably best," said Sharpe. "When you get back from Turkey you should have a drink with Sam. He still speaks fondly of you."

"I'm not sure I could go back to being a cop, Razor."

"It's not like it was, Spider. The National Crime Agency means business. It's a lot more professional than SOCA ever was."

"We'll see," said Shepherd.

"You be careful out in Turkey," said Sharpe. "You can't trust the ragheads."

"It's Turkey, Razor, not Iraq. The Turks will be in the EU before long."

"And won't life get interesting then?" said Sharpe. "Like I said, be careful." He ended the call.

Shepherd put his mobile on the coffee-table and stretched out on the sofa. It had been almost five years since he'd left the Serious Organised Crime Agency to work for MI5, and he'd never given any thought to going back to the police. But maybe Sharpe was right, maybe it was time to get out of intelligence work. He'd always trusted Sam Hargrove, and it might be fun to work with Razor again. One thing for sure, life with Razor was never boring.

When the Syrian civil war first erupted and thousands of refugees fled the country, the shortest and safest route to the safety of Europe was by land to Greece. Syria had a 125-mile border that ran along the River Evros in the north of Greece. Refugees poured across, mainly at a six-mile strip of farmland close to the town of Nea Vyssa. But in the winter of 2012 the Greeks built a barbed-wire fence to block the exodus. It was more than twelve feet tall, fitted with thermal-imaging cameras and guarded by Greek soldiers. The refugees had had to find another way to Europe, and resorted to the sea.

Most aimed for the Greek island of Lesbos, which could be reached by boat across the Aegean Sea, close to the Turkish town of Ayvacık, in Çanakkale province. By 2015 thousands of refugees were daily cramming into boats filled to over-capacity to make the crossing, usually hiding in olive groves during the day and making their way down to the beaches under the cover of darkness. A whole industry grew up to ferry them to Lesbos, with armed gangs charging for a place on a boat, a life vest, food and water. Everything had to be paid for.

After the EU had persuaded the Turks to beef up security at Ayvacık, many of the traffickers had moved on to pastures new, though a steady stream of refugees tried to make their way to Lesbos, come what may.

Mohammed al-Hussain's passage to Europe wasn't in the hands of a trafficking gang so he didn't need to sit on a leaking dinghy packed with other refugees. His minders avoided Ayvacık and drove instead to the small fishing port of Küçükkuyu, a popular holiday destination for Turks, with bustling seafood restaurants and gift shops. Every Friday a popular farmer's market brought shoppers from miles around. During the day families played on the beach and swam in the sea, and the bars were busy until late at night.

The drive from Akçakale had taken a full twenty-four hours, though they had broken the journey at a farmhouse midway. There, a Turkish family had shown him to a white-washed bedroom with a comfortable single bed. Al-Hussain had asked if he could wash and was taken to the villa's only bathroom where a bath was run for him, and he was given clean towels. Afterwards he prayed, then sat down with his minders in the kitchen where the woman of the house, her face hidden behind a cloth niqab served them a meal — meat, cheese and fruit, with bread rolls fresh from the oven. She poured them hot mint tea, then left them alone. There was little in the way of conversation between the men. They were Turks and al-Hussain was Syrian, and while he was grateful for their assistance and support, he knew nothing about them, not even their names. They ate in silence, but after he had retired to his bed, he could hear them talking and laughing in the kitchen. He was dog tired and they let him sleep for six hours before one gently shook him awake and told him it was time to go.

They arrived at Küçükkuyu late at night. The driver parked the pick-up truck down a quiet alley, then slipped away into the darkness. Al-Hussain and the two other IS men waited, the only sound the clicking of the engine as it cooled. Fifteen minutes later the driver returned and opened the rear door so that al-Hussain could climb out. He led him along the alley, across a market square, then down a sloping street to the harbour where fishing boats were bobbing in the water, preparing to go out before first light. The yacht was at the far end, well away from the fishing fleet. The two other fighters followed some way behind, their weapons hidden under their coats. They stayed on the pier as the driver took al-Hussain down a flight of stone stairs. Two men were waiting at the rear of the yacht, strapping Asians with closely cropped beards.

"I will leave you here," said the driver. "These men will take you to Greece. There you will be handed over to the next team. The men have Greek passports. In the event you are stopped, they will explain that you are their English friend and they are taking you sightseeing. You have your passport."

Al-Hussain nodded.

The man embraced him and kissed him on both cheeks. "*Fi amanullah*," he said. May Allah protect you.

"*Jazak allahu khair*," replied al-Hussain. May Allah reward you with all good things.

The two men reached out to help him climb onto the boat. He turned to wave at the driver but the man had already slipped up the steps and disappeared into the night.

"Are you OK, brother?" asked one man. He spoke with a heavy Greek accent. Al-Hussain could tell they weren't Syrian, Iraqi or Iranian, but other than that he was none the wiser as to their ethnicity. Pakistani or Bangladeshi, maybe Afghans. Not that it mattered: they were Muslims, committed to the Islamic State, which meant they were his friends and comrades.

"I am well, brother," said al-Hussain in English. "I need to wash, and to sleep."

"We have prepared the main cabin for you," said the second man. They were both wearing dark linen shirts and shorts with leather belts from which hung knives in scabbards. "We shall set sail in about an hour when the tide is favourable." They showed him to the hatch.

Al-Hussain was not looking forward to the voyage. It was the first time he had ever been on a boat, and even tethered to the harbour wall, it was unpleasant as the craft rocked from side to side.

A few hours after Mohammed al-Hussain had left Turkey by boat, Spider Shepherd landed at Istanbul airport. There were long queues at Turkish immigration and when Shepherd eventually reached the front his John Whitehill passport was carefully scrutinised. The officer checked his certificate of medical insurance, which had been processed by the MI6 paper handlers, then went through every page of his passport again, quietly sucking her teeth. Eventually she stamped it and waved him through.

He had flown from Heathrow to Charles de Gaulle airport in Paris, then waited there for a little more than three hours, more than enough time to check that he wasn't being tailed. He'd eaten a late breakfast and drunk three cups of coffee. The first leg of his trip had been economy but he had been booked into business class for the second and wasn't too stiff as he walked out into the arrivals area. He'd dressed casually in a blazer and blue jeans and put on a pair of impenetrable Ray-Bans in preparation for the blinding Turkish sunshine. He was carrying a large brown canvas camera bag containing some basic camera equipment, a change of clothing and a washbag.

He scanned the waiting crowds looking for the man who was supposed to be meeting him — Derek Shuttleworth, one of MI6's men in the British Embassy. Within seconds he had spotted him, mainly because he was holding an iPad showing JOHN WHITEHILL in capital letters. Every few seconds it flashed. Shepherd cursed under his breath. Whitehill wasn't his real name but, real or not, Shuttleworth shouldn't have been broadcasting it to the world. He walked over to the man. "Put that away, yeah," he muttered.

"Sure, yes, absolutely," said Shuttleworth. He was a good three inches shorter than Shepherd, thin but with a middle-age spread that tugged at the buttons of his charcoal grey suit. He was wearing mismatched socks and Shepherd wondered if that was a fashion choice or a mistake. He had a thin moustache, deep-set eyes and flecks of dandruff on his shoulders. He was in his late thirties. He wasn't wearing a wedding ring and his nails were bitten to the quick.

"I'm Derek Shuttleworth," he said, in a voice loud enough to be heard ten feet away.

"Yes, I know," said Shepherd, tersely. "What's the story?"

"I've got you on a relief flight to Suruç. It's not fancy but it's the quickest way there. Fancy a coffee?"

"Here?" He couldn't believe the MI6 officer was planning to brief him at an airport coffee shop.

"Sure. You can grab a sandwich — there won't be anything on the plane."

They went into a café where Shepherd took a corner table and sat facing the entrance, automatically checking to see if anyone was paying them any attention. Everything looked clear and he assumed that Shuttleworth had been professional enough to make sure he wasn't being followed. But meeting at airports was never a good idea — everywhere was covered by CCTV and there was a constant stream of faces to be monitored. Shuttleworth collected a couple of coffees. He'd asked if Shepherd wanted anything to eat and Shepherd had declined but he put a couple of sandwiches and a chocolate muffin on his tray before making his way to the cashier. Shepherd saw him pocket the receipt so he guessed he'd be putting the meeting on expenses.

"Good flight?" asked Shuttleworth, as he placed the tray on the table and sat down.

"It was okay," said Shepherd. "So, tell me your impressions of Yusuf."

"Bit shifty, to be honest," said Shuttleworth. He held out a sandwich packet but Shepherd shook his head. Shuttleworth peeled it open and smelt the contents before taking one out. "Very hard to tie down on specifics. Wouldn't show me anything on paper. Seemed to be more interested in what we could do for him." He took a bite of his sandwich, smearing mayonnaise across his moustache.

"And he wants what? Passports and safe passage?"

Shuttleworth nodded. "For him and his family. And money."

"How much?"

"Millions. I said I couldn't talk about money. He said to get him someone who could."

"What's his background?"

"Run-of-the-mill people-trafficker," said Shuttleworth. "Mainly helping high-worth individuals who have money but no connections. He can fast-track them into Europe without them having to paddle across the Mediterranean in a leaky dinghy."

"No al-Qaeda or Islamic State contacts?"

"Depends on what you mean by contacts," said Shuttleworth. He wiped his mouth with his sleeve. "He goes back and forth to Syria, no question of that. He flies to Damascus and goes into the country by road. He has to come across Islamic State when he does that."

"So he pays them off?"

"Perhaps."

"Or he works for them."

"Equally possible," said Shuttleworth.

Shepherd wasn't happy about the man's casual demeanour or that he hadn't much grasp of what was going on. Yusuf's loyalties could prove to be a matter of life or death and it wasn't good enough to say "perhaps" or "possible". Shepherd needed facts and Shuttleworth didn't seem to have many.

"Could this be a set-up? Could he be giving us false intel to send us on a wild-goose chase?"

"He'd hardly do that if he wanted us to take care of his family."

"You met the family?"

Shuttleworth shook his head. "No."

Shepherd sighed. "Then for all we know he doesn't have one. He could be an Islamic State plant, feeding us false intel to tie up our resources."

"I hadn't thought of that."

"Yeah, well, when anyone offers you a gift horse, you pull its mouth wide open and take a good look inside," said Shepherd.

"You just have to check the intel, surely," said Shuttleworth. "If it's kosher he gets what he wants."

"Maybe it's a Six officer he wants," said Shepherd. "Maybe the plan is to get one of us wearing an orange jumpsuit begging for our life on a YouTube video."

Shuttleworth's eyes widened. "You think that's possible?"

"Anything's possible," said Shepherd. "That's why we need to consider our options."

"Right," said Shuttleworth. "Yes. Absolutely."

"So I'm on a supply flight to Suruç?"

"Close to Suruç. Craig Parker will pick you up at the airport and drive you to meet Yusuf."

"What are the security arrangements?"

Shuttleworth frowned. "Security?"

"My security?"

"You should be fine. This isn't a war zone."

"No, but it's bloody close to one." He grimaced. "Willoughby-Brown said I'd be protected. Bodyguards or army."

"Craig Parker has a security team. I'm sure he'd make them available to you. But, really, this is Turkey. It's a relatively safe country."

"Istanbul, perhaps. But Suruç is close to the border."

Shuttleworth shrugged. "I felt perfectly safe there."

Shepherd resisted the urge to snap at the man. He sipped his coffee. "So do you and Willoughby-Brown have a history?"

"A history?"

"Have you worked together before?"

"Ah. Yes. Right. No."

"No?"

"No, but we went to the same college at Oxford."

Shepherd nodded. "That's nice."

"It's a small world, that's for sure. Where did you get your degree?"

Shepherd smiled thinly. "I didn't." He sipped his coffee again. "How many fire extinguishers are there, and where are they, Derek?" he said quietly.

Shuttleworth tilted his head on one side. "Excuse me?"

Shepherd repeated the question.

Shuttleworth looked flustered, obviously realising he was being tested.

"If you have to look, you obviously don't know," said Shepherd.

"Why's it important?"

Shepherd finished his coffee. "It isn't," he said. He grabbed his camera bag and stood up. "Okay, put me on the plane and I'll get out of your hair."

Omar Hassan brought his motorcycle to a halt and Faisal climbed off the back. He removed his helmet and blinked several times. "Why don't you buy a car, brother?" he asked.

Omar kicked the stand into position and dismounted. "Because I like bikes," he said.

"They're dangerous," said Faisal.

"Were you scared? Don't you trust me?"

"You I trust," said Faisal. "It's all the other idiots on the road who scare me. In Pakistan I rode a bike all the time, a small Honda, but never as fast as yours."

"That's because mine is a Kawasaki Ninja ZX-10R super-bike, 210 horsepower at 13,000 r.p.m. It's supposed to be fast."

They were outside a near-derelict factory in east Manchester. A chain-link fence ran around the perimeter and the gate was chained and padlocked. Faisal nodded at a sign warning of guard dogs. "I hate dogs," he said.

Omar looked around, then checked his watch. The message in the draft folder had said the meeting was at seven thirty and he was five minutes early. Faisal put his hands on his hips and surveyed the building. "It's big enough," he said.

"You can't tell from the outside," said Omar. "But it's not overlooked and it can't be seen from the main road."

A blue Honda headed to the gate. The window wound down as Omar walked up. He nodded at the driver, a bearded Asian in his fifties wearing a white skull cap. "Good evening, brother," he said.

The man smiled, showing a gold tooth at the front of his mouth. "Good evening to you, brother. Did you watch the game last night?"

Omar nodded. "I did. Chelsea were on form."

"Who would have thought it would go to four-one?" said the man.

Omar stiffened. That wasn't what he'd expected to hear. Apparently the man saw his confusion. "Sorry, brother. My mistake. I meant three-one."

Omar studied the man's face. The rules were clear: if the phrases weren't spoken exactly as they should be, the meeting was off. But it appeared to have been an honest mistake. And the man had corrected himself quickly. "Okay, brother, show us around," he said.

The man climbed out of the car, unlocked the gate and drove through to the factory. Faisal followed him on foot and Omar got onto the bike, fired it up and rode slowly towards the building. It was brick-built with a flat roof, windowless, with a loading dock to the left and roll-up metal doors to the right. The man parked and climbed out. He was wearing a quilted jacket, baggy jeans and fingerless wool gloves. He had a set of keys and selected one to open a wooden door at the side of the loading bay.

"What was it used for?" asked Omar.

"They made something," said the man. "Back in the days when this country made things. Some machine. Who cares?" He opened the door and Omar and Faisal followed him inside. There was a sour, musty smell and piles of rat droppings by the walls. The floor was dusty, the concrete disfigured with countless stains, the walls dotted with cobwebs. "It's been empty for years. The company that owned it went bust but the liquidators went bust too and now it's in limbo."

"It's for sale, though?"

"Supposedly, but in reality, no. No one's looked at it for months. I got them to give me a short-term lease on it for cash. I said I wanted somewhere for storage, short term. They practically bit my hand off."

Omar looked at Faisal. "What do you think?"

Faisal nodded. "It's big enough. And there's plenty of room for spraying."

"The lease is for six months and I've done it through a shell company that will end up untraceable," said the man. He handed Omar the keys. "Okay, brother, I'll leave you to it."

"*Jazak allahu khayran*," said Omar. May Allah reward you with all good things.

The man grinned. "He already has, brother. He already has."

Even through the orange plastic earplugs the drone of the four turboprop engines of the Lockheed Martin C1130J Super Hercules was mind-numbing. Shepherd was no stranger to the plane, which had been around in various forms for more than sixty years. He'd flown in it hundreds of times during his time in the SAS and jumped out of one on more than a dozen occasions. Shepherd was sitting on a jumpseat attached to the fuselage, holding a plastic bottle of Evian water, the only refreshment he'd been offered by the predominantly French crew. The main hold was packed with pallets of food, medicine and water, while plastic trunks contained donated clothing and the equipment needed to keep a refugee camp running. No one had asked him for any identification, or said anything other than that he was to fasten his harness and that there were no toilet facilities on the plane.

Shepherd took a sip of the tepid water. Shuttleworth was inexperienced; of that there was no doubt. The question about the fire extinguishers had been a test, and the MI6 officer had failed. It was all about being aware of one's surroundings. Whenever you went into a new place it was vital to check possible threats and escape routes. Fire extinguishers were important: if there was an explosion or a fire then an extinguisher could be a life-saver, but it could also be used as a weapon or distraction, and could batter down a door or smash a window. Shuttleworth didn't know where they were, which suggested he hadn't given the venue the once-over. Post Nine Eleven and Seven Seven, the UK's security services had gone on a recruiting spree and standards had dropped. Shuttleworth had the confidence bordering on arrogance that suggested a public-school and Oxbridge education, but being successful at intelligence work wasn't dependent on education. More often than not it required street smarts and cunning. The fact that Shuttleworth had failed the fire-extinguisher test meant that Shepherd had to regard everything else he did as suspect, but more importantly it begged the question as to why Willoughby-Brown had entrusted the assignment to him.

The closest airport to the Suruç refugee camp was Şanlıurfa GAP, some eight hundred miles from Istanbul, which took the Hercules just under two hours. The pilots were good and the landing was as smooth as silk. After five minutes of taxiing and a further ten minutes waiting, the back ramp slowly went down, allowing the hot desert air in. Shepherd took out his Ray-Bans and put them on, then unclipped his harness, and stood up and stretched. A fork lift truck was already at the bottom of the ramp, preparing to drive up and get the first pallet.

The French aid workers were getting on with their assigned tasks and no one paid any attention to Shepherd as he walked carefully into the blinding sunshine. To his left was a line of white trucks and a dozen or so Turkish men in overalls with the name of the aid company on the back. To the right three white SUVs were similarly marked. Half a dozen casually dressed Westerners were standing in a huddle, smoking cigarettes. They were all in sunglasses and baseball caps.

Some distance away armed security guards in cargo pants and waistcoats carried their weapons of choice: Glocks on the hip and American-made M4 carbines held to the chest.

A good-looking guy in khaki cargos and a faded denim shirt stood alone. He had wraparound sunglasses and jet black hair that he kept flicking away from his face. His shoulders and forearms suggested he worked out a lot.

He smiled. "John?"

96

Shepherd nodded.

"Craig Parker." He had a firm handshake and offered to carry Shepherd's camera bag. Shepherd shook his head and followed him to a black Jeep, parked behind the SUVs. Next to the Jeep a white Toyota Landcruiser contained four young Western men wearing khaki fatigues and wraparound Oakley sunglasses.

"We're about fifty kilometres from the camp," said Parker, as he climbed into the driving seat. "It'll take us about an hour." He started the engine and headed for the airport exit. The Landcruiser followed.

Shepherd gestured at it. "Your security?"

Parker nodded. "They go everywhere I go. The camp is close to the border so there's always the worry that IS will launch an attack."

"You might think about telling them they should go ahead of your vehicle if they're serious about protecting you."

Parker pulled a face. "I hadn't thought of that."

"Also, they need to get out their vehicle before you exit yours. The airport is probably secure, but it's good practice. Before you get out they should be securing the area for you."

"You're right. I'll talk to them."

"Your NGO pays for them?"

"Yeah, there's a security company that does protection worldwide. They've got a good reputation. The guys with me are South Africans."

Shepherd sat back and folded his arms. They left the airport and drove down a decent highway. There was a line of rocky hills to his left and barren land to his right.

The sky was cloudless and Parker had the Jeep's air-con on full blast.

"How much are you allowed to tell me?" asked Parker.

"Not much."

"But you're not a journalist, obviously."

Shepherd forced a smile.

"Journalists aren't interested in what's happening here," said Parker. "All they care about is the ones going to the UK. They ignore the millions of refugees here who are just grateful to be out of the hellhole that Syria has become."

"To be honest, Craig, I'm only concerned about the ones that are making their way to England. You work for a charity, but I don't."

"Message received and understood," said Parker.

"So, tell me what you can about Yusuf," said Shepherd.

"He's very smooth," said Parker. "Not at all what you'd expect a people-smuggler to be. Brings food and drugs into the camp, supplies for the school."

"Drugs?"

Parker smiled. "Medical supplies. Antibiotics. Whatever we need. Logistics out here aren't great. Say we run short of insulin, Yusuf can usually lay his hands on some at short notice."

"No questions asked?"

"If we've got a kid with bad diabetes, I'm not going to start asking him where he got it from."

"I'm guessing there's a quid pro quo. He helps you, and you do what for him?"

"I know what it sounds like, but we keep a close eye on him."

"While he's doing what?"

Parker sighed. "He moves around the camp, talking to the refugees, seeing what they want. He's a fixer. But he doesn't come cheap."

"False papers?"

"Officially, I don't know. Unofficially, yes. Sure. For the right price, Yusuf can get you any papers you need, and get you into any country. Pretty much guaranteed."

"So you let a people-trafficker have the run of the camp?"

"If we kept him out, there'd only be someone else. Or he'd just wait outside. It's like they say, better to have him inside the tent pissing out than outside pissing in. And Yusuf isn't one of those bastards shoving families into leaking dinghies and pushing them out into the Mediterranean. He looks for high-end refugees, people with money. And he finds them."

"And does what for them?"

"Arranges passage into Europe. Advises them on the best way of claiming asylum. Arranges paperwork, passports and the like."

"He told you that?"

"He doesn't go into details. But it's generally known what he does."

"Do you trust him?"

"Not as far as I can throw him, and he's a big guy. He's like all of them. He smiles and he nods a lot and he calls you his friend, but I've no idea what's going on behind his eyes."

"And this latest thing, he came to you?"

Parker nodded. "Said he had a problem and wondered if I knew anyone who could help."

"Why do you think he chose you?"

"I've always got on well with him. Some of the NGO guys treated him like shit. I was always respectful."

"Do you think he knows you're Six?"

"I don't think so."

"It's important, Craig. Him asking a friend for help is one thing. Putting out feelers to someone he knows is with the intelligence service is something entirely different."

"You think it could be a trap?"

"There's no need to go jumping the gun," said Shepherd. "I'm just trying to get the lie of the land. But if Yusuf is playing both ends against the middle, there might be something else going on. What did he actually say when he made the first approach?"

"We were in a bar. Yusuf is a Muslim but he likes his beer. He was a bit worse for wear and said he was in deep shit with some Islamic State people. He said he'd heard they weren't happy about him fraternising with the NGOs and were planning to take out him and his family."

"What's his family situation?"

"Wife and three kids. They're in Urfa about forty kilometres away. He's got them protected, he says, but fears for their safety. He was badmouthing Islamic State, saying they were shits for targeting him after all he'd done for them. I asked what exactly and he tapped the side of his nose. You know, Secret Squirrel, couldn't tell me."

"He said that? He said he'd been helping Islamic State?"

"Like I said, he'd been drinking. Said he needed to get out of Turkey. Said he'd only be safe in the US or the UK."

"He specifically said the UK? Not the EU?"

"He's got relatives in London. Said he'd be safer there. Anyway, he puts his arm around me, starts calling me his one true friend and did I know anyone who could help him out of his predicament."

"No mention of Five or Six? You were just a friend?"

Parker nodded. "I said I'd see what I could do and that was the end of it. He started talking about this and that. Didn't mention it again."

"And what did you do, afterwards?"

"I put in a call to London. London got Shuttleworth to call me, we talked it through and he drove down. Spent an hour with Yusuf but I got the impression they didn't click."

"Because?"

"Yusuf said he didn't trust Shuttleworth, to put it bluntly. Too smooth, he said. Too quick with the promises, too eager to see the gold up front."

"The gold being?"

"Names and photographs of Islamic State fighters that Yusuf had moved into Europe. Most of them with fake Syrian paperwork."

"So he has pictures?"

"He was fixing them up with fake passports. He says he's kept copies."

"But Yusuf wouldn't show the pictures to Shuttleworth?"

"He told him he wanted to speak to someone from London face to face. Said he wanted cast-iron guarantees. Shuttleworth wasn't happy."

"I'm sure he wasn't," said Shepherd. "Where did they meet?"

"A café in Suruç."

"Your security were there?"

Parker nodded. "Shuttleworth insisted on it."

"And Yusuf was happy enough to meet in a public place?"

"He didn't seem to mind. I assumed he thought it would be less conspicuous than at the camp."

"And where is he now?"

"Out and about, I guess. I called him this morning to confirm you were on your way."

"Does he know where we're meeting?"

"I said I'd tell him later."

"And he didn't press you for details?"

"He's fine. He just wanted to be sure you were from London. That's all he was concerned about."

Shepherd nodded. It was a good sign: if a trap was being set up for him, Yusuf would have wanted to know where the meeting was to take place. "Where would you suggest?"

"To be honest, if your cover as a journalist is good, it doesn't matter."

"I'm not sure that's true, Craig. Would Islamic State be happy for their man to talk to the press?"

"I hadn't thought of that," said Parker. "I reckoned we could say you were doing a feature on the camp and that way you could talk to anybody."

"Nah, I need a chat in private. What's your office like at the camp?"

"It's okay. It's a prefab but it has air-con."

"Private?"

"There's a few of us use it but I can make sure we're not disturbed."

"Let's do that, then. But keep your security close by, just in case. Set me up in the office first, then call him in. If anyone sees him coming and going, they'll assume he's there to talk to you."

The Greek coastguard patrol boat was about twice the length of a yacht, but it was much faster and better equipped. The two yachtsmen had seen the boat coming and had carried on heading for Greece under full sail. The wind was lacklustre at best, and even with all the sails unfurled they weren't making much more than four knots. Not that running was an option. The Faiakas Class boat was just short of twenty-five metres long, came with a .50 calibre heavy machine-gun, and could reach thirty-two knots in calm water.

The two men had their story prepared. They were a couple of Greek sailors showing their English friend the delights of the Mediterranean.

The patrol drew closer and a uniformed sailor with a megaphone shouted at them to heave to. They furled their sail and allowed the men on the boat to tie up to their yacht. Armed sailors stood looking down at them as an officer carefully made his way down a metal ladder to their deck. He was in his late thirties, totally bald with a sunburned scalp. His gun was holstered and his shirt sleeves rolled up. "ID," he said in Greek.

They handed over their ID cards. "Don't worry, we're Greek," said the older of the two men. His name was Yasir. His family had moved to Greece from Pakistan when he was a toddler and his Greek was perfect, better than his Urdu.

The officer flashed them a tight smile and returned their ID cards. "Where are you heading?"

"Piraeus," said Yasir. "The wind isn't great and we were thinking of switching to the engine." Piraeus was Greece's main port, the largest sea passenger terminal in Europe.

The officer grinned. "Fair weather sailor, huh?"

"We don't want to be out at night," said Yasir. That was a lie. The plan was to return to Greece under cover of darkness and they had night-vision goggles for just that purpose.

"Where in Piraeus?" asked the officer.

"Mikrolimano," said Yasir. It was the second biggest marina in the port, a popular location with tourists and weekend sailors. It was pretty, surrounded by tavernas and restaurants, and often used as a backdrop in Greek movies.

The officer turned to the second man. He had already checked his ID and confirmed that he was Greek, but he needed to check his language skills. "Did you stop anywhere?" he asked.

104

The man smiled and nodded. His name was Saif. His parents were also from Pakistan but he had been born in Greece, along with his three brothers and two sisters. Like Yasir, he had spent three months on the Pakistan-Afghanistan border being trained by IS before returning to Greece.

"A few hours in Küçükkuyu, just taking in the sights."

"Did you buy anything? Alcohol? Cigarettes?"

Saif shook his head. "We don't smoke or drink."

"Anyone else on board?"

"Our friend. He's below deck."

"Call him out," said the officer.

Yasir laughed. "I'm not sure he can come. He's throwing up."

The officer frowned. "Seasick? Why did you bring him on board if he's got no sea legs?"

"His sea legs are fine," saidYasir. "He had some bad chicken in Küçükkuyu. You know the Turks, not the cleanest, right?"

The officer pointed at the hatch. "I'm going to have to talk to him."

Yasir stood to the side. "Be our guest," he said. "He's in the forward cabin. But I warn you, it smells terrible. Oh, and he doesn't speak Greek."

The officer's eyes narrowed. "Where is he from?"

Yasir laughed. "Don't worry, we're not smuggling in asylum-seekers," he said. "He's English."

The officer waved for one of the armed sailors to accompany him and the two men went down the hatch. The officer wrinkled his nose at the nauseating smell coming from the forward cabin. As they walked through the galley they heard retching sounds and the slop of vomit hitting the head.

"Can you come out here, please?" the officer called in Greek. Then he repeated his request in English. There was no reply other than more retching. The officer stepped to the side and waved the sailor through. Rank had its privileges, and the closer they got to the cabin, the worse the smell.

The sailor grimaced but went forward. The door was open and inside the cabin a young Asian man was on his knees, throwing up again. "Sir, we need to talk to you," said the sailor in English.

"Okay, okay," said the man. He tried to get up, turned to face the men, and was promptly sick on the floor. "Sorry, sorry," he said, dropping back to the floor.

"What is your name?" asked the sailor in heavily accented English.

"Hammad Rajput."

"Where are you from?"

"England."

"I need to see your passport."

"My bag. On the bed."

The sailor went into the main cabin. There was a black backpack on the bed and he found a British passport in a side pocket. He flicked through to the photograph. He checked the name. Hammad Rajput. Born in Birmingham. "Date of birth?" asked the sailor.

The man looked up from the toilet. His beard was smeared with yellowish vomit. "What?"

"Your date of birth?"

The man groaned and closed his eyes. "March the fifth," he said.

The sailor nodded. "Okay." He put the passport back. "Have you taken medicine?"

The man heaved and put his head back over the toilet. The sailor chuckled and went back to the officer. "All good, sir."

He headed back up on deck. "You might want to get your friend to the hospital, have him checked out," he said to Yasir. "Food poisoning can be serious."

"We'll see how he is when he gets to port," said Yasir. "He'll probably have thrown up most of the chicken by then."

The officer climbed off the yacht and on to the cutter, and his sailor followed him. Yasir switched on the yacht's engine and steered away from the larger vessel. Five minutes later the cutter was heading back to Greece leaving a foaming white wake behind it.

It took just under an hour for Parker to drive to the refugee camp at Suruç. His company compound was outside the refugee camp. Like the camp, it was surrounded by a chain-link fence, but it was patrolled by armed guards and everyone who went in or out had to show their ID. The compound included a storage area where food, water and medicines were held before distribution, a line of Portakabins, with the NGO's logo on the door, and another of blue portable toilets. Parker slowed to a halt at the entrance and wound down the window. A guard wearing the ubiquitous baseball cap and wraparound Oakleys came up to the window. "How's it going, Craig?" he asked, in an Afrikaans accent.

"All good, Jed," said Parker. "This is John Whitehill. He's a journalist doing a story on us."

Shepherd held out his Whitehill press card but the guard barely glanced at it and waved them on. Parker drove through the gate and over to a parking area with a dozen SUVs already in it. The Landcruiser parked in front of a Portakabin with SECURITY on the door.

Parker and Shepherd climbed out of the Jeep. The heat hit Shepherd immediately and sweat beaded on his forehead. He followed Parker to one of the Portakabins, and by the time they stepped inside Shepherd's shirt was wet under the arms. The door opened into a waiting area with two plastic sofas and a coffee-table, and beyond it a desk where a young woman sat tapping on a computer keyboard. "This is Laura — she pretty much runs the place," said Parker.

The woman looked up and smiled brightly.

"This is John. He's a journalist," said Parker. "I'm introducing him to a few people around the camp."

"Can I get you a coffee?" she asked.

"I'd prefer water," said Shepherd.

"Over here," said Parker, opening a fridge packed with plastic bottles of Evian. "One of the perks of working with the French," he said. He tossed a bottle to Shepherd and took one for himself. "Come on through."

He took Shepherd down a narrow corridor and opened a door into a large office. It was stiflingly hot and he switched on an air-conditioning unit before dropping onto an orthopedic chair behind a desk piled high with files. "I'll call Yusuf, see where he is."

As Parker pulled out his phone, Shepherd sipped his water and gazed out through a large window that overlooked the camp. It was huge, with tents stretching almost as far as he could see. They had been laid out with military precision. It was surrounded by a chain-link fence but there were no armed guards and people were free to come and go. The tents had been set up in blocks separated by wide walkways, and in the middle there was a mobile-phone mast. Many of the refugees had smartphones and were sitting or standing as they tapped on the screens. Children were playing and women stood around chatting, but most of the refugees were young men. The heat was relentless. The blinding white light bounced off the soil, which was so bleached it was almost white.

"Okay, he's on his way," said Parker, putting away his phone. He stood up and went to the window. "It's a hell of a sight, isn't it?"

"How many refugees live here?"

"About forty thousand, give or take," said Parker. "To be honest, we never have an exact figure because we just don't know. They come and go, and most of them don't want to give their details."

"The Dublin Regulation?"

Parker nodded. "They're scared that if they go into the system here they won't be able to move to Europe."

Under the so-called Dublin Regulation, asylum-seekers were supposed to apply for asylum in the first

EU country they entered. Under the law, if they tried to claim asylum anywhere else, they could be returned to the first country they had applied to.

"In fact the Dublin Regulation was suspended in 2015 when the exodus was in full swing," said Parker. "Hungary just couldn't cope with the numbers pouring in so Germany said it was suspending the regulation and would take any Syrians who wanted to come. Czechoslovakia followed suit and promised asylum of passage to another country. But the refugees here think it might be a trap so they don't allow us to process them."

Shepherd shaded his Ray-Bans with the flat of his hands as he surveyed the ranks of white tents. "Are they all Syrians?"

"Most of the refugees here are Kurds who fled across the border from Kobane," said Parker. "Most had only the clothes they were wearing and what they could carry."

"There are no guards?" asked Shepherd, gesturing at the entrance to the camp. There was no gate, just a large gap in the wire through which ran a two-lane concrete road.

"They're not prisoners," said Parker. "They can come and go. Some find work. They go shopping in the town, if they have money. Those who can't work get by on the monthly vouchers the Turkish government gives them for food and basic necessities. Soap, toilet paper, stuff like that. And the NGOs provide what they can. Initially funds were flooding in but Paris put paid to that. Once the public found out that several of the terrorists who had attacked Paris had posed as Syrian refugees, well, sympathy evaporated."

"Understandably," said Shepherd.

"You know what I mean, right? Now everyone assumes that a Syrian refugee is an Islamic State jihadist in disguise. Countries that were lining up to take them are now bringing down the shutters. But I can tell you, most of the refugees in the camp are just that, refugees. People who dropped everything and ran for their lives."

"But some Islamic State fighters are using the refugee situation as a way of getting into the EU. That's a fact, Craig, you can't deny it."

"I'm not saying it doesn't happen but it's a tiny, tiny fraction of the refugee population we're talking about. One in ten thousand, maybe."

"Which, extrapolated over two million refugees, means that we could be talking about two hundred terrorists. Look at the damage half a dozen did to Paris. You can see why people are worried." He saw disappointment flash across the other man's face. "I'm not here to screw things up for you, Craig. I just want to talk to Yusuf and then I'll be out of your hair."

Parker grimaced. "If Yusuf gives you what you want and the information goes public, there'll be even less sympathy for the refugees here."

"The security services don't usually go public with their intel."

Parker flashed him a tight smile. "They do when it serves their purpose," he said. "The French were

111

bloody quick to publicise how their terrorists got into the country."

"That's the French. They always do things their own way. This isn't about messing with your work. This is about identifying potential terrorists who are planning to kill innocent civilians."

"I know, I know," said Parker. "It's just you don't see the suffering that I do. Most of these people have lost everything. The least we can do is offer them sanctuary and allow them to rebuild their lives."

Shepherd didn't say anything. There wasn't anything he could say. If the tables were turned and he was fleeing a murderous regime, he'd do whatever he could to save himself and his family. But he wasn't there to help refugees: he was there to identify and stop terrorists, and when it came to the war on terror there was no place for sentimentality. And there was no denying that the vast majority of the refugees in the camp were young, fit men. There were women and children, and a few old men with walking sticks, but everywhere Shepherd saw men in their twenties and thirties, huddled in groups, playing football or standing around smoking. Many had brand-label shirts, designer jeans and new trainers, and none appeared hungry or injured. He wondered why they didn't stand and fight for their country, and why, if safety was their predominant concern, they didn't want to stay in Turkey. But, as he had said to Parker, his mission had nothing to do with refugees and everything to do with terrorism.

There was a knock on the door, and Laura came in. "Yusuf is here," she said. She stepped aside and a portly man in a white linen suit bowled in. He had a round face and was bald except for a heart-shaped patch of hair above his forehead. There were large dark bags under his eyes and he had droopy jowls that gave him the look of a bloodhound. His lips were large and fleshy and there were rolls of fat around his neck, which glistened with sweat. His shirt had come loose from his trousers and his blue and white tie was loosely knotted and scattered with small stains, which suggested he was a messy eater.

"Yusuf, welcome," said Parker. Yusuf rushed forward and hugged him tightly, then released him and turned to Shepherd. "This is John, from London," said Parker. "The man I told you about."

Yusuf nodded excitedly. "Thank you for coming all this way," he said. He stepped forward, arms out, and Shepherd allowed himself to be hugged. He could smell garlic, tobacco and sweat. He looked over Yusuf's shoulder at Parker, who grinned at his obvious discomfort.

"I'm going to leave you two alone," he said. "I'll be doing some paperwork with Laura. Just open the door when you're done." He went out and shut it behind him.

Yusuf let go of Shepherd and sat on a small sofa under the window. It was for two people but he took up most of the space. He stretched out his feet. He was wearing sandals with no socks and his toenails were a yellowish green. Shepherd pulled the window blinds closed and sat down behind the desk.

"So, Craig tells me you help people get out of the camp," said Shepherd.

Yusuf held out his hands. "These people need help," he said. "I am grateful that Allah allows me to provide that help."

"Do you take people across the border?" asked Shepherd.

Yusuf shook his head. "That's a dirty business," he said. "And dangerous."

"More dangerous than what you're doing?"

"All I'm doing is helping refugees," said Yusuf. "That is a noble cause, which could cause no one any offence. But the border smugglers, that's the dirty end of the business. They bring people over, but they also take people into Syria, mainly foreigners who want to fight for Daesh."

"Daesh" was an insulting term that many Muslims used to describe Islamic State. It was an abbreviation of Dawlat al-Islamiyah f'al-Iraq wa al-Sham, which translated as "Islamic State in Iraq and the Levant". But in Arabic it sounded like "Sowers of discord", and Islamic State warlords killed anyone they heard using the term.

"And you don't do that?"

"I try not to deal with Daesh. Sometimes it is unavoidable, but I do not do it by choice."

"You don't trust them?"

"I don't trust anybody, my friend. Loyalties change, people move on. One day you might be dealing with a Daesh commander who decides he doesn't like the look of your face and the next thing you know your head has been separated from your body. Or the Americans decide that you are an enemy of their state and they launch a Hellfire missile with your name on it." He smiled. "No, my friend, I do what I do and that is all I do. I get papers for people who can afford it, and I arrange transport. I am a travel agent, if you like."

"What about going the other way? People helping those who want to get into Syria."

Yusuf grimaced. "Now you are talking about jihadists," he said. "That is not what I do, my friend."

"I wasn't suggesting you did. I'm just interested."

Yusuf pulled at his right ear lobe. Shepherd marked it down as a nervous gesture. "There are cafés near the border, literally within sight of the fence, where such people can be found," he said. "Going into Syria unannounced can be a dangerous business. Daesh do not take kindly to strangers, even those who say they have come to fight. The agent checks them out first, then takes a fee from them. The going rate is two hundred dollars. Or euros. For that they are taken across the border to a Daesh recruitment house. Men and women. You'd be surprised how many Western women want to be the bride of a jihadist fighter."

"Girls are always drawn to bad boys, I suppose," said Shepherd.

Yusuf laughed. "It's true, isn't it? They can be chopping the heads off Christians or setting fire to Russians and the girls just keep on coming. Violence makes them wet, they say. At the recruitment centre they are interrogated by a Daesh official. Sometimes that can take a month. If they are approved, they are moved on."

"And if not?" asked Shepherd.

Yusuf made a throat-cutting gesture with his finger. "That is not what I do, my friend. I help people get from Turkey to the West. I am not interested in helping jihadists into Syria."

"I understand," said Shepherd. "So you need to tell me exactly what information you have."

Yusuf lowered his voice and leaned towards Shepherd. "I have the details of Daesh fighters who have left here intending to go to Europe. They plan to hide among the genuine refugees."

"How do you know they are with Islamic State?"

Yusuf smiled. "I know," he said. "Trust me, I know."

"And what details do you have?"

"I have their photographs, and copies of the passports I obtained for them."

"What passports do they have, these fighters?"

"Syrian," said Yusuf.

Shepherd frowned. "You've been getting Syrian passports for Syrians?"

"No, of course not. They were Afghans. Iraqis. Two were from Pakistan."

"And these passports were fake?"

"No, real passports. A lot of the refugees leave without their papers so the Syrian government has made it easier for passports to be issued abroad. I have a contact at the Syrian embassy in Ankara. For a fee he will issue me a genuine passport in any name I require, using any photograph. It takes ten days, including the courier service."

"Expensive?"

"Very. But the passport is genuine, and if the holder can get to Europe he — or she — will have no problem claiming asylum."

"And how many of these have you done?"

Yusuf smiled. "Hundreds. It is a nice business and I have a steady stream of clients."

"So how do you know who are genuine refugees and who are IS fighters?"

Yusuf bit his lower lip. "You are going to help me, my friend?" he asked. "You will help me and my family get to England?"

"Providing the information you give me is helpful, yes," said Shepherd.

"And money?"

Shepherd nodded. "Money, too. You and your family will be taken care of, Yusuf. But the information you give me must be helpful and accurate. Now how do you know which are IS fighters and which are genuine refugees?"

"Sometimes I don't get to see them," said Yusuf. "There's a Daesh commander who moves back and forth across the border. He brings me photographs and cash and collects the passports."

"How many have you done for him?"

"A couple of dozen."

"You don't know for sure?"

"Twenty-five," said Yusuf.

"And did you ask this commander why the men weren't here themselves?"

"Of course not. You do not question men like him, not unless you want your head separated from your shoulders."

"But there are others you're sure are with Islamic State?"

"Forty-eight in total," said Yusuf.

"Okay, so twenty-five came from a Daesh commander. You know they're Islamic State. But the rest? How can you tell?"

"I just can," said Yusuf. "The really desperate ones are the ones with families. They'll do anything to get to Europe. They beg, they plead, they bribe. They offer me whatever they have." He jerked a thumb at the window. "Out there, in the camp, you can get a blow-job for medicine. Sex for ten dollars. They are desperate people, John. You have no idea." He put up his hands. "Not me, of course. But there are men out there who will take advantage of the weak and defenceless. There are fathers offering their daughters for sex. And their sons." He shuddered. "I wish I could help them all, but I do what I can. Some of the men who come to me, you can just tell they're not refugees. They're not running from anything. They don't have families. They're young, they're fit. It's their eyes that give them away. You can see what they have done in their eyes."

Shepherd understood exactly what Yusuf meant because he'd often looked into the eyes of men who had taken lives, and there was something different about them. "The men you've been providing passports for, have you helped them leave Turkey?" he asked.

"The Daesh fighters?" He shook his head. "No. And that is also suspicious. They clearly have their own transport arrangements. All they need from me is the passports."

"And when you're suspicious, you keep records?"

Yusuf smiled slyly. "My insurance policy."

"What about the men you met? Did any of them tell you where exactly they were heading?"

"Those men were not the sort to chat about their plans. But Europe, for sure. America never came up in conversation with any of them. They wanted passage to Europe."

"But not specifically to the UK?"

Yusuf shrugged. "A couple of them mentioned London. But everyone wants to go to England, don't they? In England they give refugees money and a house. They all know that. Even when Angela Merkel said they could go to Germany, most of them only wanted to go so they could get a German passport and move to England."

"But they said London? Specifically London?"

"Yes. Several of them."

"Why? How did it come up?"

"One said he had family there. Another said he had a friend who would give him somewhere to stay. Some of them were open about it. Others were more circumspect."

"You have their pictures?"

Yusuf rested his hands on his stomach. "Of course. And copies of their new passports. I have copies of all the passports. All forty-eight."

"Because you suspected they were not genuine refugees?"

Yusuf laughed. "I keep copies of all the passports I obtain. For insurance."

"But the forty-eight you're talking about. You're sure they're IS?"

"I wouldn't be bothering you with suspicions, my friend. I can imagine how upset you would be if you discovered that one of the names I had given you was a genuine refugee."

"That would be embarrassing," said Shepherd.

"The intel I have is one thousand per cent genuine," said Yusuf, quietly. "There is no doubt. I am sure that all forty-eight of the names I have are of Daesh fighters intent on launching terrorist attacks within Europe. Now, it is true I cannot say which of them are heading to the United Kingdom but we both know how Daesh hates your country and is intent on doing it harm. You cannot afford not to have these names."

"There's no need for the hard sell, Yusuf. We're well aware of the value of your intel."

Yusuf smiled ingratiatingly. "I'm not a greedy man. All I ask is passports for me, my wife and children, and passage to England. And money, of course."

"How much money?" asked Shepherd.

"How much do you think they will pay?" asked Yusuf, narrowing his eyes.

"That's not my area," said Shepherd.

"Would they pay a million dollars?"

"I wouldn't think so."

"Half a million?" asked Yusuf, hopefully.

"Possibly. It would depend on how good the intel is. If the jihadists are low-level soldiers, then maybe not much. But if they were commanders, or bomb-makers, possibly more."

"I will need money," said Yusuf. "My plan is to buy cars and rent them to Uber drivers. Maybe drive myself. You can earn good money with Uber."

"That sounds like a plan."

"So who do I talk money with, if not you?" asked Yusuf.

"Someone from London will come up with a figure after I've given my report," said Shepherd. "I need to see the intel you have."

Yusuf shook his head emphatically. "If I give it to you, it loses its value," he said. "At the moment there is no trust between us. You do not know me, I do not know you. Trust has to be earned."

"You don't have to give me anything," said Shepherd. "But I need to see it. They won't pay for intel if they're not sure it exists."

"I don't have it here."

"I wouldn't expect you to carry it around with you."

"I can take you to it. I can show it to you. But only you."

"That would work. Where?"

"I have a villa in Urfa. It is where my family stays."

Urfa was a city about forty kilometres from the camp, the capital of Sanliurfa Province. "You can take me there?" Shepherd asked.

"You will have to be alone," said Yusuf. "Only you."

"That's okay."

"You are not worried?"

"About what?"

"About being alone in a strange country? About being kidnapped?"

"Should I be?"

Yusuf smiled. "Of course not, my friend."

Shepherd returned the smile. "I've been kidnapped before," he said. "And it didn't end well for the people who did the kidnapping."

"Your government intervened? Special Forces? The SAS?"

Shepherd laughed. "No, mate. The British aren't like the Russians or the Israelis. If you fall in the shit they leave you to your own devices. It was the Yanks. The Americans. And they were doing a favour for a friend. A lot of people died, Yusuf. Just so you know."

"No one is going to kidnap you, my friend," said Yusuf. "You have my word."

"When can we go?" asked Shepherd.

Yusuf shrugged carelessly. "I can take you now. What is it you say? 'Strike while the iron is hot'? I am ready when you are."

"I'll need to make a phone call."

"Take all the time you need," said Yusuf. "But afterwards I must ask you to leave your phone here."

Shepherd nodded. "I understand," he said. Yusuf was right to be cautious: phones could be tracked, and with drones able to deal near-instant death from the skies it was only common sense to keep his home a closely guarded secret.

Mohammed al-Hussain was still kneeling down with his head over the toilet when the yacht moored in the marina at Mikrolimano. Saif went below deck to fetch him. "Are you all right, brother?" he asked.

Al-Hussain spat into the toilet bowl. "No," he said.

"We have arrived," said Saif.

"*Ashokrulillah*." Praise be to Allah.

Saif touched his arm. "We need to go now. Your transport is waiting."

Al-Hussain groaned and grabbed a bottle of water. He rinsed his mouth and got unsteadily to his feet. Saif picked up his backpack and helped him up the steps to the deck where Yasir was waiting.

"Feeling any better, brother?" he asked, gripping al-Hussain's arm.

"Is the sea always as rough as that?" asked al-Hussain.

Yasir laughed. "Brother, the sea was as smooth as silk."

Al-Hussain moaned softly. Yasir and Saif helped him off the yacht and onto the wooden pier. Two Asian men were waiting at the far end. They were dark-skinned and beardless, wearing leather jackets and faded jeans.

Saif gave al-Hussain his backpack, then hugged him. When Saif stepped back, Yasir hugged al-Hussain and

123

kissed him on both cheeks. "*Allah yusallmak*," he said. May God protect you.

Al-Hussain thanked them and walked unsteadily along the pier towards the Asians. They greeted him, then took him along to a waiting SUV.

Yusuf was an erratic driver at best. He rarely had more than one hand on the wheel and seemed to pay little attention to any other traffic on the road. His vehicle was an old Renault, its red paintwork pretty much obliterated by a thick layer of dust. It was an automatic, and Yusuf drove using both feet, his left on the brake and his right on the accelerator. Sometimes when he braked he stamped on both pedals at the same time resulting in the engine roaring as they came to a jerking halt. The passenger seatbelt was broken but he kept the speed down and there wasn't much traffic on the road.

"You live in London, my friend?" asked Yusuf, taking his eyes off the road to look at Shepherd.

"Yes," said Shepherd.

Yusuf continued to study him, one hand on the wheel, the other pulling at his ear lobe. "I have heard that Manchester is a better place to live."

"It rains a lot," said Shepherd.

There was a pick-up truck ahead of them and Yusuf didn't appear to have noticed it.

"We have a lot of rain here too," he said, "though you wouldn't think so at the moment. But the rain will come. Sometimes snow. Manchester is cheaper than London?"

124

"Sure," said Shepherd. "London is crazy. Everything is expensive." The pick-up truck was only fifty feet away and Yusuf was still looking at him. Shepherd was about to say something when Yusuf jerked the wheel and overtook the truck without even glancing at it.

"I am looking forward to living in England and becoming an Englishman," said Yusuf. "My children will do so much better at an English school. They are very excited. My wife, too."

Shepherd didn't say anything. There wasn't much he could say until he'd seen the information Yusuf had.

"You know we have half a million Syrian refugees in our province?" said Yusuf.

"I heard that, yes."

"One in three people who live here are refugees," said Yusuf. "The world doesn't know that, I think. Or doesn't care."

"People care," said Shepherd. "They just don't see what can be done."

"Many here are protesting, but they have no solution. In a perfect world they'd be sent home, but how can we do that when we know what will happen to them in their own countries? This could bankrupt our country. So far we have spent six billion dollars taking care of refugees. And we lost another two billion that Syrian tourists used to spend here. And the war means we no longer export to Syria. That has cost us another six billion dollars." He shrugged. "I don't know how much longer Turkey can sustain those costs."

"It won't be your problem, though, will it?" said Shepherd. "You'll be out of here."

"Please don't misunderstand me," said Yusuf. "I don't want to leave Turkey any more than the Syrian refugees want to leave their country. But, like them, I have no choice. If I stay here, Daesh will kill me eventually. I am sure of that."

"But you're helping them."

"I help them for money, not because I agree with what they are doing. And they think I don't suspect. They think they are so much smarter than everyone else so I won't know what they're up to. But eventually they will realise I am not as stupid as they think I am and at that point they will kill me. So I have no choice. I have to leave. If I do not leave I will die and I am not prepared to allow that to happen."

"Have you had a direct threat made against you?" asked Shepherd.

"Not to my face, no," said Yusuf. "But I have heard that one of the IS commanders is not happy with the work I am doing for the refugees. He thinks that by helping the refugees I am working against Daesh."

"But you've been helping them."

"I think there is a power struggle going on within Daesh and it has put me and my family in the firing line. That is why you must help me."

"That's why I'm here, Yusuf. You show me what you have and, if it's good, it'll be your ticket to England."

Yusuf beamed. "Just what I wanted to hear, my friend. Just what I wanted to hear."

It took just under forty-five minutes to reach Yusuf's villa. It was on the outskirts of Urfa, surrounded by a barbed-wire-topped wall. There was a metal gate that rolled back as he approached and Shepherd saw two men in long robes cradling AK-47s. Yusuf drove up to the villa as the gate rattled shut behind him. It was built of whitewashed stone with a flat roof and ornate metal bars over the windows. CCTV cameras were mounted above the front door. The two men climbed out of the Renault. "You have security here but not at the camp?" asked Shepherd.

"I would not be allowed armed guards at the camp," said Yusuf, waving at one of the men. He put a hand on Shepherd's back, guided him to the front door and pushed it open. Beyond, a hallway led to a small courtyard with a stone fountain in the centre. There were large spreading plants in terracotta pots and more plants in baskets hanging from metal brackets. Several wicker chairs and sofas stood around an oval glass table. Yusuf waved at one of the sofas. "Please sit, my friend. Do you smoke?"

"Smoke? No."

"I am very fond of the pipe," said Yusuf. "I hope you do not mind." He waved at a brass and wood hookah at the side of the table.

"Go ahead," said Shepherd, sitting down.

Yusuf smiled his thanks, then disappeared through a side door. Shepherd looked up at the sky. It was a brilliant blue and cloudless, but the courtyard was cool, and the gushing fountain gave it the feel of a spa. The grey flagstones seemed ancient, worn glass-smooth over the years. On the far side a flight of stone steps led to the upper floor. Yusuf returned with a portly middle-aged woman wearing a black tunic and hijab.

She smiled at Shepherd and picked up the pipe. "Would you like water?" asked Yusuf. "Tea? Something stronger? I have some excellent malt whisky."

"Iced water would be fine," said Shepherd.

Yusuf spoke to the woman in Turkish and she disappeared into the kitchen with the pipe. He sat down in a wicker chair with a spreading back that made it look as if he had wings.

"Is that your wife?" asked Shepherd.

Yusuf laughed. "No. You think . . .?" He laughed again and shook his head. "She is the maid, my friend. One of the maids. My wife, she is a beautiful woman. My wife and children are not here, my friend. They are in a safe place, with more guards than I have here."

"And why aren't your family here?" asked Shepherd.

"It's not safe."

"It looks fairly secure to me."

"Looks can be deceiving," said Yusuf. "We are still close to the border. And there are thousands of Syrian refugees nearby, any one of whom could be loyal to Daesh. I am happy enough to rest my head here at night, but I would not be able to sleep soundly knowing that my children were in the next room. That is why I need to move them to England. Only there will they be safe."

"Have you been to England?"

"No, I have not been lucky enough to make the journey. But I love your country, Mr Whitehill. The English are good people. Fair people. There is no better country in the world." He spread his hands. "I love Turkey, and I will always be a Turk, but in my heart of hearts I wish I had been born in England. Do you like cricket, Mr Whitehill?"

"I prefer football."

Yusuf patted his chest. "I have always loved cricket. I love to watch the game. How can that be, Mr Whitehill? Why, as a child, was I so drawn to cricket, the game that the English invented? I sometimes think that in a previous life I was an Englishman."

"That might explain it," said Shepherd.

The maid returned with the pipe. She had prepared it with hot charcoal and tobacco and placed it next to Yusuf. He reached for the hose and sucked on it, then blew smoke at the sky. He sighed and nodded his approval at her. She hurried off.

The smell of the tobacco wafted over to Shepherd. It was sweet with a hint of apple. "Yusuf, I don't want to rush you but I'm going to need to see the intel you have."

"Of course, my friend. Just let me enjoy my pipe for a minute or two."

For the first time Shepherd began to worry. It was as if the Turk was playing for time. The maid returned holding a brass tray on which were a glass of iced water along with two ceramic bowls, one containing shelled peanuts, the other cubes of what looked like sugar-dusted Turkish delight. She set the tray on the table in front of Shepherd.

"Please, help yourself, my friend," said Yusuf.

Shepherd picked up the iced water. He was thirsty and drank almost half of it in one go. Yusuf took another contented pull on his pipe, then put down the hose. He pushed himself up out of the chair. "I will get the information," he said.

"Excellent," said Shepherd.

Yusuf rubbed his hands together. "How many will you need? To prove that my information is good?"

"I need to see everything," said Shepherd.

"Everything? You expect me to give you all that I have?"

"Not give, Yusuf. Just show it to me. I won't take notes or photograph anything. Just bring it to me, show me that it exists, then you take it away. I'm not going to try to steal anything." He gestured at the doorway. "You have men with guns out there. It's not as if I could run away with anything, is it?"

"I just worry, my friend. That information is my ticket to England and I don't want to lose it."

"I understand," said Shepherd. "But you have to see it from my boss's point of view. You're asking for a lot and we would be remiss if we didn't confirm that you're in a position to deliver on your promises."

"That is fair," agreed Yusuf. He disappeared up the stairs.

The maid returned with a jug of iced water. She refilled Shepherd's glass, then placed the jug on the table, picked up the bowl of Turkish delight and offered it to him. He smiled and shook his head but she continued to prod the bowl at him until he took a piece and nibbled it. As she headed out of the courtyard, Yusuf came down the stairs holding a sheaf of papers. They had been folded twice as if he had been keeping them in an envelope.

130

He sat down next to Shepherd. Shepherd reached for them and Yusuf gave them to him, albeit with reluctance. He bit his lower lip and rubbed his hands together as he watched Shepherd flick through the sheets.

There were forty-eight, each a photocopy of a Syrian passport. All the passports had been issued in Ankara to Asian men. The youngest was eighteen, the oldest thirty-seven. Shepherd passed his eyes over each one. He didn't have to try to remember the details: providing he looked at it, the information would be in his memory for ever. "The dates of birth, are they genuine?" he asked.

Yusuf wrinkled his nose. "I don't know. But I was given them. And the names. The place of birth was put in by my man in the embassy."

Shepherd continued to examine the sheets. "And these are real passports, not fakes?"

"They are genuine. The real thing. The details are in the system. And they can be renewed."

Shepherd gathered together the papers, and handed them back to Yusuf, who grabbed them and folded them in half. "So it's good?" he asked.

"Yes," said Shepherd. "It's good."

Yusuf grinned like a schoolboy who had just been told he'd passed an exam. "So I can come to England?"

"That's what I'll be recommending to my boss," said Shepherd.

Yusuf beamed. "That is just what I wanted to hear." He held up the sheets. "Let me put these away."

"Go ahead," said Shepherd. He leaned over the table, poured himself more iced water and glanced at his watch. It was just before four o'clock. He wanted to be back at the camp before dusk. Parker had told him a supply flight would head back to Istanbul that evening. He sipped his water. The maid reappeared and spoke to him in Turkish. Her eyes were almost black and when she smiled he could see that several of her back teeth were missing. He figured she was asking him if he wanted anything and he shook his head. "*Teşekkür ederim*," he said. Thank you. That was just about all the Turkish he knew.

She picked up the dish of Turkish delight and prodded it at him again until he took another piece and popped it into his mouth. As she left, Yusuf came down the stairs. He'd changed his suit and was wearing a clean shirt. Shepherd assumed they were about to leave so he stood up but Yusuf sat down in his chair and reached for the tube of his hookah. Shepherd looked at his watch pointedly, but Yusuf didn't seem to take the hint. He sucked at the hose, then blew smoke at the flagstones. "So, what do you think of my country, my friend?" he asked.

"I haven't seen much of it," said Shepherd. "The airport and the camp, and your house, of course."

"This isn't my house," said Yusuf. "I rent it. I sleep here but it's not my home."

"You don't mind leaving Turkey?"

Yusuf took a long pull on the pipe and blew a cloud of sweet-smelling smoke. "I will miss Turkey, of course,

132

but I can always return, knowing that my family are safe."

"And what about Turkey?" asked Shepherd. "What will happen here, do you think?"

"Who knows? Something must happen. Turkey can't afford to keep paying for all the refugees who are coming, not without help. The cost will bankrupt the country unless Europe pays to deal with the problem. They can't all stay here, that's for sure. This province is very conservative. We have Turks, we have Arabs, we have Kurds. Good people. The Syrians ..." He shrugged. "You have to understand, they are not the same as us. They are what you might call our country cousins. Their morals are ... How would you say? Looser."

"Looser?"

"Underage girls are married off to older men for money. Or they sell themselves on the streets. The men, they're lazy, they're aggressive, they can't be trusted. Don't get me wrong, they're refugees and they need our help, but we can't take them all in, not without destroying what we have."

Shepherd nodded. "So what's the answer?"

"Daesh must be fought and defeated," he said. "And we Turks cannot do that, not on our own. NATO must do it. They must send troops to fight Daesh and do what needs to be done."

"You know that's probably not going to happen?"

"It will have to happen, eventually," said Yusuf. "Do you know how many fighters they have?"

"Estimates vary," said Shepherd.

"Two hundred thousand," said Yusuf. "With a war chest of billions. You know how many soldiers Italy has?"

"A hundred thousand, give or take."

"Exactly," said Yusuf. "And Spain, less than that. And Daesh is growing while the West cuts back on its armed forces. So let's look ahead a few years. If nothing is done, Daesh will continue to grow. What happens when they have half a million fighters and they invade Spain or Italy? Would the Italians be able to hold them back? Would the Spanish? Of course not. NATO would have to act, and that means the Americans. But would the Americans be prepared to send hundreds of thousands of men to fight in Europe?"

"There's a long way to go before that'll be necessary," said Shepherd.

"It will happen," he said. "Daesh wants to control the world. And unless the world fights back . . ."

Yusuf drove Shepherd back to Suruç and stopped outside Craig Parker's Portakabin. The two men climbed out of the car. "I will wait to hear from you, my friend." Yusuf embraced him. "But, please, do not leave it too long. I fear for my family, and the sooner they are in England, the better."

"I'm leaving for England tonight. As soon as I've spoken to my boss someone will be in touch," said Shepherd.

"But we are good?" asked Yusuf.

"Yes," said Shepherd.

Yusuf beamed and hugged him again. "You are a good man, John. Thank you." He got back into the Renault, still grinning, and waved as he drove off.

Shepherd waved back, then headed inside. Laura was at her computer and she beckoned him through.

Craig Parker jumped up from his desk when Shepherd opened the door. "How did it go?" he asked.

"It was okay," said Shepherd, sitting down.

"Can you help him?"

"I don't see why not. Do you really think he's in danger?"

"I don't know," said Parker. "He said he fears for his safety and the safety of his family, but I haven't heard it from anyone else. But then I wouldn't, would I? The thing is, he's hardly low-profile. He's well known in the camp so I'm sure he's on Islamic State's radar."

"He says he's been threatened. By an IS commander."

"That's what he told me. And it's perfectly possible, so he's put his family in a safe house."

"If he really feared for his life, wouldn't he just pack up and go?"

"He needs the money," said Parker.

"So he's putting money ahead of his family's safety."

"It's tough out here, John," said Parker. "He doesn't have many choices."

One of Shepherd's phones vibrated. He took it out and looked at the screen. It was the Terry Taylor phone and the caller had withheld his number. "I've got to take this," he said. "Do you mind?"

"Sure, of course, go ahead," said Parker.

Shepherd smiled and held up the phone. Parker got the message. "Ah, right." He stood up. "I'll be outside."

Shepherd waited until Parker had left before taking the call. "Yeah?"

"Terry, it's Howard. The brothers want me to give you a briefing."

"How's tomorrow?"

"Today would be better," said Wedekind. "The Mayfair again — say, six?"

"I'm out of the country, mate. Back tomorrow."

"Where the fuck are you?"

"I had some business to take care of. I can do tomorrow, first thing."

"Tommy didn't say anything about you being out of the country."

"Well, I'm not staff yet, Howard," said Shepherd. "If you want you can give me the SP over the phone and I'll head straight out there."

"Tommy doesn't want business discussed over the phone, ever," said Wedekind. "You'll have to learn that. Anyone discusses anything other than face to face, they're out."

"Understood. So what time's good for you tomorrow?"

"No time's good for me tomorrow," snapped Wedekind. "That's why I wanted to see you today."

"Howard, mate, I'm sorry. Totally my fault. Look, let me buy you lunch tomorrow. Or dinner. On me. Anywhere you want."

"Sheekey's. Lunch. And I'll be drinking champagne."

"As many bottles as you want, Howard."

"You can count on it."

The message in the draft mail folder said the meeting was to be in Heaton Park again at eleven in the morning. Omar replied, explaining that his father queried time off so an evening meeting would be preferable. Within minutes another message had appeared: 7 *p.m.*

Omar ran the same counter-surveillance measures as he had last time when he travelled from his home to the park by bus, tram and on foot. Once he was sure he wasn't being followed he turned into the park. It was starting to rain and he had brought a small collapsible umbrella with him. He opened it and held it over his head as he walked to the bench. The man was already there, sitting under a large red, green and yellow striped golfing umbrella. There was a black kitbag at his feet.

Omar sat down. The rain was still spitting and all but the most committed dog-walkers had left the park. "I will need more money," said Omar. He reached into his coat and handed the man several printed sheets. "I can't find anything usable for under three thousand pounds. The best ones are closer to ten. Six tens are sixty grand."

The man nodded. "We knew you would need additional funds. Are the buyers happy to accept cash?"

"Most prefer it. I've been asking for discounts for cash and no one knocks me back."

"Sixty thousand isn't a problem," said the man. "Just remember what I said about receipts. How much work is required?"

"They all need light bars but I can buy those second-hand and fit them myself. Of the ones I'm looking at, three are white so we'll need to respray but I have a good guy for that."

"And the premises we arranged for you? They are suitable?"

"They're fine. Well away from prying eyes."

The man pushed the kitbag towards Omar with his foot. "There is thirty thousand pounds in there. Be very careful with it, brother. You can tell me when you need more and we will meet again, but you must bring receipts with you."

Omar reached down, picked up the kitbag and placed it on his lap.

"This guy who is helping you. You trust him?"

"He is a good man. He has met my imam and they have talked."

"I know that. I was asking if you trust him."

"I do."

"With your life?"

Omar frowned. "What do you mean, brother?"

"You were trained by us. We know you. This man, we don't know."

"He is a good man and a good jihadist. He has no family here. He has refugee status and his paperwork is all good."

"But he has family in Afghanistan?"

Omar nodded. "A wife and children."

"A family can make a man vulnerable to pressure," said the man. "If he is caught, it can be a lever to open his mouth."

"Faisal wouldn't talk. But we won't get caught. We're careful. And all we're doing at the moment is buying vehicles."

The man smiled. "Of course. But there will come a point when the true purpose of those vehicles is realised. You are committed to our cause, brother, and you will die before you reveal its secrets. But this Faisal, will he be as steadfast?"

"I think so."

The man's smile widened. "Is that worth betting your life on, brother? I know I wouldn't bet my own on 'I think so'. I would want to be sure." He wiped his hands on his coat. "But no matter. We can talk about this again closer to the time. For the moment we are happy for you to use Faisal." He stood up. "Send me a message when you need more funds." He walked away before Omar could reply.

Shepherd arrived back at Heathrow airport just after nine o'clock in the evening. It had been a rushed journey. Craig Parker had driven at breakneck speed to the airport where the Hercules had been warming up its engines as Shepherd boarded. It had got him into Istanbul just forty-five minutes before a Turkish Airways direct flight to London. The plane was almost full and the only available seats were right at the back by the toilets. It wasn't a pleasant flight, only marginally more comfortable than the jumpseat on the Hercules, but he'd been in worse places and was just grateful to get back to London.

He caught a black cab to Battersea, showered and fell asleep as soon as his head hit the pillow. He was woken by the sound of his mobile ringing. He sat up and peered at the screen. Seven o'clock in the morning. The number was being withheld but it was his work phone and he could think of only one person who would call him at that hour. "Hello, Jeremy," he said, running his hand through his hair.

"How did you know it was me?" asked Willoughby-Brown.

"Lucky guess."

"How did it go?"

"All good," said Shepherd.

"You saw his intel?"

"Yes."

"Excellent. We need to meet, obviously. You're still averse to coming into Thames House?"

"I'd be happier meeting elsewhere."

"How about breakfast?"

"Sure, if it's out of the way."

"Ah, I was going to suggest the Savoy."

"Of course you were. There's a greasy spoon two roads down from where I am. The tables at the back are tucked out of the way. I'll see you there at eight thirty."

"Sounds salubrious."

"It isn't. But the grub's good."

"I'll be there," said Willoughby-Brown.

Shepherd shaved, showered and pulled on black jeans. He made himself a coffee, then spent the next half-hour at his laptop, typing out the details of the passports Yusuf had shown him. Then he grabbed his coat and headed out. Willoughby-Brown was already sitting at a table at the back, facing the door, which annoyed Shepherd: he needed to keep an eye on anyone coming or going and couldn't do that with his back to the door. That meant Willoughby-Brown was an idiot who didn't know basic tradecraft or he'd done it deliberately to put Shepherd on the back foot. Shepherd decided not to make an issue of it and sat down. A Polish waitress came over. Willoughby-Brown ordered tea and toast, Shepherd a full English and coffee.

"Not worried about your waistline, Daniel?"

Shepherd smiled. "What do you weigh?"

Willoughby-Brown grinned and patted his stomach. He was at least twenty kilos overweight whereas Shepherd was fit and trim. "Fair point," he said. "But I've earned these extra pounds."

"By sitting at a desk?"

"That's where the real work is done, these days."

"I wish I'd known that before I went all the way to Turkey to interview an asset," said Shepherd. "We could have done it by email."

"There's no need to get frosty with me, Daniel," said Willoughby-Brown. "I was just making the point that you're unlikely to keep your admirable physique eating a full English."

"I haven't eaten anything since I was on the plane yesterday afternoon, and I barely touched that. Plus I'll be out running later today."

"You run every day?"

"Pretty much. Got into the habit with the SAS. It's the best exercise there is."

"I always get bored on the treadmill. Even when you're watching the TV, it just feels like wasted time."

"You need to run outside. Your feet have to be on the road or grass, hitting a real surface, not a rubber band."

"Maybe I'll give it a try," said Willoughby-Brown. But Shepherd could tell from the man's voice that it was never going to happen. Willoughby-Brown was no more likely to go for a run than he was to sprout wings and fly around the café.

The waitress came over with their drinks. Willoughby-Brown added two spoons of sugar and stirred methodically. "So, do you think Yusuf is in serious danger or is he over-egging the pudding?"

"He says there's an IS commander after his blood," said Shepherd. "But he drives to and from his villa in a battered old Renault with no security. There's security at his villa, but just a couple of guys with Kalashnikovs. I would have thought if he really believed his life was in danger he'd have more. On the other hand, he's moved his wife and children to a safe location. But that's not really the point, is it? He's trading safe passage for the intel he has, and the intel seems good to me."

The waitress returned with their food. She put a plate with two slices of toast in front of Willoughby-Brown and Shepherd's full English in front of him. Two eggs, two sausages, bacon, mushrooms, beans and fried bread. Shepherd pushed the fried bread to the side of the plate.

142

"And exactly how good is his information?" asked Willoughby-Brown, buttering his toast.

"He showed me copies of all the passports he's fixed up for the ones he thinks are jihadists. He doesn't know about my memory, obviously — I just took a quick look and gave them back."

"But you have all the information? Passport numbers, dates of birth, all the good stuff?"

Shepherd put down his knife and handed Willoughby-Brown a blue plastic thumb drive. "I transcribed everything I saw onto this," he said.

"What about their photographs?"

"I can remember them all. And I'd recognise them if I saw them."

"What about working with one of our artists? Could you get them to draw the faces?"

"I don't see why not. But it might be easier to liaise with the Syrian government. All the passports were issued by the Syrian embassy in Ankara. We have the names and dates, so they'd be able to supply the photographs."

"I'm not sure how cooperative the Syrians would be, frankly," said Willoughby-Brown. "But we have other options." He weighed the thumb drive in his palm. "And that's all he has? The forty-eight here?"

"That's all he showed me."

"That's not what I'm asking, Daniel. Do you think he's holding something back for a rainy day? Something he can produce down the line to squeeze a little more out of us?"

"I don't think so, no." Willoughby-Brown slipped the thumb drive into his pocket, then pointed at one of Shepherd's sausages. "Are you going to eat that?"

"I was planning to, but help yourself."

Willoughby-Brown picked up the sausage and took a bite. "So the well is dry, effectively."

Shepherd frowned. "I don't follow you."

"I mean we have everything he has. You saw all his intel. Everything you saw you've passed on to us. There's nothing more to be had."

Shepherd's eyes narrowed. "You're not suggesting what I think you're suggesting, are you?"

Willoughby-Brown grinned, took another bite of sausage and swallowed. "And what do you think I'm suggesting, pray tell?"

"You're considering throwing Yusuf to the wolves."

"And that would be a bad thing, why?"

"Are you serious?" said Shepherd. "The guy risks his life to help us and you're going to turn your back on him?"

"Well, now, to be fair, he's not approached us out of the goodness of his heart. He wants money, he wants passports, he wants transport. His total bill will be close to a million pounds by the time he's finished. So let's not harp on about his altruism. And let's not forget that he's been instrumental in helping what he admits are forty-eight IS fighters into Europe. Do you think he'd be coming to us if he wasn't in the shit?"

"It's a betrayal, Jeremy." He put down his knife and fork. He'd lost his appetite.

144

"That's subjective, Daniel. If you were to talk to Islamic State, they'd probably say Yusuf is betraying them. We're in the betrayal business. That's what we do."

"Since when?" said Shepherd. "He's a source. We protect our sources."

"No. We use our sources in the best interests of our country. We've done that. We've spoken to him and he gave us his intel. That would seem to me to bring the matter to a close."

"Jeremy, will you listen to yourself? If you betray Yusuf after what he's done for us, no one will ever trust Five again."

Willoughby-Brown laughed. "I hardly think Yusuf will go around telling everyone what happened. I mean, come on now. What's he going to say? That he showed us intel on Islamic State and we didn't pay him? He'd be signing his own death warrant. No, he'll keep quiet. And he still has his intel. Maybe he can get the French to take him in."

"You're a bastard, you really are."

"Sticks and stones, Daniel."

"You planned this right from the start, didn't you? You sent me because of my memory. You knew that once I had sight of his intel we wouldn't need him."

"You're overthinking things, as usual."

"Is that why you sent Shuttleworth?"

Willoughby-Brown looked confused. "What do you mean?"

"Shuttleworth's an idiot. Presumably you know that. You sent him precisely because he wouldn't be able to handle Yusuf. Yusuf recognised Shuttleworth for what he was and demanded to see someone from London, and that allowed you to send me. Yusuf thought he was running the show but actually it was you, being your usual devious self."

Willoughby-Brown chuckled. "Now you're entering the realms of fantasy," he said. "Look, in a way it serves him right. If he'd played his cards a bit closer to his chest, he wouldn't be in this state, would he?" He finished off the sausage and wiped his hands on a paper napkin.

"He's only got himself to blame?"

"Exactly."

"I was being ironic, Jeremy."

"I wasn't. He's a people-trafficker, Daniel. He trades in other people's misery. And he knew he was helping jihadists get into Europe. He knew it and he went ahead and did it, for cold, hard cash. He took copies as an insurance policy, not because he wanted to help the West. If he hadn't felt threatened we'd probably never have heard from him. He should count himself lucky I don't pick up the phone and call the Americans. They'd grab him and put him in an orange jumpsuit any day of the week."

Shepherd shook his head grimly but didn't say anything. He knew it would be pointless. Willoughby-Brown grinned, obviously thinking he'd won the argument. "So, at least now you can get back to concentrating on the O'Neill brothers. You caught the sun while you were in Turkey. You'll need a story for that."

146

Shepherd stood up. "Are we done?"

"Oh, come on, Daniel, don't leave angry."

Shepherd would have liked nothing better than to smack him in the mouth but he knew that if he did it would be the end of his career. He walked out of the café and stormed off down the street.

Mohammed al-Hussain spent the night in a terraced house on the outskirts of Athens. The men who had picked him up at the marina spoke limited English but they were friendly and did all they could to make him comfortable. They had prepared a bed for him in the basement, given him a prayer mat and shown him the Qibla, the direction of the revered shrine in Mecca's Great Mosque. They provided food — lamb kebabs, deep-fried cheese, pitta bread and grapes — and left him alone. There was a small shower room where he washed and cleaned his teeth. When he had dressed again, he went into the main room and prayed, ate most of the food and climbed into bed.

They woke him early the next morning with a tray of bread, boiled eggs and goat's cheese and told him that in two hours they would be leaving for the airport. He showered, prayed, then ate his breakfast. Later they came with a change of clothing — a dark blue suit, which fitted him perfectly, a white shirt and a blue tie. They gave him a pair of black shoes, which were comfortable albeit a little loose, and a briefcase containing brochures from hotels in Athens, menus from several restaurants and a change of clothes.

147

They took him upstairs and outside to a waiting Toyota saloon. One of the men who had met him at the marina sat in the back with him but said nothing during the journey. When they reached Athens airport the man gave him an Air France business-class ticket and an envelope containing several hundred euros. Al-Hussain got out of the car and walked into the terminal without a backward look.

Shepherd took the tube to Piccadilly Circus and spent fifteen minutes wandering around Leicester Square. His anti-surveillance was more out of habit than a serious worry that he was being followed. Sheekey's was in St Martin's Court, the heart of the capital's Theatreland. It was an old-fashioned fish restaurant and oyster bar, and he had been there many times over the years. He arrived at the restaurant five minutes early but Howard Wedekind was already sitting at a corner table with a half-empty bottle of pink champagne in front of him.

"You weren't joking about the bubbly," said Shepherd, as he sat down opposite the accountant.

"I'm having the lobster, too," said Wedekind.

Shepherd put up his hands in mock-surrender. "Whatever it takes to keep you sweet, Howard."

"What was so important that you had to flee the coop?" asked Wedekind. "You knew that Tommy had a job for you. You give me all that guff about wanting to be on the team, then bugger off."

"I was away for a day, Howard. Something that needed to be taken care of." A waiter appeared at his shoulder and began pouring champagne into a flute. Shepherd waved for him to stop. "Gin and tonic, please."

The waiter began reeling off a list of gins but Shepherd held up a hand to silence him. "Whichever bottle is closest to the barman's hand will be fine," he said.

The waiter nodded and walked away. Shepherd leaned closer to Wedekind. "A guy owes me money and I needed to sort it out," he said. "I didn't want to tell Tommy because it makes me look like a prick."

"What's the story? I can't believe somebody didn't pay you for a job."

Shepherd chuckled. "Nah, he's an accountant. They're all robbing bastards in my experience, no offence."

"None taken. But how come he owes you money?"

"He's been doing a bit of laundry for me. Taking my cash and getting it into the banking system for seventy-five pence on the pound. Except the last two payments didn't make it into my Jersey account."

Wedekind shook his head. "Seventy-five pence on the pound? Are you serious?"

"Best deal I could get," said Shepherd. "The guy before that only gave me sixty pence on the pound. Though to be fair he got the money into my account within forty-eight hours and he never let me down."

"The percentage you're paying I'm not surprised," said Wedekind.

"I'm getting a shit deal, then?"

Wedekind sipped his champagne. "Yes," he said.

"Can you get me a better one?"

"Maybe."

"Would you? You can take a cut, obviously."

"I'd have to talk to the boys. I work for them, remember."

"Yeah, but I'll be on the team so it'll all be in house," said Shepherd.

"Let me give it some thought," said Wedekind. "How much are we talking about?"

"Half a mill a year, give or take. Pounds and euros."

"And this guy you went to see, what's the story?"

"I met him through a friend of a friend. He vouched for him. But, like I said, a hundred grand's gone walkabout."

"Bearing in mind how you make your money, why would he take the risk of upsetting you?"

The waiter returned with Shepherd's gin and tonic. He waited until the man had set down the drink and left before continuing. "I didn't tell him, obviously. And neither did the guy who introduced us. He thought I was just a self-employed businessman trying to hide money from the taxman." He grinned and raised his glass. "Which is sort of true, but not the whole truth."

"And you resolved this?"

"Let's just say if the money isn't in the bank by close of business today he'll be at the receiving end of my expertise." He winked and sipped his drink.

"If you don't mind me asking, where does he put your money?"

"Some in Jersey. Some in the Isle of Man. The usual places."

150

Wedekind grimaced. "I'd be wary of the usual places," he said. "They're not as safe as they used to be. Under the new EU rules they have to open their books to the taxman, and they do."

"Most of the accounts are in other names."

"That'll help muddy the water. But if they ever come after you, a false name or two won't stop them."

"So what would you do?"

"Hypothetically?"

Shepherd laughed. "Hypothetically."

"There's no problem in having accounts in Jersey or the Isle of Man, but you need to make them company accounts. Or ideally put the money in a trust fund. As soon as the Revenue see a trust fund, they know they've got a fight on their hands and, more often than not, they won't bother. They're typical bureaucrats, mainly. They get paid to do their job no matter how well they do it." He swirled the champagne in his glass. "If I was running the Revenue I'd be putting them on commission. You'd soon see them perk up if they knew they'd get to keep ten per cent of anything they found. But they don't so, like most bureaucrats, they'll always look for the easy life."

"And you make it more complicated. Is that it?"

Wedekind smiled. "The more complicated the better," he said. "You can have your Jersey account, along with a debit card and a credit card feeding off it. But you make it a company account and have the business incorporated offshore. Belize, maybe, or the Cayman Islands. You throw some local property into that company but then have it owned by another offshore company, ideally one which is then owned by a trust fund." He shrugged. "It takes a bit of time to set it up but it's worth the effort."

"And how do you get the money into it?"

"Some offshore banks will still take cash," said Wedekind. "From people they trust."

"And you could set up something like that for me?"

"Not me personally, no. It's specialist stuff and it has to be done right."

"But you know people?"

"Of course."

"And these people, they could set something up for me?"

"In theory, sure. But I'd have to talk to Tommy and Marty first."

"You couldn't get them to do it for me on the QT?"

Wedekind chuckled drily. "You don't play that sort of game with the brothers, Terry. Trust me on that." He pushed a menu towards Shepherd. "I've already ordered," he said. "Oysters, then lobster."

Shepherd didn't bother opening the menu. He waved over the waiter and asked for smoked salmon, then fish pie.

"And bring us another bottle of the bubbly," said Wedekind. "This one will be dead soon." The waiter repeated the order and walked away. Wedekind drained his glass and refilled it. "So, Gibraltar, you've never been?"

"Never needed to. But I know the SP. British-owned, the Spanish want it, bit of a tax haven."

Wedekind nodded. "The brothers have money there and some property, including a couple of hotels. All locked away in offshore companies, obviously."

"Obviously," repeated Shepherd.

"They also have an online casino based there. Blackjack, slots, poker, all the usual stuff. Their guy over there is a Spaniard, Carlos Garcia. Carlos is a nice enough guy, a bit lazy but, then, all the Spaniards are, right?"

"I guess so."

"It's always *mañana, mañana,* tomorrow, tomorrow. But with the brothers, as you know, if they want something done they want it done yesterday. Anyway, earlier this week the head of security was shot. No one seems to know who did it or why and Garcia is being less than forthcoming. We've had a look at the books and it seems he's let some of the high-rollers run up tabs. Big tabs. One of them is close to two hundred thousand euros in the hole. The client's a Russian. Lives in Marbella. Been a client for going on a year, all fine and dandy, then for some reason Garcia gives him a tab and now the Russian won't pay him back."

"So I'm debt-collecting?"

"Would you just shut up and listen for a minute?" snapped Wedekind. "It's not just about debt-collecting. If it was, the brothers have a dozen guys they could send and those guys wouldn't be swanning around taking care of their own personal business as a priority."

"Sorry," said Shepherd, raising his glass.

Wedekind waved away the apology. "I'm just fucking hungry," he said. "I didn't get breakfast this morning."

153

He sipped his champagne. "Anyway, the brothers want to know what the fuck is going on over there and obviously they want to keep it at arm's length."

Shepherd smiled thinly. "Got it."

"They want you to fly over and calm things down. Shootings will draw attention to us and the brothers hate that. Put a lid on it. And find out what the story is about tabs. They should all be paying up-front."

"I'll fly today."

The waiter came over with Wedekind's oysters and Shepherd's smoked salmon.

"How heavy can I get?" asked Shepherd, once the waiter had left.

Wedekind leaned across the table. "Don't kill anyone," he whispered. "But you don't have to pull any punches. The brothers want this stamped on, and stamped on hard."

Shepherd raised his glass. "That's what I do best," he said.

Mohammed al-Hussain walked out into the arrivals area at Paris Charles de Gaulle airport. A middle-aged clean-shaven Asian in a black leather bomber jacket and tight jeans was holding up a piece of cardboard with the name RAJPUT on it. Al-Hussain nodded at him. "Welcome to Paris, bruv," said the man, folding up the piece of cardboard and putting it into his jacket pocket.

"You are English?" asked al-Hussain.

"Yeah, bruv. I'm taking you on the Eurostar. Business class, so it's all good." The train was preferable to flying into London. Security was less stringent on the Eurostar than at the airports, and passports weren't checked as thoroughly.

"So you are coming to London with me?"

The man nodded. "That's the plan, bruv. You hungry? We can grab some food here or, if you can wait, they'll feed us on the train."

"I can wait," said al-Hussain.

"No problem," said the man. "We'll get a cab to the Eurostar terminal."

He headed for the exit and al-Hussain followed him. "What is your name?" he asked.

"Sunny," said the man. "Sunny by name, sunny by nature."

Shepherd flew to Gibraltar on British Airways. Business class had been full and he ended up sitting halfway down the plane, over the wing. He had a good view of the Rock as the plane came into land, topped by a white radar dome and aerial towers, and behind it the three-hundred-acre nature reserve that was home to the famous Barbary apes. The limestone cliff was peppered with the holes used by cannons to defend Gibraltar going back to the seventeenth century, and a single Union flag fluttered from a pole at the peak. As they taxied back to the terminal he caught a glimpse of a blue-grey RAF Hercules parked by a hangar.

The plane came to a halt and stairs were pushed up to the front and rear, which meant that Shepherd was one of the last off. The sky was overcast but it was a good ten degrees warmer than it had been in London.

The queue from Immigration wound onto the tarmac and there seemed to be just one officer handling EU arrivals while another dealt with non-EU passengers, including a dozen or so Filipino men who were presumably flying to work on one of the many cruise ships that visited Gibraltar. It took Shepherd longer to get through Immigration at Gibraltar than it had at Heathrow after his last flight. Even with no luggage to collect, it was almost an hour before he walked into the arrivals area.

Carlos Garcia was easy to spot: he was tall and thin with a greasy comb-over and a well-tended goatee. He was carrying the jacket of his grey suit and wearing a grey shirt with the sleeves rolled up, showing forearms matted with thick black hair. He grinned, revealing unnaturally white teeth. "Terry, how was your flight?"

"Flight's a flight, mate," said Shepherd, playing the role of Terry Taylor, hard man, to the hilt. He wasn't in Gibraltar on a social visit: he was there to sort out a problem for the O'Neill brothers and, if necessary, crack some heads together. "Where's your motor?"

Garcia's smile hardened a little. "Outside," he said.

"Lead on then," said Shepherd, brusquely. "I haven't got all day."

Garcia took him outside, crossed a road to a car park and led him to a lime-green Lamborghini. Shepherd stared at it in amazement. "You're shitting me," he said.

"It's a beauty, isn't it?" said Garcia, misinterpreting his reaction.

Shepherd looked at him contemptuously. "You drive this all the time?"

Garcia frowned. "What's wrong with it?"

"It's a bloody pimp-mobile," said Shepherd. "Aren't you supposed to be keeping a low profile?"

"This is Gibraltar," said Garcia. "Here, if you've got it, you flaunt it." He unlocked the door and climbed in.

Shepherd squeezed himself into the passenger seat. The car was left-hand drive. Gibraltar was a British Overseas Territory, but as it was on the tip of Spain, driving on the left wouldn't have made much sense. "Yeah, well, where I come from, if you flaunt it, someone's likely to try to take it off you," he said. "Do you know what car Tommy drives when he's in the UK?"

Garcia shook his head as he started the engine. Shepherd could feel the vibration coming up through the seat. A stereo system that must have cost several thousand pounds kicked into life, filling the car with a Spanish love song at full volume. Garcia flashed Shepherd an apologetic smile and turned the sound down.

"Tommy has a Volvo estate," Shepherd continued. "With a kid's seat in the back."

"I didn't know he had a kid."

"He doesn't, that's the point," said Shepherd. "No one pays attention to a guy in a family car. He blends. This is a red rag to a bull, mate. If I were you, I'd lose it."

Garcia flashed him a tight smile. "I understand."

"It's about staying below the radar," said Shepherd. "You can have as much money as you want, but the trick to keeping it is not to let people know you've got it." He folded his arms. "So, your head of security was shot?"

"Only in the leg. It wasn't life-threatening. He probably won't even have a limp."

"What's his name?"

"Jake. Jake Rosenfeld."

"He's a Brit?"

Garcia shook his head. "American. Used to work in Vegas."

"And forgive my ignorance but you don't have any premises so why do you need security?"

"It's more website security, making sure we're not hacked. He's a systems guy."

"And who shot him?"

"We don't know."

"And where is this Jake?"

"Home. They let him out of hospital this morning."

"Okay. You need to take me there now. I want to talk to him."

Garcia edged the Lamborghini out of the car park. "How long have you worked for the O'Neills?" he asked.

"Why do you need to know?" said Shepherd. "This isn't a fucking job interview."

Garcia flinched as if he'd been struck across the face. "I was just making conversation."

"Yeah, well, I haven't flown all this way for a social chat," said Shepherd. "I'm here because the shit has hit the fan and somebody has to clean up your mess."

"Terry, you don't know me, I don't know you. But I've known Tommy and Marty for years. I'll talk to them and put it right."

"They want you to talk to me, Carlos. That's why I'm here. They're not going to talk to you over the phone."

The Spaniard threw up his hands. "It's nothing, Terry. It's a storm in a teapot."

"Teacup."

Garcia frowned. "What?"

"It's a storm in a teacup."

Garcia nodded enthusiastically. "Exactly. That's what it is. Just explain to Tommy and Marty that it's a storm in a teacup. I'll handle it."

Shepherd shook his head. "You need to talk to me, Carlos. I'm here to help."

"Really, I don't need your help. I can handle this."

"You handling it got your head of security shot. How is that handling it?"

"Terry, please, it will blow over."

"And, according to your records, you've let a client run up a two-hundred-thousand-euro tab."

The road they were on cut across the airport's single runway. "He'll pay it back," said Garcia.

"When? *Mañana*?"

"Soon."

"Tell me, Carlos, do you think this client is the one who had your head of security shot?"

The Spaniard concentrated on the road and said nothing, but Shepherd could see that he'd struck a nerve.

"His name is Stefan Bazarov?"

Garcia nodded.

"Why isn't he paying?"

"He says we cheated him. He was playing poker and he says we were cheating."

"And were you?"

Garcia looked over at him. "Of course not. Online casinos operate on trust. If people suspected we were cheating, we'd lose our whole customer base."

"But Bazarov thinks you're cheating?"

"That's what he says, yes."

"And because of that he had your head of security shot?"

Garcia grimaced. "Not exactly. No."

"Carlos, you need to stop fucking around here. Your balls are on the table and I'm the guy holding the cleaver. You need to tell me what's going on so I can get it sorted."

"Okay, okay," he said. "Stefan ran up a debt. My fault. He was a good customer, one of our best, so when he asked for credit I said yes. That was fine for a couple of months until his payments stopped going through. I mentioned it to Rosenfeld and he said he'd sort it out. I thought he meant he'd talk to Bazarov but he got some Serbs involved. They went to talk to the Russian and roughed him up. Nothing broken, just worked him over."

"You knew about this?"

"Not before it happened. Not until Jake got shot. I went to see him in hospital and that's when he told me."

"Who shot him? Who actually pulled the trigger?"

"He doesn't know. But he thinks they were Russian."

"And this Bazarov. Who is he?"

"Just a client."

"A client who can get someone shot. Who is he, Carlos? Russian Mafia?"

"Just a Russian client. That's all I know. You think I'd pick a fight with the Russian Mafia?"

"I don't know what to think, Carlos. That's why I'm talking to you and not giving you the kicking you so richly deserve. He lives in Marbella, the Russian?"

Garcia nodded.

"You've got an address for him?"

"Sure."

For several minutes Garcia drove in silence. "How much trouble am I in, Terry?" he asked eventually.

"I'm not sure yet. Soon as I know, you'll know."

It took less than five minutes to drive from the airport to the tower block where the American lived, overlooking Gibraltar's Ocean Village complex, with shops, restaurants and apartment blocks around a large marina. The largest vessel by far was a massive white cruise ship that had been converted into a hotel, dwarfing the yachts around it. Garcia parked the sports car in the block's car park and they walked up a flight of stairs to Reception. There was no doorman but a big man in a dark suit was sitting on a sofa reading a newspaper. He nodded at Garcia, who nodded back.

"He's one of yours?" asked Shepherd.

"Jake wanted extra security," said Garcia, as they walked towards the lift.

"The head of security needs security," said Shepherd. "That sort of defeats the point, doesn't it?"

"As I said, Jake's more about system security. This is a new situation for the two of us." They got into a lift and Garcia pressed the button for the top floor. When the door opened, a second, slightly bigger, man in a slightly darker suit was on the landing. He nodded at Garcia.

"Who's paying for the extra security?" said Shepherd. "Because I'm pretty sure the O'Neills don't know about it."

"Jake's handling it." There seemed to be only two apartments on the top floor and Garcia took Shepherd to the one on the right. He pressed the bell, and a few seconds later the door was opened by a guy in his thirties with a cast on his left leg. He was holding a steel crutch. He had blond hair tied back in a ponytail, there was a cut on his lip and his right eye was bruised. Despite his injuries he smiled and welcomed them.

"This is Terry, the guy I told you about," said Garcia.

"Come in," said Rosenfeld. "The place is a bit of a mess. I'm not up to clearing up after myself at the moment." He gestured with his crutch for them to go inside.

The apartment was impressive with floor-to-ceiling windows on three sides and spectacular views over the marina, the sea beyond and across to Spain. There were long black leather sofas set around a glass table that was supported by two brass figures of naked kneeling women and on the wall by the door was a large oil painting of two naked women entwined around each other. The coffee table was littered with take-away containers and pizza boxes. Rosenfeld smiled apologetically. "I'm not much good in the kitchen either." He dropped down onto one of the sofas and waved his crutch at the other sofa. "Please, sit. Carlos, help yourself to a drink from the fridge. I'll have a beer."

Garcia headed for the kitchen. "What do you want Terry?" he asked.

"I'm good," said Shepherd, sitting down. He looked over at the American. "So tell me what happened?"

Rosenfeld grinned. "It's nothing. It looks worse than it is."

"I don't care what it looks like, I want to hear what happened."

"You presumably know what happened. A client decided to welsh on a debt and when I tried to collect I got shot." He gestured at the cast. "It's no big deal. I can still work, the cast is just there to protect the stitches. Like I said, it looks worse than it is."

"Jake, I couldn't care less about the state of your fucking leg," said Shepherd.

Garcia returned with two bottles of beer. He gave one to Rosenfeld. "It was a problem, but it's over now," said Garcia, sitting down next to Shepherd.

"It's over when I says it's over," said Shepherd. "From where I'm sitting, it looks to me as if you're in the middle of a gang war. And that's not good for business."

"Who the hell are you, exactly?" asked Rosenfeld.

"I represent the owners."

"Yeah, well I work for Carlos."

He looked over at Garcia, clearly looking for support, but Garcia turned away and sipped his beer.

"And Carlos works for them. Listen, I'm on your side here. I want to find out what happened and make sure it doesn't happen again. I'm guessing you don't want another bullet in the leg."

"They won't shoot me again," said Rosenfeld.

"I wasn't talking about the Russians," said Shepherd. "I mean that if you keep fucking me around like this I'll put a bullet in your other leg myself."

Rosenfeld looked surprised and glanced over at Garcia. The Spaniard was studiously avoiding him.

"So, what did you do to set them off?"

"Look, I talked to him, told him that he had to pay. He refused. So I spoke to some people who collect debts."

"Serbs?"

"Yeah. They're based in Estepona, midway between here and Marbella. They collect debts for ten cents on the Euro. The guy I spoke to is called Goran Kolarac. He said he'd get our money back. Guaranteed it."

"So you were paying them what, twenty thousand Euros?"

"That was the idea."

Shepherd looked over at Garcia. "You were happy at this?"

"I didn't know," said Garcia.

"You told me to do what was necessary, and that's what I did," said Rosenfeld.

"Those Serbs, you've used them before?"

Rosenfeld shook his head. "I was introduced to Kolarac through a friend of a friend. I thought it would help. Bazarov wasn't going to pay. He said we could whistle for it."

"And the Serbs did what? Beat him up?"

"Roughed him up a little, that's all."

"For fuck's sake, Jake, what did you think that would achieve?"

"I thought if he knew we were serious, he'd pay back what he owes."

Shepherd gestured at the man's injured leg. "So much for your plan, hey?"

The American was clearly embarrassed.

"So where are we with the Russian?"

"In what way?" asked Garcia.

"Is he done now? Or was he hoping for more than a bullet in the leg?"

"You think he might hit us again?" Garcia looked nervous.

"That's what I'm asking you," said Shepherd. "And what about the Serbs? Are they now off the case?"

"They're in hospital," said Rosenfeld, quietly.

Shepherd squinted at him. "Run that by me again."

"They were shot. Three of them. The three that went around to see Bazarov. They got shot worse than I did."

Shepherd stood up and paced over to the window. Navigation lights were twinkling on the boats in the harbour. Shepherd turned back to the room and glared at Garcia. "So we're in the middle of a gang war. Is that what you're telling me?"

"It's over. It happened three days ago."

"Have you spoken to Bazarov since?"

Garcia shook his head.

"So how do you know it's over? How do you know he's not got a couple of guys sitting outside waiting to put a bullet in you? Or me? And what are we going to do about the money? The O'Neills want that money, Carlos. Do you understand me? They're not going to take no for an answer."

Garcia and Rosenfeld looked at each other. "I don't think he's going to pay," said Garcia, quietly.

"Well, someone's going to have to. How much do the brothers know about the technical side of what you've been doing?"

"Not much," said Garcia. "All they're interested in is the bottom line. And we've been making money, hand over fist. If it hadn't been for Jake getting shot . . . So what happens now?"

"I'll talk to the Serbs, make sure they don't take it any further." He looked at Rosenfeld. "Have they been paid?"

"They were going to keep their share when Bazarov paid them."

"Except Bazarov has no intention of paying. And if you ask him again, I'm guessing you'll get more than a bullet in the leg." He turned back to the window and folded his arms. "The Serbs are going to need paying. That means you two are going to have to come up with the twenty thousand euros. You need to give me the cash, I'll give it to them and, hopefully, they'll see there's no point in taking it any further."

"Twenty thousand?" said Garcia. "You expect me to hand over twenty thousand?"

"They need paying, Carlos. And I'm not using my money. Plus, I'll tell you now, if the Russian doesn't come up with the two hundred grand, you'll have to."

"You're crazy!" spat Garcia.

"It's not crazy, it's Plan A. The brothers will want their money so if the Russian doesn't pay up you'll have to. Plan B is that I put a bullet in your head and another in Jake's. Because if the O'Neills find out what you've been doing they're going to want you dead. It might be me they get to do it, it might be someone else, but as sure as I'm standing here, that is what's going to happen if they don't get their money."

Garcia wiped his face with a hand. He was sweating and there were damp patches on his shirt.

"I want the twenty thousand now," said Shepherd. "I can give that to the Serbs. I'll talk to the Russian and see how the land lies. Have you got the cash?"

The Spaniard nodded. "I can get it."

"I need it now."

Garcia looked at Rosenfeld. The American's eyes widened. "Are you serious? You want my money?"

"I don't care who gives it to me but I'm not leaving here without the twenty grand."

Rosenfeld glared at Shepherd, but then the fight went out of him and he sighed. "Fine," he said. He pushed himself up off the sofa and hobbled into the bedroom.

"I'm sorry about this, Terry," said Garcia.

167

"You and me both," said Shepherd.

Rosenfeld returned with a bundle of notes, which he handed to Shepherd. "I'm not walking outside with that," said Shepherd. "Get me a bag or something."

Rosenfeld limped back to the bedroom.

"What do I do now?" asked Garcia.

"Stay out of trouble and wait for me to call you," said Shepherd.

"Thank you, Terry," said Garcia. "I appreciate what you're doing."

"Don't thank me yet," said Shepherd. "This could still all turn to shit."

Rosenfeld came back with a small washbag. "How about this?" he asked.

"It'll do," said Shepherd.

Rosenfeld put the money into it, zipped it up and gave it to Shepherd. "You're welcome," he said, bitterly.

Shepherd glared at him. "There'll be time for please and thank-you when this is sorted," he said. "Until then your best course of action is to keep your mouth shut."

The immigration officer who examined Mohammed al-Hussain's passport was a Sikh, his head covered with a pale blue turban. Further along he saw a Chinese woman and beyond her a West Indian. The Sikh handed the passport back and motioned for al-Hussain to walk on. Al-Hussain smiled and moved away from the counter.

Sunny was at the next counter, saying something to the Chinese woman. He loved to talk. They had sat facing each other in business class and Sunny had talked incessantly for the first fifteen minutes. He had talked about sport, movies he had seen, girls he had been out with, food he had eaten. Al-Hussain had grunted occasionally but hadn't replied. Nothing Sunny had said was dangerous. There had been no hint in his incessant rambling of who they were or why they were going to London, but al-Hussain had found it distracting and annoying.

They were served a meal and Sunny talked all the way through it, whether or not there was food in his mouth. Eventually, after their trays were taken away, al-Hussain was able to get some peace by pretending to sleep. They had walked together along the platform at St Pancras and Sunny had followed him to the immigration checkpoint. He clearly intended to stand behind him and al-Hussain had to tell him to join another queue. It wasn't a good idea to go through Immigration together and Sunny should have known that.

Al-Hussain walked out into the station and looked around. There didn't seem to be anyone waiting for him, which meant he had to stay with Sunny. He didn't like the Brit and would have walked away there and then, but he didn't know where he was supposed to go so he stood where he was and waited. "All right, bruv," said Sunny, coming up behind him.

"What happens now?" asked al-Hussain.

"Our ride's outside." Sunny headed towards the exit and al-Hussain kept pace with him. On the pavement, Sunny looked around and spotted a grey Vauxhall

Astra. "That's us." He waved at the driver and the car edged towards them.

Al-Hussain climbed into the back and put his bag on the seat, then slammed the door. Sunny got into the front and twisted around. "This is Ash," he said.

Ash flashed al-Hussain a thumbs-up. Sunny grinned. "It's all right, bruv, he speaks good English."

"Yeah? Is that right?" said Ash.

"Where are we going?" asked al-Hussain.

"Sheffield," said Ash.

"You heard of Sheffield, bruv?" asked Sunny.

Al-Hussain shook his head. "No."

"It's a shit-hole," said Sunny, "but that's where we have to take you."

Shepherd couldn't be bothered to arrange a rental car and he didn't want to be seen driving around in Garcia's green Lamborghini. Rosenfeld had a Honda CRV parked in the basement of his apartment building so Shepherd took the keys and went down in the lift to the car park. As soon as he was in the vehicle he took out his mobile phone and tapped out a number. Amar Singh, one of MI5's most able technicians, answered on the third ring. "Amar, can you talk?"

"Give me a second."

Shepherd heard footsteps then a door opening and closing. "Go ahead," said Singh.

"I need a favour. Are you in the office?"

"For the foreseeable future," said Singh. "I'm babysitting two bugging teams and overseeing a facial-recognition job that's gotta be done PDQ."

"Can you grab a few seconds to check someone out for me?" said Shepherd. "A Russian by the name of Stefan Bazarov. He's living in Spain at the moment. I've never heard of him so see what you can dig up. From what's gone down I'm thinking Russian Mafia."

"Okay, I'll sit down at a terminal now. One thing, is this official or on the QT?"

"You think I'd use you for an off-the-books operation?"

Singh laughed. "Do you really want me to answer that, Spider?"

"I find your lack of faith disconcerting," said Shepherd. "Joking apart, it's official but I don't have time to go through channels. There'll be no comeback. Willoughby-Brown's running the operation."

"That must be fun for you," said Singh.

"I'm going to be driving for a while. Can you send screenshots to this number?"

"Not a problem," said Singh. "Soon as I can."

It took Shepherd just minutes to leave Gibraltar. The last flight had long left so the barriers across the main road leading to Spain where it cut across the airport runway were up. There was no passport check leaving Gibraltar but he had to show his passport to a black-uniformed Spanish officer, who asked him to open the boot of the CRV. The officer took a quick look inside, presumably checking for cigarettes, which were much cheaper in Gibraltar than Spain, then motioned for Shepherd to be on his way.

The Spanish roads were good and it took Shepherd just over half an hour to get to the hospital where the injured Serbs were being cared for. The Hospital Quirón de Marbella was on the seafront, right next to the fishing port. The Serbs were in three rooms but Shepherd was interested in only one man, the one Rosenfeld had said was the leader, Goran Kolarac. There was one nurse on duty and a fifty euro note and a promise to keep his visit short got him Kolarac's room number. Kolarac's room was south-facing with a view over the Mediterranean but as it was now dark there wasn't much to see. When Shepherd walked in, Kolarac was watching cartoons on a wall-mounted TV. He was a hefty guy with bulging forearms and a square jaw that looked as if it could take a punch or two. His left leg was bandaged and raised in the air on some sort of trapeze device, presumably to keep the pressure off it. There was a drip on a rack at the side of his bed and a tube leading into his left arm.

Kolarac's eyes widened when he saw Shepherd and he reached over to grab his water jug. Shepherd held up his hands, palms outward. "I come in peace, Goran," he said.

"Who the fuck are you?" growled Kolarac, still ready to throw the jug.

"I work with Jake Rosenfeld," said Shepherd. "I want to talk about what happened."

"I got shot, that's what fucking happened," said the Serb, putting the water jug back on the bedside table. "You tell Rosenfeld I want to talk to him."

172

"He's been shot, same as you."

"Yeah? Serves him right."

A blonde nurse appeared. "Is everything all right, Mr Kolarac?" she asked.

"I just brought him some grapes," said Shepherd. "I won't keep him long."

"It's all right, Sandra," said Kolarac. "It's just a brief visit. He's going soon."

"You need to rest," said the nurse. She looked at Shepherd. "Mr Kolarac is a very lucky man. He almost lost his leg."

She smiled at Kolarac and left.

"Of course, if I'd been really lucky I wouldn't have been shot in the first place," Kolarac growled.

Shepherd reached inside his jacket and Kolarac tensed. Shepherd smiled. "Chill, Goran. I'm on your side, remember?" He pulled the washbag from his pocket and tossed it onto the bed. "There's twenty thousand euros," he said. "That's what you'd have been paid if you'd got the money from the Russian."

Kolarac frowned. "You're paying me?" He unzipped the washbag and ran a finger over the banknotes.

"Rosenfeld is."

"He should have told me who the Russian was."

"He didn't know."

"How could he not?"

"He was just a client."

"He's a fucking Russian gangster."

"You know that for sure?" asked Shepherd.

"The son of a gangster, anyway. His father's a big shot in Moscow. Drugs. Extortion. Prostitution."

"What's the son doing here?"

"He got into an argument with some hoods in Moscow. His father sent him here until things cool off. That's what I was told. But that was after they did this to me."

"Did Jake know this?"

"If he did, he didn't tell me. I found out yesterday."

"And what happened? How did you get shot?"

"I was walking to my car after a night out. Two guys pulled up on a motorbike, both with full-face helmets. The passenger had a gun. One shot. Then off they went."

"Did they say anything?"

"They didn't have to."

"And your other guys?"

"Two of them. Same. One got shot twice." He grinned. "Dragan is a big fucker and when they shot him he charged at them. Almost made it but then they shot him in the stomach."

"Is he okay?" asked Shepherd.

"Like I said, he's a big guy and the shooter was using a .22. He'll be fine."

"Same shooter, you mean?"

"No, we were all shot at about the same time. It was coordinated. A professional job."

"But no one was killed, right?"

"It was a warning."

Shepherd sat on the edge of the bed. "You understand why he did what he did, right? You roughed him up for a debt he reckons he didn't owe."

"He had me shot."

174

"True. But not killed. If he'd wanted you killed he could have had it done. You sent him a message and he sent you a message back. The question is, what happens now?"

"If he wants a war, I can give him one."

"I'm sure you can. But what do you think the father will do if you kill the son?"

"I'm not scared of a Russian gangster."

"That's good to know, but it's not about who's scared of whom. It's about who does what and next time it might not be a few flesh wounds. What happened was an error of judgement on Jake's part, but he's learned his lesson. What we need now is for everyone just to take a deep breath and assess where you are. You roughed up the Russian. He fought back. And, let's be honest, you'd have done the same. If the Russians had burst in and roughed you up, you'd have hit back."

"Damn right."

Shepherd gestured at the washbag. "You've got your money. Here's what I'll do. I'll talk to the Russian and make sure this doesn't go any further. You and your guys put this down to experience. No one seems too badly hurt."

"I'm in fucking hospital," said Kolarac.

"Flesh wounds," said Shepherd.

"I got shot in the thigh. They could have severed an artery — I could've died."

"Could've, would've, should've," said Shepherd. "They were obviously pros. They could've crippled you if they'd wanted. Or worse. And, if they come back, you won't be so lucky the second time."

Kolarac opened his mouth to argue, then closed it. He lay down. "I hear what you're saying."

"Good," said Shepherd.

"But this hospital isn't cheap," said Kolarac.

"I'll make sure it's taken care of."

Kolarac frowned. "How much did Rosenfeld know about the Russian?"

Shepherd shrugged. "Not much. He thought Bazarov was a rich client who'd defaulted and that was all. I doubt Bazarov would broadcast that he was Russian Mafia."

Kolarac nodded slowly. "He's an idiot, the American."

"He should have checked, I agree, but he won't be making the same mistake again, I can promise you that." He pointed at the bag of money. "So are we good?"

Kolarac nodded again. "Yeah. We're good."

Shepherd held out his hand. "Always a pleasure dealing with a professional," he said.

Kolarac shook it. "Likewise."

Omar took off his helmet and pulled a printed sheet out from inside his green leather racing jacket. "We're looking for number thirty-eight," he said to Faisal.

They were in a suburban street in Birmingham, about four miles north of the city centre. It had taken Omar two hours to drive down from Salford, resisting the urge to let the bike rip on the M6. He had kept to the speed limit the whole way, only moving into the outside lane when overtaking.

"There it is," said Faisal. He pointed at a house to their left. It was semi-detached with a path that led to a garage at the rear.

The vehicle they had come to see was parked at the side of the house. It was white, but that wasn't a problem, and as Omar walked along the pavement, he could see the bodywork was in good condition. He knocked on the front door. It was answered by a man in his thirties, wearing a baggy green pullover and brown corduroy trousers. Omar thought of a walking tree. "I phoned you this morning," he said.

"Ah, right, yes," said the man. He stepped out of the house.

Faisal was already peering in through the passenger window. "It's not locked!" called the man. Faisal opened the door and climbed in.

"Mind if I have a quick look?" asked Omar.

"Sure, help yourself," said the man. "It runs fine — my uncle lived twenty miles away and I drove it over last week. The battery had gone flat but after I charged it she started first time. They run for ever, those things."

The man stood by the house while Faisal and Omar checked out the vehicle. The engine was sound, the bodywork was pretty much perfect, though the interior had been stripped, presumably in preparation for the conversion to a camper van. "Looks good to me," Omar said to Faisal.

Faisal nodded in agreement.

Omar got out and walked back to the front door. "I'm definitely interested," he said to the man, who was now smoking a cigarette. "Where did you get it from?"

"It was my uncle's. He was always planning to turn it into a camper van but he never got around to it. He passed away last year and my aunt asked me to get rid of it."

Omar nodded. "That's cool," he said. "I mean, sorry about your loss and all, but I can definitely take it off your hands. The advert says six. Would you take five for cash?"

"The advert says six. That's pretty much what he paid for it."

"I know, but cash is king, right?" said Omar. He pulled an envelope from his pocket and showed the man the hundred fifty-pound notes inside.

The man licked his lips. "Let's say five and a half."

"Okay," said Omar, handing the man the envelope and pulling out his wallet. "But I'll need a receipt." He smiled. "Not for tax. I'm buying it for someone else and he'll want to see how much I paid."

"No problem," said the man. Omar gave him another five hundred pounds. The man disappeared into the house and reappeared a few minutes later with a handwritten receipt and the keys. Omar took the receipt and tossed the keys to Faisal.

The man gave him the V5C log book. "Now, it doesn't have an MOT," he said. "And it's not insured. I took a risk and it was fine, but it's yours now so it's up to you. Oh, and I'll need your details for the DVLA."

"No problem," said Omar. He gave the man a piece of paper with a fake name, address and telephone number on it. "Pleasure doing business with you." He put his helmet back on. Five minutes later he was following Faisal on the M6, heading north.

Shepherd's mobile phone buzzed as he was getting into his car outside the hospital. It was a text message from Amar Singh. Just one word — *Done* — and half a dozen screenshots.

Shepherd flicked through them. Stefan Bazarov was twenty-six years old and had a criminal record going back to his teens, mainly arrests for assault, drug use or motoring offences. None of the cases had ever gone to court, presumably because of the influence of his father, Viktor.

Unlike the son, Viktor Bazarov had served several prison sentences, including twelve years for murder when he was in his twenties. That had been his last conviction, and since his release in the late nineties, he had never returned to prison. It wasn't because he had turned over a new leaf — a Europol file detailed the rapid growth of Bazarov's criminal empire and suggested that it had been made possible by the Russian's paying off high-ranking police officers and judges. Shepherd smiled to himself as he read the Europol report — it seemed that Bazarov had a lot in common with the O'Neill brothers. He was thought to have been behind several dozen murders in Moscow, and his criminal activities spanned extortion, drugs, prostitution and fraud. According to the report, there was little or no chance of him being brought to justice, not without a comprehensive clear-out of the corrupt officials currently running the city.

There was a report in Russian from the Moscow police accompanied by a translation. It detailed a fight in a Moscow nightclub three months earlier in which a young man had been shot. Witnesses had identified Stefan Bazarov as the killer but Bazarov was believed to have left Moscow and his whereabouts were unknown. The victim was named as twenty-three-year-old Timofei Ivakin. He had been shot twice and was dead when he arrived at the Botkin Hospital, close to the Dinamo Metro station. There was more detail in a report filed by an MI6 officer working out of the British Embassy. The intelligence report was a weekly summary written five days after the murder. It identified the victim as the son of another Russian gangster, a former KGB officer, who had turned to crime when the Soviet Union imploded. His name was Leonid Ivakin and, according to the MI6 report, he was in the process of legitimising his empire, moving away from his criminal activities and concentrating on his property and business interests. The death of his son had brought him back into the public eye for all the wrong reasons, and the fact that Ivakin was trying to downplay his criminal connections was the only reason there hadn't been instant retribution against the Bazarov family. The MI6 officer's assessment was that at some point Ivakin would be seeking revenge for the death of his son, and if that were to happen it would bring him into conflict with Stefan Bazarov's father.

Shepherd put the phone away. Now Stefan Bazarov's presence in Marbella made perfect sense. Presumably his father had exiled him to Spain until he had sorted out the situation in Moscow.

Garcia had given him Bazarov's address and he tapped it into the sat-nav. It was a villa on the outskirts of the town on a hill overlooking the bay, a twenty-minute drive from the hospital, and was surrounded by a high wall. There seemed to be just one entrance, with a wrought-iron gate and next to it a small stone guardhouse.

Shepherd drove up to the gate and wound down his window. A small brass grille was set into the wall with a button below it. Shepherd pressed it twice.

"Who are you?" growled a voice.

"I'm here to see Stefan," said Shepherd.

"Who are you?"

Shepherd decided he, too, could play the repetition game. "I'm here to see Stefan."

"He doesn't see visitors," said the man. "Move your car away from the gates."

"Why don't you move it?" Shepherd wound up the window and climbed out of the Honda as a large man in a black leather jacket stepped out of the guardhouse. He was a couple of inches taller than Shepherd, but several kilos heavier, with bulging forearms and a shaved head that was criss-crossed with rope-like scars.

"Move the fucking car," growled the man. He had a heavy Russian accent and spoke slowly, as if he was reading from a script.

"Like I said, you move it."

"What is your fucking problem?"

"No problem," said Shepherd. "I just want to see Stefan."

"You know him?"

"I'm a friend of a friend."

"He doesn't see friends of friends," snarled the man. "Now move the fucking car."

"You're very brave on the other side of this gate," said Shepherd.

The man sneered. "Are you fucking serious?"

Shepherd shrugged. "It is what it is."

The man went back inside the guardhouse. A few seconds later a metal door set into the wall opened and he stepped onto the pavement. He seemed bigger closer up. He had a strong jaw and a heavy brow that suggested he wouldn't be too fazed by a punch to the head. "I'm not going to tell you again," he said.

"I need to talk to Stefan about some guys he had shot."

The bodyguard reached into the pocket of his jacket and took out a small black automatic. "Yeah? Well, if you don't fuck off, you'll be the one who gets shot."

"Where is he? Is he home?"

The man pointed the gun at Shepherd's face and his finger tightened on the trigger. "You don't listen, do you?"

The gun was small. A Glock 42 with a standard six-shot single-stack magazine. It was easily concealable and close up would do the job. It wasn't a gun that Shepherd would use unless he had to. The man looked like a professional but he hadn't pulled back the slide, which meant he was carrying the weapon in his pocket with a round already chambered. Even with the Glock's safety trigger that was never a good idea. There was no safety switch on the Glock: instead it had a trigger safety, a lever next to the trigger, which, when it was in the forward position, blocked the trigger from moving backwards. The trigger safety and the trigger itself had to be pressed simultaneously for the gun to fire, and that required a pull of between eight and nine pounds. It could be that the man was bluffing and didn't have a round chambered but Shepherd wasn't willing to gamble his life on it. The nearest villa was a hundred yards or so away: if the gun did go off, noise wouldn't be a problem.

A car came down the road, its headlights on main beam. It slowed as it approached the villa, then came to a halt fifty feet away from the gate. It was a red Ferrari and its engine roared as the driver gunned the accelerator.

"Get back in your car and fuck off," said the man with the gun.

Shepherd jerked his thumb at the Ferrari. "That's Stefan?" He turned and waved at the car. "Hey, Stefan!" he shouted. "I need a word!"

The man shoved him with his free hand. "Get back in your car."

Shepherd ignored him. "Come on, Stefan! We need to talk."

The driver's side door opened and a man in his late twenties climbed out. High cheekbones, glossy slicked-back hair and a carefully cultivated five o'clock shadow. With his tie-less buttoned-up grey shirt and black Hugo Boss suit he looked as if he'd stepped out of the pages of a fashion magazine. He shouted in Russian and the man with the gun shouted back.

"Stefan, I just need a conversation with you. Can we go inside?"

As Bazarov walked towards the gate, the man shoved the gun into the small of Shepherd's back. Shepherd held up his hands.

"Who the fuck are you?" asked Bazarov.

"The name's Terry. I work for Jake's bosses."

Bazarov frowned but didn't say anything.

"Jake Rosenfeld. You shot him in Gibraltar."

"I don't shoot people."

Shepherd smiled easily. "I know people in Moscow who say different."

"What the fuck does that mean?" snarled the Russian.

"I should just shoot the fucker, boss," said the man with the gun.

Shepherd kept his hands up but looked over his shoulder. "You really don't do threats very well," he said.

The man looked confused, not understanding.

"Here's how it works," said Shepherd. "You threaten once, then you act. Otherwise it looks like you're not serious." He turned back to Bazarov. "Stefan, I don't have all night. This idiot with the gun. Is he a friend?"

Bazarov shook his head impatiently. "What the fuck's wrong with you?"

184

"Is he a friend? Do you want me to kill him or hurt him?"

The man prodded the gun into Shepherd's back again. "Kill me? You think you can fucking kill me?"

"Your call, Stefan," said Shepherd. "I'm easy either way."

Bazarov stared at Shepherd and the two men locked eyes. Bazarov was a couple of inches taller than Shepherd, and wider, and the Russian wasn't used to being stared down. On the surface Shepherd was relaxed but his heart was pounding as adrenalin coursed through his system. The Russian recognised the confidence of a man who was no stranger to violence and eventually he nodded slowly. "Don't kill him," he said quietly.

Shepherd had decided that the man behind him wasn't a professional. No true professional would prod someone in the back with a gun. Shepherd was breathing tidally, waiting for the gun to prod again. He was just about to take a second breath when the gun pressed into his back and he turned quickly to his left. His left hand came down as he moved, pushing the gun away. In less than a second the gun was no longer a threat. In fact, it was working against the man holding it because now the weapon was useless and the hand was occupied.

The Glock didn't have a hammer so there was no point in grabbing it. Instead his fingers clamped around the man's wrist. Shepherd continued to turn, his right hand forming a fist. The left hand continued to force the gun away as he punched the inside of the man's elbow and felt it crack. As the Glock slipped from the man's grasp Shepherd grabbed it. He was right up against the man, close enough to smell the garlic on his breath, and brought his left elbow up to hit the man's jaw, hard. As the man staggered back, Shepherd transferred the gun from his left hand to his right and slammed it against the side of the man's head, then kicked him in the stomach. The man fell to the ground with a loud thump. Shepherd aimed the gun casually at the man's chest. "Bang, bang," he said. "You're dead."

Bazarov clapped sarcastically. "Krav Maga?"

Shepherd shrugged. "It's a move I came up with myself," he said. "It only works when the guy with the gun gets too close."

The bodyguard lay on the ground, holding his injured arm and gasping.

Shepherd held out the gun to Bazarov. "I'm not here to fight, Stefan. I'm here to talk."

Bazarov took the gun, looked disdainfully at the injured bodyguard, then waved at the villa. "Over a drink," he said.

"My thoughts exactly," said Shepherd.

"You're going to have to move your car."

"I can do that."

Two more heavies in leather jackets and jeans walked out of the villa and started jogging towards the gate. One was reaching inside his jacket, presumably for a weapon. Bazarov shouted at them in Russian and they stopped. He waved them back inside and they obeyed immediately. Shepherd climbed into the Honda while the Russian went to the Ferrari. A few seconds later the gate rattled open and Shepherd drove up to the villa. The two bodyguards watched him with hard eyes, their hands inside their jackets. Shepherd winked at them as he drove by.

"What do you drink?" asked Bazarov, standing by a marble cabinet. He took two crystal tumblers down from a shelf.

"Whatever you're having is fine by me."

"I drink Scotch."

"Scotch is fine."

Bazarov pulled the cork from a bottle of twenty-five-year-old malt. He half filled the tumblers and handed one to Shepherd. "Straight is the only way to drink malt whisky," he said, raising his glass.

"Couldn't agree more." Shepherd clinked his glass against the Russian's and the two men drank. They were standing in a large room on the second floor of the villa with floor-to-ceiling windows overlooking the sea. Two bodyguards stood either side of the door. The one Shepherd had hit had disappeared, presumably to get medical treatment. The Glock Shepherd had taken off him was lying on a square marble coffee-table.

There were two large white leather sofas. Bazarov took one and waved with his glass for Shepherd to sit on the other.

"You former military?" asked Bazarov.

"In a previous life," said Shepherd.

"The man you hit was Russian Special Forces," said Bazarov. "Spetsnaz. You've heard of Spetsnaz?"

"Sure. But with a thousand or so men in a Spetsnaz brigade and dozens of brigades, I'm not sure how special they'd be. Your guy didn't seem that special."

Bazarov laughed. "Good point," he said. There was no disguising his Russian accent but it had a smooth edge, probably the result of an international education. "You could have killed him, right, with his own gun?"

"I wouldn't have needed the gun," said Shepherd. He sipped his whisky.

"So you're what? Former SAS?"

"I'm not applying for a job, Stefan," said Shepherd. "I'm here to talk about the men you had shot."

Bazarov shrugged carelessly. "It can be a dangerous place, Marbella," he said.

"No question of that," said Shepherd. "I'm here to see if we can make it a little less dangerous. You had Jake Rosenfeld shot. His bosses aren't happy about that."

"They were cheating," said Bazarov. "Then the American had the cheek to send Serbs to threaten me."

"What did they do, exactly?"

"I was in a nightclub, down at the marina. They came into the VIP section and pushed me around. In front of everyone. Shouted that if I didn't pay up they'd break my legs. Do you think I could let something like that pass?"

Shepherd sipped his whisky.

"Of course not," continued Bazarov. "So I gave them a taste of their own medicine. They have only themselves to blame."

"They don't see it that way, of course," said Shepherd. "The Serbs were just doing the job they'd been hired to do. And you did owe the company money."

"They were cheating," said Bazarov again.

"What makes you think that?"

"I don't think. I know. Things were happening that shouldn't have been, not in a legit game. I'd have a pair of aces and go all in. Some newbie would match my bet, then fill an inside straight. Nobody does that."

"It's a game of luck."

"Do you play?"

"I've played."

"Do you win?"

"Fifty-fifty."

"Then you're not playing properly. There's an element of luck but poker is basically a game of skill, of playing the odds and the percentages. I am a good player. And the way I was being beaten . . ." He threw up his hands. "They were cheating."

"So why run up a tab?"

"When I first started playing it wasn't rigged. It was only when I moved up to the high-roller tables that it started to happen. I chased my losses for a while but then it became clear they were cheating. I'd have a pair of kings and I'd go in heavy. Two or three would stay with me to see the flop. The flop's got nothing but there was an outside chance of a flush maybe, or a straight, so I'd go all in. One guy stays with me and he's chasing a straight. Who the fuck does that? It makes no sense at all. But time and time again I'd lose. Now, you get that nonsense in cheap tournaments or when just a few dollars are at stake, but I was playing for thousands and I was supposedly playing against professionals. No way would they make stupid calls. So I was being conned. No question."

"And you refused to pay?"

"Of course. They were fucking cheating. Had to be. Then they had the balls to come and push me around. You think I should just let that go?"

"I understand your position, Stefan. But the reason I'm here is to put an end to it. My bosses run the business and just want things to go back to the way they were."

"They started it," said Bazarov.

"They didn't know what was going on, I can promise you that," said Shepherd. "What about your father? Does he know what happened here?"

Bazarov's eyes narrowed. "What the fuck does my father have to do with any of this?"

Shepherd stared back at him. "I was just asking."

The Russian's eyes narrowed even further, until they were just slits. "Do you know my father?"

"Not personally, no."

"What the fuck does that mean? 'Not personally'. What are you getting at?"

"It's a straightforward question to help me ascertain what the position is here, that's all. The men who shot Rosenfeld and the Serbs, I'm guessing your father didn't send them because I can't think he'd send hitmen from Moscow just to fire warning shots. Am I right?"

190

Bazarov pointed a finger at Shepherd's face. "You need to be very careful when you talk about my father. He doesn't like being talked about. Especially by people who don't know him."

"I've got nothing but respect for him," said Shepherd. "But I'm guessing that this is a personal problem between you and the online casino. Your father isn't involved."

"I don't need my father to fight my battles."

"I'm not saying you do," said Shepherd. "From where I'm looking, I don't think you want him to know, right?"

"What the fuck do you mean by that?"

"Your father sent you here because of the shit that went down in Moscow. You shot Timofei Ivakin and witnesses identified you. Now, I know you and your father aren't worried about the cops, but the boy you killed was the son of another Moscow gangster and that's why your father sent you packing. What did he say? Lie low until he's taken care of it? What's he planning to do? Pay his way out of it or kill Leonid Ivakin?"

"You need to be careful when you talk about my father."

"Yeah, you said. The question that comes to my mind, though, is this. Just how mad is your dad going to be if he finds out you've been shooting people again? Did he say keep a low profile, keep your head down? Because that's not what's happening, is it?"

"He wouldn't want me being ripped off," said Bazarov.

"No doubt," said Shepherd. "But the whole point of sending you to Marbella was to keep you below the radar. If you start a gang war here in Spain, Leonid Ivakin might hear about it. Then what? Does he send people here to take care of business? Then it gets very messy, doesn't it?"

"This is starting to sound like a threat."

Shepherd shook his head. "I've no interest in threatening anyone, Stefan. I'm a peacemaker. That's why I was sent here, to make the peace. My bosses aren't happy that their head of security has been shot, but providing that's the end of it I think they'll be okay to let it drop. The question is, do you plan to take it any further? Because if you do, my bosses will take action. And it won't be peacemakers they send."

"That's definitely a threat," sneered Bazarov.

"Stefan, I know you're a hard bastard. I know you can hurt people. You've shown you have no problem with taking a life. Could you kill me? I'd say no. You try and you'll end up dead, I can pretty much promise you that. That's not a threat, it's a statement of fact. But could you kill Rosenfeld? Of course you could. And Carlos Garcia. He'd be dead tomorrow if you wanted it. But what I'm saying is that if this does escalate, if people do start to die, then other people are going to notice. In London and in Moscow. I'm here to try to stop that happening."

"By shooting me?"

"What bit of 'peacemaker' don't you understand, Stefan? Look, the online casino may or may not have ripped you off. Rosenfeld acted rashly by sending the Serbs in to do a spot of debt-collecting."

"They pushed me around," said Bazarov. "They disrespected me."

"And they realise the error of their ways. As does Rosenfeld. It was a mistake, and if it's any help, you have my apology for what happened. They did what they did without the approval of their bosses in London. No one is going to be pressing you for the debt to be repaid."

"There is no fucking debt," snarled Bazarov.

Shepherd held up his hands. "No argument here," he said. "That's not an issue any more. The issue is where we go to from here. I've spoken to the Serbs and they won't be taking it any further."

"Because they're scared."

"They're not scared. But they weren't aware of who you are and who your father is. So far as they're concerned, you were just a client who had reneged on a debt. Here's the thing, Stefan. There is no debt, the Serbs have no quarrel with you. I just want your assurance that the matter's closed and we can put it to bed. We don't need anyone to be shaking hands but we do need to know that there's no bad feeling."

Bazarov nodded slowly. "I've made my point," he said. "Providing my point is well taken, there's no bad feeling. We can all move on."

Shepherd smiled. "I was hoping you'd say that."

"But tell me one thing. If I hadn't agreed, if I'd wanted to go to war, would you have shot me?"

Shepherd smiled. "That's not what I do, Stefan," he said.

Bazarov returned the smile but his eyes were ice cold. "I'm not sure that's true," he said.

The drive from London to Sheffield took almost four hours, including a short toilet break at a service station on the M1. Their destination was a semi-detached house in a cul-de-sac. Just before they reached it they passed a large brick mosque with twin minarets. It had the look of an industrial building and if it hadn't been for the green tops of the minarets they would have passed for chimneys.

"That's the Madina Masjid," said Sunny.

"It's a good mosque, brother," said Ash. "You have a lot of friends there."

"No," said Mohammed al-Hussain. "I have no friends in England."

"I mean brothers who support what you're doing. Many of the brothers there have been for training in Pakistan."

Al-Hussain leaned forward. "No one must know I am here," he said.

"Sure, yeah, of course, brother," said Ash, hurriedly.

"Bruv, you can relax, we'll take good care of you. Me and Ash, we trained in Pakistan. We know how it goes."

Al-Hussain didn't say anything. He had taken a dislike to Sunny but there was nothing to be gained by antagonising him.

"We did all sorts of good shit out there. Fired AK-47s and saw them let off RPGs. It was the dog's bollocks, hey, Ash?"

Ash smiled thinly but he still didn't speak.

When they arrived, Ash stopped the car in front of the garage at the side of the house. Sunny got out and opened the up-and-over door. Ash drove in carefully and Sunny brought the door down behind them.

Ash got out and switched on a long fluorescent tube that flickered for several seconds before filling the garage with a clinical white light. Al-Hussain stepped out of the car, holding his bag, and Ash took him through a side door into a large kitchen with a circular table and four chairs. Two more Asian men were sitting there, both in their twenties, with long, unkempt beards. One was wearing a knitted skull cap.

"This is Jay. And Adam."

The two men nodded but didn't get up. There were glasses of water on the table and a bowl of peanuts. The shells lay scattered over the table and on the floor.

"This is Hammad," said Ash. "Can I get you a drink, Hammad? Or food?"

"Perhaps later," said al-Hussain. "At the moment I would like to bathe, to pray, and then to sleep."

"There is a room prepared for you upstairs," he said. "Tomorrow we can take you to the weapon."

"It's not here?"

Ash shook his head. "We were told it had to be kept in a safe place until it is needed."

Al-Hussain nodded. "Of course. That makes sense."

Sunny was letting himself in through the front door as Ash took al-Hussain upstairs. "You all right, bruv?" he asked. "You got everything you need?"

"I'm fine," said al-Hussain.

Ash showed him into a bedroom at the rear of the house. There was a single bed, a dressing-table and a cheap wardrobe. At the foot of the bed there was a neatly folded yellow towel, a bar of soap and a small bottle of shampoo. "I hope this is okay," said Ash. By the pillow al-Hussain saw several mobile phones, still in their boxes, and a dozen sim cards. "They said we were to provide you with phones," said Ash. "We paid in cash at different shops."

Al-Hussain placed his bag on the floor. "Thank you," he said.

"No need for thanks. We're all happy to be involved. Finally we get to do something."

"Things worth having are worth waiting for," said al-Hussain. "Where is the Qibla?"

Ash hesitated, frowned, then took out his iPhone. "I've got an app with a Qibla compass," he said apologetically. "I've not been here long." He studied the screen of his phone, then pointed at the wardrobe. "That way," he said.

"Do you have a prayer rug?"

"I'll bring one up, brother. And if there is anything else you require you only have to ask. We are here to serve you."

"Thank you," said al-Hussain again.

Ash stepped forward, put his hands on al-Hussain's shoulders and kissed him on both cheeks, then hurried from the room. He left the door open and al-Hussain closed it.

The afternoon traffic heading for Gibraltar was backed up for more than a mile to the border. Shepherd had spent a few hours in a cheap Spanish hotel getting some sleep, then snatched a sandwich and coffee before heading back to catch the first BA flight to London, scheduled for just after three p.m. After he had sat for a full thirty minutes in the queue without moving, he decided he'd be better off walking. He pulled off the main road, found a parking space, called Garcia on his mobile, then walked to the border.

His passport was barely looked at on either side, and after he'd crossed to Gibraltar it was only a few hundred yards to the airport terminal. Garcia was waiting at the coffee shop in the airport and stood up when he saw Shepherd walk towards him. "Is everything okay?" he asked. He mopped his brow with a white handkerchief as if he was surrendering to enemy forces.

Shepherd sat down. They were next to a floor-to-ceiling window overlooking the runway and the Rock beyond it. The BA plane had arrived from London and passengers were disembarking onto the tarmac. A queue had already formed to Immigration. Shepherd passed Rosenfeld's car keys to Garcia. "I left the car in Spain," he said gruffly. "Next to the blue building. The traffic was a nightmare."

"The Spanish are offended at something your foreign secretary said, so there's a go-slow," said Garcia. "Don't worry about the car. I'll have it collected."

"Get me a coffee, will you?" said Shepherd.

"What sort? Latte? Espresso? Cappuccino?"

Shepherd waved him away. "Surprise me." As Garcia scurried over to the counter, he sent Willoughby-Brown a text message with his flight number. He needed to talk to the man and he preferred face to face.

Garcia returned, carrying a tray with two coffees and a cheese baguette. Shepherd sipped his coffee while Garcia bit into the baguette.

"So what's happening?" asked Garcia. "Is everything okay?" His handkerchief was back in his hand and he mopped his brow again.

Shepherd shrugged. "It depends on how you define okay. Why didn't you tell me the Russian was refusing to pay because the games are rigged?"

"They're not rigged."

"Bazarov says they are."

"Most players who lose blame the system. They're just shit players." He dabbed at his forehead.

"He seems pretty sure. You need to tell me what's going on, Carlos."

Garcia looked pained. "You're asking for operational details and I don't think I can discuss those with you."

"Well, you need to rethink that because, the way things stand, I'll be going back to tell the brothers you've fixed the game. Or do they already know? Was it their idea?"

Garcia shook his head. "They don't know." He picked up a coffee but his hand trembled and he put it down again.

"You need to tell me what's happening," said Shepherd. "Is Bazarov right? Did you rig the game?"

"It's not rigged. That's not what happens."

Shepherd sighed. "Stop pissing around, Carlos. Cut to the chase."

Garcia took another bite of his baguette. "Look, sometimes our player levels are down and we keep our numbers up using automated accounts. It makes us look busy and that pulls in more business. Once our levels are up we pull out the automated accounts."

"Fake players?"

"Not fake. They're playing but they're using the company's money."

"So the computer's playing?"

"Yes. That's it. Just until the level of genuine players rises."

"And how does the computer know how to play?"

"Jake set up sub-programs, each acting as a separate player."

Shepherd sat back and folded his arms. "Let me get this straight," he said. "A high-roller logs on to play but there aren't any other players. Rather than telling him, you let him play against the computer."

Garcia didn't say anything.

"So, your mark could be sitting at a table with five or six players but he's the only real player. All the rest of the hands are being played by a computer? Your computer?"

Garcia nodded but didn't look up.

"And presumably the computer knows exactly what to do. When to fold, when to raise?"

Garcia nodded again.

"So the computer is always going to win. And if the computer is playing five hands against the mark's one, it's a foregone conclusion, isn't it? The only hand that is going to be betting is the winning hand. The computer isn't going to bet a losing hand, is it?"

"It plays to win," said Garcia.

"So the Russian was right. The game is rigged."

"It's not rigged. The mark . . ." He rubbed his hands together. "He's not a mark. He's a client. He plays his hand, the computer plays the others. If the client has the best hand, he'll win."

"Except the computer will always fold a losing hand and only play a winning hand. It can presumably see all the hands."

"Not the client's."

"But all the other hands." He pointed at Garcia's face. "You know this is cheating. You can play with words as much as you want but we both know what's been going on."

"But not all the time," said Garcia. "It's a temporary measure, and it only kicks in when traffic is low."

"Do the O'Neill brothers know about it?"

Garcia screwed up his face. "They don't want to be bothered with the nitty-gritty. All they care about is the bottom line and we're making money."

"That's changed since Jake took a bullet in the leg, Carlos. They can't afford to have a bloody gang war going on in Gibraltar. Online gambling is supposed to be a legitimate business and you've turned it into a gang war."

Garcia picked up his cup again but the shaking was worse and coffee slopped onto the table. He put it down and mopped up the spill with a serviette. "That was Jake's fault. He sent the Serbs to get the money. He didn't tell me until afterwards."

"Yeah? Then you need to keep him on a shorter leash," said Shepherd. "You're supposed to be running the show. The brothers will hold you accountable."

"How much trouble am I in, Terry? Am I fucked?"

"You're not totally fucked. If you do the right thing now you might get out of it in one piece."

"I'll do whatever it takes," said Garcia.

"That's good to hear," said Shepherd. "Bazarov is prepared to let sleeping dogs lie," he said, "and, considering who his father is, that's a win-win situation for you and Jake."

Garcia nodded but didn't say anything.

"Kolarac has taken the money, but you're going to have to pay the Serbs' hospital bills. They're not exactly happy, but I think they know that, tough as they are, they can't win an all-out war with the Russians."

Garcia forced a smile. "So it's all okay?"

"It's getting there," said Shepherd. "You need to put two hundred thousand euros into the company account. I'll say the money's back and leave it at that. If you want to tell the O'Neill brothers that the Russian paid up, that's between you and them. I'm pretty sure they won't ask any questions."

"What about the Serbs being shot? What will you tell them?"

"They won't know about the Serbs and I don't see that I need to be the one to tell them."

"And what do I say about Jake?"

"Providing they get the cash back I don't think they'll care much. If they press you, just say things got heated and a gun went off, almost by accident, but now everyone's cool."

"They'll be happy with that?"

"They'll be happy that the money's been paid and everything's back the way it used to be. But you have to make sure there's no repeat of this. You can get away with it once, if you're lucky, but if it happens again . . . The ball's in your court."

"We'll rethink the automated players," said Garcia.

"I assume by 'rethink' you mean you'll stop doing it," said Shepherd. "If the brothers find out you've been cheating you'll soon have them on your case."

"We were only trying to maximise profits," said Garcia.

"And you ended up in a gang war," Shepherd reminded him. He sipped his coffee. "You need to keep a tighter grip on Jake. Initiative is all well and good but getting those Serbs involved was a big mistake." He put down his cup and stood up. "Hopefully we won't be seeing each other again," he said, and walked away, leaving Garcia mopping his brow.

Yusuf felt the van lurch to the left, then rattle over rough ground. "Please, this is some mistake," he said.

"You have the wrong man." Something had slammed against the side of his head, stunning him. He had seen only two men but he knew there were more. The two he had seen had appeared in front of him as he walked out of the coffee shop. One had produced an AK-47 from under his robes. The other had a handgun. An old revolver. Then the sack had been pulled over his head and he had been bundled into a van that smelt of rotten fruit. As it had driven away he had been rolled onto his belly, his wrists tied behind his back. No one had spoken and at least an hour had passed. He had asked what they wanted, had offered them money, but the only response had been the blow to his head.

The van slowed. Then he heard the beep of a horn and the sound of a gate rattling back. The van drove forward, turned sharply to the left and braked. The rear doors opened and he was dragged roughly outside. He stumbled, and one of the men holding him cursed. He had lost one of his sandals and his bare foot scraped across rough concrete. Behind him he heard the van drive away.

A door banged open and he was thrown forward. He tripped and fell, turning at the last second to avoid smashing his face. He lay there, panting. He heard voices. Then he was dragged to his feet and the hood was ripped from his head. He stood blinking, trying to focus. He was in a large room facing a window that looked into a walled yard. There was a figure in front of him. Yusuf screwed up his eyes and shook his head. There was another figure to his right, holding something. A video-camera. "Please, who are you and what do you want?" he asked.

The two men who had him by the arms pushed him down to his knees.

"We know what you did, Yusuf," growled the man in front of him.

Yusuf recognised him from articles in the online edition of the *Zamar* newspaper. He was a Turk, Mohammed Demir, but for the last few years he had been in Syria, leading a battalion of more than four hundred Islamic State fighters. He was in his thirties but looked much older: the fierce desert sun had turned his skin the texture of old leather. He had a long, straggly beard and his cheeks were pocked with old acne scars. He was wearing a grubby white kaftan and had a webbing ammunition belt around his waist.

"*Assalamu alaykum wa rahmatu Allahi wa barakaatuhu,*" said Yusuf.

Demir stared down at him with unblinking brown eyes. "*Wa alaykum alsalam,*" he growled. And upon you be peace. "Tell me, Yusuf, how do those words not burn your mouth? How can you wish me peace when you have been plotting against me and my Islamic State brothers?"

Yusuf frowned. "There's some mistake, brother. I am a good Muslim. I wish you no harm and you surely know how much I have done to further the cause of your brothers in arms."

Demir stuck his thumbs into his webbing belt and thrust out his chest. "You are a traitor to Islam, and you will burn in Hell," he said.

204

"My friend, there has been some mistake. I am on your side. I hate the infidel with a passion that burns like the sun. I am a true Muslim and as such would never, ever side with the infidel, please, you —"

Demir slapped him across the face and Yusuf tasted blood. "You demean yourself with your lies," said Demir.

"Please, there has been a mistake. May Allah strike me dead if I am lying."

"Allah would not bother himself with the likes of you," said Demir. "We shall do that. And you will die like an infidel dog and your corpse will be treated with contempt."

"Please, don't do this," begged Yusuf.

"If you want forgiveness, ask it of Allah, for it is only Allah who can judge you," said Demir. "But I think you will be pleading to deaf ears."

"I have money," said Yusuf. "Or papers? You want passports? I can get you passports for any country you want."

Demir sneered at him. "What use do I have for a passport? Do you think I showed a passport to come here? The world belongs to Allah and his servants need no passports." He fumbled in his robes and pulled out a smartphone. He tapped on it and grinned. "I want you to see this. I want you to see the results of your treachery. You need to know what your actions have caused." He turned the screen towards Yusuf. It was his wife, her eyes wide and fearful, her cheeks wet with tears. "Esma," he whispered. "Please, no."

Two men were holding her, forcing her to her knees. There was a third man behind her, with a knife.

"Please, no," said Yusuf.

"They raped her first, and as they raped her they told her what you had done."

Esma was begging for her life. Yusuf closed his eyes. It was a recording, it was in the past. His beloved Esma was dead already.

"Open your eyes," said Demir. "She died because of you. The least you can do is to see how she met her end."

Yusuf opened his tear-filled eyes. The man with the knife grinned savagely as he placed the blade against Esma's throat and whipped it to the side. Blood spurted down her neck and Yusuf groaned. The man with the knife was holding her hair and he jerked her head back and sawed with the knife, hacking through the flesh and bone until the head came away and the body slumped to the floor. The man grinned as he swung it around. Esma's eyes were still open.

"Your fault," said Demir. "You are to blame."

Whoever was holding the phone began to move. They had killed her in the main bedroom of the villa. Yusuf could barely breathe. It was as if a steel band around his chest was tightening. The phone lurched as the man walked down the corridor. Heading for the bedrooms where his children slept. "Please, no, don't do this," he said, though he knew that it had already been done. He looked up at his tormentor. "Kill me now," he said. "If you have any mercy in your heart, kill me now."

206

"Your children were told what you did, and they were told that they were paying the price for your greed and dishonesty."

"Please, just end it now," muttered Yusuf. "Kill me now."

"They were raped, too. The boy and the girls. They screamed and they begged for their lives but they were told that there could be no mercy for them because of what you had done. You betrayed your faith, you betrayed your Muslim brothers, and they paid the price."

A door was pushed open. It was his son's room. Little Hasan. The phone went inside. There was a figure on the floor. Naked and smeared with blood. It wasn't Hasan. It was Ayse. Eight years old. Her hair was covering her face.

Yusuf looked away. "Just kill me," he whispered.

"The boy seemed to enjoy it, my men tell me. Was he gay, do you think? Such a sin to have a gay child. Your only son was gay, and he died being fucked up the arse so I doubt he'll be going to Heaven any time soon."

Yusuf sobbed uncontrollably.

"Your daughters weren't so happy, I'm told. They died screaming and begging and saying it wasn't fair. It wasn't fair that they were being punished for something you did. That's what they said. They were told to beg forgiveness from Allah for your actions and they did. They were such good little girls, weren't they? So unlucky that they had you for a father. Think of their last moments, Yusuf. Beaten. Abused. Raped. Because of you, Yusuf. Because of what you did."

All the strength had drained from Yusuf and if it hadn't been for the two men holding his arms he would have slumped to the floor.

"Look at the screen, Yusuf. See what you have done."

Yusuf raised his head and moaned when he saw the two blood-stained figures lying across the bed like broken dolls. He howled with despair and then a hand yanked his head back and out of the corner of an eye he saw the flash of the blade that would end his life. His last thought was of his wife and children, the horrors they had endured. It had been his fault. He deserved to die and to be cast into the fires of Hell for eternity.

Shepherd switched on his phone as he walked off the plane. There was a text from Willoughby-Brown: *Am in the car park. Level 3.*

Shepherd was using his Terry Taylor passport and joined the ePassport queue. The MI5-supplied passport was real, it was just the details that weren't, and the automated facial-recognition system opened the barrier.

He walked out into Arrivals, then to the car park and went up to Level 3. He looked up and down and a minivan flashed its lights. It was the last vehicle Shepherd expected to see Willoughby-Brown using and he frowned as he walked over. As he drew near, a side door slid back, revealing a plush interior with two large leather armchairs at either side of a polished table. Willoughby-Brown was sitting at the rear, facing a flat-screen television, with a laptop on the table in front of him. He grinned and indicated the seat facing him as Shepherd climbed in. The door closed electronically.

"There's water on your right and snacks on the left," said Willoughby-Brown, as the van moved off. "All mod cons."

"This is an office car?" asked Shepherd.

"For a certain paygrade, yes," said Willoughby-Brown. "London traffic being what it is, you can get work done while you're on the move." He gestured at the screen above Shepherd's head. "I have access to all but the most sensitive files and it has a built-in encrypted sat-phone. I sometimes think I could park it in my driveway and work from home."

"Sounds like a plan," said Shepherd.

"The only downside is that smoking is *verboten*. It's classed as a place of work. Not for me but for the driver." He gestured at the man behind the steering wheel, who was insulated from them with a thick glass panel. "Soundproof and bulletproof," said Willoughby-Brown. "There's an intercom you use to talk to him. And the sides can withstand an RPG. How about that?"

"Amazing," said Shepherd.

"And we'd survive a landmine," said Willoughby-Brown. "Not that we're expecting landmines in the capital."

"It could happen," said Shepherd.

"Well, let's look on the bright side, shall we? How did you get on? I hope you didn't go all SAS on the Rock."

Shepherd looked sideways at him, scornful of the attempt at humour. Back in 1988 the SAS had killed three IRA terrorists in Gibraltar as they were planning a car-bomb attack at the changing of the guard ceremony outside the governor's residence. All three were shot after being challenged and were later found to be unarmed, and no bomb was ever found on Gibraltar, though a large amount of explosives were later discovered in a car across the border in Spain. So far as the SAS were concerned, it was a valid operation, and an inquest in Gibraltar ruled that the men had acted lawfully. Either way, Shepherd didn't think it was something to be joking about. He smiled thinly, refusing to rise to the bait. "Before my time," he said.

"Obviously," said Willoughby-Brown. "So you didn't have to shoot anybody, I hope." The van accelerated away from the airport.

Shepherd settled back in his seat. "All good," he said. "I sorted everything out for the brothers so hopefully that'll open a few more doors for me. Something you need to know is that Wedekind says the brothers have money in Gibraltar, along with property including hotels."

"Good to know," said Willoughby-Brown.

"The downside is that he's confirmed they're being clever about tucking assets away. They use trusts and all sorts of financial shenanigans, he says. And I get the feeling he doesn't know too much about it."

"I thought you said he was their money man."

"He's one of their money men. And they use him to pass on instructions. But the serious money-laundering is done by someone else."

"That's annoying," said Willoughby-Brown.

"I've asked for an introduction but he's going to have to clear it with the brothers."

"Which will take time."

"I can't try to speed things up — I'll look too desperate. But I get the feeling that Wedekind is in regular touch with them, so his calls or emails might point the way. But even if we do get him to roll on the brothers he's probably not got much hard information."

"They're a devious bunch, that's for sure."

"That's why they've survived for so long," said Shepherd. "Even with all the work we've put in, most of what we've got is hearsay. On the subject of hearsay, Marty pretty much confirmed the family has judges and cops on the payroll."

"Names would be nice."

"I'm working on it. I'd hoped that some of them might have been stupid enough to go to the boxing do, but no such luck."

"I was wondering if we should put a ruse in play."

"A ruse?"

"Nothing major. But we could get the cops to start an investigation aimed at one of their operations. Then see who tries to access the file."

"I think most bent cops would see that coming a mile off."

"Have you got a better idea?"

"I think we just have to take it slowly. Let me win their trust."

"We can't let this go on too long, Daniel. I've got other tasks mounting up."

"It's your call," said Shepherd. "But there's no doubt that the family is responsible for a good wedge of the crime that goes on in South London. And they've been responsible for at least six murders over the past decade."

"There's no doubt they're valid targets," said Willoughby-Brown. "And the millions they have tucked away is a prize worth taking. But I'm starting to realise why the cops have never managed to make any headway."

"Yeah, well, the fact they have cops and judges on their payroll helps," said Shepherd.

The van picked up speed as it headed along the M4 to central London. "Oh, while I've got your undivided attention, your biannual psych evaluation is overdue," said Willoughby-Brown.

"I've had a lot on my plate. As you know."

"Absolutely. But you know as well as I do that unless the psychologist signs you off every six months you can't work undercover. Health and safety nonsense, I know, but rules is rules."

"No problem," said Shepherd. "It'll be good to see Caroline again."

Willoughby-Brown shook his head. "We stopped using Caroline Stockmann a while back," he said. "We're taking a more scientific approach, these days."

He handed Shepherd a business card. "This is the company. Call and ask for Miles Davies."

"Like the jazz musician?"

"What?"

"Miles Davis. Played the trumpet."

Willoughby-Brown frowned. "Why would I ask a trumpet player to give you your psych evaluation?"

"I meant the name. With an e or without one?"

"With."

Shepherd slipped the card into his pocket. "Definitely not the same guy, then," he said sarcastically. His phone rang and he pulled it out. It was his son. "Do you mind if I take this?" he asked. "We've been playing phone tag for days."

"Go ahead," said Willoughby-Brown.

Shepherd pressed the button to talk to Liam. "Are you okay?" he asked.

"I'm fine. Where are you?"

"London. Are you at school?"

"It's half-term, Dad. I told you, remember?"

"Sure, yes. Of course." Shepherd grimaced. Though his memory was practically infallible, birthdays and special occasions often passed him by unless something prompted him to remember. "So you're at home?"

"I just got here," said Liam. "Katra came to get me. Dad, when are you home?"

"I'm not sure, why?"

Willoughby-Brown was tapping away on his iPhone but he could hear every word, which made Shepherd a little uncomfortable.

"I need to talk to you about something."

"Are you in trouble?"

Liam sighed. "You always think the worst."

"Well, put me straight. What do you need to talk to me about?"

Liam sighed again, deeper this time. "Fine," he said. "University."

"Everything's okay with your studying, right?"

"Everything's fine. I'm a bit behind in maths but I've been given some extra work to do and I'll get back on track."

"So what's the problem?"

"I just want to talk it through with you, Dad, that's all. And I don't want to do it over the phone."

"When are you back to school?"

"Next week."

"Okay, I'll try to get home over the next few days."

"Thanks, Dad," said Liam.

"I've got to go. I'll call again this evening," said Shepherd. He hung up and put the phone away. "Sorry," he said to Willoughby-Brown.

"Is he okay?"

"I think so. Something about university. Nothing major."

"Can you get away? What about the O'Neills?"

"I'll have to have a meet with Wedekind, that's for sure. But as he gave me the Gibraltar job I don't think I'll have to report to Tommy and Marty. I might be able to get away tomorrow afternoon."

"Kids, hey?"

"Have you got any?" Shepherd didn't even know if Willoughby-Brown was married. In fact, he knew next

214

to nothing about the man who had his career in his hands.

Willoughby-Brown shook his head. "Never had the time or the inclination," he said.

Shepherd wondered what he had meant. Was he gay? Or did he mean he was married and just hadn't got around to having children? Shepherd knew there was no way he could ask a direct question, so he looked out of the window as Willoughby-Brown concentrated on his iPhone.

Mohammed al-Hussain rose at dawn, showered and trimmed his beard, then prayed for ten minutes before going downstairs. Jay and Adam were in the living room playing a video game, which seemed to involve them shooting and killing as many people as possible. It was almost certainly American, he thought. The Americans loved to glamorise war. They turned it into movies and computer games as if it was trivial, but al-Hussain knew that war was a serious business. Life and death, literally. Turning it into a game was disrespectful to the dead and to the living.

He went into the kitchen. Ash was scrambling eggs and had slices of bread under the grill. There was a carton of orange juice on the table with a jug of milk. "Eggs okay?" asked Ash.

"Eggs will be fine, thank you," said al-Hussain, sitting down at the table. He was wearing a blue polo shirt, one of half a dozen he had found in the wardrobe, and a pair of jeans. "The clothes, they told you my size?"

Ash nodded. "We were told to get you anything you might need," he said. "And if we've forgotten anything, please ask."

He took the toast from under the grill, slapped it onto a plate and put it on the table with a tub of butter, then spooned eggs onto another plate and handed it to al-Hussain, who poured himself a glass of orange juice.

Ash helped himself to eggs and sat opposite him. "When you've eaten, we'll take you to see the weapon," he said.

"Good."

"Where are my eggs?" asked Sunny, charging into the room.

"In the fridge," said Ash.

"You didn't cook for me?"

"You were in bed."

"Well, I'm up now."

"I'm not your chef, brother," said Ash.

Sunny sat down and buttered a slice of toast. "Where's the jam?"

Ash pointed at one of the cupboards. "In there."

Sunny got up, grabbed a jar of strawberry jam and sat down again. "So, you good to go, bruv?" he asked al-Hussain.

"I hope so, yes."

"This is the first time you've been to England, right?"

Al-Hussain nodded.

"What do you think?"

"I haven't seen much of it."

"It's a great country," he said. "But it'll be better under sharia law. How long do you think it'll be, bruv, before we're in charge? Our imam says fifty years but I think it'll be sooner than that."

Al-Hussain kept his eyes on his plate.

"I think twenty years. Maybe twenty-five. It's the birth rate, that's what'll do it. Good Muslims have lots of children. Ten or twelve with one wife. And they have more than one wife, right? So one good Muslim can have twenty children, maybe more. But the *kafir*, most of them are sterile. They can't even produce one kid." He smeared jam across his toast and took a bite. "They have one, we have twenty," he said, through his mouthful. "It's just a matter of time before we outnumber them, innit?"

Al-Hussain finished his eggs and put down his fork. He drank his juice, then nodded at Ash. "I'm ready," he said.

Shepherd usually varied his journey from London to Hereford between the M40 and the M4, depending on what his BMW's sat-nav told him. He climbed into the car and discovered from the sat-nav that he'd get to his home fifteen minutes earlier if he went via the M4. Assuming the device wasn't lying, he'd be in Hereford at just after three o'clock that afternoon. He headed west, listening to light jazz on the radio, wondering what he would say to Liam. He'd spent so much time playing at being Terry Taylor that he'd given little thought to his son, one of the many downsides of working undercover. Terry Taylor didn't have children

217

so he had to banish all thoughts of Liam while he worked. If someone asked him about kids he had to answer automatically, without thinking, because if he hesitated — or, worse, was caught in a lie — then his entire legend could come tumbling down.

Liam had been doing well at school and was expected to get good A-level grades, certainly good enough for most decent universities. It had been a while since he had spoken to his son about his career plans but in their last conversation Liam had said he was interested in video-game design. With the way the world was going it was probably as good a career as any. The problem in offering advice to his son was that Shepherd's own career path had been fairly random. He had joined the army because he wanted travel and excitement, then switched to the SAS when he realised that regular army life wasn't as exciting as it was portrayed in the recruitment advertising. He'd been happy enough in the SAS but his wife had begged him to leave when Liam was born because he was away from home so much. That was when he'd joined the police and been co-opted into an undercover unit. From there he'd moved to the Serious Organised Crime Agency, and when his then boss Charlotte Button had moved to MI5 he had moved with her. None of that had been planned so Shepherd really had no right to expect Liam to have his career mapped out.

It was when he crossed the M25 that he spotted the tail. Two men in a grey Toyota. They were good — they did nothing that made them stick out — but he made a habit of varying his speed and checking his mirror.

218

When he accelerated, the Toyota would hang back but eventually catch up with him. When he slowed, so did the Toyota. There were always several cars between them and Shepherd's BMW and no matter how slowly he went they matched his speed. That meant they were alone: if there had been several they'd have taken it in turns and the Toyota would have dropped back at some point. He used his phone on hands-free to call Willoughby-Brown and quickly updated him.

"You think they're working for the O'Neills or is there something else I should know about it?" asked Willoughby-Brown, when Shepherd had finished.

"I'm in Taylor's BMW, my own car's in Hereford," said Shepherd.

"This is unfortunate."

"It would have been a hell of a lot more unfortunate if I hadn't spotted them," said Shepherd. He gave Willoughby-Brown a description of the car, and the registration number. "I'll drive to Reading Services and stop there," he said.

"How do you want to handle it?"

"In a perfect world I'd just swing back to London, but I really need to see my boy. They stick pretty much to my speed so how about this? I'll wait at Reading, and make it look as if I'm there for a meet. Then I'll head back to London on the M4. If you can get a patrol car fixed up, I'll go over the speed limit, take them with me, and the cops can pull them over with blues and twos. That way we hold them up and get a definite ID. I'll leave at the next junction and head back to Hereford on the M40."

"Sounds like a plan," said Willoughby-Brown. "But what if they've put a tracker on the car?"

Shepherd grimaced. Willoughby-Brown was right. If they'd attached a tracker to the BMW they'd know where he went even if they lost sight of him. The fact that they had stuck close to him suggested they weren't using a tracker, but it wasn't definitive proof. He could dump the car and get to Hereford by train, but if he did that and they were tracking the vehicle, he might have some explaining to do down the line.

"How about I get one of our tech guys to run out and check the car? If the car's clean you can be on your way. If not we can plan how to proceed."

"That would work," said Shepherd.

"So where do we do it?" said Willoughby-Brown. "There isn't time to get it done at Reading and the next service area eastwards is Heston, between junctions two and three."

"It's a long way but it would make sense," said Shepherd. "I was aiming for a meet here, the person didn't turn up so I headed back to London. I stopped off to use the toilets at Heston. If there's a tracker it would all seem logical. But if I head up the M40 they're going to know something's wrong, especially after the cops have stopped the car."

"Heston it is, then," said Willoughby-Brown.

"Maybe I should switch cars, too," said Shepherd. "It might have been a mistake to use it in the first place."

"I'll have a replacement ready for you at Heston," said Willoughby-Brown.

"Not the bomb-proof van," said Shepherd.

"You jest," said Willoughby-Brown. "That's way above your paygrade. Stay put, I'll send you a text when the cops are in place." He ended the call.

Shepherd looked in his rear-view mirror. The Toyota was still behind him, five cars back. He glanced at his speedometer. He was doing just under the speed limit. At that rate it would take him less than half an hour to reach the service station. He settled back and concentrated on the traffic ahead of him.

Ash parked at the side of the road and turned to Mohammed al-Hussain. "This is it, brother." He pointed at the mosque in the distance. Ten years before, the building had been a pub, but as the area had been taken over by Muslims, the brewery had been forced to put it up for sale. A group of local Muslim businessmen had found the money to buy it, applied for planning permission and within a year it was a mosque.

"The imam knows about this?" asked al-Hussain.

"He lets us use the room for meetings," said Ash. "Other than that, he doesn't want to know. But he's one of us."

Sunny nodded in agreement. "He's all right, bruv. No need to worry. He's the one who arranged for me and Ash to go to Pakistan for training."

Al-Hussain looked over at the mosque. Sunrise prayers had taken place just after eight o'clock in the morning and Zohar prayers weren't due until midday so the street was quiet. "Okay," he said.

The three men got out of the car and walked across the road into the mosque. There were racks in the hallway and they removed their footwear. There was a small bookshop to the right full of copies of the Koran and various religious works. Al-Hussain saw at a glance there were no controversial volumes to attract the attention of the authorities. The prayer hall was off to the left presumably, in what had once been the main bar. At the end of the corridor double doors opened into another corridor off which were several smaller rooms. There was a sign on one of the doors: STUDY ROOM. It was locked but Ash had a key. He opened it and switched on the lights. There were four wooden tables each with four plastic chairs, and a whiteboard on one wall on which were written several Arabic phrases. A thick purple curtain had been drawn across the window.

Ash locked the door behind them. Sunny pushed a bookcase across the wooden floor and knelt down. He took a small knife from the pocket of his jeans and prised up a loose board that had been covered by the bookcase. He reached into the hole and pulled out a long package wrapped in sacking, carried it over to one of the tables and laid it down. He and Ash watched as al-Hussain carefully unwrapped it to reveal a metal transit case with two catches. He flicked them and opened the case to reveal the twin of the rifle he had used in Syria, with a Schmidt & Bender 10×42 telescopic sight, a chunky suppressor, mount, bipod, magazines, a sling and a cleaning kit.

He took out the rifle and examined it. It appeared to be brand new.

"They make shit-hot guns, the Yanks," said Ash.

222

"It's British," said al-Hussain.

"I was told it had been brought in from America," said Ash.

"It would have been bought there, yes, but that is because it's almost impossible to buy in England even though they manufacture them here. All guns are illegal in the UK."

"What's it called?" asked Sunny, stroking the barrel.

"It's an L115A3." Al-Hussain picked up the telescopic sight. It was slightly different from the one he'd used in Syria, but it was good and would do the job.

"That's a mouthful," said Ash.

"Its nickname is 'Silent Assassin' because it can be used at such a long range. The targets never hear a thing. Best sniper rifle in the world. Some guys who shot at the Olympics designed it."

"It looks the business," said Sunny. "Can I have a go?"

"It's not a toy," said al-Hussain, putting the sight back in the case.

"I know that," said Sunny. "But we fired all sorts of shit when we went to Pakistan. AK-47s and RPGs, the lot."

"This is different," said al-Hussain. "It's sensitive. It's the difference between a knife and a scalpel. Anyone can kill with a knife, but a scalpel has to be in the hands of a surgeon."

Sunny laughed. "That's what you are, bruv? A surgeon?"

Al-Hussain nodded. "It's how I like to think of myself, yes."

"Fuck me, bruv, you're so far up your own arse it's not true." He laughed.

Al-Hussain's face hardened but he said nothing. He looked at Ash. "I need to fire it."

"Here?" asked Sunny.

"Of course not here," snapped al-Hussain, his eyes still on Ash. "I need to be outside, somewhere I can shoot for eight hundred metres."

"We weren't told that you needed to practise," said Sunny. "No one said, did they, bruv?"

"It's not about practising," said al-Hussain. "The sight has to be calibrated. I've never used this weapon before so I won't be used to it."

"What do you need?" asked Ash.

"Somewhere we won't be disturbed and where no one will hear the gun being fired. As I said, I need to fire at over eight hundred metres."

"We can do that," said Ash. "We've run training exercises for brothers before they go out to Pakistan. We do it in the Peak District. Midweek this time of the year there won't be anyone around. The place we used was well away from the walking trails and I know a valley that will trap any sound."

"Tomorrow?"

"Yes, of course. If that's what you want."

Al-Hussain folded the stock of the rifle and put it into the case.

Sunny took out his mobile phone.

"What are you doing?" asked al-Hussain.

"Taking a picture, bruv."

"Why?"

"I'll put it on our Facebook page."

"Facebook page?"

"Don't worry, bruv. It's not under my name. It's an account we use to encourage recruits."

"You post on social media?"

"Sure, bruv. Everyone does. And a picture of a gun like this, shit, it'll go viral in no time."

Al-Hussain closed the lid. "No pictures, no social media, no nothing," he said. "And you need to stay off social media. Facebook, Twitter, Instagram, they're all monitored. What we're doing is too important to be jeopardised by a Facebook posting."

"Okay, bruv, no problem," said Sunny, putting away the phone. Al-Hussain handed the case to him and he replaced it in the hole in the floorboards.

"So, you can arrange a trial firing tomorrow?" al-Hussain asked Ash.

Ash nodded. "Not a problem."

"I'll need some fruit, too."

"Fruit?" repeated Ash.

"I'll give you a list."

Shepherd indicated left and slowed to leave the motorway. The Toyota also slowed and indicated a left turn half a dozen cars back. He parked and made a show of looking at his watch, then walked into the main building. He ordered fish and chips and coffee and carried his meal to a table by the window, overlooking the car park. He couldn't see the Toyota. If they were pros, one would stay with the vehicle and the other would come inside, but the fact that he had spotted them in the first place meant they were less than professional.

He ripped open a couple of sachets of ketchup and smeared it across his chips. He looked around casually but no one was paying him undue attention. He sipped his coffee, then began to eat. The fish was surprisingly good, though the chips were slightly soggy. He was halfway through the plateful when his phone buzzed to let him know it had received a message. It was Willoughby-Brown: *Call me.* Shepherd picked up the phone and rang him back.

"The car's registered to a Chris Batey of Beckenham, and nothing's known," said Willoughby-Brown. "We can't find any connections between him and the O'Neill brothers either."

"Well, they turned off into Reading Services when I did," said Shepherd.

"Have you had eyes on them?"

"They didn't park near me. I don't want to walk around the car park because then they'll know I'm on to them."

"This might have nothing to do with the O'Neills, you realise that?"

"Sure. But the car is in the name of Terry Taylor and I've been based at the Battersea flat for going on three months. I can't see it can be anyone else. But you're right, we need to keep an open mind."

"And if it is the O'Neills, do you think you've done anything to arouse suspicion?"

"Everything's been as good as gold," said Shepherd.

226

"They might just be checking on you before they take the next step," said Willoughby-Brown. "A final look-see before admitting you to the inner sanctum."

"Or it could be Wedekind doing it off his own bat. He's going to be vouching for me on the money-laundering and might want to make sure he's not setting himself up for a fall."

"How do you want to play it?"

Shepherd looked at his watch. It was after one o'clock. "I think we stick with Plan A," he said. "Can you get a patrol car to pick them up between junctions eleven and ten? I'll get them to speed and they can be pulled over. I'll head back to Maidenhead and take the A404 up to the M40."

"I've a car on standby," said Willoughby-Brown. "I'll get it ready to go at the roadside."

"Make sure they keep them tied up for some time," said Shepherd. "I don't want them catching me up."

"I think I can smell alcohol on their breath from here," said Willoughby-Brown. "Okay, you stay put until the car's in place. I'll let you know when they're ready."

Shepherd ended the call and made a point of checking his watch again and frowning. If he was under surveillance he wanted to make it look as if he was waiting for somebody and they were late.

He finished his fish and chips, then bought himself another coffee and a copy of the *Daily Telegraph*. He went back to his table and spent the next fifteen minutes reading the paper, looking out of the window and checking his watch. Eventually his phone buzzed again. A message from Willoughby-Brown: *Good to go.*

Shepherd peered at his watch again, faked another frown, then finished his coffee and closed his paper. He picked up his car keys and walked to the exit. A man sitting alone at a table by the door grabbed his phone and made a call. It might have been a coincidence but as Shepherd left the building the man rushed off in the opposite direction. Shepherd let him go. If he was the tail, the cops would take care of him on the motorway.

A few minutes after leaving the service station and heading back to London, Shepherd drove past a police patrol car parked at the side of the motorway. He accelerated smoothly and took the BMW up to eighty. The Toyota kept pace with him but stayed about two hundred yards back. He eased down on the accelerator and gradually got the speed up to ninety. The Toyota accelerated too. Shepherd had to move into the outside lane and the Toyota was forced to follow suit. That was when the patrol car behind them hit the blues and twos. At the sound of the siren the Toyota slowed and indicated it was pulling over. Shepherd grinned and kept going.

Once he was sure the Toyota had pulled over he slowed the BMW and drove the rest of the way to Heston Services at just over the speed limit, spending most of the time in the outside lane. If the cops did their job right they could detain the Toyota for up to half an hour.

228

His mobile phone rang when he was ten minutes away. It was Amar Singh. "You can't keep away from me, can you?" he said.

"Must be love," said Shepherd. "Are you going to clean my car?"

Singh laughed. "I've got your replacement and I'm to drive the Beamer back to London. Where are you?"

"About ten minutes away. You?"

"I'm at Heston already."

"Excellent. Look, park behind the coaches. Somewhere quiet."

"No problem."

Shepherd kept the BMW at a steady eighty to the service station, keeping a close eye on his rear-view mirror. He moved to the left and slowed for the exit, then drove along to the coach parking area. He saw a grey Audi TT sports car, and as he parked next to it, Amar Singh climbed out, immaculately dressed as usual, this time in a black Hugo Boss suit, pink shirt and red tie. He shook hands with Shepherd. "You've got a tail, I'm told."

"Picked them up in Slough and they were with me all the way to Reading. They stuck close so I'm hoping the car's clean." He gestured at the Audi. "Is that my replacement?"

Singh tossed him the keys. "Be careful with it."

"How is this in the car pool?"

"It isn't. It's mine. I didn't have time to get one from the pool and I know you're a careful driver."

"Are you sure?"

"It's a bit late to be asking me that now," said Singh. He took a small black box with three stubby antennas on it and walked slowly around the BMW, staring at a series of small lights. He bent down to examine the underside of the car, taking care not to dirty his trousers, then ran the box over the boot and the bonnet. "Nothing I can see," said Singh, "and this thing will pick up pretty much anything."

Shepherd gave him the keys. "Thing is, you have to just drop this at my place in Battersea. Whatever you do, don't drive it around."

"You don't trust me?" Singh looked hurt but grinned when Shepherd started to explain. "I'm only pulling your chain, Spider," he said. "Willoughby-Brown explained the situation. I'll put it back in your parking space and make sure no one sees me." Shepherd gave him the keycard for the car park. "Any idea when you'll be back?" asked Singh.

"Two days, max," he said.

"If you need anything, give me a call," said Singh.

The two men shook hands and Shepherd climbed into the Audi. A few minutes later he was powering his way towards Hereford.

Omar parked his bike at the back of the unit and took off his helmet. The main door was locked so he took out his key and let himself in. "It's me," he shouted, as he locked the door behind him, realising immediately how stupid it was to announce himself. The police would have charged in with guns and stun grenades, not let themselves in with a key.

He could hear the hum of the compressor powering Faisal's spray gun. There were three vehicles in the unit now, all bought with cash. Two had been in the colours they needed. The last had been the exact make and model they wanted but had been all white so Faisal was having to respray it.

Omar went to the far end of the unit, which had been sealed off with sheets of polythene hanging from the ceiling. A ghostly figure was walking back and forth as he gave it its first coat of yellow paint. Omar put his helmet and gloves on a metal table and waited for Faisal to finish.

After a few minutes Faisal turned off the compressor and placed the spray gun on the floor. He parted the polythene sheet, then took off his goggles and dust mask. He was wearing paint-spattered overalls and rubber gloves. "You missed all the hard work again," he said.

"My dad said I had to stay late," said Omar. "We've got jobs backed up but he's too tight to hire anyone else."

Faisal grinned. "I'm joking," he said. "Spraying's an art. It's got to be done right."

Omar nodded at the vehicle behind the polythene sheeting. "How's it going?"

"Yellow's done. I'll let it dry, then do the green. You should be able to fix the lights tomorrow. What about the plates?"

"I haven't been given the numbers yet but I've a guy lined up to make them for me. He's in Stretford so they can be here within an hour."

Faisal took off his gloves and picked up a bottle of water. "I'm starving," he said.

Omar glanced at his watch. "We've got to be in Lancaster by seven but we can stop for a bite on the way," he said.

"What state is it in?"

"The advert says it's a runner but the fittings have been removed. The paintwork is good, so I don't think it's going to need a respray."

"Have they told you when they'll be needed?"

"No, but as soon as I know so will you."

"It's going to be big, isn't it?"

Omar grinned. "Huge."

It was starting to get dark when Shepherd arrived at his house in Hereford. He parked in the driveway and climbed out, just as Liam appeared at the front door. His son looked admiringly at the Audi. "A TT? Nice."

"It's a loaner, so don't get too attached," said Shepherd.

"What about the R8? You should get one."

"Are you serious? They're over a hundred grand. Who pays a hundred grand for a car?"

"People who like cars," said Liam.

Shepherd gestured at the BMW X5 parked at the side of the house. "You can't beat an SUV," he said. "They're tough, they're safe and you can take them off-road." He ruffled his son's hair. "When you come up with the money to buy a car you can have what you want. Until then, the R8 can wait."

"Can I drive the TT?"

"It's not mine. A friend lent it to me."

"I'll be careful."

"Let me think about it. Where's Katra?"

"Supermarket."

"You can make the coffee, then."

"I'm not sure I've got the recipe."

Shepherd joke-punched his arm. "Then that very expensive private education is going to waste," he said. They went into the house and along to the kitchen. Liam switched on the kettle and set out two mugs. Shepherd leaned against the fridge. "So what's happening?" he asked.

"What do you mean?"

"On the phone you said you wanted to talk about university."

Liam took a deep breath as if he was steadying himself, then let it out slowly before speaking. "I don't want to go to university," he said.

"What?"

Liam held up a hand. "I know, I know, but hear me out, Dad. I don't think a degree is going to do me any good. It's a waste of three years and it'll cost a fortune. Nine grand a year plus living costs."

"You can live here."

"Dad, Herefordshire doesn't have a university. Not yet, anyway. And the one they've got planned is mainly for engineering. Living at home and commuting isn't an option. So we're looking at almost twenty grand a year to get me through university. That's a shedload of debt to be saddled with."

"I'll chip in," said Shepherd.

"I know you would, but that's not what I want," said Liam. "Even if I did get a degree, there's no guarantee that I'd find a job at the end of it. Not a real job, anyway. A third of graduates are working as cleaners, office juniors and road sweepers six months after leaving university. And seven per cent don't work at all."

"That may be true, but if you've got a degree, you've got more chance of getting a job than someone who hasn't been to university."

"Perhaps. But there are plenty of guys who've been mega-successful without doing a degree."

"So you want to be the next Bill Gates or Richard Branson, do you?" There was an opened packet of Jaffa Cakes on the table. Shepherd took one and popped it into his mouth, whole.

Liam laughed. "No. An entrepreneur I'm not. But I do know now what I want to do."

Shepherd waited expectantly. Liam was looking at him and Shepherd could see he felt strongly about whatever it was he was going to say. "I want to join the army."

It was the last thing Shepherd had expected to hear and his mouth fell open. "What? The army? Since when?"

"I've been thinking about it for a while. I've talked to the recruiting people and got all the details. It's what I want to do, Dad."

"I thought you wanted to work in the video game business."

Liam laughed. "Yeah, when I was a kid. I also toyed with the idea of being an astronaut. And a superhero."

Shepherd shook his head, trying to clear his thoughts. He opened his mouth to speak but closed it when he heard the front door open.

"Liam? Whose car is that in the driveway?" shouted Katra, their au pair.

"It's Dad's!" Liam replied. "We're here, in the kitchen."

They heard hurried footsteps in the hallway and Katra burst in, laden with full carrier bags. She was wearing tight jeans and a baggy sweatshirt, and her dark hair was pulled back in a multi-coloured scrunchie. "I'm sorry I wasn't here," she said. There was virtually no trace of her Slovenian origin in her accent, which was hardly surprising as she had been with the family for more than a decade.

"It's okay," said Shepherd. "Liam struggled to remember the recipe for coffee but he got there in the end. We're just waiting for the kettle to boil."

Katra put the bags on the table. "I'll do that," she said. "How long are you staying?"

"Tonight for sure, don't know about the day after."

"You're working hard?"

"Always." He nodded at Liam. "Let's go out in the garden," he said. He grabbed a couple more Jaffa Cakes and went outside. Liam followed him. There was a football and Shepherd kicked it across the grass. Liam ran after it, dribbled it and passed it back. Shepherd grinned at his son's skills and returned it to him. "Remember when I was tiny and just couldn't kick?" asked Liam. "I kept falling over."

"You remember that? You couldn't have been much more than two and a half."

"I remember Mum laughing at me."

"You were funny. But you got better quickly. Do you still play at school?"

"I prefer rugby." He lifted the ball up to his knee and bounced it onto his head. He kept it up for several seconds before letting it drop to his feet and kicking it back to Shepherd.

"Which part of the army are you interested in?" asked Shepherd.

"The Army Air Corps," said Liam. "I want to fly helicopters if I can but I'd be okay as ground crew. You know I love cars, and choppers are way more fun. Plus I'd get to travel the world."

"And a degree wouldn't increase your chances?"

"Not really. I can join up straight from school. If I get selected for flight training I could be flying within a few months."

Shepherd kicked the ball back to Liam, harder than he'd planned, but Liam caught it effortlessly with his left foot. "You realise you could end up serving in one of the trouble spots?" said Shepherd. "Afghanistan, Iraq, Syria. Who knows where over the next few years? It's all very well saying you want to travel, but six months in the desert fighting jihadists is no fun."

"It's not supposed to be fun, Dad. It's about learning a skill and serving the country. I love this country and I want to protect it."

"You don't have to join the army to do that."

"Become a copper, you mean? It's almost impossible for someone like me to join the cops at the moment. They're only recruiting minorities. And they insist you spend years working as a special constable first." He shook his head. "And everyone says it's a lousy job, these days. Form filling and meeting targets." He grinned. "Plus they're not big on choppers."

"The army isn't all excitement either," said Shepherd. "There's a lot of hanging around, waiting for officers to make up their minds."

"Not so much if I'm a pilot."

"I wouldn't be too sure of that," said Shepherd. "Pilots follow orders, too."

"I know," said Liam. He kicked the ball back to his father. Shepherd was a fraction slow and the ball went past him. He hurried after it. "The thing is, the skills I learn will stand me in good stead my whole life. Helicopter pilots can work anywhere. Oil rigs, sightseeing, commercial flights. All over the world. Same for the support crew. A good helicopter mechanic can work all over the world. And if I do go the mechanic route, I'd get to service the Land Rovers and all the big trucks. I only have to sign up for four years. If I like it I'll stay in. If I don't, I won't."

"But how much do you know about what a soldier does?" Shepherd kicked the ball back to Liam but timed it badly and it shot off to the side. "Sorry," he said.

Liam retrieved it, tapped it from foot to foot, then sent it back to Shepherd.

"The primary function of a soldier is to kill the enemy," said Shepherd. "That's what it comes down to. You with a weapon facing another man with a weapon. And one of you dies."

"The days of the trenches are gone, Dad."

"You could be a mechanic out in the desert, but if a hundred IS fighters come at you with AK-47s, you'd have to drop your spanner and pick up a gun. If you're a pilot and you're flying in a hot area, a missile could bring you down. It's not just travel and adventure, it's danger and fear, injury and death. You could be minding your own business walking down a deserted road one minute and get your leg blown off the next. You could be on patrol with your mates and a sniper a mile away puts a bullet in your head. In an instant your whole life is over." He kicked the ball back to Liam. Liam trapped it easily.

"I hear you," said Liam. "But the death rate in Afghanistan works out at about thirteen in a thousand. That's just over one per cent."

"Which is great if you're not in that one per cent. But think how I'd feel if you came home in a body-bag."

Liam smiled. "Unbelievable," he said.

"What?"

Liam picked up the ball and threw it at his father, hard. Shepherd caught it — it stung his hands. "How do you think I feel when you're away? Never knowing where you are or what you're doing or what danger you're in. I know you're a cop and not a soldier any more, but you run risks, don't you? All the time."

Shepherd had never told Liam that he no longer worked for the police. Even family and friends weren't supposed to know that he was an MI5 officer, so when he had moved to the security service he hadn't told anyone. But whether he worked for the Met, the National Crime Agency or MI5, Liam's point still held good. Undercover work was always dangerous and he realised that Liam was right. "True."

"How do you think I feel at school when a teacher calls me over? You know my first thought? That I'm going to be called into the head's office and told that something's happened to you. That I'm an orphan. Did you ever think of that?"

"Actually, yes. I did."

"But despite that you continue to put your life on the line."

"Yes."

"So it's the same. You'll have to deal with it."

"This isn't payback, is it?"

Liam laughed. "You're amazing. You think I'd join the army to get back at you?" He shook his head scornfully. "This isn't about you, Dad. It's my life. My career."

Shepherd tossed the ball back. "Stupid thing to say," he said. "Sorry."

"I want to do this, Dad. I've talked it through with the school and with the army, and I can enlist now if I want."

"You'd need parental permission."

"That's hypothetical," said Liam. "I'm going to finish school, obviously. So I'll be eighteen by the time I sign up. But suppose I'd decided I wanted to join now? Would you have let me?"

"I'd try to talk you out of it," he said. "Not having a degree is one thing, but not finishing your A levels would be crazy."

Liam dropped the football onto the grass and kicked it over to Shepherd. "I know that. I'll finish my A levels, maybe travel for a few months, then sign up. They've already said I can join as an officer, assuming I get the grades I'm expected to get. There isn't much difference between an officer with a degree and one without, certainly not worth all the money the degree costs."

"Okay. But what about joining the Territorials?" He kicked the ball to his son.

"Because I don't want to be a part-time soldier. And they don't let part-timers fly helicopters."

"Sounds like you've really thought it through."

Liam flicked the ball up and headed it towards Shepherd. He caught it on his chest and let it fall to his feet. "I have."

"What about the medical?"

"I went to see the school doctor and he did all the tests they'll do. I'm fine. Better than fine. And I've been training, Dad."

"Since when?"

"Over the last year. I still play rugby but I've been doing extra running and weights work."

Shepherd was impressed at Liam's thoroughness. He seemed to have covered all the bases.

"Dad, there's one thing you haven't mentioned," said Liam.

"What's that?" asked Shepherd.

"You left university to join the army, remember? You just walked away and signed up as a squaddie. You weren't even an officer. If either of us has made a dumb decision, that would be you. At least I've thought it through."

Shepherd chuckled. It was a fair point.

"So, are you okay with this? Do I have your blessing?"

"Even though you clearly don't need it?"

"It's not about needing it. It's about wanting it."

Before Shepherd could answer, Katra came out carrying two mugs of coffee. "Did you know about Liam wanting to join the army?" asked Shepherd, as he took his mug.

"I said he should talk to you before he did anything," said Katra, folding her arms. "It's a big decision."

"Huge," agreed Shepherd.

"So what do you think, Dad?"

Shepherd nodded thoughtfully. "I need to sleep on it," he said.

Mohammed al-Hussain woke at a soft knock on the door. "I'm awake," he said, sitting up and rubbing his eyes. He squinted at his wristwatch. It was five a.m.

"We're leaving in twenty minutes," said Ash through the door. "Do you want something to eat?"

"Just tea." He grabbed his towel and washbag and headed for the bathroom. It took him less than ten minutes to clean his teeth, shower and dress. Ash had a cup of tea ready for him, and Sunny was eating an egg sandwich. He wiped his mouth with the back of his hand. "You okay, bruv?"

Al-Hussain nodded and picked up his cup. "What's the plan?" he asked Ash.

"We'll drive you to the practice area," he said. "On the way we'll meet Adam and Jay. They'll collect the weapon and give it to us. We'll complete the practice, then return it to them. We come back here, and they'll replace it in the mosque."

Al-Hussain nodded. In Syria his weapon stayed with him all the time. It was always at his side, even when he slept, but in England it made sense to keep it at a distance until it was needed. If he was caught in possession of a firearm it would all be over.

"Did you get the fruit?"

"In the fridge," said Ash. "Do you want some now?"

"Bring it with us," he said.

Sunny finished his sandwich, wiped his mouth again, then opened the door to the garage. Al-Hussain followed him and got into the car, holding his backpack. Sunny opened the garage door as Ash climbed into the driver's seat with a blue carrier bag, which he passed to al-Hussain. "There's your fruit," he said. Al-Hussain put it on the seat next to him.

Ash drove out of the garage. Sunny closed the door and got into the front. "Rock and roll," he said, beating a rapid tattoo on the dashboard with the flats of his hands.

Ash headed west, away from the house. Sunny switched on the radio and flicked through the channels, eventually settling on a station playing pop music.

Al-Hussain would have preferred silence but the music was preferable to Sunny's inane chatter.

Ten minutes later Ash turned into a supermarket car park, looking for Jay and Adam's car. It was still dark but a dozen vehicles were parked up "There they are," said Sunny, pointing at a white van with the name of a florist on the side.

The bay next to the van was empty and Ash reversed in so that the boot was furthest away from the building. Adam was in the van driver's seat and gave Ash a thumbs-up. Sunny got out of the car and walked around to the back. Ash pressed a button and the boot popped up as Jay opened the van's rear doors. Al-Hussain twisted around in his seat. Jay jumped down from the van, took two steps to the car and put the case containing the rifle into the boot. Sunny slammed the lid and got back in. As soon as he'd closed his door, Ash moved off. It had taken just a few seconds and no one had been in the vicinity to see the handover. Ash turned onto the main road and headed for the Peak District.

Liam groaned as Shepherd switched the bedroom light on. "What time is it?" he said, rubbing his eyes.

"Time to get up," said Shepherd.

Liam peered at the curtains. "It's still dark outside."

"But not for long. See you at the car in five minutes. Dress for a run."

"A run?"

"You want to be a soldier? You can show me you've got what it takes."

"Are you serious?" asked Liam, sitting up, but Shepherd had already gone.

He was standing at the back of the X5 when Liam came out, wearing a sweatshirt, tracksuit bottoms and trainers. Shepherd grinned. They had dressed the same, pretty much, though Shepherd was wearing his old army boots and two pairs of socks. He had put a rucksack and a smaller back-pack into the boot and slammed it. "Get in," he said.

Liam got into the passenger seat while Shepherd sat behind the wheel.

"Where are we going, Dad?" asked Liam.

Shepherd tossed him an Ordnance Survey map. "You tell me," he said, as he drove away from the house.

"Can't we just turn on the sat-nav?"

Shepherd threw him a withering look.

"Okay, okay," said Liam. He unfolded the map, checked the road signs that flashed by. Realisation dawned. "No way!"

Shepherd grinned.

"You're taking me to the Brecon Beacons?"

Shepherd's grin widened.

"To do what, exactly?"

"You tell me."

Liam's eyes widened. "The Fan Dance?"

"Why not? You said you'd been training. You said you were fit."

"Army fit, not SAS fit."

Shepherd laughed. "The Fan Dance is just to see if you're ready for Selection," he said. "The Long Drag is the real test, but we'll save that for down the line."

Liam settled back in his seat. "Bring it on," he said.

The Fan Dance formed part of the Fitness and Navigation phase of the SAS's selection process. It was a fifteen-mile trek up and down Pen y Fan, a three-thousand-foot peak. From one side to the other, and back again. It was a speed march and recruits had to do it in less than four hours and ten minutes, though Shepherd had never taken more than three and a half. The Long Drag was a more serious affair, a forty-mile march in full gear, which had tested Shepherd at the peak of his fitness.

It took just less than an hour and a half to reach the Storey Arms Mountain Rescue Centre. Shepherd parked a few feet away from the red phone box, where the SAS usually gathered before starting the Fan Dance. He and Liam climbed out and walked to the back of the vehicle. Shepherd opened the door and handed Liam the backpack. "On Selection you carry a Bergen, total weight thirty-five kilos. But I'll let you off with energy bars, four litres of water and a foil blanket." He took out his old rucksack, filled with bricks wrapped in newspapers. It had been more than a year since he'd used it, but it slipped easily over his shoulders and his body automatically accommodated the weight.

"Okay, this isn't a race, not against each other," he said. "You're testing yourself.

"Dad, if you want a race, I'm up for it."

Shepherd laughed. "I admire your enthusiasm, but stay within earshot of me." He pointed at Liam's trainers. "The forecast is warm so you'll be fine in those. But the weather can change quickly up there. If it starts to rain I've got boots for you in my rucksack."

Liam nodded.

Shepherd could see the lad was enthusiastic but over-confidence could be dangerous on Pen y Fan. "Pace yourself."

"How fast can you do it, Dad?"

"My record is just over three hours but that was fifteen years ago. I'll be happy if we're back here in four."

Liam looked at his watch. "Ready?"

Shepherd grinned. "Hell, yeah." He slammed the door of the SUV, then turned to see that Liam was already sprinting away. In the first two miles the terrain climbed around two thousand feet so he doubted that the boy would be able to keep up the blistering pace for long. He headed after him, his boots thudding on the ground. Liam led the way for the first half-mile, Shepherd staying about fifty feet behind him. Then there was a downward slope and Liam picked up the pace to a shallow river. The terrain was uphill again after the river, but steeper, and Shepherd easily caught up with him.

Liam was breathing heavily but not panting, and he slowed to a fast walk. It took almost forty minutes to reach the summit by which time their faces were bathed in sweat. Shepherd clapped him on the shoulder. "Quarter of the way," he said.

Liam stopped and surveyed the view. On the other side of the hill a group of five men, not much older than Liam, was heading up towards them. They were all wearing full mountain gear and carrying lengths of pipe. Obviously soldiers training for Selection — on the real thing, the men had to carry their Bergens and weapons. They were climbing Jacob's Ladder, the rock-strewn hill that separated the peak from the Roman road below.

Shepherd pulled a bottle of water from Liam's backpack, opened it and gave it to him. Liam drank half and handed it back. He wiped his mouth on his sleeve. "Ready? Or do you need more time to rest?"

Shepherd put the empty bottle into the backpack and zipped it up. "After you," he said.

Liam headed down the hill at a slow jog. After ten minutes they reached the group of guys who were working their way up. They were all lean, fit and sweating profusely under the weight of their Bergens and pipes. "Well done, guys, keep it going," said Shepherd.

The guy at the front, tall, with an unruly mop of ginger hair, grinned. "Thanks, sir."

The four guys behind him all wished Shepherd and Liam good morning as they continued up.

Liam was about twenty feet ahead of Shepherd when he reached the top of Jacob's Ladder and Shepherd called for him to be careful and watch his step. The rocky incline was the most dangerous part of the hike, treacherous in the wet and a death-trap in the dark. But the weather was good and the rocks were dry so, provided they were careful, it was a simple enough descent. Again, over-confidence could lead to a slip or a fall. The first rocks were huge with drops of a couple of feet, but then it became more of a staircase and eventually an uneven track. From there it was a downhill slope all the way for going on five miles, traversing towards a lake and woodland before eventually hitting the road.

By the time they reached it Shepherd was about fifty feet behind Liam and his shirt was soaked with sweat. It had been a long time since he'd exercised with the bricks on his back and even longer since he'd done the Fan Dance. Most of the time he ran on the flat and he was finding the slopes, uphill and down, challenging to say the least.

On the road it was a long, slow descent to the turnaround point. Shepherd checked his watch and nodded appreciatively. "Ninety-two minutes," he said to Liam. "Not bad."

Liam was bent double with his hands on his hips, breathing heavily, but when he straightened up he was grinning. "Ready to go back?" he asked.

"Rehydrate first," said Shepherd. "Even if you don't actually feel thirsty you need to keep putting water into your system." He took off his pack and pulled out two bottles of water. He gave one to Liam and opened the other. Shepherd held out his bottle and Liam tapped his against it before they drank.

"How many times have you done the Fan Dance, Dad?" asked Liam.

"Too many to remember," said Shepherd.

"And if you fail this, you don't get into the SAS?"

"You don't even get onto Selection," said Shepherd. He waved his bottle up at the peak. "Those guys we saw had the right idea. If you're serious about passing Selection you need to come out here half a dozen times, and at different times of the year. Today's a nice day but it can be as hot as hell up there, or freezing cold, with rain, fog and even snow. Selection always seems to be at the hottest or coldest time of the year, never like it is now."

They finished their water and Shepherd flattened the two empty plastic bottles, then slotted them into pockets on his rucksack. He looked at his watch again and clapped Liam on the back. "Off we go," he said, but Liam had sprinted off before he finished the sentence. Shepherd grinned and ran after him.

They reached the bottom of Jacob's Ladder just as the five guys they'd seen earlier were descending. They passed them at the midway stage. "Good time, guys, well done," said Shepherd. "Keep it up."

"We intend to, sir," said the ginger-haired lad, who was now number two in the string. All five were sweating but none appeared over-exerted.

"Do you have a Selection date?" asked Shepherd.

"Yes, sir," said the lad. "This winter."

"Wrap up warm," said Shepherd, and the five guys laughed as they headed down the rocks.

By the time they reached the top, Shepherd was breathing heavily. Liam was waiting for him, hand on hips. "Having trouble?" he asked.

"All good," said Shepherd. He took off his rucksack, pulled out two bottles of water and two energy bars.

"Want to change packs?" said Liam.

"Now you ask! When it's downhill all the way!"

Liam laughed and bit into his bar. He chewed as he looked out over the rolling hills and farmland. "Is this where they do Escape and Evasion?" he asked.

"That's right," said Shepherd. Escape and Evasion was the final stage of SAS Selection. Recruits were dropped in the countryside and expected to escape detection for three days. They had to make their way to a series of checkpoints, feeding themselves off the land and finding water where they could.

"Does anyone not get caught?"

"Some," said Shepherd. "But it doesn't make any difference. Even if you escape detection you still have to report for TQ."

"TQ?"

"Tactical questioning. It's where they rough you up and interrogate you."

"And you can only answer with your name, rank, serial number and date of birth."

Shepherd nodded. "Anything else, you have to say, 'I'm sorry but I cannot answer that question.' Say anything else and you've failed."

"Was it bad?"

Shepherd grinned. "It wasn't pleasant. But it's not supposed to be."

"Have you ever been interrogated for real?"

Shepherd took a final bite of his energy bar, and drained his water bottle. "Let's save the war stories for later." He put away his wrapper and bottle and waited for Liam to finish, then tucked his rubbish into the rucksack. He grunted as he hefted it onto his back.

250

"Last one down's a sissy," said Liam.

"Just be careful," said Shepherd. "These hills can be unforgiving, even on a day like this. Watch where you put your feet — it's way too easy to twist an ankle out here." Liam had already started down the hill and Shepherd headed after him.

The final run home was simple enough and, despite Shepherd's warning, Liam was able to keep a slow jog for much of the way. Shepherd followed, breathing heavily but not in too much pain. His feet were fine — he'd had the boots for years and they fitted perfectly — but the slope was playing havoc with his hips and calves. His back was burning, too, the result of the heavy weight on it. By the time he reached the river, Liam was already on the other side, munching another energy bar. He had a bottle of water and gave it to Shepherd after he had splashed across.

"You okay, Dad?" asked Liam.

"Do you want to race the last bit?"

Liam laughed. "I don't want you having a heart attack."

"Cheeky bugger," said Shepherd. He pointed off in the distance. When Liam turned to look Shepherd ran off, the rucksack bouncing against his back.

"Cheat!" shouted Liam, and hared after him.

The terrain was uphill for a few hundred yards and Liam made no headway, but then there was a slope down to where they'd left the car, and though Shepherd was running flat out he could hear Liam gaining on him. He didn't look around and concentrated on where he was placing his feet: even though the ground was relatively smooth there were plenty of traps for the unwary that could result in a fall and a twisted ankle. His chest was burning and his legs felt like lead but he kept up the pace. A mile passed. Then another. They were both still running, but they'd slowed to a jog.

Ahead Shepherd could see the car park and the red phone box that was the traditional finish point. He pushed himself harder but he could hear Liam's heavy breathing behind him and then they were neck and neck. Liam grinned at him. "Gotcha!" he said.

Shepherd was too tired to reply. There was a hundred yards to go and he grunted and ran faster but Liam was already pulling ahead. He gritted his teeth and increased the pace but there was no catching his son and Liam reached the phone box a good five seconds before Shepherd. He hugged it, then turned around, took off his backpack and slid down until he was sitting on the ground, legs splayed.

Shepherd took off his rucksack and pulled out two more bottles of water. He unscrewed the top from one and handed it to Liam, who drank gratefully as Shepherd sat down next to him. He patted his son's knee. "You did well. Really well."

"Thanks, Dad."

"I mean it." He looked at his watch. "We did it in three hours and ten minutes. That's faster than my first time."

"And I beat you. Let's not forget that."

"I let you win."

"You did not."

252

Shepherd laughed. "No, I didn't. You beat me fair and square. Seriously, well done."

"I've got to make a confession," said Liam. He swallowed another mouthful of water. "This isn't my first time."

"What?" Shepherd's jaw dropped.

"I've done the Fan Dance a couple of times. During the last school holidays. I got Grandad to drive me over."

"And you never told me?"

"I wanted to prove to myself that I could do it. If I'd failed, I'd probably have knocked the army idea on the head, but my first run was okay."

"Wait a minute. Your grandad drove you here and never mentioned it to me?"

"I asked him not to."

"So you told him about wanting to join the army before you told me?"

"To be fair, Dad, you haven't been around much this last year." He opened his backpack and took out an energy bar.

Shepherd nodded. "I guess so."

"I told Grandad I wanted to train and he said he'd help." Liam offered the energy bar to Shepherd but Shepherd shook his head. Liam ripped open the wrapper and took a bite.

"And what about you joining the army? What did he have to say about that?"

"He said it wouldn't have been his choice of a career, but that you had had a life most people could only dream about."

Shepherd's eyebrows shot up. "He said that?"

"I don't think you know how much he admires you, Dad. And Gran. They both think the world of you."

Shepherd's cheeks reddened and he covered his embarrassment by drinking some water. He hadn't spent much time with his in-laws over the past few years — usually it was a matter of saying hello and goodbye when he dropped off Liam. If he was honest with himself, he had to admit he often felt uncomfortable around them. He had married their daughter and she had died, killed in a senseless traffic accident when Liam was just seven. They had always been a rock when it came to Liam and he couldn't have managed without them when his son was a youngster. But Shepherd always felt guilty in their company, as if he was in some way to blame for Sue's death.

"I always thought they resented my job," said Shepherd.

"They understand how important your work is. Sure, they don't like it keeping you away from home but Grandad said you only get one life and you have to do what makes you happy. He worked in a bank and he was happy with that, but he said he always wished he'd worked on a cruise ship."

"A cruise ship? A life on the ocean waves?"

Liam laughed. "I know. He wanted to be a cruise-ship captain. But his dad said the bank was a safe place to be and he took his advice."

"I never knew that."

"You should sit down and talk to him some time, Dad."

254

"I will. Think you can manage to get to the car or do I have to carry you?"

Liam got to his feet and groaned as he bent to pick up his backpack.

"You'll feel it more tomorrow," said Shepherd.

"But I passed, right?"

Shepherd held up his hand. Liam grabbed it and helped him to his feet. "It's what you want to do?"

Liam nodded. "Yes."

"No question? No doubt?"

"I've thought about it long and hard, Dad. Went through all my options with the careers teacher at school."

"And what did he say?"

"She. Mrs Peters. Like you, she said go to university first but she couldn't argue with the economics of the degree. These days, it doesn't make sense, unless you want a career that needs specialist knowledge. I can be a soldier now. I'd be good at it, too." He grinned. "It's in my genes, remember."

"Your mum wouldn't have allowed it, you know that. She hated me being in the SAS."

"She was married to you. I'm not married so I don't have a wife who's worried about me. If I ever do find a woman I want to marry, I'll think about leaving. Look, Dad, I'm not saying I want to be a soldier for the rest of my life. But right now I do. I might stay in for five years, ten, maybe longer, but what I learn while I'm a soldier will be way more helpful than anything I'd learn at university. And I'll be earning from day one."

Shepherd stared at him for several seconds. "When did you get so grown-up?" he said eventually.

"While you were off doing whatever it is you do," said Liam. "I am grown-up, Dad. I'm old enough to make my own decisions."

"I couldn't be more proud of you." Shepherd held out his hand.

Liam grabbed it. He had a firm grip, Shepherd realised. A man's grip. The two men shook, then Liam hugged his father. "Thanks, Dad. For everything."

Mohammed al-Hussain carried the case up the hill. Ash followed him. He had a pair of binoculars in a leather case hanging over one shoulder. They had left the car in a sheltered field a hundred yards from the road. The sun had just come up, there had been no other vehicles around, and the nearest house was miles away.

Sunny had headed off in the opposite direction with the bag of fruit.

They were in a valley, and much of it was still in shadow. Al-Hussain stopped and turned to check on Sunny's progress. He was just over five hundred metres away, heading for a stone wall that wound its way across the hillside on the far side of the valley. Al-Hussain had explained to him several times what he had to do because there was no mobile-phone coverage in the valley and he'd be too far away to hear either Ash or him shouting.

He headed up the slope again, treading carefully. It wasn't especially steep but there was dew on the grass, making it slippery. When they reached an area that was pretty much flat, al-Hussain stopped and looked around. "This will do," he said. He put the case on the grass, then took a blanket from his backpack and spread it over the ground.

Ash took out his binoculars and trained them on Sunny. He was a hundred metres from the wall and appeared to be finding it hard going.

Al-Hussain knelt down and opened the case. He flipped the folding stock open and locked it into place, then attached the sight and screwed the suppressor into the barrel. He rested the rifle on the case and slotted five rounds into one of the stubby magazines. He put it on the ground and loaded another.

"He's at the wall," said Ash.

It was about eight hundred metres from them, the perfect distance. Al-Hussain attached the bipod to the front of the rifle, and eased in one of the magazines.

As al-Hussain lay down and prepared himself, Ash watched through his binoculars. Sunny used both hands to place a large green watermelon on the wall. It was about twice the size of a man's head. He bent down and picked up a honeydew melon. It was slightly smaller than the watermelon, the size of a child's head. He placed it three feet away from the watermelon. Further along, he positioned a grapefruit, then an orange.

"Not going for a grape, then?" asked Ash, lowering the binoculars.

"I have shot a man in the eye from this range," said al-Hussain. It wasn't a boast, it was the truth.

"Where was that?" asked Ash.

257

Al-Hussain realised he had said too much so he ignored the question and concentrated on adjusting his sights.

In the distance, Sunny walked away from the fruit. He took a dozen paces then turned and waved at them to show he was ready. "You can start when you want, brother," said Ash. He focused his binoculars on the largest fruit. "Watermelon first, right?" he said.

"Of course." Al-Hussain sighted on the watermelon, took a breath, released half of it, then slowly squeezed the trigger. The rifle kicked, the suppressor reducing the sound to a dull pop, and a second later he saw a divot appear in the grass behind the watermelon.

"High and to the left," said Ash, but al-Hussain was already adjusting his sights.

He took aim, regulated his breathing and fired again. That bullet missed, too, but he didn't see where it had gone.

"Still high and to the right," said Ash.

He fired again. Another miss.

"Not as high but still to the left," said Ash.

Al-Hussain adjusted his sights, steadied his breathing, and pulled the trigger a fourth time. A chunk of watermelon tore off the left side and fell to the ground.

"You hit it!" shouted Ash. "Man, that was awesome. You hit it."

"Yes, but I was aiming dead centre," said al-Hussain. He made a small adjustment to the sight and fired again. This time the watermelon burst apart and splattered over the grass. In the distance, Sunny pumped the air and whooped.

Al-Hussain pulled out the magazine, slotted in the second, then took aim at the honeydew melon. He took a breath, released half of it and squeezed the trigger. As soon as the bullet left the barrel he knew that the shot was good and a second later the yellow melon exploded.

Two seconds later he hit the grapefruit, dead centre.

"Brother, you are amazing," said Ash.

Al-Hussain said nothing. He moved the barrel to the right until Sunny's face was in view. He centred the crosshairs on Sunny's chest. He pulled the trigger and felt no more emotion than when he had been aiming at the fruit. The rifle kicked. A second later Sunny's chest imploded and blood splattered across the wall behind him as he slumped to the ground.

Slowly, Ash took the binoculars away from his face and stared at al-Hussain in horror. "What the fuck did you do, man?"

"I had no choice," said al-Hussain, cradling the rifle. "He talked too much. He had become a liability."

"You killed him."

"He killed himself by his behaviour."

"You can't do that."

"I can and I did."

"You just decided to kill him? Just like that?"

"My mission is what is important. Nothing can be allowed to jeopardise it. He talked too much. And what he was saying about social media. Does he not know that everything is scrutinised, these days? Everything. You saw him take a photograph of the gun. Do you not see how irresponsible that was? How dangerous?"

"We told him not to do it."

"He should have known. He was a liability, and you know that, don't you?"

Ash said nothing.

"You know I am right," said al-Hussain.

"Tell me, brother, how do I know you won't shoot me as well?"

"Do you talk too much?" asked al-Hussain.

"Fuck, no," said Ash. "I keep my mouth shut and I don't use social media. I'm not into Twitter or Facebook or any of that crap."

"Then you're not a liability." He folded the stock of the rifle and slid it into the backpack. "Come on," he said, heading down the hill.

Ash hesitated, then followed him. It took just over half an hour to reach the wall and Ash was out of breath. Al-Hussain was made of sterner stuff and hadn't even broken a sweat. He bent down and pulled a black rubbish bag from his backpack and handed it to Ash. He pointed at the mess on the wall. "Clear it up as best you can," he said.

As Ash picked up the shattered bits of fruit, al-Hussain took a kitchen knife and knelt down next to Sunny's body. He rolled it over. There was no exit wound. He let the body roll back, then stuck the knife into the chest wound.

"Bruv, what the fuck are you doing?" asked Ash. "He's dead. Leave him be."

Al-Hussain continued to slice into the wound. "I need the bullet," he said. "We can bury the body but we need to take the bullet with us."

260

"Brother, you are one cold motherfucker," said Ash. Al-Hussain looked over his shoulder and Ash took a step backwards. "Okay, okay," he said. "Whatever you want is fine by me." He bent down and grabbed a piece of watermelon. Juice smeared across his hand, like watered-down blood, and he shuddered.

Shepherd had breakfast with Liam before heading back to London. Katra made them Liam's favourite cheesy scrambled eggs and toast, then disappeared upstairs.

"Dad, what's going to happen to Katra?"

"What do you mean?"

"She was crying in her room yesterday. She was saying we wouldn't need her any more. You won't sack her, will you?"

"Of course not. You'll still come back from time to time. And this is my home. Even if we moved we'd still need a housekeeper. I can see that maybe we won't need the house in Hereford but if we got a place in London, say, she could move with us."

"Grandad and Gran won't be happy if we do that."

Shepherd laughed. "They'd miss you, sure. Me maybe not so much. But it's not too far from London. We can always get up to see them. Who knows? Maybe you'll end up in the SAS and we can keep the house."

"I don't know that I want to be in Special Forces, Dad. But, yeah, we'll see. Maybe you should have a word with her."

They finished their breakfast and Shepherd went upstairs. He knocked on the door to Katra's room but she didn't reply. He knocked again but there was still no answer. "Katra, it's Dan. Can I talk to you?"

A few seconds later the door opened. Shepherd stepped inside but Katra was back on her bed, curled up. He sat down next to her. "Are you okay?"

"I'm fine," she said, her voice shaking.

"What's wrong?"

"Nothing."

"You're worried about your job? Is that it?"

She rolled over and looked at him. Her eyes were red and her cheeks were wet with tears. "My job?"

"About Liam leaving and you having no one to look after."

"I don't care about my job," she said, wiping her eyes with the back of her hand. "It's you and Liam I care about. But you're hardly ever here and Liam's going and . . ." She sniffed. "You're my family and I'm losing you. I don't know what to do."

"You're not losing us," said Shepherd, but even as he spoke he realised she was right.

"If Liam's in the army you won't need the house. You won't need me."

"Liam will still come home. So will I. We'll still need looking after."

She sat up and swung her legs over the side of the bed. "I'm being stupid."

Shepherd put his arm around her and kissed the top of her head softly. "You're not."

She looked up at him. "You know I love you."

He smiled. "I love you, too."

262

"No," she said. "I mean it." She moved her head closer to his and before he knew what was happening she was kissing him. For a second or two he resisted, but then he reached up and stroked her hair as he kissed her back. Then it was Katra who broke away, red-faced and flustered. "I'm sorry, I'm sorry," she said.

He laughed. "Why?"

"I'm so stupid."

"I told you, you're not."

She stood up. "I'm so sorry."

Shepherd stood up and tried to put his arms around her but she stepped back, her eyes brimming with tears. "Please just go, Dan," she said.

"Katra, there's nothing to be sorry about."

"I'm so confused."

Shepherd laughed. "You and me both."

"Now you're laughing at me."

"I'm not. Really. Look, we need to talk, but I have to get back to London. Once my job's done I'll come back and we'll talk it through."

"Okay."

He held out his arms. "Hug?"

She let him take her in his arms. As he held her she turned her face up to him and this time he kissed her without hesitation.

"How did it go?" asked Liam, when Shepherd walked back into the kitchen.

"It went okay," said Shepherd. He glanced at his watch. "I've got to go."

"You always have to go, Dad," said Liam. "It's what you do."

Shepherd's Terry Taylor phone rang as he was driving past Swindon. He took the call on hands-free. It was Howard Wedekind. "Where are you?" he asked.

"Just out doing some shopping. What's happening?"

"Got a job for you, if you're interested."

"For you or the brothers?"

"Would that make a difference?" asked Wedekind.

Shepherd faked a laugh. "I just want to know who's paying the bill."

"It's company business," said Wedekind.

"What do you need doing?"

"Not on the phone, Terry. Never on the phone."

"Where and when?" asked Shepherd. He was still some fifty miles away from London.

"I could come around to your place this evening," said Wedekind.

"My place?"

"Is that a problem?"

Shepherd frowned. Wedekind had always chosen to meet in public places before. He hoped it was a sign that he was now trusted and not something more sinister. "Of course not. What time's good for you?"

"Six? I've got a meeting at four thirty in the City and I could drop by on the way home."

"Perfect," said Shepherd. "I'll get some wine in."

"It's not a fucking date, Terry. There's some stuff I need to show you so I want a bit of privacy, that's all."

"All good, Howard," said Shepherd.

The line went dead. Shepherd used the hands-free to call Willoughby-Brown. "Wedekind is coming around to the flat this evening."

"Why?"

"Good question," said Shepherd. "He could be checking me out. Thing is, I didn't give him my address and he didn't ask for it."

"You think that's a worry?"

"We set the legend up so it would check out," said Shepherd. "I would have thought he'd ask me for my address, though."

"Maybe he wants you to know that he knows," said Willoughby-Brown. "Playing mind games."

"It's possible," said Shepherd. "If he was going to do me any harm he'd hardly do it where I live. He could just as easily invite me to somewhere isolated. Anyway, he says he wants a private chat so I'll take him at his word. The good news is that we can get him on video." Amar Singh and two other MI5 technicians had wired the Battersea flat for sound and vision before Shepherd had moved in. It could be monitored live, with everything recorded.

"So what time will he be there?"

"Six."

"We'll be watching. Check in before to make sure there are no technical issues."

"Will do," said Shepherd. He ended the call.

Shepherd arrived back in Battersea at just after two o'clock that afternoon. He had called ahead and asked

Amar Singh to arrange to return the Audi but as he drove down the road to the apartment block he spotted the grey Toyota, which had been following him, parked at the side of the road. Shepherd cursed under his breath and turned his head away as he went by. Singh was standing in front of the building, his hands in the pockets of his pale blue Ted Baker suit. Shepherd made a left turn and found a parking space, then phoned Singh.

"Bit of a problem, Amar," he said. "I've parked around the corner. The guys who were tailing the BMW are across the road from you. Walk away and I'll call you later."

"Do you need back-up?"

"Terry Taylor wouldn't have back-up," said Shepherd. "I could do with a gun, mind."

"Can't help you there," said Singh. "There's an Uzi pen in the glovebox of the Audi, though."

"I'll give that a go," said Shepherd. He ended the call, opened the glovebox and found the pen. It was made by the people who manufactured the renowned submachine-guns. The heavy-duty lightweight aircraft aluminium was so strong that the pen could pierce wood if wielded with enough force, and on the end there was a durable carbide glass-breaker. He slipped it into his jacket pocket, climbed out and locked the Audi. It was a chilly day but that wasn't why the hairs were standing up on the back of his neck. Who were they? And were they tailing Dan Shepherd or Terry Taylor? He doubted they were cops because MI5 had access to all the Met's databases and would have picked up anyone running the plates of the BMW. It was more likely to be someone checking up on him on behalf of the O'Neills, and Wedekind clearly knew where he lived. But if they were working for Wedekind, why sit outside the block on the day that Wedekind himself was going to visit?

The bigger question was, how should he react? As Dan Shepherd, his best course of action was to note that he was being followed but not to show he knew they were there. But if Terry Taylor didn't spot a tail, he'd look like an amateur, and that would be bad for his reputation. The even bigger question was what they thought had happened to them on the motorway. Had they realised he'd called in the cops, or did they think being pulled over was simply bad luck? There was only one way to find out and that was to confront them.

Shepherd walked to Tesco Express where he bought a bottle of milk, bread, a jar of Gold Blend coffee, lighter fluid and a cigarette lighter. He headed back towards his apartment building, swinging the carrier bag as if he didn't have a care in the world.

He came up behind the car, taking the pen from his pocket. The man in the passenger seat was reading a newspaper. The driver was tapping his fingers on the steering wheel. They both had their seatbelts on, which would hinder any movement.

He transferred the can of lighter fluid and the lighter into the right-hand pocket of his jacket. As he drew level with the rear of the car, he dropped the carrier bag and slammed the glass-breaker into the corner of the rear passenger window. There was a dull crack and the window exploded into a shower of cubes. Both men jumped. Shepherd shoved the pen into his pocket and pulled out the can of lighter fluid. He unscrewed the cap and squirted the contents over the men, concentrating on their faces, then tossed it into the car and pulled out the lighter. They were wiping their faces and the air was thick with fumes. The passenger grabbed for his seat belt buckle but Shepherd hit him on the back of the head.

"If I flick this lighter you'll both go up in flames, so put down your hands and sit quietly," said Shepherd.

"Get the fuck away with that!" shouted the passenger.

"What the fuck are you doing?" shouted the driver.

"Shut up and listen!" hissed Shepherd. "If you don't want to spend the next week in a burns unit, sit the fuck still."

They quietened but they both stared nervously at the lighter.

"Who are you working for?" asked Shepherd.

"We're just sitting here," said the driver. "We don't work for anyone."

Shepherd flicked the lighter and both men yelped. "Okay, okay!" shouted the passenger. "Howard sent us to keep an eye on you."

"Howard who?"

"Howard Wedekind."

"Since when?"

268

"Two days ago," said the passenger. "Now put that lighter away."

"Why did he want you to follow me?"

"He didn't say."

"Fuck that! He must have told you something!" Shepherd flicked the lighter again.

"I swear!" said the passenger. "He just said he wanted to know where you lived, where you went, who you met."

"What are you? Private detectives?"

The passenger shook his head. "We do due diligence checks, that's all, mainly on companies but individuals as well. Please, just take the lighter away."

"Listen to me and listen to me good," said Shepherd. "If I see you anywhere near me again, I'll do more than splash you with lighter fluid. Do you understand?"

Both men nodded.

"Now get the hell away from me. And don't come back."

He straightened, the lighter still in his hand. The driver started the engine and the car sped off. Shepherd put the lighter back into his pocket and picked up his carrier bag. He went into the building and made himself a cup of coffee. He had drunk half of it when his phone rang. It was Howard Wedekind. "We should talk, obviously," said Wedekind.

"The sooner the better," said Shepherd.

"I'll cancel my meeting and come around now, if that's okay with you."

"I'll be waiting," said Shepherd.

Ash drove all the way from the Peak District to Sheffield in silence. The first time he spoke was when they were turning into the supermarket car park. The florist's van was parked in the same bay it had occupied that morning. "What do I tell the brothers?" he asked. "They'll want to know where Sunny is."

"Tell them nothing."

"They'll want to know. They'll wonder why he didn't come back with us."

Al-Hussain shrugged. "Tell them he was needed on another operation. People move around. He moved. It's not a big thing."

Ash parked next to the white van. He popped the boot and climbed out. Al-Hussain watched in the wing mirror as Ash took out the rifle case and passed it to Jay, who disappeared inside the van and slammed the rear door as Ash got back into the car.

"Did they ask?"

Ash started the engine. "No."

"So all is well," said al-Hussain. "*Inshallah*."

Ash didn't speak again until they were passing the Madina Masjid. Men were queuing to go inside, wearing traditional clothing and skull caps. "Do you know when it will happen?" he asked.

"Soon," said al-Hussain.

"Do you know where?"

"It is better that I don't," he said. "The fewer people who know, the fewer people can betray us."

"Does that mean we aren't trusted?"

"It's not about trust. Say the intelligence agencies were looking at you. They will read your emails, listen to your calls, monitor your text messages. They will bug your car and your home. If you say or write anything they will know. But if you know nothing, they will discover nothing. If we were caught today and interrogated, tortured, even, there is nothing of any use that we can tell them."

"That makes sense," said Ash.

"Of course," said al-Hussain. He folded his arms and looked out of the side window.

"I'm not like Sunny," said Ash, quietly.

Al-Hussain said nothing.

"I get that he talked too much," said Ash. "And I told him he should stay off social media. He wouldn't listen."

Still al-Hussain was silent.

"Are you sure you're not going to kill me?" Ash asked, his voice trembling.

Al-Hussain turned to him slowly. His eyes were as dull and lifeless as those of a dead fish. "Why do you say that, brother?"

"You killed Sunny. I saw you do it. That makes me a witness."

"Are you going to tell anyone what you saw?"

"No. Never. Of course not."

Al-Hussain shrugged. "So you have nothing to worry about."

"I am loyal, brother. I will happily die for Islam. And I will do nothing to jeopardise our mission."

"I know that, brother. You are thinking too much."

271

"I've never seen a dead body before. Not close up. Not for real."

"Not when you were training in Pakistan?"

"We trained with weapons. We studied. We didn't actually kill anyone. I mean, I've seen videos and shit but never in the flesh."

Al-Hussain nodded. "Killing a man is a big thing," he said. "Especially a Muslim. But sometimes it has to be done. For the greater good."

"Can I ask you a question, brother?"

"Of course."

"What does it feel like? To take a life?"

"It depends," said al-Hussain. "I took no pleasure in killing your friend. He was a Muslim, he was a jihadist. But he was a fool, and a dangerous one. Killing him was a necessity so I feel no guilt but I am sad for having taken the life of a Muslim. Before, in Syria, I was killing our enemies and I took pride in that. But not pleasure. I do not kill because I enjoy it, brother. I kill because we are fighting a war against the crusaders who want all Muslims dead. I am fighting to protect our people and killing is part of that."

"Do you feel guilty about taking lives?"

"Why should I? The Koran is clear that all Muslims must fight those who fight against us. The West is our enemy. They are killing our people around the world. In Afghanistan, in Iraq, in Syria. And when Muslims are not being killed, they are being oppressed. It is our duty to fight back. So, no, I feel no guilt. And neither should you, brother." His eyes narrowed. "Are you having second thoughts? About what we have to do?"

"No, definitely not," said Ash, hurriedly. "We have to kill the infidels, we have to show them we are strong."

"Good man," said al-Hussain, patting Ash's leg again. "You are a good Muslim. Allah will reward you."

They arrived at the house. Ash drove up to the garage, climbed out and opened the door, then got back into the car and drove slowly inside. Al-Hussain got out and shut the door, then the two men went through to the kitchen. "Are you hungry, brother?" asked Ash. "I can cook."

"That would be good, brother, thank you," said al-Hussain. "I shall bathe first." He went upstairs and retrieved his mobile phone from under the mattress. He tapped out the number he had committed to memory. A man answered and they spoke in Arabic. "The weapon is ready," said al-Hussain. "And so am I."

"You took care of Sunny?"

"I did."

"Were there any problems?"

"None."

"You will be collected soon, brother. *Alhamdulillah w AShokrulillah.*" Praise and thanks to Allah.

"*Alhamdulillah w AShokrulillah,*" repeated al-Hussain. He ended the call, removed the sim card from the phone and went along to the bathroom where he broke it in half and flushed it down the toilet.

The intercom buzzed and Shepherd checked the CCTV monitor. It was Wedekind. He pressed the button to admit him. Two minutes later the bell rang and he went to the front door. Wedekind was wearing a tweed jacket and grey trousers and carrying a scuffed leather briefcase. He looked apprehensive and started speaking the moment Shepherd opened the door. "Obviously I need to apologise," said Wedekind. "And I do, unequivocally."

"Come on in, Howard," said Shepherd.

"You're angry, I understand that. But you have to understand that I needed to carry out due diligence."

Shepherd opened the door wider but Wedekind stayed where he was.

"You understand that, Terry? It was nothing personal."

"Howard, stop babbling and come inside before my neighbours start to wonder what's going on." He gestured with his thumb for Wedekind to come inside. When Wedekind hesitated, Shepherd grinned. "Howard, if I was planning to hurt you, I'd hardly do it in my own flat."

Wedekind forced a smile and walked into the hallway. Shepherd closed the door, then led him into the sitting room. "Drink?" he asked.

"No, thanks," said Wedekind, sitting down on one of the sofas. "Look, obviously I need to explain what's been going on."

Shepherd sat in an armchair. There were three hidden cameras in the room, two of which covered the sofa, and half a dozen concealed microphones that ensured anything said in the room was relayed back to Thames House. "I'm listening."

Wedekind raised his hands. "I was carrying out due diligence, nothing more. We're doing business with you so we need to know if there are any problems."

"You had two men sitting in a car outside my apartment," said Shepherd. "That's not due diligence. What were you hoping to achieve?"

"We just wanted to be sure that you were . . ." He failed to finish the sentence.

"What, Howard? What were you scared of?"

"Not scared, Terry. Curious. You say you want to work for the brothers, and that's great, but you can't expect us to take everything you say on trust. What do we know about you? I mean, really know about you?"

Shepherd didn't say anything. It was better to let the man talk because Wedekind was nervous and nervous people tended to say too much.

"You could have all sorts of problems, and if you join the brothers, those problems might come with you. You can understand they wouldn't want that, can't you?"

Shepherd shrugged.

"I know Paul vouched for you and that's great, but he doesn't know everything there is to know, does he?"

"Like what, Howard?"

"Drugs, for instance. Do you have a drugs problem? Do you owe a dealer who might be after you? Do you sell drugs? And if you do, are the cops on your case?"

"You think I sell drugs?"

"We don't know, do we? That's why we carry out due diligence. That's all it is, Terry. We run checks on anyone we deal with."

"Let me get this straight," said Shepherd. "You checked with the cops? That's what you're saying, right? You did a PNC check on me?"

"We had you checked out, yes."

"You had a tame cop run my name through the Police National Computer?" Shepherd sat back and folded his arms. "Why the fuck would you do that?"

"I told you. Due diligence. You don't need to worry. It was one of the guys we use all the time. He doesn't know he's checking, just tells us what's there, that's all."

"All you had to do was ask me, you know that."

"It doesn't work that way, Terry."

"You don't think that having two goons sitting outside my apartment might cause me problems?"

"They're not goons, Terry. They're investigators. And you terrified them."

"Serves them right. They were lucky I didn't set fire to them. And, trust me, if I ever see them again I will." He glared at Wedekind, though it was disconcerting staring at the man because his wonky left eye was looking off to the side.

"Message received and understood, Terry."

"I'm serious, Howard. I don't appreciate being spied on."

Wedekind's smile vanished. "Understood."

"Tell me, was this your idea or Tommy or Marty's?"

"Due diligence is down to me."

"Now, hang on a minute, do the brothers know you were having me followed?"

"They trust me to do my job," said Wedekind.

"Don't fucking play with words, Howard. Just answer the question."

Wedekind took a deep breath. "Tommy and Marty deal with people they don't know through me. I insulate them from any problems. Only when I can vouch for you one hundred per cent will they even think about dealing directly with you. That's why due diligence is necessary. The brothers aren't aware of the specifics, but they know I'll be checking you out."

Shepherd frowned. "How long had your guys been tailing me?"

"A couple of days."

"They followed me to Reading, right?"

Wedekind folded his arms. "Yes."

"That explains why my guy didn't turn up," Shepherd snarled. "He must have seen them. Just them, or were they mob-handed?"

"Just them. They followed you to the service station but they got nabbed for speeding on the way back to London."

"Have you any idea what the fuck you've done?" spat Shepherd. "I was there to meet a guy who owes me thirty grand for a job I did. He was supposed to pay me. I waited but he didn't turn up and his phone's off now. He must have seen your guys and thought it was a set-up."

"I'm sorry about that, Terry."

"Sorry doesn't cut it!" he snapped. "If I lose that money, it's down to you."

"Calm down, Terry, please."

Shepherd stood up abruptly and Wedekind flinched. "I'm not going to fucking calm down!" he shouted. "You might have cost me thirty grand, and I'm not having that!"

"Okay, okay," said Wedekind. "I'll put it right."

"Damn right you will!" Shepherd bunched his right hand into a fist. "I should beat the crap out of you now, I really should."

He took a step towards Wedekind and the man flinched again. "Terry, please."

Shepherd relaxed and took a deep breath. "I'm serious, Howard. If my guy's done a runner and I don't get my money, it's down to you."

"Yes, agreed. Now, please, sit down."

Shepherd threw Wedekind a final withering look, then dropped into his chair.

"I apologise, Terry. It won't happen again."

"Damn right it won't," said Shepherd. "I need a fucking drink." He stood up and went over to a drinks cabinet. "You?"

"I'm fine," said Wedekind. Shepherd poured himself a gin and tonic, shielding the glass with his body so Wedekind couldn't see how little gin went into it.

"So, what did you want to talk about?" Shepherd sat down again.

"The brothers have another job for you, if you're interested."

"Sure." He sipped his drink. "What do they have in mind?"

"Similar to the Larry McGovern job. Take care of business and make sure no one finds them."

"Them?"

"A father and son. They've been giving the brothers all sorts of grief."

"No kids," said Shepherd. "I made that clear from the start."

"The son's twenty-eight," said Wedekind. "A Scouser by the name of Karl Palmer. They call him Lippy because he talks too much. His dad's Gerry. They ripped off a delivery the O'Neills had arranged. Container-load of marijuana coming on the cross-Channel ferry."

"They must have balls, ripping off the O'Neills," said Shepherd.

"They might not have known — but when they were told they didn't seem fazed. Tommy sent an emissary to negotiate for the return of the consignment but they broke his legs and bust his spleen. They took the view that they rule the roost in Liverpool and there's nothing the brothers can do to them."

Shepherd sipped his drink as Wedekind reached for his briefcase. He opened it, took out a couple of photographs and passed them to Shepherd. One was of a slightly overweight man in his fifties with a greying mullet and a sweeping grey moustache. The son also had a mullet but his hair was a shade of dark brown that looked as if it might have come from a bottle. He was wearing a denim jacket with the arms hacked off over a black leather motorcycle jacket. "The son's a biker?" asked Shepherd.

Wedekind nodded. "So's the father. A group called the Outlaws."

"They can be dangerous, bikers." He turned over the photograph of the father. The man's name and address were on the back.

"You can do it, though, can't you?"

"Sure. I know Liverpool well enough. It's just a question of timing."

"You won't be alone on this one," said Wedekind. "I'll put you in touch with another guy we're using. His name's Mark Ashton. He's based in Manchester."

"What the fuck?" said Shepherd. "I fly solo."

"Yes, of course, but the father and son tend to stick together. It's too tough a job for one."

"Yeah? Well, with respect, that's not your area of expertise, is it? I work best alone, end of."

"Tommy and Marty don't want any fuck-ups."

"I don't fuck up," said Shepherd. "I never have and I never will. I don't see how you can expect me to work with a stranger. That's asking for trouble."

"Mark's never let us down before. The brothers would use him more down here if they could but he prefers to stay up north."

"Howard, you can't take two professionals who've never worked together and assume they're going to get on. Everyone works differently."

"They do. You can sit down with Mark and work out how best to proceed."

"How best to proceed? The best way to proceed is to let me get on with it."

Wedekind forced a smile. "The brothers want a two-man team. If you're telling me you can't work as part of a team, I'll relay that back to them. But I think we both know how they'll react to that." He looked at Shepherd expectantly. "It's your call, Terry."

Shepherd glared at him, then took a long pull on his drink. He put down the glass, his eyes still on Wedekind. "Fine," he said eventually.

"Excellent," said Wedekind.

"How do I go about meeting this Ashton?"

"I'll arrange something," said Wedekind, standing up and grabbing his briefcase. "And, once again, my heartfelt apologies for what happened earlier."

"Yeah, well if you fix me up with the money thing I'll let bygones be bygones."

Shepherd showed Wedekind out and called Willoughby-Brown. "Did you get all that?" he asked.

"Every word, sound and vision," said Willoughby-Brown. "Nice job on muddying the waters re the M4."

"Did you know they'd done a PNC check on Terry Taylor?"

"That was news to me. You're flagged so we should be told as soon as it happens. Either he was bluffing or there's a problem. I'll check, obviously."

"Do we have enough now?"

"We're getting there," said Willoughby-Brown. "We have enough to pull in Wedekind, certainly. But the brothers aren't tied up yet."

"What do you think about this new job?" asked Shepherd.

"It could be another test," said Willoughby-Brown. "Or it could be they think of you as a team-player."

"He didn't buy the 'I work best alone' story."

"Taking out two targets needs two operatives, at least."

"Sure. But we're not going to be able to fake it if I've got a sidekick."

Willoughby-Brown chuckled. "To be honest, Daniel, I got the impression that Wedekind regards you as the sidekick."

"Semantics aside, you get my point?"

"I do, I do. We can hardly fake it if you're part of a team. Let me make some enquiries about Mark Ashton before we decide what to do. We might be able to take him out of the equation."

"We have Wedekind on video planning a murder. That's enough to nail him for conspiracy."

"Sure. But that's, what, somewhere between five and eight years? Out in four at the most. Is that likely to be enough to get him to give evidence against the O'Neills? I think not."

"So offer him witness protection?"

"It's four years, Daniel. Plus if we do show our cards, he'll know where he was recorded, which blows your cover."

Shepherd gritted his teeth in frustration. It wasn't what he wanted to hear but he knew Willoughby-Brown was right.

"Let me give it some thought," said Willoughby-Brown.

"Not too long," said Shepherd. "If they come for me I'm going to have to bail and then it'll be over."

"I hear you," said Willoughby-Brown. "My thinking cap is on. Oh, and while I have you, Miles Davies will see you tomorrow."

"Seriously? In the middle of this?"

"If you think about it, the timing is pretty much perfect. You're in town and all you're doing is waiting for the call. Miles will see you first thing. It's unlikely that the job will be that soon."

"I suppose so," said Shepherd.

"You'll be fine, Daniel," said Willoughby-Brown, and ended the call.

Omar finished washing the grease and oil from his hands and grabbed a paper towel. The door burst open and Zack walked in, clearly angry. "What are you doing?" he asked.

"What does it look like I'm doing?" said Omar, tossing the screwed-up towel into the waste bin.

"We've work backed up," said Zack, putting his hands on his hips and jutting his chin, like their father did when he was angry. "You need to help Toby with that gearbox. It has to be done by first thing."

"I've got to go," said Omar, taking his motorcycle jacket and helmet.

"You have to stay here," said Zack. "There's work to be done."

Omar tried to push past his brother but Zack grabbed his arm. Omar reacted instinctively. He had been taught unarmed combat by hardened jihadists in the desert and Zack was weak and flabby. In less than a second Omar had his brother up against the lockers, his face squashed against a metal door. Zack yelped in pain as Omar yanked his arm up behind his back. "Don't you dare lay your hands on me," hissed Omar.

"I'm sorry — I'm sorry!"

Omar knew he had gone too far and released his grip. Zack twisted around, rubbing his injured arm. "What the fuck was that?"

"I'm sorry," said Omar. "You caught me by surprise."

"What was it? Kung fu?"

"I dunno. I wasn't thinking."

"Bruv, are you okay?"

"Of course I am. I've just got stuff on my mind, that's all."

"Yeah? Like what?"

Omar's mind raced. He needed a lie and a good one. He wouldn't get away with the dental ruse again, but he needed some reason why he was leaving early. He had to take delivery of the fourth and final vehicle and had promised to pick it up at six.

"I've got a problem with a girl."

Zack frowned. "What girl?"

"I met her a few months back. English girl."

Zack's face broke into a grin. "You fucking an English girl, bruv? You always said you weren't into that." He punched Omar's arm. "You sly fuck."

Omar pretended to be embarrassed. "It's not funny," he said. "Girl says she's pregnant."

"You serious?"

284

"Says she's pregnant and swears it's mine but I think she's a slag, so who knows?"

"What are you going to do?"

"She says she wants to see me to talk it through. I thought I'd give her money to get rid of it." He put his hand on Zack's arm, "Don't tell Dad — he'll kill me."

"I won't. But be careful, bruv. She could be scamming you. Make sure you see her pee on a stick before you do anything. Bitches lie, you know that."

"I will, bruv. Thanks. So are you okay if I push off?"

"Yeah, you go and take care of business. I'll help Toby." He pointed a finger at Omar's face. "And don't forget. She pees on a stick before you do anything."

Omar thanked him and rushed out. He felt nothing but contempt for his brother. Zack was weak and a fool, but lying was better than confrontation. If Zack found out what he was really up to he'd turn him in. Omar had no doubt about that. He was a bad Muslim, a traitor to Allah, and one day he would pay the price for his disloyalty. But not today.

Shepherd had the black cab drop him around the corner from the address on the business card Willoughby-Brown had given him. The company that Miles Davies worked for was in the Shard, the tallest building in London. Their offices were about halfway up and the views were spectacular, though Shepherd barely noticed. He wasn't happy about having his psychological evaluation done by a new face. He'd always got on well with Caroline Stockmann and her no-nonsense approach. His evaluations with her had generally consisted of a chat over a few drinks in a pub. That didn't mean she wasn't professional: she was as sharp as a whip and didn't let anything get past her, but she made it more of a social occasion than an official visit.

The company that Willoughby-Brown was sending him to was called Mind-Set and had a logo of a lightning bolt zigzagging through the outline of a skull. The lift opened into a minimalist reception area, as gleamingly white as an operating theatre, with a tall blonde girl, wearing a headset, standing behind a plinth with a computer screen on it. "Can I help you?" she said, in a voice so flat and emotionless that he thought she might be mechanical.

"I'm here to see Miles Davies." He couldn't say the name without instantly being reminded of the jazz musician.

She smiled and tapped on a keyboard. "Your name, please?"

"Dan Shepherd."

"Please take a seat, Mr Shepherd. I'll let him know you're here." She smiled again, and her face went professionally blank. It was very disconcerting, and Shepherd looked at her closely, just to check that she was a real, breathing, human being. Her skin was flawlessly white, her eyes were unnaturally blue and her hair glistened like plastic.

There was only one place to sit: a low white sofa that was just inches off the floor. When Shepherd sat down his knees were above his waist and he knew he'd have trouble getting up. He wondered if it was a psychological trick, a way of putting visitors off balance. If it was, it didn't bode well.

"Can I get you something to drink, Mr Shepherd?" The blonde receptionist was smiling again. She had perfect teeth.

"No, I'm fine, thanks."

The smile vanished and she tapped on her keyboard. Shepherd wondered if she was recording his refusal to accept a drink. A large screen on the wall to his left showed a constantly changing pattern of swirling colours that seemed totally random. He stared at it until he felt light-headed and had to tear his gaze away.

"Mr Shepherd?"

He hadn't heard the woman walk up to him. She was a near-twin of the blonde behind the lectern, though this girl was a brunette. She was tall and model-thin, wearing a black suit and high heels that put her pretty much on tiptoe. Like the blonde, her eyes were dull and flat, though she had a toothpaste-commercial smile.

"Yes?"

"I'll take you through to Dr Davies," she said, and motioned towards two glass doors at the far end of the room.

Shepherd grunted as he pushed himself up off the sofa, and followed her through the doors. It was as minimalist and impersonal as the reception area, with white walls, steel bookcases and leather and stainless-steel chairs. Miles Davies was sitting behind a desk with only an Apple computer and a steel Newton's cradle on it. Davies's head was as smooth and shiny as the steel balls on the desk ornament, and the skin glistened in the sunlight streaming through the window behind him. It was only when he stood up and walked around the desk that Shepherd discovered how tall the man was — well over six feet. He had a slight stoop, as if he was ashamed of his height, and several inches of bare wrist stuck out of his jacket. He was in his forties, with ears like mug handles and deep creases across his forehead.

"Miles, good to meet you," said Shepherd, holding out his hand.

"Thanks for coming, Mr Shepherd," said Davies. "I'm Dr Davies in the office. It prevents any confusion." He waved Shepherd to the chair facing his desk. "Please, take a seat."

Shepherd sat down, wondering why the psychologist was so averse to using first names. Caroline Stockmann had always been Caroline. And all the psychologists he'd met before her had used their first names.

Davies sat in his chair, which was several inches taller than Shepherd's. "So, we'll have a quick chat and then I'll run you through some tests," he said. He had the bland, featureless accent of a BBC newsreader.

"Tests?"

Davies held up his hands. "There's no need to be worried," he said. "Just a few profiling programs that we've developed."

"I wasn't worried," said Shepherd. "Just interested. In the past the interviews have always been oral."

"We take a more scientific approach here," said Davies. "But don't worry, it's quite painless. So, you've been undercover for how long now?"

288

"On my present case, or as a career?"

"Well, both, I suppose."

"The present case, going on six months. As a career, well, I started working undercover for a Home Office unit in 2000, moved to SOCA, and then to my present position."

"Always undercover?"

"Pretty much. Though sometimes I'm running teams rather than being undercover myself."

"And would you say it's getting easier or harder as the years go by?"

Shepherd shrugged. "The same, I suppose."

"And has the nature of your targets changed over the years?"

"Of course," said Shepherd. "We only heard of al-Qaeda after Nine Eleven and Islamic State is a recent phenomenon. But organised crime and overseas agents have always been with us."

"Do you do much undercover work in the fight against jihadists?"

Shepherd smiled. "I'd stick out in a mosque, wouldn't I?"

Davies didn't smile. If anything his eyes became a little colder, and Shepherd saw his attempt at levity wasn't appreciated. "But, yes, in jihadist cases I tend to be running agents or helping in undercover operations."

Davies nodded slowly. He wasn't taking notes and Shepherd wondered if the conversation was being recorded.

"Tell me a bit about your current task," said Davies.

"It's the long-term penetration of a South London crime family," he said. "Drugs, extortion, fraud. They're a close-knit team, which is one of the reasons they've been so successful for so long. I'm posing as a hired killer and, if all goes to plan, they'll invite me into their inner circle."

"It sounds dangerous."

"It can be."

"You sound confident."

"I've been doing it for a long time."

"Familiarity breeds contempt?"

"No. I'm never complacent about the danger I'm in. But I'm a professional and I minimise the risks at all times. Wherever possible I'm around other people, or there's back-up close by."

"What if these criminals asked you to walk with them down a dark alley?"

"A lot would depend on what had happened up to that point," he said. "I'd be reading their body language, trying to get a handle on what was going on. Is the walk down the alley logical? Do they go ahead of me? Are they carrying? I'd be tapping into my subconscious feelings. Am I worried? Tense? Or does it all feel okay? It's a dark alley but do I have back-up close by? If there's doubt, I might test them. Lag behind to see how they react. Take out my phone, see if that provokes a reaction."

Davies smiled without warmth. "Must make for quite a bit of tension."

"Tension is a good thing," said Shepherd. "It keeps you on your toes."

"It can also result in high blood pressure, which in turn can lead to heart attacks and strokes."

"I have a yearly physical. Everything was just fine last time."

"The body can cope with increased levels of stress for long periods, then suddenly snap," said Davies. "Like putting a rope under pressure. Everything seems okay until one day the rope breaks."

"And you think that's my situation?" said Shepherd. "I'm reaching my breaking point?"

"You sound defensive, Mr Shepherd."

"I'm just trying to get a handle on your thought process here," said Shepherd. "Physically I'm fine. I can handle any stress that the job throws at me, but you make it seem like I'm about to implode."

"I don't mean to give that impression," said Davies. "I'm trying to get a handle on your thought processes, too, and the best way of doing that is to ask you questions. I'm sorry if it upsets you."

Shepherd smiled. "It doesn't upset me," he said, but even as the words left his mouth he knew he'd sounded defensive. He put up his hands, but that was a defensive move and he lowered them. "Ask away," he said.

"Oh, I think we're done," said Davies.

"That's it? That's all?"

"No, I mean we're done with the verbal questions. I'd like you to work through our programs now. They'll let us know what's going on in there." He stood up, walked around the desk and showed Shepherd to the door. He took him back through Reception and along a corridor where he opened the door to a small, windowless room. There was a table with a computer on it against one wall, and a high-backed orthopedic chair. Shepherd sat down in front of the screen. The firm's logo featured in the centre of a pale blue background.

"It's all done through the mouse," said Davies. "As soon as I've left the room, click on the logo. There's no rush, no time limit. Just answer the questions and perform the tasks presented to you. Any questions?"

"How long does it normally take?"

"That's up to you," said Davies. He left and closed the door behind him. Shepherd sighed, then stretched. He felt the tension in his neck and moved his head from side to side. He looked around the room. There was no sign of any camera and the walls were bare, but Shepherd was sure he was being watched. It wouldn't just be the way he performed on the tests that would count, but how he approached them. He took a breath, then clicked on the logo. A note filled the screen. He would be given two choices and he was to click on the one that most applied to him. Did he understand? YES or NO? He wondered what would happen if he clicked NO but he just smiled and clicked YES. The first question was simple enough. DO YOU PREFER TO GO FOR A WALK OR READ A BOOK?

Shepherd tilted his head to one side. He was quite happy doing either activity, and it was rarely a decision he had to make. Sometimes he'd do both, go for a walk, then read. It was a pointless question, except he doubted that Dr Miles Davies would waste his time on questions with no point. The answer would give a clue

292

to Shepherd's character and state of mind. Reading a book was more cerebral. Going for a walk suggested he favoured physical activity, which was probably how he felt. Was there anything wrong with that? Probably not. He clicked GO FOR A WALK.

The second question was equally bland. DO YOU PREFER TO EAT ALONE OR GO FOR A MEAL WITH FRIENDS? Obviously the sociable alternative was the preferable answer, even though Shepherd was perfectly happy eating on his own. He rattled through fifty or so either-or questions, then stopped as he stared at the screen. DO YOU PREFER TO READ A BOOK OR GO FOR A WALK? It was the first question he'd been asked, this time in reverse. He smiled to himself. The program was obviously checking to see how consistent his answers were but, considering his photographic memory, it wouldn't be a problem. He rushed through the questions on autopilot.

The next part of the test was more complex. He was shown a series of photographs and asked to choose from a number of options as to what the photographs showed. The first was of a man standing in front of a crying woman. There were four choices. THE MAN HIT THE WOMAN. THE MAN IS COMFORTING THE WOMAN. THE WOMAN IS THE MAN'S WIFE. THE WOMAN IS ASKING THE MAN FOR HELP. Shepherd frowned. The test appeared to be asking for a judgement based on emotion rather than fact. He stared at the photograph, then saw that both the man and the women were wearing wedding rings. And there was no reddening of the skin or marks that suggested she had been hit. The man was reaching out to the woman in a gesture that was definitely not threatening. She wasn't looking at him so Shepherd figured she wasn't asking him for help. He was trying to comfort her. He clicked that option and a second photograph flashed up. There were more than two dozen in all, and Shepherd spent several minutes on each, trying to use logic rather than gut feeling to choose the best option each time.

The next section was a series of TRUE/FALSE questions, most of which seemed to be asking for an emotional response. He answered them quickly and honestly.

The final section was based on the Rorschach inkblot test where a series of what appeared to be computer-generated inkblots flashed up on the screen along with six choices as to what Shepherd thought the design might represent. His hand tensed on the mouse, as he wondered what the purpose was. The Rorschach test was rarely used in the UK, though American psychologists tended to rely on it. The problem was that it wasn't an either-or test: there was no correct answer. What the test did was to get an indication of how the person thought, and when the psychologist showed the cards physically, he or she had the chance to ask follow-up questions. Getting Shepherd to choose the best answer from six made no sense.

Shepherd had seen the Rorschach inkblots before and he knew what the most common answers were. There were ten official ones, five of black ink, two of black and red ink, and three were multi-coloured.

Shepherd frowned as he studied the first shape. It looked like two hawks, standing back to back, but hawks wasn't a choice. Birds was. As was a bat. Two women talking. A kite. Trees. Children talking.

Birds would have been his first choice. But maybe he was supposed to personalise it and see people. Women or children? And the more he looked at it, the more it did look like a bat with outstretched wings. He was about to click BAT, then hesitated. Was he choosing too quickly? Or too slowly? And was he supposed to be taking the same time over each figure or were some supposed to be more difficult to identify? He chose the bat. The second shape looked like a horse's head and that was one of the choices so he clicked on it straight away. There were another dozen shapes and he stopped overthinking, clicking through them instinctively. As he clicked on the last one, the screen went blank. For a moment he thought something had gone wrong. Then a note flashed up: THANK YOU FOR COMPLETING THE TEST. SOMEONE WILL BE ALONG TO COLLECT YOU SHORTLY. HAVE A NICE DAY.

Shepherd wondered if "Have a nice day" suggested that the program was American. He sat back in his chair and stretched out his legs. Then he rubbed the back of his neck but stopped when he remembered that was a sign of tension. He looked at his watch and regretted it: that would show impatience. He smiled to himself and folded his arms, but that was defensive so he put them on the chair but that felt too stiff. He crossed his legs, which felt a bit more comfortable.

A minute passed and he realised that the delay was part of the test. They were seeing how he would react to being left on his own. He resisted the urge to grin. He was more than capable of playing the waiting game. Another minute passed. Then another. Shepherd was certain he was being tested. How should he react? He wanted to get up and pace around, but that would send out the wrong message. Or he could simply get up and walk out. Unless they had locked the door. Had they? And if they had, how was he supposed to react? It was probably best not to know if the door was locked because he wasn't sure how they would expect him to behave. Kicking it down might suggest he was aggressive. He had been told to wait until someone came to collect him, so it might be a test of his ability to obey instructions. But his job entailed using his initiative, and following instructions blindly could end badly. He stopped himself frowning. If they were watching they'd be studying his every reaction to see how he was feeling. He looked at his watch. Five minutes. Fine, he thought. He took out his mobile phone and swung his feet onto the desk. He tapped out Liam's number. For once his son answered immediately.

"Just calling to see how you are," said Shepherd.

"All good."

"What about the army papers?"

"It's in hand. I've spoken to the careers teacher and she's helping me."

"Was she happy?"

"Once I'd made up my mind she was really supportive. She said the school always tries to get its pupils to go on to further education but that in my case she thought I'd made the right decision."

"That's good."

"Yeah, it turns out she was an army brat. Her dad was in the Royal Engineers for most of the time she was a kid. We had a long chat about absent fathers."

"I'm sorry about that, Liam," said Shepherd. "I wasn't much of a dad, was I?" Immediately the words left his mouth he regretted it as he remembered he was probably being recorded.

"You were okay. When you were around, anyway."

"I get why you think it's an interesting career. Just be aware of the havoc it can cause to your nearest and dearest."

"Dad, I already told you I'm not planning to get married, not for a while anyway."

The door opened and Shepherd swung his feet off the table. It was the brunette, She smiled brightly and held the door open for him. "Got to go, Liam. I'll try to call you tonight."

"Love you, Dad."

"Love you, too," said Shepherd. He put the phone away and saw that the brunette's smile had widened. "My son," he explained.

She led him down the corridor. Shepherd assumed that he was going back to talk to Dr Davies, so he was surprised to find himself back in Reception.

"I thought I'd be seeing the doctor," he said.

"Dr Davies will be sending his report in later," she said.

"And I don't get a goodbye handshake?"

She held out an elegantly manicured hand. "Goodbye," she said.

Shepherd shook her hand. It was as cold as ice.

Mohammed al-Hussain was sitting on his bed reading his copy of the Koran when there was a soft knock on his door. He got up and opened it. It was Ash. "There's someone here to see you," he said. "Downstairs."

"Who is it?"

"He didn't say."

"You let a stranger into the house?"

"He's a Muslim, brother."

"You think there are no Muslims in the police?"

"He knew you were here, brother. If you want I can tell him you've gone out."

"It's too late for that," said al-Hussain. He put his hand on Ash's shoulder. "We have to be careful, brother. We have to be watchful. Nothing must get in the way of what we have planned."

"I understand, brother."

Al-Hussain went downstairs. The visitor was a bearded Asian man in his fifties with a bushy beard and straggly eyebrows. He was wearing a long coat over baggy trousers and Timberland boots. He was gazing out of the window and turned when he heard al-Hussain in the hallway.

"*Assalamu alaykum*," said the man.

"*Wa alaykum alsalam wa rahmatu Allahi wa barakaatuhu*," replied al-Hussain.

The man stepped forward and kissed him on both cheeks. "You are well, brother?"

298

Al-Hussain nodded. "I am."

The man waved at the sofa. "Please, sit."

Al-Hussain did so, and the man sat next to him. "Azmar al-Lihaib sends his regards," he said.

"Thank you," said al-Hussain.

"My name is Mahmod Abbas and I am here to facilitate the next stage of this operation," said the man. "I am told your weapon is suitable."

"Very suitable."

"And I understand you have calibrated the sights."

"It is ready."

"We will be moving you to London tomorrow. A new team will support you."

"When will I be told what I am to do?" asked al-Hussain.

"Just before it happens," said Abbas.

"It is disconcerting not to know."

Abbas smiled. "Of course. But for reasons of security, the fewer people who know what is planned, the better. But you can be sure that we will be using your skills to their full advantage." He leaned towards al-Hussain and lowered his voice to a hoarse whisper. "We understand why you had to kill Sunny. Under the circumstances it was the right thing to do." He looked left and right as if he feared being overheard, then leaned even closer. "The three men who are looking after you here. Do you think they will be a problem?"

"The one called Ash. He saw me kill Sunny."

Abbas nodded and smiled. "Ash is highly regarded. That is why he was chosen to be one of your minders."

"I sense he has doubts," said al-Hussain. "If he were ever to be put under pressure . . . But I will be leaving soon so perhaps his weakness will not be an issue. *Inshallah*."

"Do you think he should be dealt with?"

Al-Hussain looked pained. "It might be best."

"And the other two?"

Al-Hussain gave the slightest of shrugs. "If Sunny and Ash disappear, they might become suspicious."

"So all three, then?"

"It might be best," repeated al-Hussain.

"*Innaa lillahi wa inna ilayhi raaji'oon,*" said Abbas. To Allah we belong and to Him is our return.

"*La hawla wala quwwata illa billah,*" said al-Hussain. There is no strength or power except Allah.

The ringing of his mobile phone woke Shepherd from a dreamless sleep. He sat up. It was his work phone and the caller's number was withheld. He put it to his ear. "This is Angela," said a woman, in clipped no-nonsense tones. "Please confirm."

It was the MI5 control centre. Angela wasn't her real name. It was Monday so it could be any name, so long as it began with the letter A. Tomorrow would be B, Wednesday C and so on.

"Bravo Echo Sierra," said Shepherd. The three-letter designation changed every month.

"Is it safe to talk?"

"I certainly hope so."

"We've had a call from Turkey, a Craig Parker. He's on our list and we have confirmed his identity. He's asking to speak with John Whitehill."

"I'll call him," said Shepherd.

"Do you have a pen?"

Shepherd smiled to himself. "Yes," he said. It was easier to lie than to explain about his memory.

The woman read out Parker's phone number and Shepherd repeated it back to her without hesitation. She thanked him and ended the call.

Shepherd had half a dozen mobile phones on his side-board. He picked up a throwaway model he hadn't used before and tapped out the number. It rang through to voicemail but Shepherd didn't leave a message. He called again and this time Parker answered.

"Craig, it's John. You were trying to get hold of me."

"Have you heard what's happened to Yusuf?"

"Yusuf? No. Nothing. Why?"

"He's dead. Islamic State killed him, there's a video and everything. They hacked off his fucking head."

Shepherd put a hand up to his face and closed his eyes.

"They butchered his family, too. His wife and kids. They raped his wife and his daughters. One of them was eight, John. She was fucking eight years old. And they killed his son. Killed them all."

"I'm sorry," whispered Shepherd, knowing how lame the words sounded.

"They accused him of being a traitor, said this was a warning to anyone who thought about betraying Islamic State."

"Shit."

"They knew Yusuf had been helping you."

"Me personally?"

"No. But they know he was talking to the security services. They said that Yusuf had been passing intelligence to the British. How could they know that, John?"

"Maybe he talked out of school."

"He was careful. He was bloody careful."

"I'm sure he had enemies out there. Competitors who'd do him harm. How did they get to his family?"

"Stormed his villa and killed his guards. Then killed the family. And they buggered his son. What sort of animals do that?"

"That's what we're up against," said Shepherd. "That's why we have to win."

"Yeah. Well, I'm at the airport. I'm leaving right now."

"They know about you?"

"How could they not? Yusuf and I used to hang out all the time at the camp."

"But you haven't been directly threatened?"

"They're not stupid. They're not going to broadcast their intentions, are they? But I'm not giving them the chance to put me in an orange jumpsuit and hack my head off."

"I'm sorry."

"Yeah, well, sorry doesn't cut it. I'm now totally fucked in the region. Anywhere Islamic State operates I'll be at risk. How the fuck did this happen?"

"I don't know," said Shepherd.

"This could be the end of my job, you know that?" said Parker. "My bosses are going to want to know why I'm bailing out."

"Tell them Yusuf was a friend. They'll understand. He was getting you pharmaceuticals, right? Islamic State have killed him and that puts you at risk. They can take you out of the field."

"That's not the point," snapped Parker. "I want to be in the field. I want to be where I'm doing the most good, not hiding behind a desk. But if I go anywhere in the region I'll be a marked man. Fuck it, this is so fucking unfair."

"It's not the end of the world. Look, you're already drawing a Five salary. It would be easy enough to work for them full time. Or for Six."

"Be a spook full time?"

"Why not? You've been on the payroll for years. We need people like you, Craig. You know what's happening on the ground."

Shepherd heard an announcement in the background. "They're calling my flight," said Parker. "I've got to go."

"Ring me when you get to London," said Shepherd. "We can talk it through."

"I'm not going to London," said Parker. "I'll be in the Philippines working on the typhoon-relief project. I'll be there for a while."

"Well, get in touch whenever," said Shepherd. "And I'm sorry about Yusuf."

"You and me both," said Parker. The line went dead.

They came for Mohammed al-Hussain just after dawn. He had already washed and prayed, had packed his bag and was reading his Koran when Ash walked upstairs and told him it was time to leave. Ash hugged him, kissed him on both cheeks and wished him well. There was no sign of the other two men in the house and it was Ash who took al-Hussain outside to the waiting car.

There were two Asians in the front and he climbed into the back. The driver only spoke twice, once to ask al-Hussain if he wanted to listen to the radio and again two hours later to ask if he needed to use the bathroom. Al-Hussain said no to both.

After three hours, they reached the outskirts of London and drove to Tower Hamlets. It was like another country. Everyone he saw on the pavements was Asian. There were women in hijabs and even full burka. Most of the men, young and old, were bearded and a lot wore traditional clothing — long robes, baggy trousers and skull caps. There were as many Arabic and Urdu signs as there were English, and every butcher announced that his meat was halal.

They drove to an area of terraced houses, the streets lined with old cars and vans, litter blowing across the pavements. Groups of young men stood on street corners smoking cigarettes, and most of the women were accompanied by young children or were pushing prams.

The car turned down a narrow alley and slowed to walking pace as it bucked and bounced over the rough surface. Stained brick walls were dotted with rotting wooden doors leading to backyards. A stray dog left it until the last moment to scamper out of their way and glared at them resentfully as they went by.

They stopped midway down the alley. The passenger got out and used a key to unlock a door, pushed it open and disappeared inside.

The driver turned. "Are you okay, brother?"

Al-Hussain nodded.

"Salman is just checking that the house is secure," he said.

Al-Hussain nodded again.

"You speak English?" asked the man.

Al-Hussain smiled. "Yes."

"Salman will stay with you. I will leave you here."

The door opened and Salman motioned for al-Hussain to join him. He grabbed his backpack and opened the door.

"Good luck, brother," said the driver. "*Baraka Allahu fika*." May Allah bestow his blessings on you.

Al-Hussain thanked him and got out of the car with his bag. Salman kept the door open for him, then locked it behind them. The yard was cluttered with two wheelie bins, several rusting bicycles stacked together, an old fridge and sheets of stained plasterboard. Salman hurried past al-Hussain and opened a glass-panelled door that led into a kitchen. It was filthy, with a grease-stained cooker, grimy work surfaces and a stainless-steel sink piled high with dirty dishes. "Sorry about the mess," he said. "We were planning to clean today but then we got the call to come and get you."

Al-Hussain said nothing. The place was disgusting, which meant the man had no military training. Soldiers did not live like pigs, wallowing in their own filth.

The kitchen led into a hall. There were stairs to the left, and to the right a sitting room from which came the sound of shooting. "That's Addy," said Salman.

Addy was a bearded Asian in his late twenties, wearing a grubby *shalwar kameez*. He was bare-footed and his toenails were yellowing and engrained with dirt. He was staring at a large TV and playing a shoot-'em-up video game, blowing away soldiers with a carbine. As Salman stepped into the room, Addy was throwing a digital hand grenade that exploded, killing three men in a fiery blast.

"Addy," said Salman.

Addy flinched, then smiled when he saw Salman. His smile broadened when he spotted al-Hussain in the hallway. "Hello, brother," he said, putting his video controller on the table and standing up. He embraced al-Hussain and kissed him on both cheeks. "I didn't hear you arrive."

Al-Hussain said nothing, but he didn't like the way Salman and Addy were behaving. They were living like animals, and Addy hadn't even noticed people coming in through the kitchen. There appeared to be no security procedures in place, which was worrying, but there was no point in confronting the two men with their stupidity. "Where is my room?" he asked.

"Upstairs," said Salman. "I'll take you."

He led al-Hussain up the stairs to the front bedroom. Al-Hussain sighed. "I should be at the back," he said.

"The back?"

"The front bedroom is overlooked. People will see me move around. I need to be at the back."

306

"That's where we sleep," said Salman.

"Then we need to change rooms," said al-Hussain. "I cannot sleep here."

"Okay, okay. Sorry. I'll move our things."

"I shall wash while I wait," said al-Hussain.

Salman showed him where the bathroom was. Al-Hussain's heart sank when he saw the state it was in. If anything, it was even more disgusting than the kitchen. The bath was stained, there were smears of toothpaste across the shelf above the sink and the shower curtain was spotted with black mould. "Is everything all right, brother?" asked Salman.

Al-Hussain forced a smile. "Everything is fine, brother. Please prepare my room. And perhaps you wouldn't mind cleaning it and changing the sheets."

"I don't think we have any clean sheets," said Salman. "We haven't done any laundry for a while." He smiled. "We don't have any women in the house."

Al-Hussain's voice hardened a fraction. "Then go out and buy some, brother," he said. "Now."

Shepherd called Willoughby-Brown's mobile. It rang half a dozen times, then went through to voicemail. He ended the call and dialled again. Voicemail. He sent a text message. *I need to talk to you. Urgent.* He left it two minutes and called again. This time Willoughby-Brown answered. "I'm in a meeting, Daniel," he said tersely.

"I need to see you. Where are you?"

"I'm at Vauxhall Cross all afternoon."

The MI6 building at Vauxhall Cross was the headquarters of the British Secret Intelligence Service. It was at 85 Albert Embankment, south-west London, overlooking the River Thames.

"I'll see you at Vauxhall Pleasure Gardens in one hour," said Shepherd.

"Daniel, I'm in meetings all afternoon."

"If you're not there I'll come into the building and drag you out," said Shepherd. He ended the call. Talking to his boss like that probably wasn't a great career move, but just then he didn't care whether or not he continued to work for Willoughby-Brown.

Fifty minutes after he'd made the call, Shepherd took the tube to Vauxhall, carrying out only basic counter-surveillance measures. He paced around the perimeter of the park, partly to confirm that he wasn't being followed but mainly because he had energy to burn. His heart was pounding and he could feel the adrenalin surge kicking in.

He walked into the park and across to where a group of teenagers were kicking a ball on a tarmac football pitch. Another group wearing near-identical Puffa jackets were watching and handing around a hand-rolled cigarette. Shepherd was too far away to tell if it was marijuana or not, but from the reverence with which they treated it, he figured it probably was.

There was an empty bench but he didn't feel like sitting. He looked at his watch. Willoughby-Brown was five minutes late. Shepherd wasn't sure if he should try to carry out his threat because he was fairly certain he'd be stopped at Reception if he turned up without an appointment, even with his Home Office ID.

He took out his phone and checked the screen to see if Willoughby-Brown had tried to contact him but there had been no calls or messages. As he slipped the phone back into his jacket pocket, he saw the man striding across the grass, coat flapping around his knees. Shepherd walked towards him, trying to get his thoughts in order. His heart was racing with the same intensity he felt prior to a firefight. He was angry but controlled, and while verbally attacking his boss wasn't the best career move, there was no way he could let Willoughby-Brown get away with what he'd allowed to happen to Yusuf.

Willoughby-Brown stopped by a bench but didn't sit down. He waited for Shepherd to walk up to him, his hands thrust into the pockets of his coat.

Shepherd opened his mouth to speak but Willoughby-Brown beat him to it. "I don't take kindly to being spoken to like that, Daniel," he said. "You work for me, remember. Not the other way around."

"I work for MI5," said Shepherd. "I just happen to report to you. That can change."

"Indeed it can," said Willoughby-Brown. "But insubordination isn't going to help you career-wise, no matter who you report to."

"Yusuf Yilmaz is dead. Did you know?"

"He mixed with some very dangerous people."

"Yeah? Well, his wife and kids were in a safe house and they died too."

"He was a people-trafficker, Daniel. He worked for Islamic State. With the best will in the world it was never going to end well."

"So you knew?"

"Of course I knew."

"And you didn't think to tell me?"

"Your part in that operation is over. You went over, you debriefed him, you passed the information on, end of story."

"How is that the end of the story? I went over to negotiate his package. We were offering him passports and money in exchange for his intel."

Willoughby-Brown shook his head. "No. That was what he was demanding. We never agreed to anything."

"We gave him the impression we were agreeing terms."

"Again, that's not the case. You might have given him that impression but all you were supposed to do was have sight of his intel."

"Which I did, and I gave the intel to you."

"Exactly. And then there was no point in doing a deal with him."

"Because you had what you wanted. That's theft."

Willoughby-Brown chuckled. "Oh, come on, now you're being ridiculous." He took a packet of small cigars from his pocket and lit one. He began to walk, giving Shepherd no choice other than to follow him. "I understand that you're upset, but your empathy is misplaced. Yusuf Yilmaz was no hero. We owed him nothing."

"He came to us for help."

Willoughby-Brown blew a tight plume of smoke at the ground. "No. He came to us to make a profit from his dealings with Islamic State. If he'd asked us to get his family out, that would have been a request for help. But have you forgotten he wanted a million dollars? He wanted paying."

"We could have negotiated."

"We didn't need to. He was trying to sell us something we already had."

"You're going around in circles," snapped Shepherd. "He's dead. His family are dead, and you're playing with words."

"I'm sorry about his family," said Willoughby-Brown. "But you can't blame Five for that. He should have protected them better. He knew they were targets."

"You're blaming him? You're unbelievable."

"Daniel, everything that has happened is a result of the choices he made. No one forced him to become a people-trafficker, and no one forced him to deal with Islamic State. At the end of the day all his choices were about making money. And as I said, when he came to us, it was money he wanted. He was betraying the people he'd been working for. Your sympathy is misplaced."

"We promised to help him."

"No, we didn't. We were negotiating. But he was a fool and gave away his bargaining power."

Shepherd shook his head angrily. "You were setting him up to betray him. That's why you sent me. You knew that once I'd seen his intel it no longer had any value."

"I knew he wouldn't let us make copies. So it made sense to send someone who could at least remember what he'd seen. And it was his call. He could have refused. He could have shown you just one."

"If he'd shown me one and held back the rest, you'd have flown him and his family to London?"

"Possibly. It wouldn't have been my call."

"So now you're blaming me? You're saying the fact that I told him to show me all the passports resulted in his death? And the death of his family?"

Willoughby-Brown stopped walking, stuck his cigar between his lips and reached into his jacket pocket. He pulled out a sheaf of photocopied sheets and handed one to Shepherd. "You remember this guy?"

It was a police photograph of an Asian man in his twenties, two side views against a scale, showing that he was five feet nine inches tall, and a front view. Bearded, hooked nose, dead eyes. Shepherd frowned. He'd seen that face in one of the passports Yusuf had supplied to Islamic State.

"I can see from your face that you do," said Willoughby-Brown. He gave Shepherd a second sheet. Another police mugshot. Another bearded man. Another face on a Syrian passport that Yusuf had provided. "And this guy. They both made it to Germany. They were in Cologne when they dragged a nine-year-old girl into an alley and beat her almost to death. They were caught before they could kill her and they were carrying the Syrian passports Yilmaz had arranged. The local police examined their phones and

312

found all sorts of IS material. Videos of beheadings, tutorials on IEDs, all sorts of nasty stuff."

Shepherd recognised the second man, too. "What's happening to them?" he asked.

"They'll be charged. Hopefully convicted. The little girl they attacked is still in hospital. The doctors doubt she'll ever be able to have children of her own. All sorts of internal damage." He blew smoke. "Do you feel like telling her parents you wanted to give a million dollars to the man who sent those two animals to rape their daughter?"

"That's a bit simplistic and you know it."

"I know that if Yilmaz had come to us when he'd first been approached by Islamic State we could have tracked them and picked them up once they arrived in Europe. Or kept them under surveillance. They got to Cologne six months ago. Who knows what else they've done? Rapes have gone through the roof in Germany since the migrants poured in."

"Yusuf couldn't have known what they'd do. You can't blame him for that."

"Actually, yes, I can. And I do. He knew he was supplying passports for Islamic State fighters, not refugees. That's why he kept those copies, the ones he showed you. He knew what he was doing and don't try to tell me he didn't."

He handed over several more photocopied sheets. It was a Europol report, written in French with an English translation. Shepherd quickly read through the English version as Willoughby-Brown smoked his cigar.

It was dated 19 November and detailed the police raid in Saint-Denis the previous day when armed police had killed Abdelhamid Abaaoud, the Islamic fundamentalist who had organised the attacks in Paris that had killed 130 people. The attacks had been well-planned and coordinated with three suicide bombers near the Stade de France in Saint-Denis, followed by more suicide bombings, mass shootings at restaurants and cafés, and culminating in an attack on the Bataclan theatre in Boulevard Voltaire, where gunmen wearing suicide vests mowed down eighty-nine people with AK-47s.

Shepherd read through the details of the police raid and its aftermath, and felt a chill run down his spine as he studied the list of terrorists who had died along with Abdelhamid Abaaoud. He recognised one of the names. He looked up at Willoughby-Brown, confusion etched on his face. Willoughby-Brown nodded. "You see it now?"

Shepherd opened his mouth but words failed him.

"One of the men Yilmaz got a passport for was working with Abdelhamid Abaaoud and died with him. We don't know for sure what his role was in the Paris attacks, but I do know this, Daniel. If Yilmaz had given us those names earlier, we might have known what was being planned. And if we'd known about it, maybe, just maybe, the French could have stopped it. As it is, Yilmaz played a part in the murder of a hundred and thirty innocent civilians in France. A small part, perhaps, but a part nonetheless. So you won't find me shedding a tear over his demise. I feel bad for his

314

family, but the guilt for that lies on his shoulders, not mine."

He held out his hand and Shepherd gave the papers back to him.

"I get that you're not happy about what happened to Yilmaz but you need to remember two things. One, he brought it upon himself. And two, we have yet to see how many of the Islamic State fighters have come our way. Because all the signs are that what happened in Paris is going to happen here and if it does . . ." He left the sentence unfinished and put the papers back into his coat. He took another drag on his cigar, then flicked ash onto the grass. "I have to say I resent the way you spoke to me, but I understand your frustration and I'll let it pass this time." He flashed Shepherd a cold smile. "Consider this a yellow card, Daniel." He looked at his watch. "Now, as much as I enjoy open-air chats, we'll have to end it here. We need to talk again soon because the results from your psych evaluation are in, but not today." He tossed the remains of his cigar away. "And I'll need an update on the O'Neill operation at some point." With that he turned and set off towards the MI6 building.

It was only when Shepherd was walking out of the park that he realised Willoughby-Brown had been expecting his outburst. Why else would he have been carrying the details of the Cologne rape and the Paris terrorist attack in his coat? He cursed under his breath, annoyed with Willoughby-Brown but even more annoyed with himself.

       ★   ★   ★

Shepherd had just microwaved himself a Marks & Spencer ready-meal when his Terry Taylor phone rang. It was Paul Evans. "How's it going, mate?" asked Evans.

"All good," said Shepherd.

"What are you up to?"

"Just about to tuck into sausage and mash," said Shepherd.

"Fuck that for a game of soldiers," said Evans. "I'll pick you up outside in half an hour."

"Business or pleasure?"

Evans laughed. "Bit of both." He ended the call.

Shepherd finished his meal, drank a coffee and was outside on the pavement five minutes before Evans pulled up in his Range Rover. There was another man sitting in the front passenger seat and Shepherd climbed into the back. "This is Billy," said Evans.

Billy twisted around in his seat and shook hands with Shepherd. He was in his late twenties with close-cropped blond hair and a strong jaw. "How's it going?" He had a strong Belfast accent.

"Billy's over from Ireland for a few days," said Evans.

"Yeah?" said Shepherd, settling back in his seat and trying to work out what was going on.

"He used to work for me but missed the old country too much," said Evans.

Billy laughed. "Yeah, that'll be right. My ma's getting on and she wants me close by."

"Sorry to hear that," said Shepherd.

"No, she's fine. Fit as a fiddle. But my sister's in Chicago and my brother's out in Australia so I'm all she's got. My da passed away a few years back."

"Where are your family, Terry?" asked Evans.

"My dad walked out when I was a kid," said Shepherd. "My mum died when I was a teenager."

"Brothers? Sisters?"

"I was an accident. Dad married Mum when he got her pregnant, then walked out when he decided he didn't want to be a father. Or a husband." The Terry Taylor background was second nature to Shepherd — it had to be so that it sounded completely natural whenever he talked about it.

"Still, you turned out all right," said Evans.

"Yeah," said Shepherd. "I guess." They were heading east, staying south of the river. "So, what's the story, Paul?"

"Collecting some money we're owed," said Evans. "This is just a chat but I needed back-up."

"I'm not carrying," said Shepherd.

"Bloody hell, Terry, chill," laughed Evans. "It's a chat. If it was going to be heavy I'd have told you."

They drove through Camberwell and on to Peckham, where Evans parked the Range Rover across the road from a large pub. The three men climbed out. "You'll get a kick out of this," said Evans, patting Shepherd on the back. They walked to the pub's entrance where two huge men with shaved heads and spider-web tattoos on their necks were standing guard. A wooden blackboard had been set up at the side of the door: CLOSED FOR PRIVATE FUNCTION.

"Paul, long time no see," said one of the men. He held out his hand and Evans shook it. Then they bumped shoulders. Evans introduced Shepherd and the man nodded but didn't offer to shake hands.

"What time's he on?" asked Evans.

"Eleven," said the bouncer. "He's coming in the back way, through the kitchen. You know how it works. If the lefty tree-huggers know he's around they'll be out like flies around shit."

Shepherd and Billy followed Evans inside. It was an oblong room with a bar running pretty much its full length. At the far end there was a raised stage with a large-screen TV on the wall, flanked by flags bearing the cross of St George. A banner reading ENGLAND RULES had been strung above the television. The bar was almost full and customers three deep were fighting to attract the attention of the half-dozen bar staff.

Evans jerked a thumb at the bar. "Get them in, Billy," he said. "I'll have a beer."

"Me too," said Shepherd.

Evans headed to the bar. "So why are we here?" Shepherd asked him. He gestured to the crowd at the bar. They were mainly young men in bomber jackets with shaved heads and tattoos. "Not your sort of place, I'd have thought."

Evans grinned and gestured at the stage. "I'm here to talk to the guy they've come to see," he said. "Simon Page. You heard of him?"

Shepherd had. In fact, a few years earlier, he'd seen the man in action. Back then Page had been deputy chairman and chief fundraiser for an anti-immigration organisation called England First. Shepherd had been undercover and had gone along to a meeting with Jimmy Sharpe. "England First, right?"

Evans nodded. "Used to be. He's set up his own group now." He pointed at the sign. "England Rules. He borrowed some money from Tommy to set the thing up." Before Evans could say anything else there was a cheer at the far end of the room as two men in shiny black bomber jackets opened a door. They were followed by Simon Page. His chestnut hair had greyed at the temples since Shepherd had seen him. He was wearing an immaculate double-breasted suit and a red and blue striped tie. Behind him, a younger man in a blue blazer and grey trousers was carrying an aluminium briefcase.

The whole pub was cheering now and a group of skin-heads in olive combat jackets and cherry red Dr Martens boots began chanting Page's name. Page stepped onto the stage and raised his arms, smiling broadly. The man in the blazer had sat down at the side of the stage and taken a laptop computer from the case. He opened it and plugged a wire into the USB slot.

Another man, older and wearing a tweed jacket with leather patches on the elbows, stepped onto the stage holding a microphone. He put up a hand for quiet. "Ladies and gentlemen, thank you for coming out this evening to listen to our guest. He needs no introduction. He's a true patriot, a man who believes in his country and who is prepared to fight for it. Listen to what he has to say, and dig into your pockets to give whatever you can to support him." He held out his hand to Page. The two men shook. "So, ladies and gentlemen, I present Simon Page."

The crowd cheered and applauded as the man handed the microphone to Page and stepped off the stage. Page stood with his feet shoulder width apart, his chin up, as he basked in the adulation. He stood still and waited for the crowd to fall quiet. Only then did he put the microphone to his mouth. "I'm proud to be English," he said. "I'm proud of this country and I'm proud of the people of this country. Are you? Are you proud to be English?"

The crowd roared and cheered. Page smiled and waited for the noise to subside.

"There's a lot to be proud of," he said. "The English have fought and died for this country. My own grandfather died fighting Germany, and so did his brother. They gave their lives for the freedoms we have today. But the England they fought and died for doesn't exist any more."

He nodded at the man in the blazer, who tapped on the laptop keyboard. A picture flashed up of a London street scene, some time in the 1940s or 1950s. It was in black-and-white. People were standing at a bus stop. It was drizzling and most were carrying umbrellas. The men wore long coats and hats, the women skirts, with hats or headscarves. A double-decker bus had pulled up and a man was standing to the side to let a woman get on first. "This is the London they died for," said Page.

He waved at the man in the blazer and the image changed. It was a view of present-day London. A street market. Everyone in the picture was Asian or black. All of the women were wearing burkas. "This is London today, my friends. And if my grandfather and his brother saw this, they'd be spinning in their graves!"

A group of skinheads at the front began shouting at the screen. "Fucking Pakis! Paid bastards!"

Page walked over the stage towards them and wagged a finger at them. "No lads!" he shouted. "No insults! Name-calling gets us nowhere!"

The skinheads fell silent. Page continued to talk directly to them.

"The days of free speech in this country are long gone," he said. "The powers that be are taking away the freedoms that my grandfather and his brother died protecting. You can't abuse them because of their colour or their nationality. You use words like that in a public place and the police can and will arrest you. So, no name-calling! And remember that actions speak louder than words!"

The skinheads began shouting, "ENG-ER-LUND," at the tops of their voices and Page strutted around the stage, pumping his fist into the air.

When the cheering subsided, he pointed at the picture on the screen. "How did we get to this place?" he asked his audience. "How did we go from a London where everyone was English to a London where there are no white faces? How did that happen?"

"Immigration!" shouted someone behind Shepherd.

Page nodded. "Exactly," he said. "Immigration. So let's talk about immigration, shall we?"

A picture flashed up on the screen behind Page and he turned to look at it. It showed a group of Asians behind a wire fence. "You know what this is?" he asked, turning to face his audience. "That's the border between Syria and Turkey. What do you see?" He turned back to the screen and began pointing at faces. "Women," he said. "Old women, mothers, young girls. Families. Men holding toddlers, women clutching babies." He looked back at the audience. "That is what refugees look like, my friends. Families fleeing for their lives. And what do refugees do when they reach safety?"

The picture changed. It was a refugee camp. It wasn't the one that Shepherd had visited because the tents were smaller and arranged haphazardly. There were families gathered in groups and children everywhere, many of them smiling at the camera. "They thank their God that they're safe and they set about making a life for themselves. That's what thousands of Syrian refugees are doing in Turkey. It's the country next door, plenty of mosques for them, plenty of people who are just like them. Good schools, reasonable hospitals, and it's safe. So safe that my sister-in-law went there on holiday last year with her family. She had a great time."

He looked back at the screen and another picture flashed up, this one of a beach packed with holidaymakers lying under striped beach umbrellas. "This is Turkey," said Page. "People pay good money to go there on holiday and, from what my sister-in-law says, they have a ball." The picture changed. A group of holidaymakers in a bar, raising their wine glasses. Another picture. Holidaymakers around a swimming pool being served drinks by beaming waiters. "Turkey

322

is generally safe, it's prosperous, the people are friendly. And if the bureaucrats in Strasbourg get their way, Turkey will be joining the EU sooner rather than later. So, if you were a refugee, wouldn't you stay there? Maybe as a stop-gap until things improve back home, or maybe apply for Turkish citizenship? That's what refugees would do, right?"

He waved at the screen and the picture changed.

The image was of a rubber dinghy packed with Asian families wearing bright orange lifejackets. A man was holding the tiller of a small outboard motor. "So, why do these so-called refugees pay traffickers for places on boats like this to get from Turkey to Greece? Turkey is a safe haven. Turkey will give them a place to live, food and medical treatment. But that isn't good enough for them. They want more. They want to be in Europe. So they put their families in leaky boats and risk the lives of their children to sail to Greece. But even Greece isn't good enough for them."

The picture changed again. The new one was of hundreds of Asian men walking through farmland. It could have been Hungary, Bosnia maybe.

"Now look at this picture," said Page. "What do you see? Do you see families? Do you see children? What do you see? Fit, healthy men, that's what I see. Men who could be fighting for their country. But what are they doing?" He turned to point his finger at the screen. "I'll tell you what they're doing. Some of them are heading for Germany because they've been told they're welcome there. But most of them are on their way here. They want to come to England, because in England we'll give them a house and money and expect nothing in return." There were jeers from the crowd and he turned back to them. "These are not refugees. Refugees would have stayed in Turkey. If they were refugees and wanted to be in Europe, they could have stayed in Greece." He waved at the screen. "Here they're in Hungary. A perfectly safe country. Are they stopping there? No. Why? Because they're not refugees. They're migrants. The idea that these people are refugees, fleeing for their lives, is bollocks. Do they look scared? Are they running? Do they look like they're starving?"

Another picture flashed up. A group of Asian men sitting on a wall studying smartphones. "They're not running," said Page. "They're travelling. And I'll ask the question again. Why aren't these healthy, fit males fighting for their country? When the Germans invaded France, did millions of French cross the Channel to England? No, they didn't. And in the darkest days of the Second World War, did the British get into rubber dinghies and flee to Ireland? No, they did not. They stood and they fought. They fought for their country. My grandfather gave his life for this country. He died in France, with a gun in his hand. He didn't run. I'm sure he could have done. I'm sure he could have got onto a boat and sailed to America if he wanted. But he didn't. He fought for his country." Page jabbed his finger at the picture on the screen. "Why aren't these men fighting for their country? Do we want these cowards in our country, living in our council houses and taking our benefits, clogging up our schools and our hospitals?"

There were angry shouts of "No!" from around the room.

Page raised a fist into the air. "No, we don't!" he shouted. "Enough is enough! It's time for the English to fight back!"

The audience cheered. Shepherd looked at Evans, who was standing with his arms folded, his face impassive. Evans must have felt his gaze because he turned to grin at Shepherd. "He knows how to work a crowd, doesn't he?"

Shepherd didn't say anything. He still wasn't sure why they were there. Evans had never struck him as a racist.

The cheering subsided and Page was speaking again. "Now, the papers will say that our organisation is racist, that I'm racist," he said, almost as if he had read Shepherd's mind. "They say that anyone who stands up for their country is racist. But this isn't about being racist. I'm not racist and our organisation isn't racist." He shaded his eyes and peered at the crowd. "Where's Tony?" he shouted. "Where are you, mate?"

"Over here!" shouted a voice by the bar. Everyone turned to look at a big black man, who was waving both hands over his head. He was in his fifties, his hair greying, but his body showed he spent a lot of time in the gym.

"Tony, tell them how long we've been mates," shouted Page.

Tony grinned, showing a wall of gleaming teeth. "Forty years, give or take," he replied.

"That's right," said Page. "Tony and I were at school together. Best mates for four decades." He pointed at him. "I love that guy. I'd fucking die for him. So the next time anyone calls me a racist, or calls our organisation racist, you can tell them what-for."

The crowd erupted with applause. People were slapping Tony on the back and shaking his hand.

"Because this isn't about race," said Page. "This is about culture. About being British. Don't get me wrong. I'm happy for foreigners to come and live here, if they're needed. Doctors, nurses, teachers, if they have skills we need then let's welcome them. But if they come, if they want to live in our country, they have to adopt our ways. If you want to live in Britain, you have to want to make Britain great. That should be a given. Here's what I say, guys. If you want to live in England, you should be happy going into an English pub and drinking a pint of English beer. And you should be able to sit down and eat a full English breakfast."

"Too fucking right!" shouted a skinhead at the front.

"The problem is, we're letting people in who don't want to belong. They don't want to be English. They don't want to drink our beer or eat a full English." He shaded his eyes and looked at the bar. "What about you, Tony? What do you think about the full English?"

"I fucking love it!" shouted Tony, to cheers and applause.

Page turned to the screen, which was filled with a picture of a group of elderly Asians sitting in a line outside a café, smoking hookahs. Above them there was a red canopy with white Arabic writing on it. Page

326

pointed at the picture. "Do you know where that is? Kabul? Baghdad? Islamabad? No. It's Edgware Road, not two miles from here."

Another picture flashed up. A market street packed with Asians. "That's Southall," said Page. "Let's play Where's Wally, shall we? But instead of looking for Wally, let's play Where's the White Face?" He folded his arms and stared at the picture for several seconds. "Well, I can't find him, can you?"

There were cries of "No!" from around the room.

"This isn't multi-cultural," said Page. "This is an invasion. An invasion that our politicians are happy to see."

Another photograph flashed up. It had been taken in a school. The teacher was Asian and all the pupils were Asian or black. "Do you know where that photograph was taken? Africa? South America? Jamaica? No. Tower Hamlets. That's a London school. How many white faces do you see in that picture?"

There were cries of "None!"

"Exactly," said Page. "This is London. The capital city of our great country. Can you tell me why there are no white children in that class? How can that happen? How can that be allowed to happen?"

The picture changed. A country church, with a vicar saying goodbye to parishioners. Men in suits, women in coats and hats, smiling children. All white. "This is an English church. This how the English worship. As families."

Another picture. A mosque. Worshippers were praying in the street outside, all Asian men. "This is how our new arrivals worship. There are now so many that the mosques are full and they have to pray in the streets. Do the police move them on? No. They don't. Can you imagine what would happen if we all went outside and blocked the road? They'd be here mob-handed in minutes and they'd start cracking heads. But Muslims? No, they can do what they want. Why? Because this country is soft on Muslims. We allow them to slit the throats of the animals they eat, we allow them to have as many wives as they want, and we pay for them to breed. It's time to say enough is enough!"

Shepherd's eyes narrowed as he stared at the photograph. In it, he saw two Asian men in their twenties, bearded and wearing skull caps. One had his hands in his pockets and the other was holding an apple. Shepherd recognised both men. He had seen them on Yusuf's Syrian passports.

The crowd burst into applause. Page waved for them to be quiet. "So, what can you do? That's what you want to know, right?"

"Kill them!" shouted a skinhead.

"Burn them out!" shouted another.

"Hang them!"

"Throw them out!"

"Send them back to the desert!"

Page held up his hands. "I'm not condoning violence," he said. "We're better than that. But these people need to be shown that they're not welcome. They need to know that we don't want them here. If we make life unpleasant for them, they'll stop coming." He paused while his audience cheered, then raised his hand for quiet. "There's a lot you can do. You can fly the English flag, the cross of St George. You can take pride in the fact that you're English. You need to vote for politicians who see things our way."

"UKIP, UKIP!" chanted one of the skinheads. More joined in and eventually Page had to raise both hands in the air to quieten them.

"And we're not just talking about general elections. We have to start thinking locally. It's the local councils who decide if a pub gets turned into a mosque. It's the local councils who can close down Muslim halal abattoirs. Control the local councils and you can start to control your community."

Shepherd moved towards the stage, trying to get a better look at the picture on the screen. He was certain they were among the men Yusuf had arranged passports for, but he wanted to know where the photograph had been taken. He tried to get past two heavy-set skinheads but they were so caught up in cheering that his way was blocked. By the time he'd pushed through the picture had changed to a selection of newspaper cuttings. The headlines were damning:

ASYLUM SEEKER RAPES TODDLER
MIGRANTS IN GANG RAPE TERROR
ASYLUM SEEKER RAPES
AND KILLS TEENAGER

"This is what they do when they get here!" shouted Page. "They don't respect us, they don't respect our culture. So why do we tolerate them here?"

"Throw them out!" shouted one of his supporters.

"Burn them out!" shouted another.

Shepherd felt a hand on his shoulder. It was Evans. "You all right, Terry?"

"Just trying to get a better look," said Shepherd.

A pretty girl wearing a white dress with a red cross on it pushed her way towards them holding up a bucket with DONATIONS on it. Shepherd took out his wallet and dropped in a ten-pound note.

"What are you doing?" asked Evans.

"Supporting the cause," said Shepherd.

"You daft bastard, we're not here to give him money," said Evans. "Come on, we're going out back." He gestured towards a door at the side of the bar and headed towards it. Shepherd looked over his shoulder. Billy was behind him.

Shepherd followed Evans into a kitchen with stainless-steel appliances, metal work surfaces and a hissing stove. Two cooks in chef's whites were working there and didn't look up as Evans led Shepherd past a walk-in refrigerator and pushed open a fire door that led to the alley behind the pub. There were two large rubbish skips, both piled high with filled plastic bags. A Mercedes was parked further down the alley, exhaust feathering around the boot.

Billy pushed the door shut. Evans took out his cigarettes and lit one, then offered the packet to Billy. They walked to stand behind the skip so that the driver of the Mercedes couldn't see them.

"What's going on, Paul?" asked Shepherd.

330

"We're here for a little chat with Mr Page," said Evans. He blew smoke up at the night sky.

"Do you want to tell me why?"

"Page went cap in hand to Tommy six months ago. He wanted to set up on his own but didn't have any financial backing. That group he was in was getting too bad a press and he was only number two so he couldn't make the changes he wanted. He asked Tommy for a loan and Tommy gave him a couple of hundred grand."

Shepherd raised his eyebrows. "That's a hell of a loan."

"Page showed Tommy the England First books. Money pours in. There's subscriptions and donations, most of it in cash. So Tommy agreed a repayment schedule and gave him the cash. But Page hasn't been paying and he's stopped calling Tommy back so . . ."

"How heavy are we going to get, Paul? I told you I wasn't carrying."

Evans grinned and slapped him on the back. "I'm just going to have a chat, Terry. Give him a gentle reminder that debts have to be paid."

Evans finished his cigarette and flicked away the butt. Billy's followed a few seconds later, hitting the ground in a scatter of sparks. Evans was just taking out the packet again when the kitchen door opened. One of Page's bodyguards appeared, a big man in a shiny black bomber jacket and jeans. His head was shaved and he had a cross of St George tattooed under his left ear. He held the door open and Page stepped out. The man in the blazer was behind Page, carrying the metal briefcase.

Evans stepped out from behind the skips. "Hello, Simon."

A look of surprise flashed across Page's face, but he smiled and held out his hand. "Paul, I thought I saw you in the crowd. How's it going?"

The second bodyguard came out and closed the door. Evans shook hands with Page. The bodyguards stiffened as Shepherd and Billy came into view.

"Friends of yours, Paul?" asked Page.

Evans ignored the question. "Tommy sends his regards," he said.

"Is there a problem, Mr Page?" asked the bald bodyguard.

"Everything's fine, Andy."

The second bodyguard walked over to stand beside Andy. He folded his arms and gave Evans the bouncer's stare. The man with the case looked confused, as if he had no idea what was going on.

"Well, you say that, Simon, but if Tommy doesn't get what he's owed, that's a problem, isn't it?" said Evans.

"He'll get his money, Paul. You know I'm good for it. And so does Tommy."

"Tommy's worried that you've missed the last three payments. And you don't return his calls. That's disrespectful, Simon."

Page's smile was forced now. "I've been busy, that's all. I'm speaking two or three times a night."

"We're all busy, Simon. But we pay our bills."

Page put his hands up as if he was trying to soothe a spooked horse. "Paul, the money's coming. It's a cash-flow thing, that's all. We're bringing in money every night."

"Yeah, about that. You were collecting cash in there."

"For running costs. Expenses."

"Yeah? Well, paying your debts is an expense. Hand it over."

Page opened his mouth as if he was going to argue but then he turned to the man in the blazer. "Ollie, give Mr Evans the cash."

Ollie knelt down on one knee and opened the case. As he took out a brown envelope Shepherd saw the laptop computer he'd been using for the presentation. The man stood up and gave the envelope to Evans.

Evans took it, opened it with his thumb and nodded as he saw the notes inside. "No coins?"

Ollie looked at Page and Page nodded. Ollie dipped into the briefcase again and pulled out a carrier bag with a few dozen pound coins in it. He gave it to Evans, who handed it to Billy. "I reckon that's a couple of hundred quid at most," said Evans. He looked up at the sky. "So that means you still owe . . . How much would you say? Two hundred grand, plus interest?"

"I'll pay Tommy back, don't worry about that."

"You think I'm worried?" said Evans. "I'm not worried, mate. You're the one who should be worried."

The bodyguard called Andy stepped in front of Page and stabbed a finger at Evans. "You need to go," he said. "Mr Page has to be somewhere."

"It's all right, Andy," said Page, reaching for his elbow. Andy shook him off, stepped forward and pushed Evans in the chest with both hands. Evans took a step back and launched a kick between Andy's legs. Andy moved to the side and the kick glanced off his left leg. He threw a punch at Evans but Evans blocked it and threw a punch of his own that hit the bodyguard square in the jaw. The other bodyguard launched himself at Billy, but Billy swung the bag of coins and hit him in the face. The bag broke and pound coins tinkled on the ground.

Shepherd heard a car door slam and turned towards the Mercedes. The driver had climbed out and was jogging towards them. He was a big man, well over six feet and built like a weight-lifter.

Evans had punched Andy again, two blows to the stomach, and Billy had the other bodyguard in a vicious headlock and was punching him repeatedly in the face. Page was standing with his mouth wide open while Ollie was hiding behind him, clutching the briefcase to his chest.

Shepherd stepped to the side and went up on the balls of his feet as the driver charged towards him. The man's neck was almost as thick as his head and his chest was like a barrel. Shepherd figured the guy would absorb pretty much anything he threw at him. The driver saw Shepherd was blocking his way and started to roar. Shepherd waited until he was almost on top of them, then brought his foot crashing into the man's knee, which snapped like a twig. He followed through with the blow so that the man fell to the ground. He rolled onto his back, then tried to get to his feet. Shepherd kicked him in the side and he fell again with a grunt.

334

Billy had turned the second bodyguard's face to mush and when he released his grip on the man's neck he dropped like a stone. Billy rushed over to help Evans and began punching Andy in the back, over the kidneys.

"Paul, come on, there's no need for this!" shouted Page, as Andy fell to the ground and the two men started kicking him.

Evans stopped, mid-kick. "This is down to you!" he shouted. "Pay your debts, mate!"

"I will! I promise!" said Page. "Just leave him be, okay."

Evans was panting with the exertion. He grabbed Billy and pulled him away from the man on the ground.

"Tommy wants his money," said Evans, pointing a finger at Page's face.

"I'll get it, I swear," said Page.

"Two days," said Evans. "You get up to date with your payments within forty-eight hours or we'll be back and next time it'll be you we kick the shit out of, understand?"

Page nodded fearfully.

"Well, fuck off," said Evans. "And take your little girl with you — he's pissed himself."

Ollie was trembling, still hiding behind Page.

"How am I going to get home?" asked Page. "Look what you've done to my driver!" He pointed to the man at Shepherd's feet.

"You can Uber it," said Evans.

"Yeah, that'll work — I get a man called Mohammed to drive me home."

"Don't get fucking shirty with me, Simon. If you'd paid what you owe you wouldn't be in this position."

"I can drive," said Ollie, his voice shaking.

"Get the keys," said Page, indicating the prostrate driver, who was moaning quietly.

Ollie knelt down and went through the man's pockets with no luck.

"The keys are probably in the car," said Shepherd. "It's still running."

Ollie stood up and headed for it with Page. They got in and drove off.

Evans grinned and lit a cigarette, then offered one to Billy. "I suppose that could have gone better," he said. His grin widened. "But it feels good, doing a bit of the old rough-and-tumble, doesn't it?"

Billy laughed, and Shepherd followed suit.

"Drinks at the Mayfair?" said Evans.

"Why not?" said Shepherd. He really wanted to get away and phone Willoughby-Brown but leaving early wasn't an option. He and Billy followed Evans out of the alley and back to the Range Rover. They drove north of the river and parked around the corner from the Mayfair.

The bar was busy but there was plenty of room in the VIP area where Marty was holding court over bottles of Cristal. He waved Evans over as soon as he saw him. They had a quick conversation, then Marty patted him on the back.

Shepherd ordered a gin and tonic from a waitress and asked Billy what he wanted. "Guinness." The waitress smiled and went off to get their drinks. A hand fell on his shoulder — Marty's. "Paul says you gave a guy twice your size a good kicking."

Shepherd grinned. "Yeah, well, you know what they say, the bigger they are . . ."

"He was an animal," said Evans.

"You and Billy didn't do so bad," said Shepherd. "And from the look on Page's face, I reckon he'll fall over himself to pay you. He damn near shat himself."

Marty chuckled. "Nice one, Terry."

"Cheers, Marty." Shepherd glanced around. "Where's Tommy?"

"Fucked off back to Dubai."

"I don't get it. What's the attraction?"

"Have you been?" asked Marty.

"A couple of times. Bloody hot and nothing but sand."

"That's what I keep telling him," Marty agreed, "but Tommy fucking loves it out there. He's got a huge villa with a pool, booze, hookers on tap, and he likes the food. Some of the best restaurants in the world, out in the Emirates."

"Plus you can't be extradited from Dubai," said Evans.

Marty smiled. "Providing you don't break any local laws, they don't extradite. Ever."

"Tommy's worried about something?" asked Shepherd.

"He's just careful. Plus he's put a few noses out of joint here over the years and it's easier to protect yourself there. He goes back and forward but Dubai is his home now pretty much."

"And his missus is OK with it?"

"He looks after her. They've been married for twenty years and we O'Neills are good Catholic boys at heart . . ." He patted Shepherd on the back. "So, you're coming to the fight?"

"Sure. Paul's got ringside seats."

"From the sound of it, maybe we should be putting you in the ring with Kuznetsov."

"Only if I can kick him in the balls," said Shepherd. "What about Tommy? Is he coming?"

"You couldn't keep him away," said Marty. He put his head close to Shepherd's ear and lowered his voice to a whisper. "Howard says you've got some laundry that wants doing?"

Shepherd nodded. "Told me the guy I use is ripping me off."

"How much do you want to put in?"

"Long term about half a mill. Short term, I've got a hundred in cash I need to get legit."

Marty nodded. "Okay, well, Tommy and I are cool with you using our guy. I'll get Howard to link you up. He's an Indian but he's good and he's never let us down."

"Brilliant, Marty, thanks. I owe you."

"Forget about it. You're one of the family now."

The waitress returned with drinks for Shepherd and Billy. Marty clapped Shepherd on the back. "You're a good guy, Terry. One of the best."

Shepherd raised his glass. "So are you, mate," he said. "I'm glad to be on your team."

"Fucking right," said Marty. "Best team in London."

Shepherd had the black cab drop him half a mile from the Mayfair. Evans and the O'Neills had called it a night shortly before two o'clock and were heading home. Shepherd had flagged down a cab but didn't want to have a conversation with the driver listening in so he gave the man a fiver, got out and called Willoughby-Brown as he walked down the street. His boss sounded half asleep when he answered so Shepherd spoke slowly and clearly. "Have you heard of Simon Page? Used to be with England First?"

"Sure. Right-wing anti-immigration anti-Muslim activist. He was a bit of a firebrand in his youth and he's on our watch list but he's reasonably well-behaved, these days. What time is it?"

"Just after two. Earlier this evening I saw him speak in South London. He had a slide presentation and one of the photographs had two of Yusuf's guys on it."

"You're sure?" asked Willoughby-Brown. He laughed but immediately corrected himself. "Sorry, I keep forgetting your trick memory. Of course you're sure. Where were they?"

"That's the problem, I don't know. They were in front of a mosque but I don't know where it was. The pictures were on a laptop and the laptop's in his car. A Mercedes." Shepherd gave him the number. "Not sure if the car is his or not. There was a driver. Page's assistant, a guy called Ollie, was carrying the laptop in a metal case the last time I saw it. He got in the car with Page."

"Brand of laptop?"

"A Sony, I think. Grey."

"How long ago did you see it?"

"A few hours. I couldn't get away any sooner."

"Any idea where the car was headed?"

"No. Sorry."

"No problem, I'm sure we've got an address on file. Okay, I'm on it." There was no trace of tiredness in his voice now: he was firing on all cylinders.

"And the brothers have given me the go-ahead to meet their main money man. Wedekind's going to arrange it. I've said a hundred grand and they're okay."

"At least that's less than half a million," said Willoughby-Brown. "But you'd better not lose it. Now what about Tommy?"

"Back to Dubai. But I'm sure he'll be back for the big fight."

"We might want to think about getting you wired up."

"No point. They always have anti-surveillance stuff around."

"So get Tommy around to your flat."

"For drinks and nibbles?" He laughed harshly. "I'm not his best mate. I've only met him a few times. Marty's a better bet."

"We want them both, Daniel. This is a two-headed monster. There's no point in just lopping off one of the heads."

He ended the call. Shepherd put the phone away and went looking for another black cab.

"I'm going to have mine rare," said Liam. "Just take the horns and hoofs off and slap it on the plate." He was the second man in the patrol, a few yards behind the Vallon man, named after the metal detector he was holding. They were only a few hundred yards from base, heading home after six hours on patrol. Liam was wearing full body armour, a tan-coloured Mark 7 combat helmet and carrying an SA80 assault rifle.

Shepherd knew that the Vallon picked up only three-quarters of the IEDs the jihadists planted — some contained hardly any metal and so escaped detection. Relying on it could be a fatal mistake. Vigilance was essential, even on the way home.

The Vallon laughed. "We're not getting steaks," he said. "It'll be Spam. Spam, Spam, Spam. Steak is a myth. Like unicorns."

"Guys, focus," said Shepherd. He was bringing up the rear. Tail End Charlie. He spent most of his time walking backwards, checking that no one was coming up behind them. No one paid him any attention. Hardly surprising: they were kids and Shepherd — even though he was in his very early forties — was the old man. Like Liam, he was cradling an SA80.

"Chips or baked potato?" asked the number-three man. He was a Liverpudlian, a big, broad-shouldered guy, carrying the patrol's heavy weaponry, a Minimi belt-fed light machine-gun.

"Let's stay focused, guys," said Shepherd. "We can talk about food when we're back at base."

"Gotta be chips," said Liam. "Loads of chips."

"You need to lay off the carbs, Liam," said the fourth man. He was another big guy, well over six feet tall with receding hair and slab-like teeth. It seemed that no matter what Shepherd said they were going to continue their conversation.

Shepherd faced the front and looked right and left for any signs that the ground had been disturbed. Rocks that had been piled up, or dips in the soil. Sometimes the jihadists poured water into the dips. Sometimes they piled garbage on top. Sometimes the IEDs were in the garbage — explosives packed into a tin can or drink carton could easily blow off a leg.

"You can't have steak without chips," said Liam. "That's like scrambled eggs without cheese."

"Guys, seriously, stop talking about food," snapped Shepherd. "Stay full on until we're back in the compound."

Again he was ignored, as if they hadn't heard him.

"It could all be bollocks," said the soldier in front of Shepherd. He was barely out of his teens, ginger-haired and stick-thin. "I can't see them flying in sirloin steaks."

"I heard it from one of the cooks," said Liam. "The horse's mouth."

"Yeah," said the Liverpudlian "That'll be fucking right. Horse meat."

Shepherd looked over his shoulder. "Guys, cut the chat!" he shouted. "This is —"

The explosion knocked him backwards and his weapon slipped from his hands. He hit the ground hard. His ears were ringing and tears stung his eyes as he rolled over and got up on his hands and knees. His throat burned and he tasted blood as he coughed. "Liam!" he shouted.

He heard a groan to his left and crawled over to him. It was the lad from Liverpool, his face and chest a bloody mess. Half his left leg was missing and all that remained of his left arm was a stump gushing blood. As Shepherd bent over the man he gasped and went still.

Shepherd struggled to his feet. The air was thick with dust and he couldn't see more than a few feet. There were no shots or shouts to suggest they were under attack. It had been a big explosion, and from the look of the Liverpudlian he had been at the heart of it. It could have been detonated by wire or the man might have stood on it. Shepherd bent down and picked up his carbine. "Liam!" he shouted.

There was no reply. Shepherd moved forward in a low crouch, expecting to hear the crack of enemy fire at any point.

"Liam!" he shouted again.

There was another body sprawled on the sand. It was the guy who had taken point with the metal detector. He was lying face down, the back of his head a bloody pulp. Shepherd knelt beside him but one glance was enough to convince him that the man was dead.

"Dad?"

Liam was off to the left, lying on his back, his carbine at his feet. He tried to sit up but fell back and grunted. Shepherd hurried over to him. "Are you okay?"

"I don't think so, Dad."

"Are you hit?"

"My stomach hurts."

Shepherd ripped open Liam's body armour and grimaced when he saw the damage to his abdomen.

"Is it bad?" asked Liam.

Shepherd didn't answer. He pulled out a trauma pack, ripped it open and slapped it onto the gaping wound.

"Dad, I'm cold."

"It's okay, Liam. We're going to get you help." He looked around but they were alone in the desert.

"I'm so cold."

"It's okay. The medics will be here in a sec." He peered left and right but couldn't see more than a few feet. "Help!" he screamed, at the top of his voice. "We need a medic! Medic!"

His voice didn't carry, no matter how hard he screamed. He looked down at Liam. His eyes were open now and he was smiling. "Goodbye, Dad."

"You're not going anywhere, Liam. Stay with me."

"I'm going, Dad. I can't stay." Blood began to trickle from between his lips. His chest heaved and red froth erupted from his mouth.

"Liam, no!" screamed Shepherd.

A bell began to ring. Shepherd couldn't see where the sound was coming from. "Medic!" he screamed, but the word was muffled, as if he was shouting underwater.

Liam began to shudder. Shepherd held him tightly. "It's okay, Liam. I'm here."

Liam gritted his teeth and the shuddering intensified. His face was ashen, his eyes closed, his chin glistening with blood and saliva.

The ringing sound was louder now. Shepherd twisted, trying to see where it was coming from. "Medic!" he screamed again — and then he was awake. His mobile was ringing on the bedside table. He gasped and sat up, his face wet with sweat. He sat panting for breath as the phone stopped mid-ring. He wiped his face with his hands, still panting. The dream had been so vivid that he felt part of him was still in the desert, cradling Liam. He picked up the phone. It was his work mobile and the caller had withheld his number. It could have been Willoughby-Brown but as no message had been left there was no way of knowing for sure.

Shepherd slid out of bed and padded over to the bathroom. He turned on the cold tap and splashed water over his face, then stared at his reflection in the mirror. The sense of relief was almost palpable. Liam wasn't dead. Any war-zone posting was months away, and even if Liam was out on patrol in a danger area, Shepherd was sure he'd be professional. He threw more cold water over his face. He had never had a dream like that before, about himself or his son. He knew why he'd had the dream: he was worried about Liam and what lay ahead. His son had chosen a career that involved putting himself in harm's way. So long as Liam was a soldier, Shepherd would worry about him every hour of every day. And for the first time he truly understood what he'd put his family through and that what went around really did come around.

Omar surveyed the four vehicles. They were identical and the paintwork was perfect. "What do you think?" asked Faisal.

"You've done a good job, brother," said Omar.

"What about the number plates?" asked Faisal. "They can't be driven without plates."

"I haven't been told yet," said Omar. "As soon as I know, I'll get them made and you can fit them."

"When will they be used?"

"Soon. That's all I know." He looked at his watch. "I've got to go."

Faisal pointed at the vehicles. "So we're done? We just leave them here?"

"Until they're needed, brother."

The camera lens looked like a button, no different from the other two on the black leather jacket. Amar Singh finished attaching the camera, stood back and looked Shepherd up and down. "Perfect," he said.

They were in a BT van parked around the corner from where Shepherd was due to deliver the hundred thousand pounds to the accountant who was going to get it into the banking system. The money was in a cheap briefcase, a hundred bundles of a thousand pounds each. Some of the bundles were of fifty-pound notes and some of twenties; they were all old and appeared random though every number had been registered. A small GPS tracking device had been built into the briefcase's plastic handle.

Singh tapped on the keyboard of his Mac computer, tapped it again a few times and a picture flickered onto the screen. It was the view from the covert lens and the image was crystal clear.

"Say something for the sound levels," said Singh.

"'Mary had a little lamb, Its fleece was white as snow . . .'"

Green bars flickered on the screen in time with Shepherd's voice. "We're good to go," said Singh.

Shepherd climbed out of the back of the van and Singh closed the door. They were in a side-street and no one had seen him get out, but Shepherd still spent the best part of ten minutes running basic counter-surveillance to make sure no one was following him, then headed to the accountant's office. His name was Sammy Patel, his company was Worldwide Equity Investments and it was based in a first-floor office with a florist on the ground floor and a minicab firm on the second. Patel wasn't known to MI5 and, other than a few parking and speeding tickets, he had a clean record with the police.

There was an old metal CCTV camera pointing down at the entrance where Shepherd pressed a button on which "WEI" had been written in felt tip. The door buzzed and Shepherd had to push it hard to get inside.

There was no carpet on the wooden stairs, and the boards creaked as he made his way up to the first floor where another CCTV camera looked down on him.

There was a sign saying "Worldwide Equity Invest-ments", and an intercom to the left of the door. He pressed the button and the door immediately clicked open into a large room with a single metal desk, behind which sat a large Indian man in a grey suit and what appeared to be a pink and yellow MCC tie. He was in his fifties with greying hair, though his eyebrows were jet black. "Mr Patel?" asked Shepherd.

The man pushed himself out of his high-backed leather chair with a grunt. "Sammy," he said. "Call me Sammy." They shook hands. "You must be Terry?"

Shepherd nodded. "Thanks for seeing me."

"Any friend of Tommy and Marty is a friend of mine," said Patel, waving Shepherd to a chair.

The two men sat down, Patel's chair squeaking under his weight. There was a window behind him but it was covered with white blinds. To his left there was a line of pine filing cabinets and to his right a large fire safe with a brass dial and a photocopier.

"So, Howard said I can be of help to you."

Shepherd put his briefcase onto the desk and pushed it across to Patel, who clicked the double locks and opened it. He smiled at the money, then closed the case. "Howard said a hundred thousand pounds," said Patel, "but that more would be coming."

"You're not going to count it?"

"Someone will count it down the line," said Patel. "I'm certainly not going to. This is a trust business, Terry. I trust you and you trust me. We're not in the business of issuing receipts, and there'll be no letters or emails. You drop the money off here and in a week or so it will be in whatever bank account you nominate, less our commission."

"And what if it goes missing?"

"It won't."

"Hypothetically?"

"It won't go missing, Terry. End of." He leaned back in his chair and spread out his hands. There was a gold sovereign ring on one finger and a large jade ring on another. "You think I could do business with the O'Neills if money had a habit of going missing?" He chuckled. "I wouldn't have lasted as long as I have if I was that careless. The important thing is that there's no paper trail, Terry. Only you and I know how much is in that briefcase. I'll get it into the banking system, and I'll move it around so much that it'd make you dizzy if you tried to follow it. Then, when it's totally clean, it'll appear in your bank account and you can do with it as you want."

"Sounds good," said Shepherd.

"Minus my commission, of course, as I said."

"Not a problem," said Shepherd. "Howard explained everything."

"Excellent," said Patel. "Now, how are you fixed for a destination account? It can be in any name you want, though obviously you'd need photo ID at some point."

"I've an account in London I was going to use," said Shepherd.

"In your own name?"

Shepherd nodded. "Sure."

"I'd advise against a UK account," said Patel. "And the US, obviously. If you want your money close to home then Ireland's a good bet, or Hungary. I used to recommend Cyprus but they did a deposit snatch a few years ago that put the wind up everybody. If you're happier about having your money further afield, I can recommend Singapore."

"What about Dubai? That's where Tommy is, these days."

"Yes, but he doesn't have his money there. I always recommend keeping your money offshore. So, Tommy doesn't have his cash there but you could quite easily use a Dubai bank if you wanted."

Shepherd pulled a face. "I suppose Dublin would be better. I can be there in an hour or two."

Patel nodded. "Dublin is a good call. I can open an account for you if you've got a passport."

Shepherd reached into his pocket, took out Terry Taylor's and handed it over. Patel stood up and used the photocopier to make a copy of it, then gave it back to Shepherd. "I'll send you a text message saying when the funds are in your bank. Any problems, you know where I am."

Shepherd stood up and they shook hands again. "Pleasure doing business with you, Sammy."

"Mutual," said Patel. He showed Shepherd out.

Shepherd went down the stairs and took the long way back to the BT van. He knocked on the rear door and Singh opened it for him. "Get it all?" asked Shepherd, climbing in.

Singh pulled the door shut and helped him take off the jacket. "Couldn't have been better. He was in shot pretty much the whole time and you even caught the cat-that-got-the-cream smile when he opened the briefcase." He unclipped the transmitter from Shepherd's belt. "Jeremy'll be over the moon, especially the way you got him talking about Tommy O'Neill. Conspiracy to launder money. Nice one."

"All in a day's work," said Shepherd.

It took a ten-man team to break into Simon Page's house. Four of them followed Page as he left the house, two on motorcycles and two in a BT van. Page left the house at just after ten a.m. when a grey Mercedes pulled up outside. The vehicle he had used the previous night had been from a car service. The driver Shepherd had assaulted was now in hospital, along with Page's two bodyguards, so the service had sent a new car and driver.

The four followers had been outside Page's home — a semi-detached cottage in Wimbledon, close to the Common — since six that morning. A search of the electoral register suggested that he lived alone, and a check of various databases came up with the information that he had divorced three years earlier and had no children. The cottage was rented and the wife now lived in Bath, her home town.

The four followers were in radio contact with the officer running the operation, Wendy Aspden. She was thirty-five, blonde, and had joined MI5 from SOCA after five years as a police surveillance operative. She was sitting in another BT van, around the corner from the house, with a laptop on her passenger seat showing the location of the four followers. She watched and waited until they were two miles away from Page's house.

Another van was parked some way down the road from the house, this one in the livery of Thames Water. The driver and passenger were wearing blue overalls and flat caps. Just ahead of the van, a car contained the lock-picker and his assistant. The lock-picker had joined MI5 straight from university but after a brief period of training he was sent off on several lock-picking courses in Europe and the United States, then spent three years working for two of London's largest lock and alarm companies. His name was Brian McAllister and he could pick any lock that was pickable and had the override codes for almost every alarm system in the capital. His assistant was a few years younger: Janet Rayner had also joined straight from university, with an English degree from Oxford.

The remaining two men in the team were on the pavement. One was carrying meter-reading equipment and his ID said he was with EDF, the electricity company. The other was dressed as a DHL employee and was carrying a parcel with paperwork showing it had to be delivered to Simon Page.

"Tango One is slowing. Looks like he's stopping at NatWest bank," said Bravo One, the follower closest to the Mercedes.

"Roger that," said Aspden. "Okay, Clive, in you go."

Clive Edwards, the "meter reader", walked down the path towards the front door. He rang the bell twice, waited until he was satisfied that the house was empty, and walked away.

"Okay, Brian, time to work your magic," said Aspden.

"Received," said McAllister. He climbed out of the car and crossed the road with Rayner. They were carrying toolboxes with the name of an alarm company on the side. They walked confidently across the road and down the path to the front door.

They had used high-powered binoculars to scope out the front door and knew that the lock was a simple Yale. There was no burglar alarm or CCTV. Page's landlord had done everything on the cheap.

"What's happening, Bravo One?" asked Aspden.

"He's gone inside the bank."

McAllister already had his pick and tension wrench in his hands. He had decided to do the lock himself. Rayner was good but time was of the essence. He inserted the tension wrench and quickly felt his way in with the pick. It took him less than thirty seconds of massaging the tumblers before the lock clicked open. Rayner nodded approval. "Nice," she said.

He held the door open for her and she went into the hallway first. "We're in," said McAllister, closing the door behind them. Rayner was already kneeling down and opening her toolbox. She took out a Fuji instant camera and photographed the hallway. She checked the print and slipped it into her pocket.

"In you go, Frank," said Aspden.

Frank Westworth, the "DHL deliveryman", strode down the path. As he walked up to the door McAllister opened it and he slipped inside. He put the parcel on a side table under a mirror. McAllister put his toolbox on the floor. They were all wearing gloves.

"Right. Let's start in the sitting room," said Westworth. He was one of MI5's most skilled searchers, with an almost psychic ability to find hiding places in any environment.

He stood at the threshold to the sitting room and smiled when he saw the Apple desktop computer and printer on a table by the window. "Looks like it's going to be an easy one," he said.

"What's happening, Frank?" asked Aspden, in his earpiece.

"There's a computer here, a desktop," said Westworth. "We might not be needing the laptop if he's got copies."

"Go for it," said Aspden.

Rayner used the instant camera to take three photographs of the room and two close-ups of the desk. She placed the photographs in a line on a coffee-table.

Westworth sat down and clicked his knuckles, flexed his fingers, then switched the computer on. It booted up within seconds. He smiled as he saw that the machine was password protected. He pulled a thumb drive from his pocket and inserted it into the USB on the side. It took him less than a minute to disable the password and start opening files.

Rayner and McAllister went upstairs. There were two bedrooms and a small bathroom. Rayner took photographs of the back bedroom, then the front bedroom. McAllister found the metal briefcase next to the dressing-table in the back bedroom. He swung it onto the bed. It wasn't locked but he could tell from the weight that the laptop wasn't in it. He opened it anyway. There were two bundles of England Rules leaflets and some business cards with Simon Page's contact details on them. He shut the briefcase and used one of Rayner's photographs to make sure he put it back exactly where it had been.

"The briefcase is here but no laptop," he said.

"No problem. Everything's on the desktop," said Westworth, in his earpiece. "PowerPoint presentations, video files, photographs. I'm making copies now."

"Well done," said Aspden. "Bravo One, how's Tango One getting on?"

"Still in the bank," said Bravo One.

Rayner went through the chest of drawers in the main bedroom and quickly checked the clothing hanging in a glass-fronted wardrobe. She found poppers, Viagra tablets and condoms in a drawer in the bedside table and took a photograph of them.

She and McAllister went downstairs and into the sitting room. "Almost done," said Westworth.

McAllister went to stand by the front door. Rayner waited until Westworth had switched off the computer and pulled out the thumb drive, then used the photograph she had taken of the desk to make sure nothing had been disturbed.

Westworth left the house first, carrying the parcel. Rayner followed soon after, the Fuji instant camera and all the prints in her toolbox. McAllister was the last to leave, locking the door behind him. Two minutes later all the vehicles had left and the surveillance team had abandoned Page, who was still in the bank.

Shepherd caught a black cab from Battersea to Charing Cross station where he took another cab to the British Museum. He went around the side, pressed the intercom by the door and looked up at the CCTV camera. The door buzzed and he walked through to the office Willoughby-Brown was using. "Sorry about the short notice," said Willoughby-Brown, "but I thought you needed to see this right away." He was wearing a rumpled charcoal grey suit. "The laptop wasn't in his house but he had a desktop, which seems to have copies of all his files. We think Page's assistant, Oliver Cooper, has the laptop. If the pictures you saw aren't here, we'll go after it."

There was a MacBook on the desk in front of Willoughby-Brown and he turned it so that Shepherd could see the screen. "His PowerPoint presentations are in that folder," said Willoughby-Brown. "I'm assuming it's one of those that they played at the pub. But there's another folder called 'Muslim London Pics' that has several hundred pictures taken at a dozen or so locations, mainly around London. Another just calls itself 'Muslims In UK'. Then there are folders for immigration in Europe, refugee camps and news stories involving immigrants. They seem to be the raw material for the presentation you saw."

Shepherd sat down and began scrolling through the pictures in the file. "This could take some time," said Willoughby-Brown. "There are literally thousands.

How about I pop out for a smoke and you can text me when you have something?"

"Sure," said Shepherd.

Willoughby-Brown grinned and stood up. "Oh, I've sorted the Karl and Gerry Palmer situation for you, you'll be glad to know. No need for you to play the hitman again."

"How?"

"A visit from the local drugs squad turned up a kilo of marijuana in their attic. They deny all knowledge of it, but they would, wouldn't they? Anyway, they're on remand and we've got Mark Ashton under surveillance so the pressure's off, for a while, anyway. We'll make sure he doesn't carry out the hit on his own."

"Were the drugs theirs or were they set up?"

"Does it matter? The important thing is that they're behind bars, which means you can't be expected to fulfil the contract." He took a packet of cigars from his jacket pocket. "Catch you later." He left the office and Shepherd clicked through the first PowerPoint presentation, but it wasn't the one Page had used at the pub and he didn't see any faces he recognised.

The second presentation was the one Shepherd had seen before and he clicked through to the photograph that had attracted his attention. He stared at it, then smiled. They were definitely faces he'd seen in Turkey. The man on the left was Amma al-Kawthari and the other was Elyas Assadi, according to the details on the passports Yusuf had shown him.

The photograph had been taken in front of a mosque, but there was nothing to say where or when.

There was nothing even to confirm that it had been taken in England. There were no other familiar faces in any of the PowerPoint pictures so Shepherd closed the file and opened the one labelled "Muslim London Pics". There were 154 and Shepherd clicked through them. He recognised some faces from MI5 watch lists and others who were known to the police, but none matched the photographs he'd seen in Turkey.

He found a copy of the PowerPoint photograph in the "Muslims In UK" folder, along with more that had been taken at the same time. The men were in three of the photographs in the folder and there was no question that they had been among the passports Yusuf had shown him. There was a better view of the mosque in one of the photographs. It was built of brick and had two tall minarets with green tops. In one of the pictures the two men were deep in conversation with a young bearded Asian wearing a long jacket and baggy pants.

Shepherd searched the three photographs for clues as to where they had been taken but came up with nothing. There was a street light in the background of one picture, which suggested it was England, and a car with the steering wheel on the right.

He went through all the folders but spotted no other faces that matched Yusuf's passports, but saw several more from MI5's watch lists. He closed the final folder and sent a text message to Willoughby-Brown. His boss returned a few minutes later with two cups of Costa coffee. "So, what you have got?" he said, pulling up a chair.

Shepherd showed him the three photographs and pointed out the two men. "That's Amma al-Kawthari and this one is Elyas Assadi."

"What about the guy they're talking to in this one?" asked Willoughby-Brown.

"Him I've not seen."

"Okay. I'll get our experts on this — that mosque looks pretty distinctive."

"So what's the plan?" asked Shepherd.

"As soon as we find out where they are, I'll get surveillance up and running," said Willoughby-Brown. "If they're local to the mosque we should be able to find them fairly quickly."

"You ran their names through the various databases?"

Willoughby-Brown nodded. "Of course. They aren't in the system — at least, not using the names that Yilmaz gave them. But unless they were planning to claim asylum as Syrians I think it's fair to assume they ditched the passports and the names when they got to the UK."

"So you think the fact they haven't asked for asylum means they're up to no good?"

"Don't you?"

"I'm afraid so. Yes."

"I don't want to bang on about it, but if there is a terrorist cell, it's down to YusufYilmaz getting them into the country."

Shepherd's eyes narrowed. "Best not go there."

Willoughby-Brown held up his hands. "It's water under the bridge," he said. "But I feel I should spell out that if Yilmaz had contacted us when he had first started helping Islamic State we wouldn't be playing catch-up now." Shepherd opened his mouth to speak but Willoughby-Brown got in first. "We'll draw a line under Mr Yilmaz, shall we? And to change the subject completely, maybe we should discuss your Mind-Set report."

Shepherd forced a smile. "What's the prognosis?"

"Apparently you're aggressive, with a tendency to belligerence. You make snap decisions and often act without thinking things through. Strong moral compass, which is good to know. Like to challenge authority, which I'm not so happy about, obviously."

"And what's the verdict?" asked Shepherd. "Have they said I can continue?"

Willoughby-Brown chuckled. "Those days are over, Daniel," he said. "That was one of the first changes I instituted when I took over here. Obviously I welcome the psychologists' insight, and I'm always happy to listen to their opinions, but I'm not having one tell me who I can and can't have working for me. It's not a case of biannuals being pass or fail any more. I regard them as a snapshot of your state of mind at a particular time. That's all. At the end of the day I'm the one who makes the decision."

Willoughby-Brown picked up his cup and slowly sipped his coffee. Shepherd could see that he was taking pleasure in dragging it out so he forced himself to relax and smile. Eventually Willoughby-Brown put down his cup. "Here's the way I see it, Daniel," he said. "When I first met you back in Sierra Leone in 1997, I thought you were aggressive and belligerent, and

360

probably prone to acting without thinking. But I also thought you were one of the best soldiers I'd ever met." He grinned. "I'd never tell you that to your face, of course. But I knew back then that one day you'd find yourself in this line of work. Not undercover, necessarily, but doing the work that really matters."

"Soldiering doesn't matter?"

"And there you go, challenging my authority again. Of course soldiering matters. But it matters less than it used to. You've worked with the drones. That's the future of warfare and you know it. But what you're doing now matters far more. If we do our job properly we can win battles without firing a shot. That probably doesn't appeal to the soldier in you, but it's a fact nevertheless. And the thing about your line of work is that traits that might seem weaknesses in the office are lifesaving out in the field. Your ability to act without thinking has probably saved your life countless times. The circles you move in, you'd be trampled over if you weren't aggressive. You have to react instinctively undercover and your instincts are good."

"Have you ever worked undercover, Jeremy?"

Willoughby-Brown smiled. "Actually I have. Several times. But I can't tell you the details as they're classified and will remain so for a long, long time." He leaned back in his chair. "When Davies says you tend to challenge authority, I think he means you challenged him. You gave him a hard time, did you?"

"With respect, he's an idiot. And his programs are ridiculous. The way the biannuals worked before made

361

much better sense. They'd sit down and talk to me, get inside my head."

"Except you're a master at disguising who you really are," said Willoughby-Brown. "Does anyone really know how you think and feel, Daniel? I mean, does anyone really know what makes you tick?"

Shepherd didn't answer.

"You present different faces to different people. You have to. Terry Taylor is Terry Taylor. Pretty much everything he does and everything he thinks is different from Daniel Shepherd. You spend most of your life hiding your real feelings. So I hardly think you'd drop your guard during a friendly chat over a couple of pints."

"You'd get closer to the truth doing that than having me spend hours on silly yes or no questions."

Willoughby-Brown chuckled. "They're a bit blatant, aren't they? White guy chasing a black guy, which one's the cop? If you say white you're a racist, so you choose the black guy."

Shepherd smiled and shook his head. "The white guy was the cop."

Willoughby-Brown's eyes widened. "Why do you say that?"

"He had police-issue boots. The black guy was wearing trainers. And the black guy had an earring. Okay, he might have been undercover but that would be overcomplicating it. The white guy was the cop. The black guy was running away from him. The test was to see if political correctness would override the facts."

"How do you know that?"

"I'm guessing."

"Davies did say you had a good eye for detail."

Shepherd grinned. "At least he got that right. So why didn't you tell me the biannual wasn't pass-fail?"

"That would have spoilt the fun," said Willoughby-Brown. "You're a good undercover man, Daniel. Better than good, you're superb. And I don't care what foibles a shrink might think you have. So long as you do the job as well as you do, you stay on the team."

"So I'm beholden to you. Is that what you're saying?"

Willoughby-Brown laughed. "That's one way of looking at it, yes. But there is another you might consider. I've got your back, Daniel. And I've had it for quite some time."

Omar's heart began to race when he saw there was a new message in the drafts folder. It was a list of four registration numbers. He licked his lips, went over to his sock and underwear drawer and pulled out his throwaway mobile. He called the number of the brother who would make the plates for him and gave him the four numbers, spelling them out carefully and telling him to repeat them back.

He was putting the phone back in the drawer when his bedroom door opened. It was Zack. "Don't you ever fucking knock?" asked Omar.

"Why? You pulling yourself off again?" asked Zack, closing the door behind him.

"I'm busy," said Omar, sitting on the bed and closing his laptop.

"Porn?"

"No, not porn. What the fuck do you want?"

"Chill, bruv. I just wanted to see how the girl thing played out."

Omar shook his head, confused. "Girl thing? What girl thing?"

"The girl you got pregnant. The one you went to see. What happened?"

"Oh, that. Yeah, it's okay. You were right. I got her to pee on the stick and there was just the one line."

"So the skank was lying?"

Omar pulled a face. "She was just trying to rip me off. Wanted me to pay for an abortion she didn't need."

"Bitch," said Zack.

"Yeah," agreed Omar. "Bitch."

"So everything's good?"

"Everything's fine."

Zack ruffled Omar's hair. "You know I love you, bruv."

"I know."

"And I'm always here for you."

"Sure." Omar smiled up at his brother but really he just wanted him out of the room so that he could leave a new message in the drafts folder to say that the registration plates were being made and would be fitted the following day.

Shepherd spent the best part of an hour making sure he wasn't being followed before heading into the pub. It was close to Hampstead Heath, hopefully well away from anyone involved in the O'Neill brothers' investigation. It was a pub he was familiar with, so he knew the location of the fire extinguishers, the emergency exits, and the fact that there was a fire door in the kitchen that led out to the car park. Caroline Stockmann was sitting at a corner table from where she could see the door and the toilets. There was a beige trench coat over the back of her chair and a woolly hat with a fur pompom on the table in front of her, next to a pint of beer. She was reading a copy of *The Economist* but she spotted him the moment he walked in. She looked over the top of her square-rimmed spectacles and smiled.

She stood up as he approached her table and for a second or two he was confused as to how he should greet her. Every previous occasion they'd met had been work-related but this time he'd phoned and asked for a chat. She had immediately pointed out that she no longer did any work for MI5 but Shepherd had offered to buy her an early-evening drink and she'd agreed. She solved his dilemma by offering her hand and he shook it.

Her glass was almost empty so he offered to buy another. She thanked him and sat down. Shepherd went to the bar and brought her a fresh pint and a Jameson's with ice and soda for himself. "Thanks so much for this," he said, as he sat down.

"No problem. I'm at a loose end this evening — my husband's in the theatre until late."

"Which play?" asked Shepherd.

Stockmann smiled. "He's a surgeon," she said. "Kidney transplants, mainly."

Shepherd realised he knew absolutely nothing about her, other than her professional qualifications. "Sorry."

She smiled. "No need to apologise. And, you know, they call operating rooms 'theatres' because that's exactly what they used to be. They had tiered seating and overhead lighting so that medical students could watch the operations."

Shepherd raised his glass to her and she clinked hers against it. "To crime," she said, and Shepherd laughed.

"So, how's Charlie, these days?" he asked.

"She's fine. Better than fine. I think the private sector suits her. She hasn't been in touch?"

Shepherd shook his head. "I'm guessing she's been told not to talk to anyone at Five." He smiled. "Though, to be fair, she isn't one to follow orders, is she?"

"You can see that Five wouldn't want her contacting current staff," she said. "They'd be worried about poaching. But Charlie Button's a professional. She wouldn't do that."

Shepherd tilted his head on one side. "You mean she'd have qualms about trying to recruit me if that's what she wanted?"

Stockmann laughed. "Now you're feeling not wanted, is that it?"

"Of course not. I wouldn't want to work in the private sector and she knows that."

"But it's nice to feel wanted?"

She was teasing him and Shepherd couldn't help smiling. "I don't need that sort of approval, as you know. But it would be nice to see her again at some point. It's just that we don't mix in the same social circles."

"Would you like me to mention it to her?"

"Good grief, no. I'm sure it'll happen at some point." Stockmann sipped her beer. "So, all's well with you?"

"Sure. I guess."

"You guess?"

"It is what it is, Caroline. I work for the government, and that's never easy. I've got a new boss and that's never easy either."

"Jeremy Willoughby-Brown?"

"You've met him?"

"No, but Charlie's spoken about him."

"He was instrumental in forcing her out."

"I think she knows that would have happened anyway."

"So she doesn't bear a grudge?"

"If she did, I wouldn't tell you. Obviously. Charlie's fine, as I said. She's not one for looking back."

Shepherd took a drink. He knew that wasn't necessarily true. Charlie had lost her husband to an al-Qaeda assassin and her lust for revenge had led her along the path that had ended with her being forced out of MI5.

Stockmann sipped her drink again, and Shepherd guessed she was leaving a silence for him to fill. "Thanks for coming, anyway."

"It's not a problem," she said. "I've often wondered how you've been getting on."

"All good," said Shepherd. "Or maybe not. If it was all good I probably wouldn't have needed to call you."

"So it's not completely social?" said Stockmann. Shepherd began to answer but realised she was joking and stopped. Instead he shrugged and she laughed. "Go on," she said. "Tell me how I can help."

"To be honest, I just need somebody to talk to," said Shepherd. "I can't tell most people what I do for a living, never mind run my problems by them. And I miss our chats."

She raised her glass to him. "That's mutual."

"You know Miles Davies?"

"The jazz musician or the psychologist?"

"Mind-Set."

She nodded. "Of course. He's very well regarded."

"I hated the whole thing," said Shepherd. "The interview all done by computer."

"Oh, there were human beings watching you, don't worry about that."

"I figured as much."

"I'm sure you already know this, but how you react to the questions is more important than the answers you give. You'll have been recorded and then your micro-expressions analysed."

"It works?"

"I assume so. Personally I prefer to do things the old-fashioned way."

"Me too."

"Was there a problem with the evaluation?"

"No. All good. Passed with flying colours."

"But that doesn't seem to have put your mind at rest."

Shepherd wrinkled his nose. "The thing is, when you did my evaluations we talked. You asked how I was feeling and I'd tell you. You'd give me a view. Guidance. I didn't get that from Mind-Set. I didn't get anything."

She flashed him a sympathetic smile, sipped again, then carefully placed her glass on its beer mat. "So how are you feeling?"

"I'm okay, I guess."

"What are you working on?"

"The long-term penetration of a South London crime family."

"And how's that going?"

"Slowly. But we're getting there."

"Winning their trust and then betraying them. That's never an easy thing to do."

"These guys are nasty pieces of work, so it's easier than usual. They're responsible for at least a dozen murders and a shedload of beatings. They're into drugs and extortion. They've ruined a lot of lives."

"But they're good to their mother?"

Shepherd chuckled. "I'm not sure that's true," he said. "They rule by fear so they have it coming."

"And what else is occupying your time?"

"I'm out in Lincolnshire with 13th Squadron, working with their drone units," he said.

"Ah, the Stabbed Cats." She smiled at his confusion. "That's 13th Squadron's nickname," she explained. "Their motto is 'We assist by watching' but, considering what they're doing with their drones, that's a tad ironic. What's your role?"

"Target identification," he said.

"Your memory, of course."

Shepherd nodded. "Basically I sit with them and make sure they hit the right targets."

"And how's that going?"

"We've a pretty good success rate."

"You don't sound enthusiastic."

Shepherd leaned back in his chair. "It's not combat."

"Well, it *is* combat. It's just not hand to hand."

"I find it a bit strange to be killing people from thousands of miles away."

"You've killed from a distance before. You were a sniper in the SAS."

Shepherd looked away and didn't answer.

"There isn't a difference, is there? A sniper pulls his trigger and someone dies half a mile away. Sometimes further. You do the same in Lincolnshire and someone dies in where? Syria? Iraq?"

"Syria at the moment," said Shepherd.

Stockmann didn't say anything.

The silence grew, and Shepherd smiled. "The old psychiatrist's trick," he said. "Fill the silence."

"I do hope you're not suggesting I'm an old psychiatrist."

Shepherd laughed. "You know what I meant."

"Because I don't like to think of myself as old and I'm a psychologist, not a psychiatrist."

"I was trying to lighten the moment," he said.

"I think we like to describe it as a technique rather than a trick," she said. "But perhaps you'd prefer it if I was more direct."

"We could give it a go?"

"I asked you if your work with 13th Squadron was successful and you complained that it wasn't combat. Do you have an issue with the drones?"

"I think I do, yes."

"Because they kill from a distance?"

Shepherd nodded.

"And that's making you think about your sniping career?"

"Wow. You go for the jugular, don't you?"

"I'm just trying to get a feeling for what's troubling you. And I can sense you are troubled."

Shepherd took a pull on his drink and discovered his glass was empty. He looked at the bar, then back at Stockmann. She was grinning. "I wasn't playing for time," he said. "It's just I've finished my drink."

She drained her glass and handed it to him. "Why don't you get us refills?" she said. "I have to send a couple of texts."

Shepherd went to the bar, bought fresh drinks and returned to their table just as she was putting her phone away. He sat down and she sipped her pint, then smacked her lips appreciatively. "Go on, then. I'm listening."

Shepherd swirled the ice around his glass. "I was a bloody good sniper, back in the day," he said. "I had a knack for it. Some people do. But I never really thought about what I was doing. You pull the trigger and hundreds of yards away someone dies. You see them go down but it's not real. I mean, it doesn't feel real. When you kill someone close up all your senses are involved. You can hear them die, smell them, feel them. It's real.

Sniping is just visual. Pull the trigger. The rifle kicks. The target goes down."

"How many men did you kill like that?"

"I never counted. Some snipers do. They keep meticulous records, dates, times, windage, distance."

"But not you?"

"It never mattered to me that much."

"But your memory is infallible, right?"

"Right."

She smiled. "So how many?"

He raised his glass in salute. "You're good," he said.

"Of course I am."

He drank, then put down his glass. "Forty-six," he said. "Though it's not possible to say they were all confirmed kills."

"And at the time the kills meant nothing?"

He nodded.

"And now?"

"I don't know. It's difficult to explain."

"Try."

He thought for a few seconds before answering. "At the time it was just a job. My kills were mainly in Afghanistan and we were killing men who wanted to kill us. Kill or be killed. I was killing them one day, but if I didn't, there was a chance they'd kill me the next."

"That's how you rationalised it?"

"I do now. Back then I didn't think about it."

"I guess that's the training," she said. "Army and SAS. You follow orders and you kill the enemy. You don't want soldiers stopping to consider their actions — it slows things up."

"Exactly," said Shepherd.

"But how do you feel about it now?"

Shepherd grimaced. "Now?" He took another pull on his drink. "Snipers are cowards. Like the bastards that plant IEDs. It seems to me that if you can't look into a man's eyes as you pull the trigger, maybe you shouldn't be doing it."

"That's quite a change," said Stockmann. "Any idea what prompted it?"

Shepherd rubbed the back of his neck. The tendons were as tight as cables. "I do, yes." He took another drink. His glass was empty again but he resisted glancing at the bar. "Not long after I left the SAS two mates of mine were killed in Afghanistan. Shot by a sniper. It might not have been the same sniper, but that's not important. Neither of them was in actual combat when it happened. One was taking medical supplies to a hospital. His name was Scotty, from Edinburgh. One of five kids. The youngest. Hell of a nice guy. He'd talked our medic into giving him a load of antibiotics and stuff and he was taking it out to a local hospital. I say hospital, it wasn't even a clinic, just a doctor and a nurse doing the best they could with no money and no resources at a time when the Taliban were running riot. Anyway, *en route* to the hospital Scotty sees a baby sitting by a pile of rubbish. Just sitting there, with what looked like blood on its arm. No one else nearby so Scotty tells the driver to stop and he runs over. Bends over the kid and bang, gets shot in the shoulder. Goes down hard. Another SAS guy runs over without thinking and he gets hit too. His name was

Bam-bam. That was what he said whenever he did the double-tap. Bam-bam. He couldn't help himself. The shot took off the top of Bam-bam's head. Dead instantly. The rest of the guys stayed in the Vector and called for back-up."

"Vector?"

"A six-by-six protected patrol vehicle," said Shepherd. "Scotty had commandeered it to deliver the drugs. The guys in the Vector realised that Scotty was still alive so they started to move it to give them cover while they got Scotty inside. They were doing that when a woman appeared from one of the buildings nearby. She walked right by Scotty and Bam-bam, picked up the baby and walked back to the house."

"It was a trap?"

Shepherd nodded. "The sniper waited until the Vector was almost in position before he put another bullet into Scotty. Into his head. Reinforcements arrived ten minutes later but the sniper was gone." He shuddered. "That was when I lost any respect for snipers."

"And it put into context what you had been doing all those years in the SAS?"

"I had a bit of a rethink, yes."

"You feel guilty? About what you did?"

Shepherd shook his head quickly. "Not guilty, no. The men I shot, all of them, deserved it. And it was kill or be killed. Not at the exact moment I pulled the trigger, but every man I killed would have killed me. And could have killed me."

"So if not guilt, what?"

"Shame, maybe. I'm not proud of what I did. I did what I had to, what I was ordered to, but I'm not proud."

"You said shame. Do you feel ashamed?"

"A bit. Yes. With hindsight I would have preferred to have killed them face to face." He shrugged. "But I don't give it much thought."

"Not consciously, no. But it's clearly preying on your mind."

"Not preying, exactly. But when I was asked to take part in this drone operation . . ." He leaned towards her. "Don't get me wrong, I know the men we're taking out deserve it. The latest were a couple of jihadists helping a sniper in Syria who would have killed a senior Syrian Army officer if we hadn't intervened." He forced a smile. "Actually, we missed him, but took out the Brits. They were helping the sniper and I've no doubt that if they hadn't been killed in Syria they'd have been back in the UK one day committing atrocities here. But there's something very disturbing about what we're doing. We sit in a container in the middle of England, press a button and two men die on the other side of the world. They probably didn't even see it coming."

"And that's disturbing why?"

"Because it reduces combat to a video game. It makes it . . . I don't know. Less real, maybe."

"You know it's real. You know that people die as a result of your actions. Same as when you were a sniper."

"Sniping was different. Yes, I killed from a distance. But they could just as easily have killed me. Same as they killed Bam-bam and Scotty."

She chuckled. "I think this might be your famous sense of fair play going into overdrive," she said. "You think drones are too one-sided."

"They are. No question. We're using missiles costing a hundred thousand dollars against men with AK-47s. It doesn't get more one-sided than that."

"Well, to be honest, the days of one-on-one combat have gone for ever," said Stockmann. "Trench warfare will never return, hopefully. Men won't charge each other with guns blazing. These days, the enemy fights with IEDs, snipers, kidnappings and beheadings. And when they're done, they merge back into the civilian population."

"It's so bloody unfair," said Shepherd. "We fight our wars in uniform, following the Geneva Convention. They fight like cowards."

"Because that's their best chance of winning," said Stockmann. "If they put on uniforms and fought by our rules they'd be defeated in weeks. They learned from the way the Viet Cong beat the Americans. You fight, drop your AK-47 and pick up a hoe. Fight like that long enough and you wear your enemy down."

"So what are you saying? We have to play them at their own game?"

"I've no idea how to fight wars. I'm a psychologist, not a general." She took another drink. "War has never been an easy business, that's for sure. But if we have to go to war, I'd rather our boys fought the good fight from the safety of an airbase in Lincolnshire than risked their lives on the ground in the Middle East."

"I suppose so."

"But in your case, that's rhetorical. There's no way you'll be sent into the desert with a gun again, is there?"

Shepherd smiled thinly. "I hope not."

"So what's really troubling you about the snipers and the IEDs? It's not guilt. You say it's shame and I get that, but that doesn't explain why it's weighing so heavily on your mind."

Shepherd looked at the bar, then back at her. "Do you want another drink?"

"Sure. After you've answered my question."

Yet again she was right. He was trying to avoid answering her. "Liam is signing up. He's joining the army."

Her eyebrows shot up. "How old is he?"

"Eighteen."

"So, no university?"

"He puts up a very good argument. And he knows his own mind."

Stockmann leaned back in her seat. "That's . . . a surprise."

"You're telling me."

"You must be in two minds."

"Why do you say that?"

"He's following in your footsteps. That has to make you proud. He admires you and what you've done. But, on the other hand, you more than anyone know the dangers."

"He's got a good head on his shoulders. And he'll be well trained."

"But none of that amounts to anything when a sniper has you in his sights."

He raised his glass to her. "Thanks for pointing that out."

"I'm just verbalising what you're obviously thinking," she said. "All this anger towards snipers, you know where it really stems from. It's Liam you're worried about."

Shepherd smiled tightly. She was right, of course.

"He's signing up to be a soldier at a time when warfare is changing," she continued. "And in the brave new world it doesn't matter how courageous you are or what skills you have. A lot of the time the difference between life and death comes down to dumb luck. To not being in the wrong place at the wrong time."

"But that's not reason enough to tell him not to sign up, is it?" he asked.

She pushed her empty glass across the table towards him. "Only you can answer that."

Shepherd was in a black cab heading back to Battersea when his phone rang. It was Willoughby-Brown. He let the call go through to voicemail while he asked the taxi driver to drop him at the nearest corner. He paid and got out, then called Willoughby-Brown. "We've tracked down the two men you recognised," said Willoughby-Brown. "The mosque in the photograph is the Madina Masjid in Sheffield. We've had it under observation since Seven Seven and we've checked recent CCTV footage and it looks as if they appeared in Sheffield two weeks ago. As I said, they haven't applied for asylum or benefits and they're not on any databases — not under those names, anyway."

"Are you going to pick them up?"

"We're keeping an eye on them, see if we can find out what they're up to."

"You're playing with fire," said Shepherd. "They're obviously here for a reason."

"Agreed," said Willoughby-Brown. "But we know where they're staying and we have our best surveillance people on them. The guy they were talking to in one of the pictures is known to us and he's putting them up in his house."

"So what do you need me to do?" asked Shepherd.

"At the moment, nothing. You can start looking for an exit strategy from the O'Neill brothers."

"Why? What's happened?"

"The Gerry and Karl Palmer thing has turned into a can of worms. When the cops went through Palmer's house to find the marijuana, they got a stack of paperwork among which they found receipts for a number of storage lockers. In the lockers they found more drugs, an Aladdin's cave of stolen goods and vehicles. The Palmers were looking at serious prison time so they asked for a deal. Seems that their robbing the O'Neills wasn't down to luck. They've had their own man in the O'Neills' organisation for years and know where all the bodies are buried." He laughed. "Not the real bodies, obviously. But their drug connections, their storage facilities, and a fair bit of intel about their money-laundering. We can add that to what we've got on Sammy Patel."

"How's that going?"

"Very well," said Willoughby-Brown. "The video footage is perfect. And him talking about Tommy O'Neill is the icing on the cake. We're still following the money and as soon as he opens the account in Dublin we can bring him in. He'll fold, he'll have no choice, and when he does he'll give up all the O'Neill money."

"So it's enough to put them away?"

"It's enough to get them on remand, that's for sure. That'll take them out of circulation for a year or two. So we can move against Wedekind on the conspiracy-to-murder charge. With the O'Neills on remand, there's a good chance we can get him to open their books. We can explain that without their assets the O'Neills lose a lot of their influence. Plus we already have Wedekind on tape, talking about Mark Ashton."

Shepherd frowned. "You'll threaten to get the video to Ashton? Is that what you're saying?"

"You make that sound so sinister, Daniel. We'll exert whatever pressure we have to in order to get Wedekind to fold. I'm sure he will."

"So your whole case is based on planting evidence, blackmail and threats?"

"That's one way of looking at it, I suppose. But all that matters is that the CPS has a case solid enough to put the O'Neills away for the rest of their natural lives. Their productive years anyway."

"And the end justifies the means?"

"I'm afraid it does, yes. You've seen how the O'Neills operate. They destroy lives. They kill people. They profit from misery. Playing by the rules hasn't worked and if

380

we continue to do so they'll never face justice. You don't agree?"

"It doesn't matter whether I agree or not, does it?"

"I don't see why it upsets you, Daniel. Undercover work is hardly playing by the rules, is it? It involves lies and subterfuge. Hardly playing fair."

Shepherd bit his tongue, knowing there was no point in arguing with the man.

"So, it'll take a day or two for the Palmers' lawyers to get a deal in place with the CPS. Then we can bring the O'Neills in. But we're going to have to talk about the timing. We have to get Tommy here in the UK. If he realises what's going on he'll go to ground in Dubai and we'll never get him back."

"He'll be back for the boxing," said Shepherd. "The Kuznetsov-Hughes fight."

"And he and his team will have to go through security, which means no nasty surprises," said Willoughby-Brown. "Perfect. Marty and Evans will be with him. We let them pass through security and sweep them up. You too, right? Best they see you being pulled in."

"Might be as well," said Shepherd. "If I'm not there, alarm bells will ring."

"Excellent. Saturday night it is. We'll pick up Wedekind separately and see if he can be turned. Patel, too. With what you've gathered over the past few months, plus the Palmers' intel, we're in good shape. Job well done, Daniel."

Willoughby-Brown ended the call and Shepherd looked at his watch. It was early afternoon, time to go home for a shower and a change of clothes before heading out for a night's drinking with Paul Evans. Drinking with Evans was easy enough. He just hoped he wouldn't get dragged along on another debt-collecting mission.

Willoughby-Brown woke up to the sound of his mobile ringing. He looked at the illuminated clock on his bedside table. It was just after five a.m. He took the call. It was Wendy Aspden. "They're on the move," she said. "They left the house before dawn and went to a local mosque. There they picked up a metal case and put it in the boot of the car. They're heading south now, to London."

Willoughby-Brown sat up, rubbing his face. "What sort of case?"

"Long and thin, three feet by a foot or so. There's no way of knowing what's inside but it looks like a gun case to me. We have photographs."

"We need to take a look at it, obviously," said Willoughby-Brown. "What's the surveillance situation at the moment?"

"We're short-handed, just two cars. But I have two bikes *en route*. We'll be fine."

"Okay. I'll get you more eyes in London."

Willoughby-Brown hung up and called MI5's duty-man in the surveillance department, told him what was needed, then headed to the bathroom to shower and shave.

Shepherd got back from a run in Battersea Park to find two missed calls, both from blocked numbers, and a terse voicemail from Willoughby-Brown. Just two words — "Call me." Shepherd tapped in his number.

His boss answered immediately. "Where are you?"

"Battersea," said Shepherd.

"Your two jihadists are in London, and we think they've got a gun."

"You think?"

"All we've seen is a case, but it looks like the sort that would contain a rifle. They had it in Sheffield and drove it down to London."

"And you're thinking what? An assassination?"

"No, we figured they were going to sell it on eBay," said Willoughby-Brown, his voice dripping with sarcasm. "Of course we're assuming they're planning to shoot someone."

"So pull them in."

"We're hoping to see who else is involved," said Willoughby-Brown. "I'll pick you up outside in ten minutes."

Shepherd showered, changed into jeans and a polo shirt, grabbed a jacket and hurried down to the pavement. Willoughby-Brown's van was already there with the engine running. The door opened and Shepherd climbed in.

As he sat down the door closed electronically and the vehicle pulled away from the kerb. Willoughby-Brown handed him a photograph taken by the surveillance team. It was of Amma al-Kawthari holding a long metal case. Elyas Assadi was standing at the back of the car, a white Toyota Prius. The picture had been taken at night but it was clearly a gun case.

A third man — the one al-Kawthari and Assadi had been talking to outside the mosque — was opening the driver's door. Willoughby-Brown tapped the third man. "Haaziq Masood," he said. "Uses the name Harry. British-born Pakistani. He went to Pakistan for six months about ten years ago, before we started regarding such family visits as a red flag. He's on the dole and seems to be living beyond his means, which suggests that someone is funding him. He rents the house from a Pakistani landlord. His name is on the utility bills and the electoral roll."

"How could they get a rifle here in the UK?" Shepherd asked. "It's a specialist weapon."

"It wouldn't be easy but it wouldn't be impossible either. You know as well as I do that anything is available at the right price. I doubt there'd be one for sale in the UK but you could definitely pick one up in the States — you'd just have to get it into this country. The thing is, it's not the weapon that matters, really. It's the man. There's no way of knowing what the gun is from the case, but if it's a sniper's rifle then a gun like that needs a professional to fire it."

Shepherd passed the photograph back to Willoughby-Brown. "Where's the gun now?"

"A house in Ealing. Masood drove them down early this morning, dropped them off and headed back to Sheffield."

"And the rifle?"

"We're assuming they took it into the house with them but there was a bit of a cock-up surveillance-wise and we didn't actually have eyes on them as they went inside."

"Run that by me again?"

"The house is on a busy road and it was the time of the school run, which made it worse. We had a car in front and a bike but Masood turned into the driveway without indicating and our guys had no chance to slow down. By the time they'd doubled back the suspects were all inside. Masood left after half an hour. He's being followed back to Sheffield as we speak and we'll be looking to see if he still has the case, but I think it's a fair assumption that he dropped it off with al-Kawthari and Assadi."

"So what's the plan?"

"Ideally we'll put a tracker on the gun so we'll always be able to follow it. And we'll keep the Ealing house under surveillance. Once the sniper turns up, we'll have him."

"You don't think the men you have under surveillance are the snipers?"

"There's no way of knowing for sure but it looked as if they were just delivering it."

"That's a guess."

"Agreed. But an educated one. They had Syrian passports so they probably came in with the rest of the refugees who flooded into Europe. There's no record of them having come by air or rail, which suggests they were smuggled in, possibly through Calais. That's a haphazard way of getting a sniper into the country. So I'm assuming these two guys are legmen and at some point they'll deliver the rifle to the sniper. Whoever he is."

"And I'm in your van because?"

"I want you on the ground with the surveillance team to see if you recognise anyone else from the passports you saw. It'll save time."

"What about the O'Neill job?"

"This takes precedence for now."

"Don't forget I've got to be at the boxing tomorrow. The main bout's at six."

"We should be done by then," said Willoughby-Brown. "But right now I need you with the surveillance team. There's a very real danger of a major terrorist incident."

The bombs had taken weeks to prepare. Work had started even before Mohammed al-Hussain had left Syria and begun his journey to England. They were relatively simple, similar to the ones made by the IRA during their campaign of terror. The main explosive was ANFO — ammonium nitrate, fuel oil. The ammonium nitrate had come from fertiliser; purification had taken time. Each bomb required 200 kilograms of ammonium nitrate, which required 600 kilograms of fertiliser. Four bombs meant 2,400 kilograms of fertiliser. Buying that much in one go would attract attention so two jihadists drove around the north of England buying individual 50-kilogram bags, forty-eight bags in total. Their names were Farooqi and Hashmi.

Farooqi was the older of the two. He had recently turned forty and was the father of three young girls to one wife and two sons to another. Hashmi was half Farooqi's age, and was studying chemistry at Reading University. Farooqi had attended a training camp in Afghanistan six months before the Nine Eleven attacks and had been involved in the preparations for the Seven Seven attacks in London, but had never come to the attention of the UK authorities.

Hashmi's training had been confined to the internet, and while he had been something of a firebrand in his youth, his local imam had explained that he should start thinking long-term. He needed to stay below the radar, to keep his fundamentalist leanings hidden from outsiders, and it had been the imam who had encouraged him to study chemistry.

Farooqi and Hashmi took the bags to a unit on an industrial estate on the outskirts of Reading, where they purified the ammonium nitrate under the watchful eye of a Pakistani chemist, who had studied at the University of Birmingham and never returned to his homeland. His name was Aleem Sayyid but his friends called him Ali. He was married with two young daughters, lived in Wolverhampton and had told his wife that his company was sending him to do trouble-shooting on a lab they had in Scotland. In fact he slept on a camp bed in the industrial unit, phoning home every evening for a before-bed talk with his children.

Farooqi and Hashmi didn't know what the bombs would be used for, but they knew they were working on

387

something big, something that would echo around the world. Unlike Sayyid, they went home each evening, returning first thing to continue their work. The task was simple and repetitive but had to be done perfectly. The main problem was to ensure that the ammonium nitrate stayed dry. Any moisture would render it inert so the purification stage was done in small amounts, just one kilogram at a time. It was filtered twice, then dried and placed in Tupperware containers. The work was slow and the men had to wear heavy masks to filter out the fumes and dust. The process reduced a kilo of fertiliser to a third of a kilo of ammonium nitrate. Working from eight o'clock in the morning until six o'clock in the evening, they managed to produce about thirty kilos of ammonium nitrate each day. There were other units on the industrial estate and the men didn't want to draw attention to themselves by working late at night so the two assistants went home. Sayyid switched off all the lights and stayed there on his camp bed, watching movies on Netflix.

Farooqi and Hashmi brought in food and water each morning, along with clean clothes and anything else that Sayyid required. They worked together, they ate together and they prayed together, united in their common aim to bring death and destruction to London, to show the infidels that nowhere was safe from the wrath of Allah.

The van turned into the driveway of a large detached house. There were two black SUVs parked outside, along with a white van and a people-carrier. The house was shielded from the road by a line of poplars and spreading rhododendrons. "We're using this as a base for the moment," said Willoughby-Brown, as he climbed out of the vehicle. "The house the jihadists are holed up in is a couple of hundred yards away."

Shepherd followed him over the gravelled drive to the front door. It was opened before they reached it by a man in bomber jacket, jeans and trainers. He nodded at Willoughby-Brown and held the door open for them.

"This is Thomas Leigh," said Willoughby-Brown. "He's one of three SFOs on standby here. We've another three in a car closer to the house."

Shepherd waved at Leigh and the man flashed him a tight smile, closing the door behind them. SFOs were specialist firearms officers, assigned to SCO19. They were the most highly trained of the Met's firearms officers, almost to the level of the SAS. The hallway had rooms off to left and right. Two men with short haircuts and casual clothing were sitting on a sofa watching television. Glocks and spare magazines lay on the coffee-table in front of them. Willoughby-Brown tapped on the door to their left and pushed it open. A middle-aged blonde woman, wearing black-framed glasses and a headset, was sitting at a table with three screens in front of her. She waved at Willoughby-Brown as he ushered Shepherd in.

"This is Wendy Aspden. She's heading up the surveillance team," he told Shepherd.

"Pleased to meet you," said Aspden, shaking his hand. "You're the man with the magic memory?"

"I never forget a face," he said, and looked at the screens on the table. The one in the centre was divided into four, each showing a different view of the target house, a neat semi-detached with an adjoining garage. To the left, a digital map of the area bore several red dots, presumably marking the positions of her team. To the right a comms screen was filled with emails and instant messages.

"How's it going?" asked Willoughby-Brown, peering over her shoulder.

"They haven't moved out of the house all day," she said. She clicked her mouse and one of the cameras switched to an infrared view. It showed three figures, two lying down in an upstairs bedroom, one sitting in the front downstairs room. "We think the two upstairs are your guys. The man downstairs is, we think, a Johnny Malik. He rented the house two months ago, a year-long lease, paid three months in advance in cash. Malik also has a lease on a car, a white Toyota Prius. It's parked in the garage."

"And the gun? Where is it?" asked Shepherd.

"We don't know," she said. "Jeremy's probably already told you that we haven't actually seen the weapon, just the case. The case was in the boot of the car that drove down from Sheffield but we didn't have eyes on it when it pulled up in front of the house. That car is now *en route* back to Sheffield. We're assuming the case is now in the house but that's all it is at present, an assumption. But as the two tangoes are in the house, I think it's fair to assume that the gun is there with them. As soon as the house is empty we'll send in an entry team for a look-see. I have one on standby."

"Anything known about this Johnny Malik?"

Aspden shook her head. "Not much. He's a cleanskin, British-born Pakistani. His parents came over in the seventies. Dad's a dentist in Bradford, Mum was a nurse. Johnny is one of eight kids. He's been to Pakistan several times but always with his parents and never for more than a week or so. Came down to London last year to study and his parents are funding him. We're assuming he was radicalised in Bradford and sent to London as part of some greater plan." She tapped on her screen and a driving licence flashed up. Malik was dark-skinned with piercing brown eyes and glossy black hair spiked with gel. "Nice-looking boy," said Aspden.

"I'm going to leave you with Wendy, Dan," said Willoughby-Brown. "If they get any visitors, I want you to see them straight away. I'll be back the moment anything kicks off."

Willoughby-Brown let himself out. Aspden gestured at a coffee-maker on a small table by the door. "Help yourself," she said. "And there's plenty of food in the kitchen."

Faisal looked at his wristwatch, a cheap Casio, and pulled a face. "What if they don't come?" he said.

"They'll come," said Omar. "It's early yet."

"You said eight."

"I said from eight. It's only quarter past."

They were standing at the door looking at the gate, now unlocked and open. The vehicles were all fuelled and ready, the freshly printed licence plates in place.

"What if they don't come?"

"They'll come, brother. A lot of planning has gone into this."

A blue Honda came down the road on the other side of the chain-link fence, slowed, and turned to drive through the gate. There were two Asian men in the car, both cleanshaven. The car stopped in front of the loading bay. The passenger got out, closed the door, and the car drove away. The man turned to Omar and Faisal. Omar waved him over. He was in his thirties, dark-skinned and wearing wire-rimmed glasses. "Welcome, brother," said Omar. He embraced the man.

"*Assalamu alaykum*," said Faisal.

The man hugged Faisal. "*Assalamu alaykum*."

"Come this way," said Omar, taking him to a table where there were four sets of green uniforms. He handed one to the man and showed him to the toilets where he could change. When he came out, Omar smiled his approval. He looked the part.

"Have you driven something like this before?" asked Omar.

"I have driven trucks," said the man.

Faisal clipped a laminated ID to the man's breast pocket. "It's the same as a truck," he said.

Omar got into the passenger seat as the man sat behind the wheel. He ran through the controls with him, then showed him the sat-nav. "Your first destination is near Reading, to the west of London.

Then you go to East London to the waiting area. Then you have your final destination."

"What do I say if I'm stopped?" asked the man.

"You won't be," said Omar. "Are you ready?"

"I am. *Inshallah*."

Omar climbed out and slammed the door. He gave Faisal a thumbs-up and Faisal raised the shuttered door to allow the man to drive out. The two men watched as the vehicle drove away. "It's begun, brother," said Omar, putting his arm around Faisal's shoulders. "It's finally begun."

Shepherd went downstairs and into the kitchen. He had slept in one of the bedrooms at the Ealing house. The previous evening he had spent playing cards with the three SFOs between popping into the front room to watch the surveillance screens. The armed cops were all good guys, tough and professional, and all had at some point trained with the SAS in Hereford, on the ranges and also in the famous Killing House. The three tangoes had stayed in the house all night, occasionally moving from room to room. But most of the time one of the men stayed downstairs and two upstairs. They had come together to pray three times — at three o'clock in the afternoon, at five thirty, and finally at just after seven. The infrared cameras had picked up the red and yellow images as they bowed, knelt and placed their foreheads on the floor.

There was a flurry of activity at eight o'clock when a moped had arrived at the house but it had turned out to be a food delivery from a local Lebanese restaurant.

Shepherd had thought about going back to his Battersea flat but decided he might as well stay put. The men had travelled to London for a purpose and he figured that purpose would be revealed sooner rather than later.

He made a bacon sandwich and took it through to the room where Aspden was still sitting in front of the screens exactly as she had been seven hours earlier when Shepherd had gone to bed. "You don't sleep?" he asked.

"I cat-nap," she said, pointing at a sofa under the window. "And I drink a lot of coffee."

"Shall I make you one?" he asked.

She grinned. "That was what I was hoping," she said.

He offered her half of his sandwich but she shook her head. He made two coffees, put them on the table and sat next to her.

"Tell me about your trick memory," she said. "Eidetic, right?"

"Yeah, pretty much. I can remember pages after just looking at them for a few seconds. I never forget a name or a face."

"Must have been a help at university."

"Not really. Remembering facts isn't a sign of intelligence. It's how you use the information. For instance, I can remember foreign words easily but that doesn't mean I'm particularly good at languages. I can read a book on astronomy and remember it, but that doesn't mean I understand it."

"That Stephen Hawking book about black holes? That was a tough read."

"Exactly. I'd be able to recall it word for word, but I wouldn't be able to hold a conversation about it." He took a bite of his sandwich and washed it down with coffee.

"You're former SAS, right?"

"How did you know?"

She smiled knowingly. "You have the look. The way you carry yourself."

"I was for a while."

"And did the memory help with that?"

"Sure. I only had to look at a map once so navigation was always easy for me. Building layouts, things like that."

"But Jeremy's using you because of your facial-recognition skills?"

"Yeah. I only have to see a face once to remember it for ever." He gestured at the screens. "The two tangoes who came down from Sheffield, I saw their faces on passports in Turkey."

"That's a useful skill," said Aspden. "The Met has a unit of super-recognisers. The memory cops, they call them."

"Humans with the right skills can still beat the computers at facial recognition," said Shepherd. "But it's not the sort of job I'd want to do, sitting staring at screens all day." He raised his coffee mug. "No offence."

Aspden laughed. "None taken," she said. "I love surveillance. I really love it. Watching people without them knowing. I mean, look at these three." She pointed at the centre screen on her table. "They're up to no good, obviously. Moving a rifle around, planning whatever they're planning, thinking we're so bloody stupid we don't know what they're up to. But all the time they're making their little plans we're watching and waiting."

"They've got a big surprise coming, that's true," he said.

"That's what I like, the look of confusion on their faces when they're confronted by the evidence," she said. "When they get arrested they think we know nothing and they try to brazen it out. Then they see what we've got on them and they can't believe it." She sipped her coffee. "But I guess you prefer the action bit. The charging around with guns and the like."

Shepherd grinned. "It's what I trained for."

"You see, I'd hate that," she said. "Guns always scare me. And I don't think I could ever pull the trigger on someone."

"You say that, but if your family was threatened you might think differently."

Her eyes remained on the screens. "Oh, sure, no question. Anyone tries to hurt my kids and I'll kill them with my bare hands. But that's something else, isn't it? That's maternal instinct kicking in. Have you got kids?"

"Just one. A boy."

"How old?"

"Eighteen."

"About to fly the coop? What's he going to study?"

"He doesn't want to go to university," said Shepherd. "He's joining the army."

Aspden looked at him. "And you're okay with that?"

He shrugged. "He's eighteen, he can make his own decisions. But, yes, I'm okay with it. It's probably the right thing for him."

She smiled. "It's in his genes."

Shepherd nodded. "You're probably right."

Sayyid and his assistants transferred the ammonium nitrate from the Tupperware containers to 45-gallon oil barrels. Ammonium nitrate alone was a powerful explosive, but by adding diesel fuel the compound became as effective as nitroglycerine. The most effective combination was 95 per cent ammonium nitrate and five per cent diesel. No mixing was required: the diesel was simply poured into the barrels and gravity did the rest.

Once they had sealed four barrels, they used grey duct tape to attach hundreds of nuts, bolts and washers. They laid down strips of duct tape on the floor and placed dozens of nuts, bolts and washers on the sticky side. Then they wound the tape around the barrels. When the bomb exploded, the metal would form lethal shrapnel.

ANFO was a powerful explosive, but it was very stable. It took a considerable kick to detonate it, but Sayyid had spent hours researching the best detonator to use. He had settled on the igniters that enthusiasts used to launch model rockets. They were freely available and even sold on Amazon. He had bought two dozen over several weeks from different sellers.

He placed them on a table in groups of six, then taped all the left-hand wires of each set together, and all the right-hand wires. He stripped the plastic from the ends of lengths of 12-gauge electrical wire, then connected those wires to the sets of leads of the igniters.

When he had finished all four, he prepared the second part of the circuit. He put together a simple circuit with a push-button trigger and a 12-volt battery. He used a small bulb to check that the trigger worked, then added a simple on-off switch so that the circuit would be totally safe while the bombs were in transit. Once in place the on-off switch had to be put in the on position and the button pressed. There was no timer in the circuit. For what had been planned, no timer was necessary.

The first vehicle arrived at just after midday, right on time. "He's here," said Farooqi.

"Open the door," said Sayyid.

Farooqi pressed the large red button that activated the metal shutter and it rattled up. The vehicle drove in and parked.

Farooqi opened its rear doors while Sayyid and Hashmi carried over one of the barrels. The driver stayed where he was as the three men lifted the barrel into the back of the vehicle. Farooqi used a length of washing line to bind it into place so that it wouldn't move around in transit.

Sayyid opened the front passenger door and climbed in. The driver was in his twenties with deep-set eyes and an unnerving cold stare. "*Assalamu alaykum*," said Sayyid.

"*Wa alaykum alsalam wa rahmatu Allahi wa barakaatuhu*," mumbled the driver. And peace and blessings of Allah be upon you.

Farooqi passed over the trigger from the rear of the vehicle. Sayyid showed it to the driver. "This is the on-off switch," he said. "It's in the off position now. That means the device is not live. When you're in position, you put the switch in the on position. Then the circuit is live. It is activated by pushing the button."

The driver nodded.

"Do you have any questions?" asked Sayyid.

The man stared blankly ahead.

"Are you okay, brother?" asked Sayyid.

The man nodded again.

"You understand what I have said to you?"

"*Inna lillahi wa inna ilayhi raaji'oon*," he said, his voice a low whisper. To Allah we belong and to Him we will return.

Sayyid patted his shoulder. "*Alhamdulillah*," he said. Praise be to Allah. He climbed out and slammed the door. Farooqi closed the rear doors and banged on them with the flat of his hand.

Hashmi pressed the button to raise the metal shutter and the vehicle reversed slowly out, a warning beeper sounding aggressively. Sayyid watched the man drive away. One down, three to go.

Salman knocked on Mohammed al-Hussain's door. The man was sitting on the bed, reading his copy of the Koran and fingering his prayer beads. "The car will be here in two hours," said Salman.

"Thank you, brother," said al-Hussain.

"Do you want anything to eat or drink?"

Al-Hussain was hungry but the kitchen downstairs was so dirty that he hadn't eaten any of the cooked food that had been offered to him. He had had some fruit the previous day and drunk the tea that Salman had prepared, but that was all. He knew he needed to eat something but when he looked at Salman's dirty fingernails he couldn't bear the thought of eating anything the man had touched. "What fruit do you have?" he asked.

"I have oranges. And a banana."

"I will eat those."

"I could cut them up and make a fruit salad."

"No," said al-Hussain, quickly. "Do not peel them, just give me them as they are. And do you have eggs?"

Salman nodded enthusiastically. "Yes. I could fry you some."

"Just boil them and bring them to me in their shells. And hot tea."

Salman sniffed and rubbed his nose with the back of his hand. "I'll bring it to you straight away," he said. He smiled and closed the door.

Al-Hussain shuddered. He couldn't understand why Salman was so careless with his personal hygiene. The Prophet himself had been clear that Islam is clean, and

400

that the followers of Islam should keep themselves clean because only clean people can enter Paradise. A good Muslim kept himself scrupulously clean, which meant that Salman was not a good Muslim.

Akram Hakim drove at just below the speed limit. The sat-nav unit mounted on the dashboard said he was two hours from his destination, an industrial site on the outskirts of Reading. The route took him mainly along minor roads, away from CCTV cameras and speed traps.

It had taken Hakim three months to reach England. It had been an arduous journey. He had started in Turkey, where he had been given a Syrian passport to disguise his Iraqi origins and a waist pack filled with euros. He had crossed the sea to Greece on an overcrowded dinghy, then taken trains across Europe until he had reached France. He had killed two men in the migrant camp in Calais, which the newspapers referred to as the Jungle. It was home to more than six thousand people, mostly young men, who wanted to make a new life in the UK. They slept in the camp as they tried to make the final leg of their journey by stowing away on lorries, cars and ferries, or sneaking on to a train at the Eurostar terminal.

When Hakim had arrived at the Jungle, it had been made up of nine camps. Every now and again the authorities would move in and close a camp down, but another would spring up elsewhere. The French were half-hearted in their attempts to stem the problem because they knew that the migrants in Calais had no wish to stay in France.

The migrants were a mixed bunch. There were Pakistanis and Afghans, Iraqis and Iranians. Most had thrown away their passports and identification documents, unless they were from a true war zone. A Pakistani or an Egyptian arriving in the UK would have a hard time claiming asylum, but a Syrian, an Afghan or a Somalian would be fast-tracked through the process.

Hakim kept his Syrian passport in his back pocket, wrapped in a plastic bag. It had earned him free rail travel across Europe. On trains in Hungary, Austria and Germany, all he had had to do was show the ticket inspectors the passport, smile, and say, "England!" and they ignored him.

The main camp was on a former landfill site three miles from Calais, which had electricity, showers and toilets. Hakim stayed in a smaller camp with little in the way of facilities, though residents received one meal a day supplied by a French charity. Conditions were bad but no one at the camp planned to stay there long. Almost everyone was looking for passage to the UK on one of the thousands of trucks that passed through Calais every day.

While he was in the camp, Hakim had met a man who knew him. The man was also an Iraqi and, like Hakim, had fought for Islamic State in Iraq, then in Syria. He was also hoping to get to England and had embraced Hakim like a long-lost brother. The man had a loose tongue and spoke loudly, reminiscing about their days in Syria. Hakim had asked the man if he could sleep in his tent and he had agreed. It was a ramshackle lean-to made of scrap wood and lined with cardboard, a stolen tarpaulin providing shelter from the rain. Another man shared the tent, a second Iraqi.

They shared what little food they had with Hakim — half a stale baguette, some rancid cheese and a bottle of water. They made plans for the final journey to England. One said he had heard of a French truck driver who was prepared to let migrants ride in the back of his truck for a thousand euros. Hakim had more than two thousand euros hidden in a money belt under his shirt, but he didn't tell them that.

He killed them both while they slept that night, strangling them with his bare hands. Afterwards he slipped away to another camp and, two days later, stowed away in the back of a truck transporting fruit. He left it at a service station somewhere in the south of England and used a phone box to call a number he'd memorised before he left Syria. Two hours later he was collected by an elderly Asian man in a small van with the name of a carpet-cleaning firm on the side.

The man drove Hakim north to Leeds where he handed him over to a Pakistani family, who had prepared a spare room for him. Hakim stayed in the room: he ate, slept and prayed there, leaving it only to use the bathroom. The family gave him a small television to watch but he never switched it on. He spent his waking hours praying, reading the Koran and preparing himself for martyrdom.

When they were ready, the father had driven him from Leeds to east Manchester to collect the vehicle he was now driving south to Reading. He was totally calm. He had no reservations about what he was about to do. There was no greater glory than dying for Islam. He was happy to give his life for Allah. Soon he would be in Heaven, while thousands of infidels would be burning in the fires of Hell and it would serve them right.

"*Inna lillahi wa inna ilayhi raaji'oon,*" he whispered to himself. To Allah we belong and to Him we will return.

Shepherd's phone rang. It was Paul Evans. Aspden was talking into her headset so he left the room and closed the door before he took the call. "Terry, mate, where are you?" asked Evans.

"Just heading out to see a guy about some business," lied Shepherd.

"You still up for this evening?"

"Sure. Of course. Wouldn't miss it for the world, mate."

"Excellent," said Evans. "The fight starts at six — the Russians want it to be shown at prime time in Moscow so a six o'clock start for the main bout but there's a couple of good ones before that so we should take our seats at about four thirty. Some of the guys are going to meet at the Mayfair for lunch and a few drinks, then we'll head over to the stadium."

"Is Tommy going to be there?"

"He landed half an hour ago. Between you and me, Tommy's got a big bet riding on the bout before the big fight. A hundred grand, Marty says."

Shepherd looked at his watch. It was just after ten a.m. "I'll try to make the Mayfair but if I'm pushed for time I'll see you at the stadium."

"For fuck's sake, mate, what's more important than a world heavyweight title fight?"

"I'll be there, but I've got a couple of things to do."

"Don't let me down, mate. These tickets are like hen's teeth."

"I'll be there, mate. Cross my heart." Shepherd ended the call and went back into the bedroom.

"Problem?" asked Aspden.

"Another job I'm working on," said Shepherd. "I might have to pop out for a few hours this evening."

"Anything interesting?"

"Boxing match, as it happens."

She turned to look at him. "Not the Kuznetsov-Hughes fight?"

Shepherd nodded. "Ringside."

"You lucky bugger," she said. "That's set to be a great fight."

"I'm not that much of a boxing fan, to be honest," said Shepherd.

"Too many rules?"

Shepherd laughed. "You read my mind."

The second vehicle arrived exactly an hour after the first. The driver was a Pakistani — Muhammad Saleem — but he had used a Syrian passport to travel through Europe. He had crossed to England in the back of a truck of oranges with a plastic bottle of water to drink and an empty one to urinate in. The driver was Spanish and the fare had been seven hundred euros, paid in cash. The man had dropped Saleem at a service station on the Ml where he had called a number he had memorised months earlier.

Saleem drove up to the factory unit and sounded his horn. The metal shutter rattled up. Two Asian men were standing there. The older one motioned for Saleem to drive forward. He edged the vehicle inside and the shutter came down, closing with a bang. Saleem sat where he was as the younger men opened the rear door. Another man appeared with a barrel on a metal trolley. Saleem watched in the wing mirror as the man pushed it to the rear of the vehicle. Saleem didn't offer to help. His orders were to stay in the driving seat, no matter what happened around him.

As the men prepared the massive bomb behind him, Saleem sat with his eyes closed, his *subha* in his right hand. There were three sets of thirty-three wooden beads and one large one on the string, making a hundred in all. The imam in his mosque in Peshawar, the capital of the Khyber Pakhtunkhwa province of Pakistan, had given him the beads on his sixteenth birthday and they had been in his possession ever since. Saleem let a bead slide through his fingers each time he recited one of the ninety-nine names for God. God The Wise, God The Compassionate, God The All-Seeing, God The Merciful, God The Good,

God The Eternal, God The Forgiving. Once he got to the large bead he would start again. It was calming, and the longer he fingered and chanted, the calmer he became.

Sometimes Saleem did a round of beads repeating the names that had extra meaning for him. Al Jabbaar: The Powerful. Al Haqq: The Truth. Al Qawiyy: The Strong. Al Mumit: The Bringer of Death. Al Muntaqim: The Avenger. His God was a strong God and a vengeful one, a God who would one day be worshipped by the entire world if Islamic State had its way. *Inshallah.*

A knock on the door jolted Mohammed al-Hussain awake. He was lying on the bed with his copy of the Koran on his chest. He blinked. "Yes?"

The door opened. It was Salman. "They are here, brother," he said.

"I shall be downstairs shortly," he said. He swung his feet off the bed as Salman closed the door. He took a deep breath to steady himself. It was time. Today was the day, and in just a few short hours he would meet his destiny. He stood up and took another deep breath, then went through to the grubby bathroom and splashed water over his face. He took his toothbrush and toothpaste from his washbag and brushed his teeth, then went downstairs with his bag.

There was a clean-shaven stranger sitting at the kitchen table with Salman wearing a quilted jacket. He stood up when al-Hussain entered the room. "Greetings, brother. My name is Jafari. I am to take you on the last stage of your journey." He embraced al-Hussain and kissed him on both cheeks. "*Assalamu alaykum.*"

"*Assalamu alaykum,*" repeated al-Hussain. He could smell the sandalwood and lemon of the man's aftershave. He placed his bag on a kitchen chair, then removed all his personal items and put them into one of the bag's side pockets. His watch, his wallet, the passport, his prayer beads. "Take care of this until my return," he said to Salman. "If I do not return, destroy everything."

Salman tried to smile reassuringly but he ended up baring his teeth like a cornered animal. "Good luck, brother."

Al-Hussain shook his head. "There is no luck, only the will of Allah," he said.

"I got what you asked me for," said Salman. He pulled a square black scarf from his pocket and unfurled it to reveal the white logo of Islamic State.

Al-Hussain smiled and took it. "Thank you, brother," he said. "It's perfect."

Jafari took al-Hussain out through the kitchen door and into the cluttered backyard. The stench from the overfilled wheelie bins almost made al-Hussain retch and he hurried through the wooden door into the alley where a blue Ford Mondeo was waiting, its engine running. A bearded Asian in his fifties sat in the driving seat with prayer beads hanging from the rear-view mirror. Al-Hussain climbed into the back and Jafari joined him. The car moved off slowly.

"Do you need anything, brother?" asked Jafari.

"Just my weapon," said al-Hussain.

"You will have that soon, brother," said Jafari. "*Inshallah*."

Shepherd went into the kitchen and called Willoughby-Brown. "I need to head out to see the brothers," he said. "They're having lunch before going to the boxing and they want me there."

"Whereabouts?"

"The Mayfair. I'll have to go home and change first — I'll need a suit. Tommy's got a bet on one of the earlier bouts so we should be there about four thirty."

"And what's happening in Ealing?" asked Willoughby-Brown.

"All quiet so far," said Shepherd. "No one's left the house and they've had no visitors."

"We need to pull the O'Neills in, that's for sure," said Willoughby-Brown. "Tommy arrived this morning on an Emirates flight so it's looking good. And I'd rather you were there when it happens. I just worry that the Ealing thing might kick off, though."

"To be fair, I'm just here to look at faces. Wendy doesn't really need me and the SFOs are good guys."

"No, I get that." Willoughby-Brown went quiet for a few seconds as he considered his options. "Okay, yes, you should be with the O'Neills. If we need a face checking we can always text you."

"And what's the story at the stadium? How are we going to handle it?"

"The Met will take care of the arrest. They'll pick you all up immediately after you've gone through security. There are SFOs on duty there anyway as part of the regular security measures and we'll make sure they're around, but we're not expecting any trouble. You'll be arrested, they'll be transferred to West End Central, you'll be put in a separate vehicle and either brought back to Ealing or wherever you're needed. Should be done and dusted by six at the latest."

"What about Paul Evans? Might be best to have him out of the way as well."

"Sure, the more the merrier."

"Sounds like a plan, then," said Shepherd.

"I'm just sorry you won't get to see the boxing," said Willoughby-Brown. "I'm told it's going to be one hell of a fight."

The third vehicle arrived forty-five minutes after the second had left. Farooqi, Sayyid and Hashmi worked quickly and efficiently and it took less than ten minutes to load the bomb into the back, then wire up the detonator and trigger.

The driver was an Afghan. His name was Pashtana Abdul, but the name on the Syrian passport he had used to travel across Europe was Nur Ismat. He had destroyed it when he arrived in the UK, hidden in the back of a van full of cheap wine that had been waved through Customs at Dover without a second glance. The vehicle had been driven by a British-born Pakistani and his brother. They ran a couple of corner shops in Bradford, and while they had never left the country for jihadist training, they had spent hours online reaching out to other jihadists. Their local imam had approached them and explained that they would be far more use if they stayed below the radar so their internet activities had ceased. From time to time they were called upon to carry out tasks, which they did without hesitation.

They had taken Abdul to a safe house in Wolverhampton where he was kept in a spare bedroom for almost three weeks before the call came for him to carry out his mission. From Wolverhampton he had been driven north by one of his minders to a factory unit on the outskirts of Manchester where he was shown his vehicle and given a sat-nav preloaded with his route.

He listened patiently as the trigger was explained to him, then shook his head when he was asked if he had any questions. He knew what he was prepared to do, and had done since the day he had left Syria. He would become a *shahid*, a martyr for Islam, and he was happy to die in the service of Allah, knowing that he would receive his reward in Heaven.

He reversed slowly out of the factory unit, performed a methodical three-point turn, and headed east, towards London, following the route outlined on the sat-nav unit.

"This is the building, brother," said Jafari, pointing to the left. Mohammed al-Hussain turned his head. There were three identical tower blocks, some twenty storeys tall. "We will be in the middle one." He handed al-Hussain a baseball cap and put one on his own head. "There is CCTV in the lobby," he explained.

The driver brought the car to a halt and Jafari climbed out, holding the door open for al-Hussain. The entrance to the building was a set of double doors with a metal keypad and console to the left. Jafari tapped in a four-digit code and the door clicked. He pushed it open and led al-Hussain to a lobby where there were three lifts. On the wall opposite a noticeboard was covered with printed sheets of paper. Jafari pressed the button for the twelfth floor. Al-Hussain knew there would be a camera in the lift so he kept his head down.

The lift arrived at the twelfth floor and al-Hussain followed Jafari out and along the corridor to the right. Jafari fished a set of keys from his pocket and opened a door. He went inside with al-Hussain. They were in a large living room. It was sparsely furnished with a dining area and a cheap floral-patterned sofa by the window, with a matching armchair. There were two framed pictures on the walls, one of a London street scene, the other of a Chinese lady in a yellow dress.

Jafari closed the door and slotted in the security chain. A door to the right led into a kitchen, and two doors to the left opened into bedrooms.

"Who lives here?" asked al-Hussain.

"No one," said Jafari. "It was rented six months ago, all paid for in advance. I have been in a couple of times over the last week to check that everything was okay, but other than that it has remained empty."

He went into the kitchen and al-Hussain followed him. It was spotless. A carrier bag filled with provisions stood on the work surface by the sink. "I wasn't sure if you would need food," said Jafari. "We have time to eat. I can cook."

"Perhaps later," said al-Hussain.

Jafari opened the fridge and took out an automatic pistol.

"Why the gun?" asked al-Hussain.

"I was told to protect you at all costs," said Jafari. He ejected the magazine, checked it, then slotted it back into the gun and chambered a round.

"And what else, brother? What else were you told to do?"

"What do you mean, brother?"

"If something goes wrong and they catch us, what then? Are your orders to kill me?" Jafari looked uncomfortable and avoided his gaze. Al-Hussain smiled. "Do not worry, brother. I understand. And, believe me, I would not want to be a prisoner in the infidels' jail. If we fail, I would rather die." His smile widened. "But have no fear, we will not fail. *Inshallah*."

He went back into the living room. Jafari followed him and put the gun on the coffee-table in front of the sofa. He took his mobile phone from his pocket and put it next to the gun.

Al-Hussain went over to the window and opened it. The stadium was four hundred metres away and from their vantage point he could see the stands at the far end and on both sides. The boxing ring had been erected in the centre of the pitch with VIP seating on all four sides. The VIP area had been walled off and security guards in fluorescent jackets were checking tickets at its entrances.

The space between the VIP area and the main stands was patrolled by dozens of security guards and a few uniformed police officers. Most of the VIP area was still empty, though the other stands were already filling up. On match day the stadium held thirty-five thousand but the organisers had decided not to utilise all of the available seating and had restricted ticket sales to twenty-five thousand.

Al-Hussain moved away from the window. The dining table at the far end of the room had six chairs around it. "I will need the table by the window," he said. "Help me."

They moved the chairs away, then he and Jafari carried it across the room. Al-Hussain lay on the table, head towards the window, then climbed off and pushed it a foot to the left. He got back on and nodded. Perfect. "What time is the weapon getting here?" he asked.

"Soon," said Jafari.

Al-Hussain rolled off the table and walked through to the main bedroom. There were two pillows on the bed but they were too soft for what he needed. There was an armchair in the corner of the room with two blue and white striped cushions. He picked one up. It was square and firm. He took it back into the living room and placed it on the table, up against the window.

"Do you want tea?" asked Jafari. "I can make tea."

414

Al-Hussain smiled. "Yes, thank you. Tea would be good." He sat down on the sofa. Not long now.

The fourth and final vehicle to be fitted with a bomb was driven by Akram Hakim, but Sayyid didn't know his name and didn't care. His role was to manufacture the bombs, install them, then return to his normal life. The vehicle edged slowly into the unit and Farooqi pressed the button to bring down the shutter.

Sayyid and Hashmi manoeuvred the barrel to the back of the vehicle as Farooqi opened the door. They lifted it inside and tied it securely in place with washing line. Once they were satisfied, they climbed out and shut the door.

Sayyid got into the front, fitted the trigger to the driver's right hand and showed him how to use it. He asked the man if he had any questions. He smiled as if he hadn't a care in the world. "All is good, brother," he said.

"*Alhamdulillah*," said Sayyid. Praise be to Allah. He climbed out and gave Farooqi a thumbs-up. Farooqi raised the metal shutter and the vehicle reversed out.

The three men stood at the open doorway and watched it drive away.

"So, we are done, brothers," said Sayyid. "It has been a pleasure working with you."

The three men embraced.

"We must clean everything now," said Sayyid, "and burn our clothing. Then we can all go home."

"It will happen today?" asked Hashmi. He hit the button to lower the shutter, which rattled down.

"I don't know for sure," said Sayyid. "And it's better we don't know."

"It has to be today," said Farooqi.

"That's not for us to worry about," said Sayyid. "Let's get this place cleaned up and then we can go."

Two dozen CCTV cameras were covering the inside and outside of the stadium, and Inspector Andrew Fielding could see their feeds on the screens in front of him. He was in the main security room of the stadium, in charge of the fifty uniformed officers on duty. Fielding had just turned thirty-two and he had spent the last three years involved in crowd security. It was challenging police work at the best of times and he had cut his teeth at some of the toughest stadiums in London, keeping apart warring fans, who seemed determined to kill each other and anyone who got between them. Not that he was expecting any trouble that evening. Boxing fans were different from football fans. Chalk and cheese. There was almost never any trouble at a match: all the violence was in the ring. But at a soccer game, where men earning millions fell to the ground clutching their legs at the merest hint of physical contact, fans could behave like animals.

The door opened. It was Ian Chapman, the football club's safety officer, a gruff fifty-something Yorkshireman. He was in overall charge of safety and security at the stadium. Fielding was in charge of the police resources, and if things went bad on a match day the safety officer would usually defer to him. But neither man was expecting trouble that evening and both were looking forward to the main bout. Fielding was sure the Russian was going to win and Chapman was behind the Brit so they'd agreed to differ and bet twenty pounds on the result. A stocky man in his early thirties, his hair cropped short and casually dressed in a black North Face fleece and blue jeans, had come in with Chapman.

"Andrew, this is is Captain Murray. SAS."

"Alex, please," said Murray.

"Andrew Fielding, Inspector. I'm running the police side."

Murray had a strong grip, and as they shook hands his jacket opened just enough for Fielding to spot a gun in an underarm holster. A large number of Russian VIPs were attending the fight and the Russian Embassy was concerned about security — so concerned that they had asked the PM's office for armed security at the event. The PM's office had pointed out that armed Diplomatic Protection Group Officers would be in attendance due to the number of diplomats who planned to be there but the Russian Embassy had offered to pay for even more and, after several days of negotiations, it had been agreed that the SAS would provide an undercover team to guard the VIP area.

"My men are outside. I just wanted to say hello and see what the story is in here," said Murray.

Fielding pointed at the bank of monitors. "We can pretty much see everywhere from the cameras," he said. "Ian's in radio contact with his stewards and I can talk to my officers."

"How many do you have?"

"Fifty inside the stadium, another ten outside," said Fielding. "I don't know if Ian's told you but every match needs a safety certificate signed off by the chairman of the Safety Advisory Group consisting of representatives from the football club, the local council, the police, ambulance and fire brigade. The SAG always grades matches according to risk — Category A is low risk, B is medium, C is high-risk, and C plus is for those games where we're almost certain that trouble will kick off. This boxing event was initially graded as A, low risk with minimal police, just ten officers on duty, but after representations from the Russian Embassy the risk assessment was raised to Category B. That means we're authorised to bring in more men but realistically we're not expecting any problems. Boxing fans are generally a good-natured bunch."

"You're searching everybody who comes in?" asked Murray.

Fielding nodded. "The organisers have placed metal detectors at all the entrances to the stadium, manned by their own security guards, and so far they seem to be doing a good job. They're acting professionally with good humour and it's not causing any problems that we can see."

Fielding's radio buzzed. He mouthed an apology to Murray and put it to his ear.

"How are things, Andrew?" It was Superintendent Stephen Enfield, the officer in charge of the Met Control Centre at Bow.

"All good, Superintendent."

"No problems?"

"We've had a few weapons confiscated, penknives mainly, and a chap claimed that his knuckleduster was a paperweight, but nothing serious. Everyone's very well-behaved — it's a pleasant change from a match day."

"Let's hope it stays that way," said the superintendent. "Have you spoken to the SAS chappie, Alex Murray?"

"He's here now."

"Excellent. He's already met with the SFOs so there won't be any embarrassing misunderstandings. Captain Murray and his team will be in radio contact with me while they're there."

"Yes, sir."

"Good man. Talk to you later."

Fielding put down his radio and apologised to the captain.

"All good," said Murray. "Ian's going to give me the tour and then I'll head down to the VIP area." He shook hands again with Fielding and left with Chapman.

Fielding dropped into one of the chairs facing the monitors. The main bout was a couple of hours away and he planned to watch it as close to the ringside as he could get. And the fact he was wearing full uniform meant that would be pretty darn close.

"Are you all right there, Terry? You're like you've got something on your mind." Tommy O'Neill was sitting at a table in the Mayfair bar with his third bottle of Cristal in an ice bucket by his side. Marty was opposite him, and a blonde with pneumatic breasts that were threatening to burst out of her red dress was running her scarlet fingernails along the thigh of his black Armani suit.

Shepherd faked a smile and patted his chest. "Indigestion," he said. "Should have done what my old mum used to say and chew before I swallow."

"I've got some Rennies if you want," said Tommy.

"Nah, I'm good." Shepherd had arrived at the Mayfair just as the O'Neills had been sitting down to eat, along with Evans and two others of their crew. After they'd polished off their steaks they'd moved to the bar and demolished half a dozen bottles of champagne between them.

Marty looked at his watch. "We should be making a move," he said. "No way of telling what the traffic's going to be like."

"Yeah, I don't want to miss the Wilkie-Okoro fight," said Tommy. "I need to see Okoro fold in the fifth. Because if he doesn't there'll be hell to pay." He raised his glass to Marty, grinned then drained it in one.

Marty waved for the bill and handed over a gold credit card, brushing away Shepherd's attempts to pay. "Nah, Terry, today's on me," he said. "After everything you've done for us recently, it's the least we can do."

Wendy Aspden reached for her phone. She had Willoughby-Brown's number on speed-dial and spoke to him through her headset. "We've got movement," she said, as soon as he had answered. She was looking at the screen in front of her, showing a thermal image of the front of the house. All three figures had gathered at the left-hand side of the hallway. "They're heading towards the garage," she said. "Looks like they're on the move."

"What about the gun case?" asked Willoughby-Brown.

"One went up into the attic and brought something down with him. I'm going to get things moving here and I'll call you back."

"I'll be linked in to your radio feed," said Willoughby-Brown.

"You want to be in at the kill?" asked Aspden, surprised.

"Try to keep me away," said Willoughby-Brown.

Aspden ended the call, opened the door and shouted across the hallway to the SFOs: "Let's get ready to move, guys. They're heading out."

Elyas Assadi placed the gun case in the boot of the Prius and got into the front passenger seat next to Johnny Malik, who already had the engine running. Amma al-Kawthari pulled up the garage door and Malik drove slowly out. Al-Kawthari closed the door and got into the back of the car.

The traffic was heavy and Malik had to wait several minutes before it was safe to edge out. He was breathing slowly, trying to stay calm. He checked his rear-view mirror, then accelerated to keep pace with the traffic. His mouth had gone dry and he wished he'd thought of bringing a bottle of water.

"Are you all right, brother?" asked Assadi.

Malik tried to smile. "I'm fine."

Assadi reached over and squeezed Malik's knee. "You're doing well."

"I'm just nervous, brother. I don't want anything to go wrong."

"Nothing will go wrong, brother," said al-Kawthari, from the back seat. "*Inshallah*."

"Everything has been planned," said Assadi, giving Malik's knee another gentle squeeze. "Do not worry. Just follow your instructions and everything will be fine."

Willoughby-Brown climbed into the back of the van and the driver closed the door electronically. Willoughby-Brown placed his transceiver on the table, pressed a button on a console and a screen folded down from the roof. There was a keyboard on a shelf behind the driver and he leaned forward, grabbed it and laid it on the table next to the transceiver. He put on the transceiver's earpiece and tapped on the keyboard. The screen flickered into life. The van had mobile Wi-Fi and within seconds he had the feed from Aspden's screen in front of him. There was a map of London and small red circles showing the locations of vehicles she had put in place.

Willoughby-Brown pressed a button to talk to the driver. "Can you hear me, Tim?"

"Loud and clear, sir."

"Excellent. Head west, north of the river, as soon as possible. No great rush at the moment. Nice and steady."

"Yes, sir."

Willoughby-Brown pressed the button on his transceiver to get to the frequency Aspden was using.

"Bravo Two has eyeball. On the A40 heading east."

"Roger that Bravo Two," he heard Aspden say. "Bravo One, prepare to take over eyeball."

"Bravo One preparing to take eyeball."

Bravo 1 and Bravo 2 were the motorcycles being used in the surveillance. Bravo 1 was a small moped. A Plexiglas screen was attached to its handlebars with a taxi route clipped to it. Anyone seeing the bike would assume it was a wannabe black-cab driver learning the Knowledge. Bravo 2 was a high-powered Kawasaki bike, its rider outfitted as a courier.

There were two nondescript saloon cars, one of which was now a quarter of a mile ahead of the Prius, the other about the same distance behind. The bikes would take it in turns to keep the target car in sight while the two cars would be ready to take up any slack if necessary.

Willoughby-Brown pressed the transmit button. "Mike One is on line," he said.

"Welcome aboard," said Aspden.

"How are we looking?" asked Willoughby-Brown.

"So far so good," said Aspden. "From the way the Prius is being driven it doesn't look as if they're taking any counter-surveillance measures. They're braking in plenty of time to stop at red lights, they indicate at every turn, and they're at a constant speed most of the time."

Willoughby-Brown pressed the button to talk to the driver again. "Tim, close to the A40 would be good."

"No problem, sir."

Willoughby-Brown called Shepherd's number but it went straight through to voicemail. He didn't bother leaving a message. Shepherd would know what it was about.

Malik clicked the indicator to show he was turning right. Off to his left were the high brick walls of Wormwood Scrubs. He drove onto the A3220 and prepared to indicate another right turn, this one taking them into the huge Westfield Shopping Centre. He glanced into his rear-view mirror but didn't notice the motorbike that was tucked in three cars behind.

He joined the queue of cars waiting to drive into the massive shopping centre: the size of thirty football pitches, it was home to more than 250 stores and parking for 4,500 vehicles.

"Bravo One, Tango One is turning into the Westfield Shopping Centre," said the voice in Willoughby-Brown's ear.

"Stay with him, Bravo One," said Aspden.

"Charlie One, Charlie Two, head for Westfield. It's going to be crowded in there."

Willoughby-Brown frowned. Attacking Westfield Shopping Centre with a rifle didn't make much sense. A rifle was a surgical weapon, designed for taking out single targets. It was hardly the weapon of choice to cause carnage in a crowded shopping centre. And if that was their plan, the jihadists would find they had bitten off more than they could chew. Since the Islamic

State terrorist attacks in Paris, the British government had increased security at shopping centres across the country. Armed police in plain clothes mingled with shoppers around the clock, and at times of high terrorist alert they were supplemented with armed SAS troopers. They would make short work of one man with a rifle. It would be different if they had been using explosives but there was no evidence of that.

Willoughby-Brown didn't want to interrupt Aspden on the radio so he sent a text message: *Westfield doesn't feel right to me.*

Aspden replied almost immediately: *Me neither.*

Shepherd travelled to the stadium in the back of a Mercedes with the O'Neills and Paul Evans. There was another car with four more of the O'Neill crew, and the two vehicles arrived at the VIP entrance at the same time. Marty led the way, tickets in hand, while Tommy followed with Evans. Shepherd held back. He took his phone out and had a quick look at the screen: one missed call, number withheld, almost certainly Willoughby-Brown. He slipped it back into his pocket. A pretty blonde in a fluorescent vest checked Marty's tickets, flashed him a beaming smile and waved for him to go through. They walked down a narrow corridor to a reception room where there were four more security guards and a metal-detector arch. "Bloody hell, this is worse than getting on a plane," grumbled Tommy.

"It's just a precaution, sir," said a young lad in a fluorescent vest that seemed several sizes too big for him. "And you can leave your shoes on. Just phones and anything metallic in the tray."

One by one they placed their belongings in grey plastic trays and walked through the arch. As Tommy was putting his phone and wallet back into his pockets, two middle-aged men in long coats walked up to him. Tommy sneered at them before either spoke, recognising them for what they were. "Thomas O'Neill, I'm arresting you on suspicion of conspiracy to commit murder, extortion, and money-laundering," said the younger of the two. He was ginger-haired with a sprinkle of freckles across his nose. "You do not have to say anything but it may harm your defence if you do not mention when questioned something which you later rely on in court. Anything you do say may be given in evidence. Do you understand what I have just said to you?"

"I want to call my lawyer," growled Tommy.

"You can do that from the station. Please turn around."

Tommy did as he was told and the detective went to handcuff him. More detectives were coming into the room. Two went towards Marty, and two headed for Evans.

"You don't need the cuffs. I'm too long in the tooth to do a runner."

"It's procedure, sir," he was told.

"Don't fuck around, Tommy," said the older detective. "It's not as if you haven't been arrested before, is it?"

"It's been a while," said Tommy. "And the last copper who put his hands on me lived to regret it, big-time."

"You wouldn't be threatening a police officer, would you now, Tommy? I thought you knew better than that."

Tommy glared at him but kept his mouth shut and allowed himself to be handcuffed.

Shepherd felt his arm being grabbed and turned to see a detective with grey hair and a dark moustache holding him. "Get your fucking hand off me," he snapped.

Another detective had read Marty his rights and was handcuffing him. Evans was also being cuffed. "This is fucking out of order!" shouted Shepherd. He pushed the detective standing next to him in the chest, hard. "We're just here for the fucking boxing!"

Shepherd was grabbed from behind and the detective he'd pushed was in his face. "Terry Taylor, you're being charged with murder, and conspiracy to commit murder."

"Fuck off!"

Shepherd's hands were cuffed behind him and he was frog-marched out of the room, down another corridor, and out to a car-parking area. Tommy was being put into one police van and Marty into another.

Evans was brought out by two burly detectives in leather jackets and he grinned at Shepherd. "Don't worry, Terry, we'll be out in a few hours. They've got nothing. Just keep schtum and let the lawyers do the talking. Tommy will handle everything."

"I want to see the fucking boxing, mate. This is a fucking liability."

Evans laughed. "They'll have it on at the cop shop. We can watch it there." Evans glared at the detective who was holding his left arm. "I'll be claiming back the cost of these tickets from the Met, and that's a fucking promise."

A security guard pulled back a metal gate and the two vans drove out. Evans was put into the back of a patrol car and driven off through the gate. Then it was Shepherd's turn. Two detectives walked him over to a Mercedes police van, opened the rear door and helped him in. Amar Singh was sitting in the back and Shepherd grinned as the door slammed behind him.

"I didn't expect to see you here," said Shepherd.

"Jeremy thought you might like to see a friendly face," said Singh. "And make sure they didn't accidentally throw you in jail."

"It wouldn't have been the first time."

Singh showed him a handcuff key and Shepherd turned around so that he could release the cuffs. He massaged his wrists and sat down. The van was already moving. Shepherd gestured at the driver. "Where's he going?"

"Just away from here," said Singh. "Willoughby-Brown wants you to call him."

"Yeah. It's turning out to be a busy day."

"Who do you think'll win the fight?"

"The Russian."

"Have you still got your ticket?"

"Are you serious?"

428

"It'd be a pity to waste it," said Singh. "It's going to be an awesome fight. I've got fifty quid on the Russian."

Stuart Smith followed the white Prius as it drove slowly through the car park. There were very few spaces to be had. Pretending to be a wannabe cabbie studying the Knowledge was a great cover on the open road but his moped with its Plexiglas map holder was out of place in the car park so he hung well back.

"Bravo One has eyeball. Tango One seems to be looking for a parking space," said Smith into his mic. The Prius turned right. The car behind went straight on. The car directly in front of Smith indicated right, then braked suddenly. Smith was so busy watching the Prius that he didn't see the stop lights go on and slammed into the back of the car.

Smith cursed. He backed up and was about to pass the car when the driver sprang out. He was a big man with tattooed arms and a diamond earring in his left ear. "What the fuck are yez playing at?" growled the man, in a heavy Glaswegian accent.

"Sorry, mate, my bad," said Smith.

He tried to move on but the man grabbed his handlebars. "Where the fuck do yez think yer going?" he said. "You need to pay for the damage."

Smith looked at the rear of the man's car. It was pristine. "There's no damage, mate," he said. He glanced at the Prius. It had moved on, still looking for somewhere to park. "Bravo One, I'm losing eyeball," he said.

"What the fuck are yez talking about?" said the man.

"Bravo Two, can you get in there?" asked Aspden, in Smith's ear.

"Bravo Two, heading into the car park."

"Mate, look, I'm sorry, I fucked up," said Smith.

The man pointed at the rear bumper. "A hundred quid," he said. "A hundred quid or I'm calling the cops."

"Are you serious?"

"You hit my car. That's an accident, right? So I'm due compensation." He rubbed the back of his neck. "I might even have whiplash coming on."

"Mate, my bike weighs a hundred kilos soaking wet. You weigh twice that."

The man continued rubbing his neck. "Yeah, I'm getting a headache. I might need a scan."

"A fucking lobotomy is what you need," said Smith. He pulled out his wallet and fished out a hundred pounds. He thrust the notes into the man's hand. "Happy now?"

"Prick," said the man, pocketing the notes. He got back into the car as Smith drove away, looking frantically for the Prius.

Malik looked right and left. "I don't see it," he said, his voice shaking. "Where are they? Why aren't they here?" The Prius was crawling along at walking pace.

Assadi patted his leg. "Relax, brother, they will be here."

"I can't see them." He banged his hands on the steering wheel. "Why aren't they here? Maybe they've been arrested."

"No one has been arrested, brother," said Assadi.

"I see them," said al-Kawthari. He pointed off to their left. A blue Transit van had been parked across two bays. "Flash your lights."

The driver was Asian and when he saw the Prius's lights flash he edged forward, then reversed back into one of the bays. The Prius reversed into the empty bay next to him.

"Good luck, brother," said Assadi, climbing out of the car. He hurried to the rear doors of the Transit. Al-Kawthari got out of the Prius and tried to open the boot. He found it was locked and banged impatiently on the rear window. Malik waved an apology and pressed the boot button. Al-Kawthari grabbed the gun case and joined Assadi at the back of the Transit. Assadi climbed in and al-Kawthari passed him the gun case, then got in after him. The van drove off.

Malik sat where he was and watched them go. His instructions were to wait in the car park for thirty minutes, then to drive back to Ealing. His job was done.

"Bravo Two, I have eyeball on the vehicle, but two of the tangoes have gone. Only the driver is in the vehicle." Willoughby-Brown frowned at the transceiver. Gone? Where could they have gone?

"Bravo Two, are the other tangoes on foot?" asked Aspden.

"I don't know, I can't see them," said Bravo Two.

"Charlie One, can you get on foot and into the mall?"

"Charlie One, roger that."

Willoughby-Brown's frown deepened. It didn't make much sense for two jihadists to be wandering around Westfield with a gun case. One, there was a good chance someone would recognise the case for what it was and report them. Two, a sniper rifle — assuming that was what was in the case — would hardly be the weapon of choice for an attack on a crowded shopping centre. The gun was slow to reload and generally sniper rifles had small magazines and weren't geared up for rapid fire. If the jihadists were planning to mount an attack on Westfield, they'd more likely go for AK-47s or semi-automatics. He looked at the screen map and pressed the button to talk to his driver. "Tim, let's go to Westfield Shopping Centre. See if you can get near to where the cars come out of the car park."

"No problem, sir."

Willoughby-Brown pressed the transmit button on his transceiver. "Mike One, I'm not convinced they're on foot. It makes more sense to me that they've switched vehicles."

"We've not seen anything like counter-surveillance before," said Aspden.

"I get that, but that's not to say they wouldn't leave it until the final run," said Willoughby-Brown. "And I can't see them arranging to meet a sniper in a shopping centre. It just feels wrong."

"I agree, I'll get Charlie Two to hang back."

"Roger that," said Willoughby-Brown. "And I'd suggest you get someone at the exit, check the drivers and passengers. I think we're in the middle of a switch."

His phone vibrated and he looked at the screen. It was Shepherd. He took the call. "The tangoes are on the move, with the gun," he said. "Westfield Shopping Centre, but I don't think that's the target. I'll get the SFOs to pick you up. How did it go with the O'Neills?"

"All done and dusted," said Shepherd.

"I just hope this operation goes as smoothly," said Willoughby-Brown.

The driver of Charlie Two was a middle-aged man in a tweed jacket, horn-rimmed spectacles and a flat cap. The middle-aged woman next to him could easily have been his wife. She had dyed blonde hair and was sitting with a blue plastic handbag in her lap. Anyone looking at them would assume they were a married couple out for a Saturday shop, but in fact they were two of MI5's most experienced followers.

"Charlie Two, we're outside the exit now," said the woman.

"Roger that, Charlie Two," said Aspden. "If they've swapped vehicles they'll be out in the next few minutes."

The driver parked opposite the exit but they were on double yellow lines and he knew they wouldn't be able to stay there for long.

Half a dozen cars came out and joined the traffic. A police car was heading their way. "We're going to have to either move or identify ourselves," said the woman in the passenger seat.

"I see them," said the driver.

"Give it a few seconds, then move on," said the woman. "We mustn't show out whatever happens."

As the driver stared at the barriers holding back the two lines of traffic leaving the centre, he saw two Asian men sitting in front of a blue Ford Transit. He didn't recognise the driver but he knew the man in the passenger seat. It was one of the tangoes. "Charlie Two, I have eyeball," he said. "They're leaving now." The woman described the vehicle and read out the registration number as the driver edged the car back into the traffic.

"Anyone else have eyeball?" asked Aspden.

"Bravo One, I have eyeball."

"That was a close call," said Aspden. "All right, everybody. Bravo One has eyeball. Note that Tango One is now a blue Transit van with at least two IC Four males on board."

Charlie Two accelerated away, putting plenty of distance between themselves and the van.

The driver of the blue Transit van was a British-born Asian. He had no idea whom he was driving or what was in the case they had loaded into the back. He had been told where to meet the men, and where to go, but that was all. His name was Rahman Naeem but only his parents used his given name. His friends and colleagues called him Ray. The van belonged to his father but it was usually Naeem who drove it, running to the cash and carry to restock the family's corner shop in Leyton.

Naeem's instructions had come through his imam, a seventy-year-old cleric who had fought against the

Russians in Afghanistan but who had lived in England since the early eighties. He was a learned man and knew the Koran by heart, but he had never lost his warrior roots. He had groomed half a dozen men at the mosque, initially tutoring them in the Koran but then educating them in the politics of Islam. Only those he trusted totally were admitted into his inner sanctum of students where he explained the aims and objectives of Islamic State.

Naeem had been one of the imam's star pupils and had begged to be allowed to go to Afghanistan for further training but the imam had advised him against it. Any young British Asian who travelled to that part of the world was immediately placed on the government's watch list. The imam had explained that Naeem would be more valuable as a cleanskin: he could operate without ever being watched. Over the past year the imam had used Naeem half a dozen times, usually driving people or delivering parcels, sometimes passing messages in person. Naeem never asked whom he was driving or what he was delivering: he trusted the imam completely.

Naeem kept a close eye on his mirrors, checking the vehicles behind him constantly. The imam had introduced him to a man from Birmingham, who had taught him about counter-surveillance, how to see if you were being followed and how to lose a tail. Naeem varied his speed, took random turns without indicating and accelerated through amber lights.

He took a circuitous route to his destination, at one point making four left turns in a row, and stopped off at a filling station, ostensibly to put petrol in the tank but the real reason was that it gave him plenty of time to look around for followers.

Only when he was satisfied that he was not being tailed did he head for the destination.

The police van braked suddenly, throwing Shepherd off balance. "This is you," said Singh. "Break a leg."

"Thanks for the lift," said Shepherd, getting up.

Singh opened the rear door and Shepherd got out. The door closed almost immediately and the van drove off. A few yards in front of him, Thomas Leigh was at the wheel of a black SUV, with Roy Graves, the senior of the three SFOs who had been at the house in Ealing, in the passenger seat. Graves flashed Shepherd a thumbs-up and waved him over.

Shepherd jogged across to the SUV and climbed into the back next to the third member of the team, Neil Walker, a former squaddie who had done two tours in Afghanistan before joining the Met.

"Nice of you to dress for the occasion," said Graves, as Leigh pulled away from the kerb.

"I was at the boxing," said Shepherd.

"The Hughes-Kuznetsov fight?" asked Walker.

"I think they're calling it the Kuznetsov-Hughes fight."

"Bollocks," said Walker. "Hughes'll walk it. And you've got tickets?"

"Ringside," said Shepherd.

"Not your day," said Walker. He handed Shepherd a transceiver.

"So, sitrep," said Graves, from the front. "The tangoes switched vehicles in the Westfield car park. We assume the gun is on board but no one saw the transfer. The tangoes are now being very cagey so something's going on. They're in a blue Transit heading east."

Shepherd put in the earpiece. "Bravo One, fall back and let Bravo Two have eyeball," said Aspden.

"How far away from the bravos are we?" asked Shepherd.

"About half a mile," said Graves. "When it became clear that the driver of the blue Transit was employing counter-surveillance techniques, Wendy had the cars pull back and the two bikes are keeping as far away as they can, one ahead and one behind the target vehicle. Oh, and just so you know, your boss is on the case. He's using Mike One."

Shepherd pulled out his phone to call Willoughby-Brown. "I'm with the SFOs now," he said. "From the sound of it, the tangoes are definitely up to something."

"Wendy's the best. They won't spot her people," said Willoughby-Brown.

"It looks as if they're on the home run now," said Shepherd. "You might want to think about possible targets in the area."

"I'm on it. I've got a map in front of me. I've already been on to the Diplomatic Protection Group and I've spoken to the PM's office. Everyone's on full alert."

"And the sniper is probably going to be shooting from a vantage point, almost certainly high up."

"Understood."

"So what's our game plan?"

"We need the sniper. That's our main concern. There's no point in pulling in the weapon or the delivery boys. If the sniper gets hold of another weapon, we're back to square one. The sniper's the prize."

"That is the building ahead of us," said Naeem. He pointed at three tower blocks immediately ahead. "The middle one." He pointed at the glove compartment. "There's a keycard in there. In an envelope."

Assadi opened the glove compartment and found an envelope with a number on it: 1214. He nodded. "Thank you, brother."

"I'll drop you outside."

Assadi climbed into the back of the van where al-Kawthari was sitting on an upturned crate, the gun case at his feet. "We're here," he said.

They turned to the right and stopped. Al-Kawthari opened the door and got out. Assadi passed the case to him, then climbed out and slammed the door. Naeem drove off immediately.

Shepherd put his finger to his earpiece as it crackled. "Bravo One, they're out of the van, which is heading back west. Two men are coming towards a tower block."

"Can you get off the bike and follow on foot, Bravo One?" asked Aspden.

"I'll try, but I don't think I'll get there in time," said the man.

Shepherd tapped Leigh's shoulder. "Let's go there — we're not doing any good here." The driver stamped on the accelerator.

"Bravo One, they're going inside. They had a key card. I've lost them. The van is still heading west."

"Bravo Two, pick up the van," said Aspden. "Charlie One, go with him. Charlie Two, you can RV with Bravo One. Mike One will be running things from there."

"Mike One, will be there in two minutes." Willoughby-Brown sounded tense.

There was a knock and Jafari picked up his gun. He tiptoed to the door and squinted through the viewer. "It's them," he said, unlocking the door and pulling it open. Mohammed al-Hussain was sitting at the table. He had closed the window but was staring down at the stadium.

Two Asian men were outside on the landing, one holding the metal case. Jafari ushered them into the flat and locked the door. "Welcome, brothers," he said.

The man with the case placed it on the table.

Al-Hussain stood up and went over to it. He flicked the double catches and took out the rifle, then carefully screwed the suppressor into the barrel. The two men stood behind him, eyes wide as they stared at the weapon. He attached the telescopic sight, then placed the gun on the table, the barrel lying on the cushion.

He took out the three magazines and loaded each one with five rounds. He placed two magazines at the side of the cushion and slotted the third into the rifle. He waved for Jafari to take away the case, then pulled the black scarf from his pocket and tied it around his head. "Brothers, we should pray," he said.

The three men joined him. Jafari showed them the direction of Mecca and they began to pray in unison.

"This is us," said Leigh, bringing the SUV to a halt. Bravo One's bike was parked on the pavement and the man himself was standing by the entrance to the block, still wearing his helmet. Willoughby-Brown's van was parked on the other side of the road and he was already climbing out.

"Guys, I need a weapon," said Shepherd. He gestured at Willoughby-Brown. "My boss there will cover any paperwork that's needed."

"No problem," said Graves. He popped the rear door and tapped a six-digit code into the keypad of a metal gun safe. He opened it to reveal two Glocks, a shotgun and three SIG Sauer 516 assault rifles. The SIG516, with its telescoping stock and thirty-round magazine, had replaced the Heckler & Koch G36 as the Met's assault rifle of choice, but Shepherd figured it would be overkill for what he needed. He took a Glock, ejected the magazine, checked it and slotted it back into place.

Graves relocked the safe as Willoughby-Brown walked over. "This isn't good," he said.

"They got inside before we could do anything," said Shepherd.

"What do you think? The roof?"

Shepherd shook his head. "Could just as easily be a flat. This has been well planned."

"So what do we do? A house to house?" He cursed under his breath.

"We need to start thinking targets," said Shepherd. He gestured at the building. "You know where we are, right? Half a mile that way is the stadium where they're holding the world heavyweight fight. It's full of Russian VIPs, and Islamic State hate the Russians as much as they hate us. And let's not forget the PM will be there."

Willoughby-Brown ran a hand through his hair. "What do we do? Evacuate? What if they're just holding the gun here?"

Shepherd glanced at his watch. "The main bout is starting soon. There'll be a riot if you try to shut it down." He gestured at the building. "There should be CCTV inside. If we can get a look at the footage, we should be able to see where they went."

Willoughby-Brown nodded. "Let's do it."

Mohammed al-Hussain lay on the table, the barrel of the rifle supported by the cushion. He brought his eye to the scope and settled his shoulder against the stock. He was breathing tidally, his chest barely moving. He centred the crosshairs on the chest of the black boxer in the ring and imagined pulling the trigger, then the bullet slamming into the man's flesh. He smiled at the reaction it would cause, shot in the heart in front of thousands of spectators, with television cameras beaming the pictures around the world.

He moved the gun a fraction, focusing on one of the trainers who was shouting encouragement at his boxer. He centred the crosshairs on the man's face and imagined it imploding as the bullet hit it, spraying blood and brain matter over the crowds behind him.

He rolled his shoulders, relaxing the muscles that had tensed in anticipation of what was to come, then settled back into the firing position. He scanned the VIP section, which was starting to fill. He recognised some of the faces. A leading Russian industrialist. A newspaper owner. An actor and his model girlfriend. Several famous boxers. The crosshairs passed over them all.

Al-Hussain moved the scope away from the ringside and scanned the terraces. He settled on a middle-aged man selling programmes. He was in his forties, balding and wearing a purple bow tie. He was holding several copies, like an oversized poker hand, and a bag over his shoulder contained dozens more. Al-Hussain slipped his finger over the trigger, took aim, held his breath, and fired.

Shepherd stared up at the floor indicators above the three lifts. One was on the ground floor, the doors open. The middle one was at the top. The final lift was on the sixth floor, coming down. There was no way of telling for sure which floor the jihadists had stopped at. Any hope of accessing the CCTV footage had been dashed when they had gained entrance to the block. There was no one on duty in the reception area, just a notice that gave a contact number for the managing agent.

"Top floor?" said Willoughby-Brown, his uncertainty showing in his voice.

"Who knows?" said Shepherd. "It'd be a guess."

The three armed officers were looking at them for guidance.

The lift that was on the way down passed the third floor. Hands were creeping towards concealed weapons. The lift passed two and one . . . Then the doors opened. An old lady reversed out, pulling a wheeled shopping basket as she muttered to herself. They watched her hobble to the doors, fumble for the exit button, and let herself out.

As the door opened they heard a helicopter overhead. Shepherd turned to Willoughby-Brown. "The Met's chopper," he said.

Willoughby-Brown understood immediately. The Metropolitan Police's Air Support Unit had three Eurocopter EC145 helicopters, each equipped with night vision and infrared cameras. He tapped his Bluetooth earpiece. "Wendy, patch me through to whoever's running Met Control over at Bow."

"Will do," said Aspden, in his ear.

"Shall we go up?" asked Shepherd.

Willoughby-Brown nodded and headed into the empty lift. Shepherd and the three armed officers followed him.

The man was lying on the floor, programmes scattered around him. He was groaning and the woman standing over him thought he'd fainted. "Are you all right?" she said. "Can I help you up?"

"My leg," he said. "My leg — it's burning."

She looked down at it — his trousers were wet with blood. She gasped and covered her mouth with her hand. "What happened?"

"I don't know. Help me — please."

The woman wasn't sure what to do. She caught the eye of a man sitting in the stand behind her. "Please help me!" she shouted. "There's a man hurt here!"

Music began to play, a Russian tune, as the Russian heavyweight made his way to the ring, surrounded by his entourage. The main bout would soon be under way.

The woman screamed again, fighting to make herself heard over the blare of the music. "Help me, please!"

Shepherd concentrated on breathing slowly as the floor counter ticked on. Twelve. Thirteen. Fourteen.

Willoughby-Brown turned to the wall and began to speak. "Thank you, Wendy." He paused, took a breath, then continued: "Superintendent Enfield, you have a helicopter in the air over the stadium?"

"We do, yes."

"I need you to get it to take a look at the middle of the three tower blocks overlooking the stadium. We believe there's a sniper in the block and at least three men will be close to the window. I'm hoping the chopper's infrared capability will find them."

"I'll get it done now," said the superintendent.

"I'll stay on the line, if I may."

444

"See how Kuznetsov always drops his right, just before he does the uppercut with his left? That's a tell, that is. As soon as Hughes spots it, it's game over." Richie McBride was sitting next to his son, trying to explain the finer points of the bout. They were up in the stands but even though they were well away from the action the seats had cost close to fifty pounds each.

Richie's son, Sean, was leaning forward with his head in his hands, watching the fight as if his life depended on it. He'd started boxing a year earlier at his local youth club, following in his father's footsteps. Richie had almost made pro. Almost, but not quite. He'd taken one too many hits to the jaw and a fracture had healed badly meaning that his fighting days had ended before they'd really started. But Sean knew how to protect his head and, even though he was only fourteen, he was clearly going to be a better fighter than Richie could ever have hoped to be.

"Hughes is going to win, no question," said Richie.

"He's tired, though."

"No, he's sweating, but that doesn't mean he's tired. You can sweat without being tired. His arms are up, and look at the way he's ducking and diving. He's fine."

A man walking down the aisle to his seat suddenly stopped and slumped to the floor. Richie looked at the man, frowning. He hadn't stumbled, or tripped. He had just been walking, then fallen to the ground.

"You all right, mate?" he shouted over.

The man groaned but didn't get up.

Sean was still engrossed in the fight as Richie stood and made his way over to the man. He was lying face down and blood was oozing from his shoulder, darkening the blue of his suit. "What the fuck?" muttered Richie. He waved at a steward in a fluorescent jacket. "Hey, there's a guy hurt here! He's bleeding!"

The steward hurried over.

The lift jerked to a halt at the top of the building and the doors rattled open. The men stepped out. Shepherd had the Glock in his hand, his trigger finger pressed against the side of the gun. The corridor ran from left to right, with emergency stairs at either end. "I've lost my bearings. Which side faces the stadium?" asked Willoughby-Brown.

Shepherd gestured at the doors opposite the lifts. "They're facing north. But there's no guarantee that the stadium is his target."

"It's a reasonable assumption," said Willoughby-Brown. His hand went instinctively to touch his earpiece. "Yes, Superintendent, I'm here."

"The room you're looking for is on the twelfth floor, fifth window from the left as you face the building," said the superintendent. "There are four people inside, one of whom appears to be lying down by the window."

Willoughby-Brown gestured at the lift. "Twelfth floor," he said. "Thank you, Superintendent. Could you get the helicopter to pull back now and clear the area? Thank you so much."

"Do I need to evacuate?"

446

"I think we have it in hand, Superintendent. But if anything changes, you'll be the first to know."

Shepherd and the three armed officers followed Willoughby-Brown back into the lift. Willoughby-Brown stabbed the button for the twelfth floor and the doors rattled shut.

Ian Chapman put down his radio and walked over to Inspector Fielding. "Andrew, something weird's going on."

Fielding turned away from the screens. "What's up?" He'd been planning to head ringside. The first round was over and it was set to be an awesome bout.

"We've got two woundings," said Chapman.

"Woundings?"

"Stabbings, by the look of it. They both happened within the last few minutes."

Fielding stood up. "What happened? Who stabbed them?"

"No one knows. We just have two people on the ground bleeding."

"Hang on, what are you saying? Someone's going around stabbing people?"

"Andrew, I don't know anything other than what I've just told you. Two people with stab wounds."

Fielding looked back at the screens. Everything seemed normal. In the ring a pretty blonde in a bikini was strutting around with a sign announcing round two. "Where are they?" he asked.

Chapman scrutinised the screens, then tapped one. "That's one of our programme sellers." Fielding went over and peered at the screen. A small crowd had gathered around a man lying on the ground. Three men in fluorescent jackets were trying to get them to move back while another steward was kneeling next to the injured man.

"I'm not sure where the other one is," said Chapman.

"Okay, I'm going to have to tell the Met Control Centre," said Fielding, reaching for the radio. "But, frankly, I'm not sure what to tell them. Do we have one nutter with a knife or is something bigger going on?"

Chapman shrugged. He had no idea.

Fielding was just about to radio Superintendent Enfield, but the superintendent beat him to it. "Andrew, we might have a problem there."

"Yes, sir, I was just going to call you. We have a number of casualties here and we're not sure what's going on."

"Casualties?"

"Two people with what appear to be stab wounds. No suspects but with severe injuries."

"Is it possible they are gunshot wounds?"

"Gunshot wounds? I don't think so. We haven't heard shots and everyone who enters the stadium is searched."

"We've had reports of a possible sniper in one of the blocks overlooking the stadium."

"A sniper?"

"That's what I'm told. Is it possible the wounds are sniper-related?"

448

Fielding waved to get Chapman's attention. "Could the woundings be gunshots?"

Chapman shook his head. "No one's reported hearing shots."

"There might be a sniper."

"It's possible, I suppose." He scratched his head. "But why?"

"We'll check and get back to you, sir," said Fielding, into his radio. "In the meantime, do we evacuate?"

"What's the state of play there?"

"Round two is just about to start."

"Do you think you could evacuate, if necessary?"

"We could try, sir, but I'm not sure we'd be listened to."

"I'll get back to you," said the superintendent.

The man stepped through the metal detector, hesitated, then walked over to the table to pick up his keys and mobile phone. He turned to wait for his friend, who came through the metal detector grinning. It must have beeped because a security guard stepped forward and began to pat him down.

Mohammed al-Hussain took aim at the man being searched, the security guard, then across to the man at the table. He aimed, took a breath, let half of it out, and squeezed the trigger. Half a mile away, the man fell to the ground in agony.

It was only then that he realised there was a helicopter outside the building, off to the left. Amma al-Kawthari was at the window, staring at it. The helicopter was several hundred yards away but the nose was pointing in their direction. "They're going to shoot us!" he said.

Al-Hussain smiled. "It is a police helicopter and they are not armed," he said. "But even if they were, they would not be allowed to shoot us. In England the police cannot attack civilians. That is the law."

"But they know we're here," said Elyas Assadi.

"Perhaps, but even if they do it is too late for them to do anything," said al-Hussain. He put his eye to the scope and focused on the helicopter. When it had first appeared he had assumed it was a random patrol but it had stayed in its present position for almost a minute and it appeared to be concentrating on the building. He could just make out the two figures but he knew there was no point in trying to shoot through the Plexiglas. Even if it wasn't bulletproof the round would almost certainly ricochet off it. He moved the rifle slightly to the right and took aim just below where the rear tail rotor was spinning. The first shot hit bang on target but didn't seem to have any effect. The second shot smacked into the tail and a few seconds later black smoke poured out and the rotor started to flicker. The helicopter began to rotate and al-Hussain took his eye away from the scope. Without the tail rotor functioning properly the helicopter was impossible to control and began to spin crazily.

It lost height rapidly, still spinning, and the lower it got, the faster it spun. It disappeared from view and a few seconds later al-Hussain heard the dull thump of an explosion as it hit the ground. His magazine was empty so he ejected it and slotted in a fresh one. He

450

already had the scope to his eye and was selecting his next target as grey smoke plumed up from the wreckage of the helicopter.

Eight doors faced the lifts, each with a number: 1202 to 1216. All even numbers. "You should hang back, Jeremy," said Shepherd, "seeing as how you don't have a gun."

Willoughby-Brown nodded. Shepherd was impressed by the man's calmness. He had seemed perfectly ready to go charging in even though he was unarmed.

Shepherd ran the numbers. The superintendent in Met Control had said fifth window from the left. There had been twenty-four windows running the length of the building, which suggested three per flat. That meant the sniper was in the second flat from the left looking at the building: 1214. Assuming all the flats were the same size. In a perfect world they would have obtained a floor plan of the building but there was no time.

Shepherd pointed for the three armed cops to take up positions either side of the door to flat 1214. There was no time for subterfuge, no time to pretend to be delivering a parcel or checking for a leak: a frontal assault was the only way to go.

"There's another one," said Chapman. "Up in the stands."

"A stabbing?"

"They don't know. He was in the middle of a row and no one saw anything. But the guy has a wound in his shoulder and is bleeding to death. We need ambulances, now. Lots of them. We've got paramedics but we need to get them to hospital."

"Ian, what the hell's happening here?" He waved at the screens. "We're not seeing anything? Who's doing this?"

"I don't know," said Chapman. A phone rang and Chapman grabbed it. As he listened, the colour drained from his face. "That's one of the stewards outside the ground," he said. "A helicopter's just crashed."

"Crashed where?"

"He's not sure exactly. He just saw it coming down at speed with smoke pouring from it."

Confused, Fielding turned to the screens, rubbing the back of his neck.

"We need to get ambulances in here now," said Chapman.

Fielding continued to massage his neck. "I'll check with Superintendent Enfield. He's Gold Commander on this."

"Andrew, there isn't time. We need to call for ambulances now and we need to get the gates open. And we need to find out where that helicopter crashed — there could be more casualties."

Fielding reached for his radio.

Mohammed al-Hussain took a breath, released half, and squeezed the trigger. The stock kicked against his shoulder and he relaxed. The bullet sped through the air at close to three thousand feet per second, friction slowing it every step of the way but it still hit its target

452

in less than half a second. The man slumped back in his seat, a look of pained surprise on his face.

Al-Hussain ejected the cartridge. He loaded a round, then put his eye to the scope and searched for another target, this time on the opposite side of the stadium.

Muhammad Saleem fingered his prayer beads as he recited the ninety-nine names for God. He had parked in a side road about two hundred yards from the stadium. He was on double yellow lines but nobody was going to give an ambulance a ticket. His mobile phone lay on the seat next to him. It buzzed to show he had received a message and he picked it up. Three words. *It is time.* He smiled to himself, took a deep breath, then pressed the switch to start the siren and flashing lights. He put the ambulance into gear, pressed the accelerator, and started to drive. The wail of the siren set his pulse racing but he calmed himself by concentrating on the names of God. Al Jabbaar: The Powerful. Al Haqq: The Truth. Al Qawiyy: The Strong. Al Mumit: The Bringer of Death. Al Muntaqim: The Avenger.

"On three," mouthed Shepherd, and the officers nodded, their guns at the ready, fingers on triggers.

Shepherd mouthed, "One, two, three," then kicked the door hard putting his full weight behind the blow. The jamb splintered but the lock held. Shepherd stepped back and kicked again. This time the door crashed inwards and he stepped into the room, both hands on his gun. The two men he had recognised in

Page's photographs — Amma al-Kawthari and Elyas Assadi — were sitting on the sofa, mouths open in shock. The sniper was lying on a table, taking aim through the open window. The fourth man was holding a gun and swinging it towards the door. Shepherd fired twice in quick succession and the double-tap hit the man squarely in the chest. Two red roses blossomed on his shirt and he slumped to the floor.

The three armed cops piled in behind Shepherd. Graves and Leigh peeled off to the left, their guns aimed at the two men on the sofa. Shepherd hoped the cops realised the men weren't armed but if they fired it would be understandable and forgivable. Walker came up behind Shepherd's shoulder.

The sniper rolled onto his back and swung his rifle around. Shepherd dropped into a crouch and pulled the trigger at the same moment as the sniper pulled his. The two cracks overlapped and Shepherd saw his round smack into the sniper's chest as the sniper's bullet whizzed past his neck. Shepherd fired again and the second shot hit the man two inches below the first. The sniper fell back and the rifle clattered onto the table.

There was a dull thud behind Shepherd. He looked over his shoulder. The sniper's round had hit Walker in the face and he had died instantly.

Graves and Leigh dragged the Asians off the sofa and threw them to the floor, face down. Leigh had his foot in the small of Assadi's back and was screaming at him to lie still.

"Get the gates open! Let the ambulances in! We've got casualties here!" shouted the security guard. He waved at the two men on the gate and they followed his instructions. Outside there were two ambulances, lights flashing and sirens wailing. "Tell them to cut the sirens!" shouted the guard. He put his transceiver to his mouth and spoke to Ian Chapman in the control centre. "The ambulances are here, sir."

"Get them in as quickly as possible," said Chapman. "The casualties need to be on the way to hospital immediately."

As the gates opened, both ambulances cut their sirens and lights, as if the drivers had read the security guard's mind. They drove through and he pointed to where they were to go. Two more ambulances were heading down the road towards the stadium, sirens wailing.

"Clear!" shouted Shepherd, and Willoughby-Brown peered cautiously into the room. He grimaced when he saw Walker's body on the floor. Leigh and the other armed cop had bound the wrists of their prisoners and were staring stony-faced at their dead colleague.

Willoughby-Brown went over to the cops. "Back-up's on the way, so you two can stand down as soon as they're here."

Leigh shook his head fiercely. "We're booking them," he said.

"No problem," said Willoughby-Brown. "I'm sorry about Neil."

He went over to look at the sniper. "The old one-two," Willoughby-Brown said, when he saw the two wounds in the man's chest. "Does the job every time."

Shepherd joined him. "I've seen him before," he said quietly.

"One of Yilmaz's passports?"

"No. He was the sniper in Syria when we took out those two British jihadists. The one who ran before the missile hit."

"Seriously? He's a long way from home."

"They all are," said Shepherd, picking up the weapon.

"What sort of gun is it?" asked Willoughby-Brown.

"It's a rifle, Jeremy."

Willoughby-Brown flashed him a cold smile. "I realise that. What is it? American?"

"It's British. An L115A3. It's a very tasty bit of kit. It holds the record for the longest confirmed kill. A corporal by the name of Craig Harrison killed two Taliban with consecutive shots at a little over nine thousand feet in Helmand Province. With his third shot he took out their machine-gun. It's one hell of a weapon."

"How good can it be if your man here kept missing?"

"Missing?"

"I'm getting the info over the radio from Met Control. Zero kills. Five shots and he didn't kill anyone. Leg wounds, shoulders. But no kills."

"That's impossible," said Shepherd. "He's the real deal. And a real sniper would have no problems with a kill shot, even at this range."

"I'm just telling you the facts," said Willoughby-Brown. "I'm hearing all the radio traffic through Met Control. There are five casualties. No deaths. The ambulances are going in now."

Shepherd frowned. "Ambulances?"

"For the casualties. They're badly injured and they need to get to hospital immediately. They've just opened the gates to let them in."

Shepherd's frown deepened. He turned towards the window, brought the sniper scope up to his eye and focused down at the stadium.

The bout was still going on, the Russian and the Brit were trading punches, toe to toe.

"They got here fast, the ambulances," said Shepherd.

"They were probably on standby," said Willoughby-Brown.

Shepherd aimed at the VIP section, packed with the famous and wealthy. He tracked to the far end of the stadium where two ambulances were moving at walking pace, blue lights flashing.

"On standby outside? Does that make sense?"

Green and yellow flashed through his scope. It was an ambulance. There was a paramedic sitting in the driver's seat wearing a green uniform. The man was Asian and Shepherd focused on his face. The breath caught in his throat as he recognised the man from the passports Yusuf had shown him in Turkey. The man was muttering to himself and there was a glazed look in his eyes. Shepherd swore. He pushed the dead sniper off the table and lay down, bringing the stock of the rifle against his shoulder.

"What's wrong?"

"Jihadists in the ambulances," hissed Shepherd. "Suicide bombers!"

Willoughby-Brown's jaw dropped but he reacted quickly. "Wendy, patch me through to Bow Control Centre, now!"

Shepherd had the ambulance in his sights again. He focused on the man in the driver's seat, knowing he'd have to fire at least twice. The windscreen would shatter but almost certainly alter the bullet's trajectory. He'd need at least two shots to be sure of a kill. He pulled the trigger, felt the stock kick into his shoulder and saw the windscreen explode into a shower of cubes. In less than a second he aimed and fired again. This time he saw the man's face implode into a red mush.

He brought the rifle around, looking for the second ambulance.

Superintendent Enfield's direct line rang and he picked it up. It was Wendy Aspden, who asked him to hold, then put Willoughby-Brown through. "Superintendent, it's all turning very nasty at the stadium," he said.

"Yes, I'm just talking to my inspector. Five wounded and our helicopter has just crashed."

"Superintendent, I'm told you have undercover armed officers on duty at the stadium."

"Several. Including an undercover SAS unit."

"You need to tell them to take out the ambulances. We believe they are bombs being driven by jihadists. They need to move now."

"What? Are you sure?"

"Superintendent, you can either be a hero today or you'll take the blame for one of the biggest terrorist atrocities this country has ever seen. The gates have been opened to allow the ambulances in but they are Islamic State terrorists. Get your men over to the ambulances now and tell them to do what has to be done." Willoughby-Brown ended the call.

Shepherd focused his scope on the second ambulance, which had just come to a halt towards the middle of the stadium. The man's face centred on the scope. It was another of the men given a Syrian passport by Yusuf. The man was holding his right hand up and Shepherd could clearly see the trigger. He went to chamber a round but his magazine was empty. He yanked it out, grabbed a full magazine by the cushion and slammed it in. He chambered a round, his heart racing. He resisted the urge to rush his shot. He aimed, he controlled his breathing, and he slowly squeezed the trigger. The windscreen exploded. He chambered a second round and fired again, catching the man in the throat and severing his spine. The head lolled to the side and the hand holding the trigger dropped. Shepherd held his breath but there was no explosion.

He took his eye away from the scope. Almost unbelievably, the bout was continuing. The two boxers were exchanging punches and the crowd were roaring, many of them on their feet.

Another ambulance was moving slowly in his direction but as he watched the stadium roof blocked it from view. Another had come to a halt close to a podium from which two TV cameras were broadcasting the fight.

"There are armed cops down there," said Willoughby-Brown.

"They'd better move quickly," said Shepherd.

He put his eye to the scope, focused on the remaining ambulance he could see and immediately recognised the driver. He aimed at the head, held his breath and squeezed the trigger. The window exploded and he ejected the cartridge and rammed home another. Aim. Breath. Squeeze. The head imploded and jerked back. Shepherd looked at Willoughby-Brown. "I've done all I can," he said. "It's up to the cops now."

Kuznetsov had Hughes up against the ropes and was hitting him hard and fast to the ribs. Hughes was grunting but taking the punishment as if he hadn't a care in the world. Then he bobbed left and hit the Russian with a devastating right uppercut that rocked him back.

Murray's transceiver buzzed on his hip and he put his hand up to his earpiece. "Captain Murray? This is Superintendent Enfield."

"Murray, receiving," said Murray. Enfield sounded as if he was under pressure.

"Terrorists have driven ambulances into the stadium, we think with bombs. You need to deal with them. Now."

Murray looked around. One of his men, Rick "Country" Lane, was about fifty feet from him. He was facing the ring but glancing from side to side, very much on alert. Murray waved him over.

"Islamic State terrorists, do you understand?" said Enfield.

"Understood," said Murray. Off to his right an ambulance was parked close to the main stand. The windscreen had shattered and the driver was slumped in his seat, his chest wet with blood.

Lane joined him. "What's up, boss?"

"Terrorist attack, ambulances," said Murray, still looking around. Off to his left, another ambulance was moving slowly. "With me," he shouted, and ran towards it, reaching for his gun.

Pashtana Abdul brought the ambulance to a halt. He was totally calm, he had long ago come to terms with the fact that he was destined to be a *shahid* and take his place in Heaven at Allah's right hand. He smiled to himself. "*Inna lillahi wa inna ilayhi raaji'oon,*" he whispered. To Allah we belong and to Him is our return.

He reached for the switch to activate the bomb and clicked it to the "on" position. As he straightened up he felt all-powerful, knowing that all he had to do was to press the trigger in his hand and he would join Allah in Heaven. He opened his mouth to say, "*Allahu akbar,*" but the words froze in his throat when he saw the two men pointing guns at him. *Kafirs*, infidels, were glaring at him with undisguised hatred. He didn't understand what they were shouting, the words meant nothing to him, but he knew what they wanted. They wanted him to surrender, to give up his mission, to become a coward and not a *shahid*, but that wasn't going to happen. He tightened his grip on the trigger but then the window exploded in a hail of bullets and he died instantly.

Willoughby-Brown and Shepherd walked out of the tower block. Willoughby-Brown's driver was standing by his van, fiddling with his smartphone. He waved at Willoughby-Brown when he saw him, put the phone away and climbed into the vehicle.

"That went better than I thought it would," said Willoughby-Brown.

"It was a disaster," said Shepherd. "Two men died when the helicopter went down, and the sniper hit how many? Five? Six?"

"Five. But they're all alive and heading to hospital as we speak. Thankfully in genuine ambulances. It could have gone a lot worse, Daniel. The bombs were huge — just one of them would have killed hundreds. The four together . . ." He rubbed his chin. "Thousands could have died. As it is, we killed the sniper, we've got six dead jihadists and two in custody. We got off lightly." He took his cigars out of his pocket and lit one. "It could have been so much worse."

"And if we'd arrested them when they collected the gun, no one would have been hurt."

"Possibly not. Except those massive bombs were primed and ready to go. If they hadn't gone to the stadium, there would have been a fallback position and they would have detonated elsewhere. Four bombs that big going off in Central London would have been a game-changer." He blew smoke towards the block. "You did well up there."

Shepherd shrugged. "I was lucky."

Willoughby-Brown shook his head. "Maybe, in that you were the right person in the right place at the right time. Only you could have done what needed to be done. But what you did wasn't down to luck, it was down to your abilities." He took another drag on his cigar. "If you hadn't been a sniper in another life, a lot of people would have died."

"I guess."

"There's no guess about it." He patted Shepherd on the back. "You're a bloody hero. I'm just sorry I can't give you a medal." He turned and walked away, heading for the waiting van.

Shepherd watched him go. His phone vibrated in his pocket. It was Liam. "Hey, Dad, what's happening?"

Shepherd smiled. "Not much. How are things with you?"

Other titles published by Ulverscroft:

BLACK OPS

Stephen Leather

When MI5 Agent Spider is asked to assume the identity of the contract killer hired to take out President Vladimir Putin, he knows he'll become a wanted man. And things are about to get more complicated: Spider is told that his MI5 controller and close friend Charlotte Button has been running an off-the-books assassination operation, taking vengeance on the men who killed her husband. Spider owes his life to Button — but this discovery will stretch his loyalty to the limit. Because he is told to betray her. Worse, he's asked to cooperate with his nemesis at MI6, Jeremy Willoughby Brown, in taking Charlie down. And he will have to cross the assassin Lex Harper, currently on the trail of two Irish terrorists, who may be able to lead him to his ex-boss . . .

FIRST RESPONSE

Stephen Leather

London is under siege. Nine men in suicide vests primed to explode hold hostages in nine different locations around the city, and are ready to die for their cause. Their mission: to force the government to release jihadist prisoners from Belmarsh Prison. Their deadline: six p.m. today. But the bombers have no obvious link to any group, and do not appear on any anti-terror watch list. What has brought them together on this one day to act in this way? Mo Kamran is the superintendent in charge of the Special Crime and Operations branch of the Met. As the disaster unfolds and the SAS, armed police, and other emergency services rush to the scenes, he is tasked with preventing the biggest terrorist outrage the capital has ever known.

WHITE LIES

Stephen Leather

Dan "Spider" Shepherd is used to putting his life on the line — for his friends and for his job with MI5. So when one of his former apprentices is kidnapped in Pakistan, Shepherd doesn't hesitate to join a rescue mission. But when the rescue plan goes horribly wrong, Shepherd ends up in the hands of al-Qaeda terrorists. His SAS training is of little help as his captors torture him. Shepherd's MI5 controller Charlotte Button is determined to get her man out of harm's way, but to do that she's going to have to break all the rules. Her only hope is to bring in America's finest — the elite SEALs who carried out Operation Neptune Spear — in a do-or-die operation to rescue the captives.

LASTNIGHT

Stephen Leather

A killer is murdering Goths with relish — skinning and butchering them. The cops aren't getting anywhere so Jack Nightingale's nemesis, Superintendent Chalmers, asks him for help. Nightingale discovers that the murdered Goths had one thing in common: a tattoo connected to the secretive, Satanic, child-sacrificing cult called the Order Of Nine Angles. As Nightingale closes in on the killers, the tables are turned and he finds himself in the firing line, along with his friends and family. The Order will stop at nothing to protect their secrets and Nightingale realises that there is nothing he can do to protect himself. It leaves him with only one way to stop the carnage — and that's to take his own life . . .